I0599005

ASSIMILATION

LONNIE BUSCH

UBiQ PRESS

No AI was used for any part of this book

This is a work of fiction. All of the characters, organizations, and events portrayed in the novel are either products of the author's imagination or are used fictitiously. Any similarity to anyone living or dead is purely coincidental.

ASSIMILATION

A UBiQ PRESS BOOK

North Carolina, USA

https://lonniebusch.com/

Cover Art by Lonnie Busch

ISBN: 978-1-964024-14-1 (hardcover)

ISBN: 978-1-964024-13-4 (paperback)

Library of Congress Control Number: 9781964024134

First Paperback/Hardcover Editions, October 2025

[CONTENT ADVISORY: Intended for adult readership and contains scenes of violence, sexuality, aliens, and language that may be uncomfortable for some readers.]

[TRIGGER WARNING: Rape]

ASSIMILATION

ONE

The warm sun.

The cool breeze off the lake.

The weak scent of my father's aftershave.

I could not see him, but I could see his shadow on the planks as he guided my wheelchair down the wooden walkway toward the boat dock. I had never been, nor would I ever be, "daddy's little girl." We didn't have that kind of relationship. I would never be his little Kercy. I was barely a girl at all. Seventeen and I still showed no signs of ever becoming a woman. I weighed eighty-eight pounds. When hair grew on my head, it sprouted in tufts, so I kept my scalp shaved. My eyebrows appeared as nothing more than short sprigs growing helter-skelter above my eyes.

Our summer cottage occupied one of the thousands of private islands in the Soshone Island area of Georgian Bay near the St. Lawrence Seaway in Ontario. I loved it here. I loved how the too blue water came together with the horizon in some distant unreachable place. How the air was crisp and unspoiled. How the afternoon breeze made the boughs of the spruce and pines sway like tall, drunken fishermen.

My father didn't speak as he rolled me along, and as much as I may have liked to be, I was not privy to his thoughts. Decking boards creaked beneath his feet, even though his stylish canvas shoes made no noise on the weathered wood. Water crashed and sprayed against the rocky shoreline in front of our house. Our white skiff bounced in the waves, bucking against the mooring ropes as if trying desperately to escape. As we approached the end of the dock, bright whitecaps opened in the blue ahead, the boards beneath my wheelchair blotched with dried gull shit.

My heart shuddered, a bit faster now as we approached the last few boards of the long pier. No railing enclosed it and the thought occurred to me that in some final act of disgust my father might actually decide to thrust my wheelchair over the edge. I would land with a splash and for just a moment, my wheelchair might shirk its responsibility to sink. And for that brief second, I would look up at him from the water, the sun behind his head, his face in shadow, his final thoughts hidden from me. Then just as suddenly as I had glimpsed him for the last time, my chair would obey the laws of physics, become an anchor dragging me down. My father would watch, me seated in my chair, the wheels rotating slowly as I sank, until my face was merely a faint bluish smudge in the depths. And then gone. Would he be smiling? Would he be aghast? Or would he have already walked away? I always wondered.

"It's a beautiful day."

My father spoke these words with the flattened affect of someone pointing out a dead mouse. Stepping out from behind my wheelchair, he positioned himself beside me. He had the slight but sturdy build of a man who worked with machinery. The truth was, he had never worked a day in his life. Wealth was as common to him as breathing. Most days he just perused the New York Times and the Wall Street Journal until he grew bored. Then he would race off to Manhattan in his Porsche convertible for destinations unknown. Forbes magazines adorned our bathroom magazine rack, but I don't think he ever read them. He really didn't care about wealth, only the freedom it afforded him. And he resented me for diminishing that freedom.

I stared at the water. My father stood post-still, a fishing rod in his right hand. I had never seen him fish, and didn't think he really liked it much, but somehow, he knew how to work the rod and reel. He prepared some kind of bait and had skewered it on a hook at the end of the line. A weight dangled two feet above the hook. I had no idea what the bait was, but it appeared to have been some kind of water creature at some point in its life.

"Do you want to try?" he said, mimicking a cast.

I didn't care about fishing either. "No, you can throw farther than I can."

"Well, Kercy, that's not really the point, is it..." His cigarette stuck to his lower lip, bobbing with each word. Using both hands, he grasped the rod firmly, flipped the bail open, then swung the rod back behind his head before whipping it forward with a *whoosh*. Within seconds the bait splashed some thirty yards away. The fishing line sliced the surface of the water back toward me as the bait sank to the bottom. When the line went slack, he handed me the rod.

"Hold on tight to the handle, Kercy," he said. "Both hands. Enormous fish out there, I'm told."

I wedged the butt of the long handle between my legs against the seat of my wheelchair, then placed my left hand above the reel and my right hand below. If a fish took the bait, I would have to use my left hand to reel it in, while steadying the rod with my right. I wasn't sure how that would work, having never caught anything before. I was at least glad for that, the part about never having caught anything. I was content to just sit and watch a few clouds crawl their way across the horizon.

"No matter what happens, don't let go of that rod," my father said. "You are strong enough to do this, right? It's important that you be good at something, Kercy, even if it is just fishing."

He took one last glance toward the infinite blue water beyond the dock, then turned and walked back to the skiff. We often went through this ritual at the lake cottage, mostly when my mother was taking a nap. She was plagued by horrible migraines and often had to lie down in the late afternoon. My father, unable to escape our private island in his Porsche, found it unbearable to be around me by himself for very long. He would take our twenty-foot skiff and buzz around Georgian Bay all afternoon. I never knew where he went. Neither did my mother, but I don't think she cared. They had not really been that close after I was born. And she would be angry with him when she woke from her nap to find me sunburned and unchaperoned at the end of the dock. My father said the sun would do my complexion good, but it only turned me red, and blotchier than normal.

Craning my neck back, I watched my father climb into the skiff. He looked so handsome standing behind the center console, his smooth black hair, his straight back, fingers wrapping the steering wheel, like someone in a magazine. I often wondered what it would feel like for him to touch me, to touch my skin, my arms, my face. At times my body ached for him to hold me, to wrap me in his arms, squeeze me to his chest. My mother hugged me all the time and it seemed our bodies meshed perfectly into one another, that we were two pieces from the same puzzle. Would it feel that way with him? Maybe if I caught a big fish, held onto the rod, fought it to exhaustion, both the fish's and mine, and let the huge creature die in the sun on the dock, maybe then.... Would that prove I was good at something?

Gulls gathered and squawked when he fired the huge Evinrude boat engine. He undid the ropes and shot away from the dock. He didn't bother waving. The birds stalked his wake, hoping for a free meal of sculpin or goby stirred up by the prop. After the skiff rounded an island to the east, he was gone. For a moment I could still hear the distant hum of the Evinrude.

What was he hoping for with this fishing routine? That an enormous muskellunge would grab the bait and drag me into the water? At the tackle store in Elico, hanging on the wall, was a mounted musky over five feet long. It had weighed over sixty pounds, armed with a mouthful of sharp teeth. I only outweighed that fish by twenty-eight pounds. I wasn't paralyzed, just woefully underdeveloped, without much strength in my legs. It wouldn't be much of a battle, with the huge monster very much at home in water, and me never feeling at home anywhere.

My father had been right about the day... it was beautiful. A couple of times I had dozed off. Luckily, I had not dropped the rod in the water. The front castors of my chair sat about a foot from the edge of the dock. That was too close. I carefully secured the rod butt beneath my left thigh, clamping my right thigh against it. With the rod steady and fixed, I released my grip on the rod handle and placed my palms on the push rings to move myself back from the edge. That's when I realized my father had not locked the brake on my chair after he handed me the rod. He must have forgotten.

I had just started moving the chair when the fishing line tightened, the rod bending toward the water. It could be I was snagged and my movement caused the reaction. Then the line jerked from the spool in short fits, the drag clicking. Seizing the rod firmly with my right hand, I used my left to set the brake on the left rear wheel. I was switching hands to set the other brake when the rod went crazy. Line ripped from the spool, the drag whining. I grasped the knob at the top of the spool, twisting it to tighten the drag and put pressure on the fish, hamper his freedom, the way my father had shown me. When I did, the rod strained and bowed against this new restriction. Something had to give... and it did. With the left rear wheel brake holding firm, the right front castor of my chair started to jerk toward the last board. The right castor was less than eight inches from the edge. The fish charged straight for deep water. The drag was too tight now, not giving the creature enough sway. With the rod held tight to my chest, my chair began to rotate slightly, pivoting on the locked rear wheel. The right castor was now within an inch of losing purchase on the wood. When I tried to loosen the drag, give the fish what he wanted— less resistance—he pulled all the harder, nearly jerking the rig from my hands.

I slid my right tennis shoe from the footplate and planted it on the dock, with little room to get footing. My impulse was to give the fish the rod and reel, let it fly from my hands and sink in the water behind the raging creature. *No matter what happens, don't let go of that rod.*

Cradling the handle in the crook of my right arm, I struggled to turn the reel handle with my left hand. I could feel my neck muscles straining, the right castor slipping forward. Tears rolled down my cheeks as I arched my back against the fish. I used every bit of strength in my right leg to find traction against the wood and push myself back from the edge. *You are strong enough to do this, right?*

Now I wasn't sure. Was I strong enough? Was I able to do anything right? *Don't let go of that rod!*

My mouth was dry and I was just about to give in when I heard my mother scream. "Kercy!" In the far margin of my vision I saw her running toward me from the cottage. I knew not to turn my head toward her, which would give the fish just the angle it needed. New resolve filled my arms and legs but the fish seemed to care nothing for my momentary confidence. It pulled harder than anything I could imagine and the right castor was now suspended in mid-air. If the left brake held, I would probably not tumble into the water. "Kercy!" my mother shouted over and over. "Let go of that damn rod!" It seemed now she was running in slow motion, her voice shrill with panic. I felt dizzy, unstable, and just when I knew the fish would win, the rod tip shot straight up, the line fell slack. The struggle was over.

In my jubilation, I turned to smile at her, holding the rod up like a trophy. *It's important that you be good at something, Kercy, even if it is just fishing.* She kept running toward me, her face still twisted in aguish. "Kercy!"

"It's okay, Mom! I'm okay!"

At that moment, the slight imbalance from my celebration caused my wheelchair to pitch forward and topple from the dock. The splash shocked me. I expected a moment, a pause, when everything stood still, like so many times before. But that didn't happen.

I was no stranger to drowning. I had drowned at least four times already in my life. My mother was proficient at CPR, bringing me back each time. And it wasn't because my parents were irresponsible, or that I was not a great swimmer, or that I was of slight build and weak; it was because I believed I could breathe underwater. Finally, at age nine, I was prohibited from going in swimming pools, lakes, or the ocean. I required supervision when I bathed; my mother no longer trusted me around water, even in the bathtub.

Regardless, I loved the water. I loved seeing with such clarity in this peculiar medium which desperately wanted to end my life. Before my first trip below the surface, I never knew the world could be so defined and colorful. When I was a young girl my mother would take me to the public pool near our home. I could read tattoos on ankles and calves as people swam by, could see individual hairs on men's legs, the colored stitching of women's bikinis, the color of their painted fingernails from the far end of the pool. Below the water my eyesight was vivid, while on land, blurry, vague and achromatic. One of my many birth defects.

My chair sank quicker than I did. For a moment I floated freely above the bottom. Suspended. What a wonderful feeling to have full movement, to drift unhindered, to cheat gravity ever so briefly. Then the colors came, beautiful fish and aquatic flowers and plants. Water was a miraculous place. One I could live in forever. But then it ended as it always did.

I coughed a few times and spit water from my mouth. When I opened my eyes my mother was kneeling over me, her hair stringy and dripping onto my chest. Her blouse was soaked, the material clinging to her bra. When she saw me breathing, she closed her eyes and seemed to be saying a prayer. Lying on the dock, I felt the boards warm against my back. I swiveled my head to find my wheelchair. I didn't see it. I looked at my left hand. The rod was clutched in my small palm. I hadn't let go of it, and wished my father could have seen me.

"Stay put, sweetheart... don't move," my mother said. She stood, still wearing her red shorts, then dove back into the water. Unlike me, she was an amazing swimmer. She had a Master's Degree in Marine Biology and was also a scuba diver with Scientific Diving Certification. She never held a job as a marine biologist, but before I was born had volunteered on research teams, diving all over the world.

Like my father, my mother had come from wealth. Her great grandfather had started a timber business in upper Ontario at the turn of the century. Even though my father had no need for money, apparently her fortune had been a big attraction to him. That, coupled with the fact that she had been told she'd never have children because of a crapped-up uterus like mine. Freedom. Unbridled freedom. According to my mom, my father married her with the idea their life would be one continuous lark of traveling, exploration and adventure. And it had been—Africa, Greenland, Malta, Greece, Spain, Australia—until my mother, against all odds, became pregnant. They had even lived on the Isle of Capri for several years, but that all ended because of me. My mother had what the medical community referred to as a geriatric pregnancy, a term assigned to any woman who became pregnant after thirty-five. My mother was forty-one when I was born, which may have accounted for some of my physical challenges. But to her, my birth was miraculous. Not so for my father, who saw her pregnancy as an unforgivable deception.

I crawled to the edge of the dock. My mother was maybe fifteen feet below, grabbing the wheelchair. She looked like a mermaid, puffs of sand swirling around her as she pulled it from the silt. She moved like a spirit, like Yemoja, goddess of all waters. My mother spent time in Nigeria and told me about her.

When she surfaced holding the arm of my wheelchair, she kicked her legs to keep from sinking, wrangling the contraption up onto the dock. It sat on its side, dripping, and for some inexplicable reason I felt sorry for it. My mother grasped the edge of the dock, and with one swift movement, shot from the water, throwing her left knee, then the right, onto the boards. It baffled me, her physical prowess.

She stood, then used both hands to squeeze the water from her hair. "Where's your father?" she asked, glancing toward the empty dock. "He took off in the boat, didn't he... damn him!"

"I held onto the rod, Mom."

She leaned over and hugged me, then kissed my head. "You did, sweetheart. You are getting so strong now. Let's get you into some dry clothes."

She helped me into the wheelchair. Even at fifty-eight my mother had the youthful beauty of someone half her age. It was no wonder my father fell in love with her. She was intelligent, vivacious, driven, warm, and strong. She was good at so many things.

As she turned my wheelchair back toward the cottage, I started reeling in the excess line. I'm not sure my father would see salvaging the rod as a victory, especially given that I hadn't landed the fish. Regardless, for me, a major triumph. My mother waited as I wound the handle on the reel. I couldn't tell if she was crying or it was water dripping from her hair wetting her cheeks. Once all the slack was out of the line, I felt resistance on the rod.

"Mom, I still have him!"

"Are you sure?"

"Yes. Look at the rod. I feel the weight."

Reeling in faster, I was surprised the fish was not fighting. Had he died from exhaustion? Or was he too tired to struggle? Or had he just given up? My mother and I watched as it came closer. It quickly became obvious it was dead, its body spinning and twirling as it came closer. It didn't look very big, either, only a foot or so long. Now I was glad my father wasn't here to see this. He would probably laugh at me for how I had struggled against this small, insignificant creature.

When the sinker reached the rod tip, I lifted the dead fish from the water and held it over the dock. "What kind of fish is that, mom?" It didn't even look like a fish.

She went over to it, inspected it a moment, then grasped it mid body and pulled it from the hook.

"Is that a fish?" I asked. It was an appendage of some sort; the bottom looking as if it had been bitten off a much larger creature. Blood dripped onto the dock.

Her expression turned dark. She studied it a bit longer, then tossed it as far as she could out into the water.

"Mom! Why did you do that? I needed to show dad!"

She turned back to me and knelt in front of my wheelchair, tears trickling down her smooth skin. She seemed to struggle for words. "I think it was the leg of a *necturus maculosus*. A mudpuppy."

My eyes had been telling me it was some kind of arm with a hand, but my mind refused to accept it. "A mudpuppy? What is that?"

"A salamander. Let's go to the house."

"That was the leg of a salamander?" I said. "Jeez, he would've been like six feet long or something, right? And that's without the tail. Do salamanders get that big?"

"Not usually, baby."

"Mom?"

"What now?"

I pointed at her stomach. "You have blood on your blouse."

She looked down and rubbed at it a second, then grabbed the push handles and started wheeling me up the walkway. My mind wrestled with all the intangibles. It was scary picturing something so large swimming beneath the serene surface. It would have been way bigger than those pike and musky mounts at the tackle shop. Could it eat a musky? Or one of those big pike? What did huge salamanders even eat? But then the most disturbing notion seized me: Something even bigger had eaten it. That's why the fight ended. Now it made sense.

"Mom?" I grabbed the push rings to stop the wheelchair. "What would be big enough to eat a six-foot salamander?"

For a moment she said nothing. I twisted in the wheelchair to find her eyes, but with the sun behind her, she was in silhouette.

"Mom?"

"I don't know, baby."

She started moving the chair again so I released the push rings. If she didn't know, who would? She was a marine biologist. She had to know. She made dives all over the world. She'd seen creatures unseen by most people except in books. Others that may never have been photographed at all. She told me once that an estimated eighty-five percent of the Earth's species are still unknown. That seemed like a lot to me.

After helping me into dry clothes, she applied aloe gel to my face, scalp and arms. My new sunburn was starting to make itself known, but the lotion felt cool on my skin. We were eating lunch when I brought up the salamander leg again.

"I wish we could have kept it to show dad," I said.

My mom chewed her sandwich and picked at the potato chips on her plate. After lunch we went into the living room where she had a complete library; books of fiction, poetry, marine biology, anthropology, countries of the world, famous cities, and science. She sat on the cushy chair that she always read in and motioned for me to come over by her.

"Are we going to do lessons?" I asked.

"No, it's still summer vacation."

I rolled my wheelchair over and she helped me onto her lap. Once I stopped squirming, she opened the picture book on ocean life. "So much about our world we still don't understand," she said, flipping to pictures of colorful yet horrific looking creatures. "These are a few of the ones we know of."

"So, how big is that one?" Enthralled by this fish with enormous teeth, I couldn't help but imagine him chomping off the body of the salamander.

"He's only about 14 inches long. Does he scare you, Muffin?"

"No." He really didn't scare me at all. "How big do muskie get?"

"The world record is almost 70 pounds. You might have tussled with a new world record."

Okay, she was patronizing me now because she didn't want to talk about the mudpuppy anymore, so I dropped it.

Later that evening when she was cooking dinner, I heard the skiff return. From the living room window I watched my dad climbing out. He squatted down and spent a few minutes securing the boat to the dock cleats. When he tried to stand up, he wavered and almost fell over. He was drunk. He must have taken the skiff to the harbor, docked it, then got in our SUV and drove to the tavern in Elico. My mom was already pissed about him leaving me unsupervised on the dock. After dinner they'd fight the rest of the evening and she'd probably sleep on the couch in the living room, next to my bedroom. She had my room special built so I didn't have to deal with the steps.

My father came inside and went directly upstairs. Within a few minutes the shower came on in their bedroom, which was just above my room. The cottage was pretty amazing, out here in the middle of nowhere it seemed, an island among thousands of islands, but with all the amenities; hot water, flushing toilets, electricity. I loved it here. Way better than New York City.

I laid on my bed reading until supper time. When my mom came and got me she sat on the bed next to me. "Sweetie, I know you're excited about telling your father about your... your adventure today, but it is probably not a good time. Your father's been drinking and he will not be easy to deal with tonight. I don't want you getting into it with him."

She sat a moment looking at me, then: "Okay? You understand?"

"Yeah, sure. No problem. Do you want to play cards after supper. Or a game? Do you want to play Sorry?"

"We'll see, okay?" She leaned in and kissed me on the forehead, then on the nose. "I love you so much, Muffin."

TWO

My parents and I ate dinner in silence. After supper my father went outside to smoke. I helped my mom with the dishes. She seemed sad this evening.

She suds the dishes as if she hadn't heard me, then rinsed them and placed them in the rack. I was several dishes behind her now. When she finished with the last glass, she pulled the plug in the sink and grabbed a towel to help me finish drying.

"Are you looking forward to getting back to the city, Muffin?" she asked.

"Not really. I love it here."

She nodded. "I know you do."

She put the dishes into the cabinets while I put silverware in the drawer. When everything was done, she told me to get the Sorry board set up.

While I was doing that in the living room, my father came in the back door through the kitchen. I thought the fighting would start straight away, but I heard him go upstairs and switch on the television in their bedroom. Satellite reception wasn't always great at the cottage, but we had DVD players for when it wasn't. My mom came in a few minutes later and sat opposite me at the coffee table.

"Are you green or blue?" she said.

"Yellow tonight."

"Then I'll be red."

After our first game she went to the kitchen and brought back Cokes and a bowl of potato chips. She pushed one of the glasses toward me.

"I'm green this time," she said. "Gotta change my luck."

"Sure, mom, like that's gonna help."

We took turns picking cards and moving our nubbins while the television played above us, sounding louder than it had earlier. I could tell my mother was trying to ignore it.

"You know we're heading back to New York tomorrow, right?" she said,

"Yeah." I moved my nubbin forward six spaces.

"I'm thinking of selling the cottage, Muffin." My mother picked a card from the stack.

I stopped and stared at her. "You can't. You can't sell it..." I couldn't believe she could even consider it. I was drawn to the summer lake house the way a salmon is drawn to the river of its birth. Every good memory I have in my life, and they are few, are connected to this place, the source of my greatest joy, my greatest hope. Maybe because it was remote and I never had to face many people. Interaction with others was not expected here. Trying to fit in wasn't necessary. Being a girl and not looking like one didn't matter on this island. Here... I was normal, no standard to measure against, the only place I've ever known true peace.

"You just can't, Mother!"

"Kercy, I didn't expect you to react like this..."

I splashed my hand across the board, sending the nubbins and cards flying through the air. I pulled myself up into my wheelchair and hurried to my bedroom, locking the door behind me. I couldn't stop crying. What hurt me most was the realization that my mother had no understanding of who I was, what was important to me. How could she not? I expected that kind of disconnect from my father, and even accepted it, but not from her, not my mother. Never had I felt so alone.

After crawling up onto my bed, I hugged my pillow to my chest and rolled myself into a ball. My sunburn was starting to hurt again and my joints ached, especially my knees and elbows. How could I live without this place? How could I make it through the winter in the city knowing I would not be spending my summer here?

I guess I cried myself to sleep because when I woke, my room was dark. The blankets were pulled up around me and I was wearing my nightgown. My mother always respected the lock on my door, even though she had a key. She must have known I had fallen asleep and came in, undressed me, covered me, and turned off the light. I was about to roll over and go back to sleep when I heard the floor creaking above me. Someone was awake in my parents' bedroom. It sounded like my mom walking across the floor. The television was still playing, but when it switched off, I heard murmuring.

The muffled conversation soon escalated into a full-blown argument. Certain words stood out: "How could you...Kercy...You left her...She needs to be more...She's not a baby...You coddle her...She's just a child...No she isn't...Wheelchair...She was sunburned...She's always something...She almost drowned...What else is new?...Fuck you!...Fuck you!...You bitch!"

The shouting soon mushroomed into a barrage of swearing and screaming and slamming and noises I had no images for. I tried to bury my head beneath the pillow and pictured them standing toe to toe, shouting into each other's mouths, their eyes aimed at one another like guns.

Then it ended.

Loud footfalls hurried down the steps.

"Carter! If you leave..." my mother shouted, "Just know we are heading back to New York in the morning whether you're here or not!" Then silence, followed by the slam of the back door. It was only moments before I heard the Evinrude fire up, then speed away. Not long after that, I heard my mother upstairs crying.

She was alone. I was alone. And I didn't like thinking that my mother and I would be better off without my dad, that life was actually more peaceful when he wasn't around.

When I woke, it was still dark outside. The house was quiet. I slid to the edge of the bed and pulled myself into the wheelchair. Rolling to the window, I saw the boat was still gone, but it was so peaceful out, the water like a sheet of black marble. The moon was just a sliver of light, as if some secret portal to another world was just beginning to open in the night sky. How could my mother ever think about selling this magnificent place? I wondered how my dad felt about it. In reality, the property had belonged to my mother's grandfather and had been in her family for decades. My dad had never shown much emotion about the island or cottage, or much of anything. He was hard to read. And where did he go when he took off into the darkness? How could he find his way around without hitting a huge slab of glacial rock? They were everywhere, lying just beneath the surface, and at times looked eerie, enormous boulders just a few feet under the water, like gigantic manatees, and with the waves rolling above them, they almost appeared to be moving.

My eyes were getting sleepy so I went back to bed. I was about to turn over and go back to sleep when I noticed someone standing near the door.

"Mom?" I said, pushing myself up on my elbow. The figure was vague and unmoving. "Dad?"

I sat up to get a better look. "Mom? Is that you?" The figure didn't move. Is that just my dresser? I wondered. But before I could question whether or not I was hallucinating, two other figures stepped forward and stood next to the first one.

"Who are you? What do you want?" I scooted backward against the headboard.

The figures approached slowly until they stood at the foot of my bed. They wore some sort of suits, it seemed, with strange shaped helmets or something. Two of the figures came to either side of my bed. They made no noise, said nothing. It was still hard to tell what they were wearing, but whatever it was it appeared to be wet. I looked over at the one to my left, the one between myself and the door, the one blocking my wheelchair. I wanted to scream for my mom, but I couldn't. Not because I was suddenly mute or anything, but because it felt like if I did, something very bad would happen, that my mother might run in to help and they'd kill her. The figure on my left moved my wheelchair away from the bed, then came closer and grabbed my wrist. Its forelimb looked like the mudpuppy appendage I hooked that afternoon on the dock, only larger. But the same scaly digits, the same weird, pearly iridescent kind of skin. Or maybe it was a suit. If only I could see its face, or its eyes, but they were hidden by some kind of shiny shield.

Just then the one on my right side wrapped its digits around my other wrist, not hard enough to hurt, but firm enough that I was unable to move. Its touch was cold, damp and slimy. It wore the same odd headgear, the same shimmering skin as the one on my left. So transfixed I was trying to see past the shield covering its face I hadn't noticed that the being at the foot of my bed was holding some kind of instrument.

I was petrified... literally. I couldn't move, as if some invisible net had been placed over me, stealing my strength, my ability to fight back, making it impossible to resist. I screamed but no sound came out, as if the entire room were packed in cotton. The creature at the foot of the bed raised its forelimbs and gripped the helmet with its glistening digits and began to wiggle the head covering back and forth on its shoulders. As it lifted the headgear off, a kind of fluid flooded out, soaking my legs and the bed. That's when I saw its face. Its eyes were almost like a puppy's eyes, big and sad and mysterious. Its skin shimmered like the others, slick, like a salamander.

When it moved the instrument closer to me, I noticed the creature's smell for the first time, like decaying vegetation and silt from the bottom of the lake. Not repulsive, exactly, but not completely fragrant either, with a presence of ammonia that burned inside my nostrils. I could not tell if the creature had a mouth.

An unexpected tranquility washed over me. I should have been frightened when the being slowly parted my legs, but the experience felt unthreatening somehow, a strange familiarity. A moment later it seemed that the creature had inserted the instrument inside me but I felt nothing. I waited, staring at it, trying to understand what was happening. That's when I saw its mouth, far back beneath its chin, opening and closing like some faulty contraption, the being struggling now it seemed, as if gasping for air, making a horrible sound, like something dying. From deep within its gullet came a guttural mewling and I wondered why the other two creatures weren't helping it. At this point, the struggling creature had become so strained it seemed unable to move, opening its mouth wider, gulping feebly, losing its connection to the world. The other two made a crackling sound, like crinkling cellophane. The being under duress, seemingly fortified by the curious noise, perked up and was able to focus again, its mouth relaxing into a more natural rhythm, its attention back to the instrument, as if monitoring or measuring something. That's when I felt a slight pinch inside me below the base of my abdomen, not pain exactly, just a sharp tweak that lasted only a second. It was shortly after that the creature removed the instrument and began to inspect it.

By then, though, the creature was battling its own physiology again, trying desperately to study the symbols flashing on the handle, its attention failing. Time was running out on this creature. When it finally succumbed to its inability to function, the other two released my wrists. Just then, as if a valve suddenly opened inside me, my once suppressed fear and anxiety sluiced through every cell in my body, churning unbearably in my chest. The pressure exploded from me in a deafening scream, a huge screeching ball of terror that ripped into my ears, reverberated along the walls of my skull. Then, as if my scream had possessed sufficient force to cause real destruction, a fissure opened in the ceiling above my bed. Other ruptures quickly snaked out, the sound of cracking, the world sagging, crumbling, chalky gray chunks of plaster raining down, falling to the floor in great plumes of smoke and dust, casting the room in a dim, ghostly light. The powdery air sunk into my lungs until I started coughing, choking.

The beings ignored my outburst as the room disintegrated around us. They were busy trying to revive the one who displayed all the signs of dying, its frail limbs reaching out, its body slowly folding to the floor. At any moment I expected my mother's bed would come crashing down from above me. The room was clogged with unbreathable air as the beings wrangled the dying one's helmet back on. By now it was hard to see, everything cloaked in a gauzy, filmy gloom. One of the creatures cradled the lifeless one in its arms and carried it from the bedroom, while the other paused at the foot of my bed to pick up the instrument, then stood upright, debris falling past its hidden eyes, staring at me, upset maybe, or agitated. I screamed again with every cell of my body...

"Wake up, Kercy! Wake up, Muffin!"

When my eyes popped open my mother was sitting on my bed, holding me. "It's okay, Muffin, you were having a nightmare."

I surveyed the room, the doorway, the window. The ceiling was intact above me, the walls aligned to a durable and predictable universe. I could breathe without issue. It was morning. After a few seconds I heard birds chittering, a breeze blowing cool air across my face, the warm light coloring everything in my room. My senses crept back slowly. My nightgown was dry. I pinched some of the material between my finger and thumb and brought it to my nose. The smell of Downy. I reached beneath the blankets and felt my underwear, then put my fingers between my legs. I was soaking wet. I brought my hand up. Blood covered my fingertips.

"It wasn't a dream, Mom!" Tears spilled from my eyes. "It wasn't a dream. It was horrible!"

My mom tried to calm me but I couldn't stop crying, remembering their smell, their touch, the peculiar instrument. My mother wiped my tears and when I looked at her face she was smiling.

"Muffin," she said. "You finally got your period. That's so wonderful, baby."

My period? I had been waiting for this day for so long, and now it was ruined by that horrid dream.

My mother grabbed some clean underpants from my dresser and helped me to the bathroom. I sat in the shower while she changed the sheets on my bed. I spread my legs a bit and looked down at myself, at the floor of the shower stall where a few drops of blood hit, a thin red trail flowing to the drain. Why had it taken so long? Then I thought about the creatures from my dream, their glistening skin, their salamander hands, the unusual instrument, like nothing I had ever seen.

After lunch, I was finally able to stop thinking about them. It was then my mother told me my father had not come back yet.

"I don't know where he is, Muffin." She busied herself clearing the lunch plates. "But we need to get back to the city. I hope he hasn't taken the car."

She stated the scenario without anger and such clarity that I figured she must have an alternate plan for getting back to the city.

"How will we get home?" I was half hoping she would say we couldn't and agree to stay up here all year. We could buy a snowmobile and explore the Soshone Islands area in winter. Drive across the frozen lake, feel the cold sting of the snow against our faces. We could stockpile food and burn fires in the fireplace and read and do my lessons in the evenings. It would be so amazing.

"We'll rent a car in Elico," she said, putting the mayonnaise in the fridge.

"You know what would be fun?"

She looked over at me. "Uh, let's see... staying up here all winter and buying a snowmobile?"

"Yes! Yes!" I was so excited she was thinking the same as me. "How did you know?"

"Because every summer you say the same thing when it's time to go back."

"What do you think?"

"I think, first, we have to call Ben and see if he can come pick us up in his boat."

My mother never asked me about the dream, and I was glad to let it drop—the palpable quality of it was fading and I didn't want to give it new life.

It was another beautiful sunny day and it seemed a sin to leave the island. Ben arrived just after four o'clock that afternoon. My mother and I had our things packed and she would pay Ben and his staff to winterize the cottage once we were gone.

"Hey there, pretty girl," Ben said, as he tied his skiff to the dock. "Did you have a fun summer?"

"I did! What's it like up here in winter, Mr. Bouchard?"

"Winter? Well, it's really kind of incredible. You know, quiet, and everything covered in snow. You and your folks thinking about coming back up after we get ice?"

"I'm working on it. Maybe you could help me."

Ben laughed and started loading our suitcases into the skiff.

"What's the biggest fish in Georgian Bay?" I asked Ben.

Ben pushed the bill of his weathered cap back on his head and squinted up at the sky. "Hmm, let's see. Well, you've got your Atlantic salmon and your lake trout, they get really big. Forty, fifty pounds or so. And of course, your muskies... but, I guess the biggest would be your sturgeon."

"Sturgeon?" I had never heard of that kind of fish. "How big do they get?"

"I've never caught one, you see, but I've seen them a hundred pounds and more and six feet long."

Six feet long? That would be taller than my dad.

"They're prehistoric," Ben said.

"Prehistoric?" my mom said, coming to the boat, not knowing what we'd been talking about.

"Sturgeon!" I said. "Ben told me they're over six feet long and a hundred pounds or more."

My mom seemed to study on that a moment. "That's right," she said, looking at me. "But they can get a lot bigger. White sturgeon can grow twenty feet long and weigh up to 1500 pounds."

I couldn't even imagine it. Twenty feet long. That was as big as our skiff. And weigh fifteen hundred pounds? I wondered how much a horse weighed. I looked up to ask my mom but she had turned her attention to Ben. "Any news?" she asked him.

"No ma'am. None of the staff has seen him." Ben spoke in a somber tone. "Your automobile's still in the parking lot, though."

My mom regarded Ben, then glanced back at me before sending her gaze out to the water.

"Liam took the boat out after you called me but he didn't have any luck," Ben told my mother. "Possible Carter drove over to Kurry Sound?"

My mom shrugged and shook her head. She chewed her lower lip, looking back toward the cottage. I knew she was frustrated with the situation.

"I could call over there," Ben added. "See if Carter might have stopped in for gas or a snack or something."

"Carter would never go to Kurry Sound," my mother said. "No taverns."

Ben pulled his lips back and let his eyes fall to the water.

"Okay, so I guess we're going back without him," my mom finally said.

"Mom! We're not waiting for dad?" I was surprised by how willing she was to leave him behind. "How will he get home?"

"He can rent a car." She reached out to take my hands. "Come on, Muffin. Let's get you in the boat."

After I was in and seated, my mom handed me a life jacket.

"Do I have to wear this?" I said.

"Are you kidding! Put it on!"

Ben folded my wheelchair and placed it toward the front of the boat, then used bungee cords to secure it. I buckled my life vest when my mom sat down next to me and gave me the look. She put her arm around my shoulders and hugged me.

As Ben pulled from the dock, I watched the cottage shrink away until it disappeared behind another island. Something sank in my belly. Over eight months I'd have to wait to come back. I tried to steer my attention away from my disappointment, toward Ben, and his boat, which seemed a lot faster than ours. He stood behind the center console, one hand on the throttle, the other on the steering wheel. I don't know how his cap stayed on his head; I guess the windshield was doing its job.

He cut around one island, then veered in close to another before shooting out toward open water. His mind must contain a map of every rock, every submerged hazard and underwater point in the Soshone Islands area. He didn't even have to slow down through Bell Letter Bay. That was the official name, but Ben called it Boat Eater Bay, on account of all the massive rocks just beneath the surface. My dad always had to idle through, which was why, most of the time, he just took the long way around Bell Island.

When we came out of Boat Eater Bay, Ben went west to an area I had never seen before. We drove around islands with no homes, natural places with incredible pitch pines and red cedars. The area was breathtaking and I was just about to say something to my mom when Ben cut the boat hard and headed for a distant island. When we reached it, he drove right past, toward an object drifting in open water. I had no idea how he even spied it.

As we idled closer it became obvious the boat was ours. Ben pulled up beside it and tied a quick knot onto one of the boat cleats. It was empty except for several crushed beer cans lying on the floor. Ben climbed into the empty skiff and looked around. He glanced back at my mother. She just stared at the boat, unaware she was squeezing me harder. She took her eyes to Ben and for a moment it seemed they were trying to communicate telepathically.

When my mother made no move to get up and drive our boat back to the harbor, Ben finally said, "We'll tow it back..."

"Thanks, Ben," she said.

Ben fixed a line to the bow eye of the skiff, then idled his rig forward until the rope between the two boats tightened, jerking his boat momentarily, our empty boat swinging around and coming in behind his. The rope was maybe twenty-five feet long. Ben eased the throttle forward until both vessels were moving smoothly across the lake.

It took much longer to get back than normal as Ben had to run half throttle the entire way. One of his employees came out to meet us at the dock, grabbing our skiff as it drifted in behind Ben's.

"Put it in an empty slip for now, Gladys," he told the woman who looked to be in her thirties. When she drove off in our boat, Ben told us she was his daughter.

"Her and her boy, Jacob, fell on some hard times in Toronto," Ben said. "Hope they can work things out up here. She's been a big help to me. The boy's still having a rough go here, new school and all."

My mom and I climbed from the boat and I thought I might see my dad waiting for us by the car. Ben grabbed our suitcases and loaded them into a large wheelbarrow that a young man rolled out from behind the office. Ben instructed him to take the bags to the red SUV in the parking lot. My mom handed him the keys and he rolled our things up the plank.

"Thanks, Liam," Ben said.

"I'll be back for the rest," Liam told my mother.

"Sure. Thanks," she said.

When my mom finished with Ben in the office, we went to the car. Liam was bringing the last of our stuff.

"Need anything else?" he said.

"Thank you... for everything," my mother said, pressing some bills into Liam's palm. "Ben told me you went out looking for my husband this morning."

Liam gave her a sad smile and hung his head. He seemed to be struggling for some words to say, but nothing came.

THREE

When she got in the car and started the engine, she must have heard me sniffle. "What's going on?"

"He's never coming back, is he?"

She drew a deep breath and placed both palms on the steering wheel. She turned her head toward me. "I don't know." Her finger gently ushered a tear from my cheek. "Here... let me help you with your seatbelt."

We drove in silence, the radio playing. I was asleep until the bright lights of the U.S. border woke me. The lines were short and it didn't take long to get through. I wiped drool from my mouth and stretched.

"I have to pee," I said.

"Yeah, me too."

We passed over the border and stopped for gas and restrooms at the first station we came to. Back on the highway, I turned the knob looking for a new radio station. I was still thinking about my dad, about the last thing he'd said to me; *It's important that you be good at something, even if it's just fishing.* I thought about the mudpuppy appendage I caught, and the horrible dream with the creatures, how their hands had looked like the appendage dangling from my hook. The images crowded out all my thoughts and I couldn't push them away. Weary from the long drive home, I reached over to find a new station on the radio, something loud and fast. Something to chase the horrible monsters from my head.

"I can't listen to that for the next several hours, Kercy," my mom said. "Find something else or I will."

I fumbled with the radio knob, the creatures standing around my bed. The smell of decay in my nostrils, the ammonia searing into my brain. The fluid pouring from its helmet. The creepy crinkling noise. My fettered wrists. Why couldn't I scream? I turned up the volume.

"Kercy, I'm not kidding," she said, shooting me looks. "Find something good or turn the damn thing off. I'm getting a headache here."

I punched the knob with my finger and the music ended. The tires on the highway beat a rhythmic noise into the car that fed my thoughts.

"Do human kinds of creatures live beneath the water up at the cottage?" I said, staring out the windshield at the highway, the yellow lines blinking past like glowing arrows racing toward the car. I wasn't sure why I believed they lived underwater; maybe because they looked slimy and wet.

"What!" my mother said a bit shocked, her eyes glinting unnaturally in the dark interior. "What are you talking about?"

"Creatures... kind of scary and weird looking?"

"No, of course not. Why?"

After a few excuses and lies about why I was curious, I finally told her my dream. It felt odd relating the details, because I could never really understand what they were doing, so it was hard to explain. But she had always been open with me about sex and everything else, even about her strained relationship with my dad, some of the problems they faced, how their love had faded over the years. After all, I had no friends, I was homeschooled, and really had no interaction with others; where would I get information about life and sex and relationships other than from her?

When I finished, she said nothing, then pulled into the next rest area we came to and stopped the car. "Do you need to go to the bathroom?" she said, turning the engine off.

"No, I'm okay."

"Do you want pop... or chips or anything? They have vending machines."

"A Coke sounds good? And maybe some Doritos."

She dug through her purse and found some cash. "I'll be right back."

When she returned with my snacks, she wore the oddest expression, like someone who had witnessed a horrible traffic accident.

I popped the tab on my Coke and offered her a drink. She shook her head and I wondered why she hadn't started the car yet. She stared out the front window, but not at anything in particular. Her eyes were fixed, yet unfocused. She reached over absently and took the chips from my hands and opened the bag for me, as if she'd heard me fumbling with the package.

"Mom? Are we gonna go?"

She nodded staring out the windshield, making no attempt to leave. Cold leached into the car. I asked her to turn the heater on. After wrestling the keys from her purse, she turned the ignition and switched the heater on, adjusting the fan to high, the rush of it drowning out the roar of the semi-trucks on the highway. After a few minutes the car was so hot I turned the fan to low and dialed back the heat.

"Are you okay, Mom?"

"Yeah, sure." She put the car in reverse and backed out of the spot without checking the rearview mirror. A driver behind her slammed on his brakes, blasting his horn. The loud trumpeting seemed to shake her from her trance. She waved at the driver as if to say sorry, then put the car in gear and guided the SUV back onto the highway.

She didn't say much the rest of the drive back to New York, mostly just asking me if I needed to pee, or if it was too warm or cold in the car. When we got back to our brownstone in Manhattan, she helped me get my suitcase to my room and told me to brush my teeth and get ready for bed. When I finished, she came in to tell me good-night. She sat on the edge of my bed for a moment, caressing my scalp.

"Scoot over," she said, then slid under the covers beside me. She pulled me to her bosom, then pressed her lips to the back of my head. I felt so safe when she held me, even though I sensed her sadness. It outweighed my own.

"Muffin. I love you so much. I won't let anything bad happen to you..."

Summer floated through my thoughts with the hollowness of an echo; the past week, everything that transpired. The image of our empty skiff drifting aimlessly—abandoned in an endless loop of water and sky.

"Is dad dead?" I asked.

I felt a tear run down the back of my head. "Mom, are you okay?" She tightened her embrace, her lips still pressed to my naked scalp.

"Muffin, we are going to work harder on getting you out of that wheelchair." Her words were soft, yet freighted with determination. Another drop ran down the back of my scalp and I pictured my bedroom filling with her tears, the bed slowly rising, floating like a raft, the walls crumbling away until we were drifting toward a big yellow moon.

"Muffin..." my mother said, her voice rife with sorrow. "I'm sorry. And I'm so sorry about your dream."

About my dream? How could she feel responsible for that? I was uncomfortable with her desperation, like she owed me something she had failed to give me, or was going to disappoint me in a way that would be devastating for us both.

It turned out to be the latter.

And it was devastating.

From that night forward my mother and I would never return to the lake cottage together. A month or so after my dad went missing, she took a part-time research position at Rutgers University in the

Department of Marine and Coastal Sciences. For several summers after landing her new position, she made numerous excuses for not returning to Ontario; the research team was going to require her attention all summer... she had to write reports and get them published... they needed further research into the effects of decades of garbage dumping into the Atlantic Ocean...

"Can't you work on them at the cottage?" I said.

"No Internet, Muffin. I need it for my research."

My summers were miserable and hot and I longed for the pristine blue waters of Soshone Islands. Then it got worse. My mother ended my homeschooling and enrolled me in a private high school where I would be at least three years older than any other student in my class and woefully underdeveloped physically and emotionally. Then finally, as if my life weren't already intolerable, she delivered the crushing blow.

"I sold it, Kercy," she said, holding my hands in her lap.

"Sold what?"

"The cottage."

"And you're just telling me now!" I jerked my hands away. "How could you! How could you sell the lake house!"

She held my teary gaze, and although I could see the hurt in her eyes over having to disappoint me this way, I didn't care. It felt like someone had reached inside me and ripped out everything that mattered, every piece and fragment that held my sorry life together in this fucking wheelchair, in this stinking fucking city.

I wanted to scream my hatred, cry my devastation. I wanted to swear, protest, break something, kill something... her resolve maddening, solid, immovable. She would endure my wrath without defensiveness or argument, without an utterance or attempt to placate my outrage, lovingly absorb everything I could hurl at her, everything I could dish out. And when I finished, she would hold me to her chest and let my tears wash over her, wait for my misery to pass, wait for some sense of peace to fill my frail body, wait for calm to restore me.

"I love you, Muffin," she said, after I had wailed and shook a good long bit in her arms. After a few more minutes, she turned to me, her eyes discolored with worry.

"I want you to promise me something, Kercy," she said solemnly.

I looked up at her, wiping slobber from the corner of my mouth.

"Promise me you'll never go back to the cottage... ever..." she said. "Even after I'm dead, Kercy... don't ever go back."

FOUR

It's been twelve years since my father vanished from our skiff in Ontario. Thinking about it now, I realize it must have been very difficult for my mother to have sold that place all those years ago. I didn't know her reasons for selling it. Maybe the memory of my father's sudden disappearance had been too hard on her. Or maybe it was something else, like worry over me drowning again; maybe she was scared of losing me to the lake. I would realize many years after her death, that something happened to her at the lake house which had forever changed the orbit of her life... and mine.

When my mother died a year ago, I inherited her entire estate. Learning how much money I now had, I immediately started chasing my dream of purchasing the cottage back, ignoring my promise to her about never returning. Even though my life had changed tremendously since those days, and New York City wasn't quite as repulsive to me as it once was, I still ached to be back on the water. It took a bit of wrangling but three months ago I purchased the lake house from the couple who bought it from my mother, as well as a new twenty-foot skiff.

It was every bit the way I remembered it. The owners had redecorated, new paint, a few additions here and there, but my mother was everywhere; the kitchen window overlooking the lake, the entry hall closet, the back door leading down to the dock from the kitchen, the floor-to-ceiling bookshelves in the living room. I pictured the lounge chair where I nestled in her lap while she read to me, the floor where we sat at the coffee table and played games, the walls hung with paintings she'd collected from traveling the world. I missed her so much.

"Here, Kercy, I'll take the tray," Gerald said, leaning over the kitchen counter to kiss my neck.

"No, you go on down to the dock. I'll be along in a minute. I just want to slice the cheese. Take that flashlight."

He smiled and kissed my lips.

"Here, take these with you," I said. "The stars are amazing tonight."

He grabbed the two beer bottles and the flashlight and walked from the kitchen. We'd been going out for only a few months and my doctoral work was taking a huge hit since we'd met. But I didn't care—all I wanted to do was spend every moment with him. Gerald was the only man, or boy, I had ever been with, sexually or any other way. Relationships were new to me, but so far, it was wonderful.

The air was crisp and clear when I walked from the back door of the cottage. I could hardly believe I now owned my most favorite place in the world. When I reached Gerald, I set the tray of food down and sat next to him. I was about to tell him we might see the Aurora Borealis when I noticed his distress.

"What's wrong?" I said.

It seemed to take a moment for him to wrangle his thoughts. "Something was out in the water. Something huge." He pointed to some vague spot in the seamless night. A moment later waves lapped at the shoreline, the wake rocking my 20-foot skiff moored to the dock.

"A boat must have gone by," I said. "It's like that all summer long, the waves crashing against the shore, the boat rocking. Not so much at night this time of year, but people still—"

"No, Kercy. I would have seen a boat. Or at least heard it. And whatever it was didn't go by... it just came up, and went back down."

I tried to smile, unsettled by his grave tone. I got up and sat in his lap and put my lips to his. It was probably a boat too far from shore to hear, impossible to see in the absolute blackness once the sun was gone. Even so, it was a bit odd for September, especially at night. Not many people came up this late unless it was to winterize their cottage and pull their yachts from the water. The weather was fickle, sometimes turning frigid overnight, and most people were done with the islands by early September.

He took his attention back to the water. "What could possibly be large enough in this ecosystem to cause that kind of disturbance just by surfacing?" Gerald said, not so much to me, but to his own professorial mind. Gerald was a geologist with an emphasis in Earth Sciences at NYU. That's where we met originally, in his class. I was taking it as part of my doctoral work in Anthropology. My interest focused on how a changing Earth affected evolution in a technological age.

The waves subsided just as he finished his sentence.

"Lots of huge fish prowl these waters," I said, knowing that no fish—not even the shy bottom-hugging sturgeon—would cause such an event, but I didn't want to keep badgering Gerald about it being a boat. "Maybe a moose."

He looked over at me. "Moose don't swim underwater, Kerse." Now he looked disturbed, not so much at me but maybe over the dwindling possibilities which could explain such an anomaly. For the past few months all we'd done was laugh, have sex, and hang out with Netflix, or play games. Nothing had gotten serious before, except for our conversations about climate change and its effects on society. We even discussed writing a book together some day. But our conversations, no matter how grave, always devolved into sex or cuddling.

Gerald and I had driven up to the lake two days earlier, and had been having so much fun, taking boat rides, making love, cooking together, but he was heading back to New York in the morning. I planned to stay for the next couple of weeks and try to get caught up on my doctoral work. But I hated the turn our long weekend was taking.

"Hey, it's getting chilly," I said, making up an excuse to go back inside. I rarely ever got cold. "Let's take our snacks and beer to the house, light some candles and take a hot bath together."

He looked over at me, then back at the water. "Yeah, it probably was a boat."

Gerald was in the kitchen melting cheese for a fondue while I was upstairs running our bath. Standing next to the tub, watching bubbles form as the water filled, I found myself in a full-blown life review, from birth to now, how far I've come from the day I was born. I remember everything about my birth, including the seven and half months leading up to it. When my mother was happy, a feeling of joy spread throughout her womb, informing every microbe of my small organism swimming inside her. When she caressed her swollen belly and softly sang to me, every ounce of me flushed with love and warmth. When she was scared, my world constricted and became troubling and cold. In the seventh month I was overcome with dread. My time inside her was coming to an end, I could sense it. It was too soon. When the contractions started, I heard my father's murmurings, hurried and frightened. Anxiety coursed through me, both my own and my parents'. We were all new to this miracle. We were all evolving. My parents had expected another month or more to prepare. I had hoped for an eternity within my dark, watery home. I would not be able to breathe in my mother's world—I knew that with certainty—and she would be lost to me forever. And when her final contraction forced me from her womb, my months of comfort came to an abrupt and jarring end.

The first words I heard upon entering the light world were, "Oh my God, what is it?" They were spoken by a nurse who was immediately dismissed from the delivery room by the attending physician who raced to start my lungs. It would be my first CPR. My father was quiet, but my mother's voice, which I had grown to cherish and rely upon, was reassuring and gentle. "Breathe my sweet little Kercy, my little Muffin." The doctor handed my wretched little body to her, every cell in it struggling for life, not in concert, but against each other. She held me to her and pressed her lips to my chest and at that moment I filled my lungs with air for the first time in my life. I felt like I would explode. Pain shot through my body, through limbs and parts I was not yet aware of. I wasn't so sure that this life everyone was fighting so hard to save was worth the excruciating torture I was subjected to.

My mother sobbed silently. My father left the delivery room. I was grotesque. Partly from being premature, but mostly from defects; syndactyly causing webbing between my fingers and toes, an abnormal fontanel which resulted in the top of my head being swollen and ruddy, my dismal, turbid complexion, and not a single hair anywhere on my body. My left ear was small, ill-formed and folded over the ear canal, closing it off. With my disfigured body still slick and wet with amniotic fluid, and my protruding coccyx bone like some prehensile creature, I had the appearance of a newt.

The first 28 months of my life were spent in the hospital. Surgery after surgery. Removing the webbing. Healing the gap at the top of my skull. Skin grafts. My mother holding me in the evenings, trying to calm my crying. Reconstruction. Stitches. Her tears and unwavering attempt to make me feel normal. Painful recoveries. Painful discoveries. Lung surgery. Open heart surgery. Bone grafts. Hundreds of thousands of dollars for experimental procedures. It was as if I had been designed for a different world.

"God, Kercy, you are so beautiful," Gerald said, coming up behind me. I was standing next to the tub, staring into the water, unaware he had come into the bathroom. He reached down and turned the water off, then wound his arms around my waist from behind, my naked body reflecting in the full-length mirror on the back of the bathroom door. He slid his palms up my ribs, tenderly kissing my neck, his fingers dark against my pale skin. I looked at him in the reflection, then let my eyes fall down over my own body, at my full round breasts, beauty I would never have believed possible and would never take for granted. My legs were my biggest miracle. They were shapely and full of form now, even though the muscles beneath the skin still lacked the consistent strength for tennis, or waterskiing... luckily, I didn't care about any of that.

Pulling the clip from my hair, I watched my lush auburn curls cascade down the sides of my face, over my shoulders. My second greatest miracle. It was only a few years ago that my scalp was still a desert terrain, random tufts of growth. I was now forever done shaving my head and wearing hats.

The operations performed when I was a baby had helped, certainly; but still at twenty, my body had yet to mature. I was weak and horribly scrawny, unable to support my weight. Because of the wreckage of my legs, doctors told me I would never walk. And with my ill-formed uterus, like my mother's, they said it would be impossible for me to conceive.

Gerald took my left earlobe between his teeth and bit gently. I bent forward, gripping the edge of the tub and Gerald's fullness filled me. I loved having sex with him and I think I could have gone for weeks without ever leaving the bed. Of course, it was affecting my performance in the doctoral program. I should have cared, but I didn't. And every time we made love I secretly thanked my best friend Cindy; if not for her, I would never have known the sexual intimacy I enjoyed with Gerald.

When Gerald orgasmed, he melted into me, using my hips like handles, pressing his abdomen hard against my bottom. I had yet to orgasm ever and had no idea what it would be like, but if it was more pleasurable than this I figured the unbridled ecstasy might kill me.

Turning in his arms to face him, I couldn't help but notice the fatigue pulling at his features. "Wow... you look rough," I said, smiling, his eyes half-open, his face haggard in the candlelight. "Are you already too old for marathon sex?"

"I'm starting to wonder..."

Gerald was thirty-five, had been married for two years, no children, divorced by twenty-five, and even though I couldn't bear to ask how many women he'd been with, I figured the number was large. He was a beautiful man, with dark green eyes and smooth skin the color of dark caramel. Gerald brought a mature and sensual pace to our sex while I treated it like a carnival ride, a tilt-a-whirl I had a whole roll of tickets for and wanted to use every one. Even so, Gerald didn't seem to mind my insatiable desire.

We snacked on toasted pita wedges and cheese fondue in the tub. When Gerald finished his beer he told me to turn around. After soaping my back, he started to gently massage my shoulders. "Please don't take this wrong, Kercy, but... I'm not sure I like this place," he said.

"What?" I spun toward him, splashing suds and water onto the floor. "It's incredible up here?"

Gerald suddenly seemed morose.

"I know Cindy's coming up tomorrow," he said. "But I don't think it's safe up here, just the two of you..."

"If I didn't know better, I'd think you were falling in love with me." I was just trying to be clever and lighten the mood, but when the words left my lips I felt so stupid. I flushed with embarrassment. This was unchartered water for me. It was obvious I didn't possess instincts to navigate a relationship. In so many ways I still felt very crippled. Gerald didn't know he was the first man I had ever been with, and I had never wanted him to know for fear he might think I was freakish and unlovable.

"I love you, Kercy."

For a moment I just sat twisted toward him. Had he said that? Without giving it too much thought, I spun around on my knees sloshing more water and suds over the edge of the tub. I knotted my arms around his neck and couldn't stop kissing him. I had been in love with him since last semester, from the moment I walked into his classroom and saw him standing at his desk. But we barely spoke then. When I ran into him during winter break at a cafe near the university, and he asked me out, I wanted to tell him how I felt, but Cindy told me to chill and take it slow. "Don't wreck it before it starts," Cindy had warned.

Was I about to spoil everything now by telling him?

"I love you so much," I said, and just then remembered he was leaving in the morning. The thought emptied me and I wasn't even sure I could be away from him. In Gerald I had found something I never believed possible and didn't want it to stop for a second, much less two weeks. There was so much I wanted to know about him, so much I needed him to know about me. But I wanted to ask Cindy first. I was in over my head.

"You okay?" Gerald said.

"Yeah, yeah... I'm more than okay."

How wreckable was this love? I wondered. How much could it withstand? Psychologists stress that children are not to blame for their parents' break ups, yet I was pretty certain I had caused the demise of my own parents' marriage. Even as a newborn, I had felt my father's disgust over me, as if I had been proof of some inferior gene he never knew he possessed. And coming from a wealthy and successful family, my father wasn't sure how to present me to relatives, so we avoided those kindred connections altogether, eventually moving from our home in Connecticut to New York City. Maybe my father figured that grotesque things had a better chance to thrive in the Big Apple, that the city was more accepting of anomalies... or maybe he secretly hoped that it would destroy those things that were unsalvageable.

While I was still in full-body hug, nearly ready to take him again in the tub, Gerald said, "Aren't you afraid?"

I eased the shifter back on my libido for a moment. Was I supposed to be afraid of love? Is that what he was asking? "I guess a little. Are you?"

He seemed confused. Was that the wrong answer? Maybe I

wasn't supposed to be frightened of it. I wanted to ask for an adult timeout to go call Cindy.

"So, you are afraid to stay up here?" he finally said.

Realizing that love didn't have to be scary brought me a moment of relief. But the lake cottage wasn't scary either. It provided me the greatest peace I'd ever know—but it seemed that he was more comfortable thinking I was frightened of the place. That was odd to me. But there was so much I had yet to tell Gerald about myself—my inability to conceive, my many birth defects, my lack of experience with other men, my odd belief that I could breathe underwater—and I didn't want to start lying on top of all my non-disclosures. But I felt I had no choice.

"Well, sure. It's pretty remote, but I'll be fine. And Cindy will be here, so..." I said, knowing I had just told him another lie. Cindy had texted me and said she'd be a few days late, that she wouldn't make it up until Tuesday or Wednesday, but I couldn't tell Gerald, not now. He'd refuse to leave, and regardless of the fact that I would be thrilled if he didn't go, I knew I'd get no work done if he stayed.

"I don't want you to worry," I said. "I'm going to be just fine."

FIVE

Gerald fell asleep before the movie ended. When I switched off the DVD player and television, the bedroom fell dark. I laid on my back and felt something pulling loose inside me, something stretching, about to fail. In a few hours I would be driving him across the bay in the skiff. I would kiss him goodbye, and he would drive from the parking lot and for a few seconds he would see me waving, a small figure in his rearview mirror. But what would he remember by the time he reached the highway? The grad student who could never get her fill of sex? What would happen in the two weeks we'd be apart? Then the strangest notion broke in: Would this be the last time I ever saw him?

I wanted to wake him, have him hold me, and then I must have fallen asleep. When I woke, I had no idea what time it was. With the bedroom so dark, it took a few seconds for my eyes to adjust, yet even before they did, I knew Gerald and I were not alone. Three beings stood in the room, dark creatures with iridescent skin, one on either side of us, and one at the foot of the bed. I shot upward trying to scream, but no sound came out, and then I realized I wasn't even sitting up, but still lying on my back, unable to move. Was this a dream? I tried to force away the gauzy overlay inside my head, as if all my senses had been packed in foam. I could barely turn my head to the side, seemingly tethered by some invisible force, like a sheet of plastic pulled tightly over my face. Shifting my eyes to the left I saw Gerald lying beside me. His eyes were wide open, terrified, as if paralyzed with fear and unable to move. He shifted his eyes toward me and I could tell he was unable to move his body. He tried to speak, struggling to part his lips, unable to make a sound. The creature next to me had a repulsive, fusty smell, dank, with a hint of ammonia that stung the lining of my nose. This all felt so familiar. The creature removed my T-shirt while the one at the base of the bed removed my sleep shorts. I was naked, helpless, and Gerald was quaking next to me, neither of us able to do anything. A moment later the creature nearest me held a bright squarish light the size of a small jewelry box over my pubic area. It was bright as the sun, but greenish in color. The lamp caused no pain as it passed a few inches above my body, up toward my breasts, then scanned back down again. In that moment I realized I was holding my breath and I exhaled and quickly filled my lungs. One of the other creatures slid something into my vagina and the one with the light started to perform another body scan, beginning at my thighs, moving to my solar plexus, my torso, my breasts, my throat. The object inside me hurt and seemed to burn as the light passed over, but I was unable to scream, my vocal cords dead. The object was withdrawn slowly from between my legs and in a moment the pain started to subside. The other creature switched the bright light off, the room falling into an eerie, milky darkness. The third one leaned over Gerald and pushed some sort of instrument up his left nostril and I could see by the way Gerald's eyes flickered the procedure was extremely painful. I shifted myself as best I could to see Gerald, to make sure he was okay, but his eyes were shut and he was either asleep, or dead. I couldn't tell. I wanted to say something to him but I felt suddenly groggy, drifting into some solid black space.

SIX

Soft sunlight painted the bedroom in a pleasing warm glow. I looked over at Gerald lying next to me, his eyes closed, his mouth soft. I got up to use the bathroom when an unsettling dread shuffled through me. Sitting down on the toilet, I was seized by a jumbled rush of disturbing images. I felt dizzy, a movie playing behind my eyes: I'm in bed, the room dark, Gerald lying beside me and I can't tell if I'm asleep or awake. Three hideous creatures are standing next to us, with instruments, a bright greenish light of some sort, and I'm naked...

A knock came at the bathroom door. "Hey, baby, you okay?"

"Yes," I said, glad to be wrenched from the unsettling vision. "I'll be out in a second."

"No worries. Just checking where you were."

Stepping from the bathroom, I felt like I was sleepwalking. Despite the fact that Gerald was standing right in front of me, I sensed some barrier I could not penetrate, an inability to reach across to him.

"Something wrong?" he said, aware I was staring at him.

"I'm not sure. Did you sleep okay?"

"Yeah, fine. You look... bothered..."

"Did you have any bad dreams...?" I asked.

He looked at me with curiosity. "I don't really have dreams... at least ones I recall..."

After a pitifully disingenuous smile, I wanted to make light of what I was feeling, but I couldn't shake the unruly images in my head, the three creatures, the light. And Gerald; I could see him now. Helpless, terrified. It pushed me nearly to tears to see him so frightened and vulnerable. The worst was, I felt as if it had actually happened.

"Are we okay?" I finally asked, feeling a frightening disconnection, not only from Gerald, but from myself, like I had become unmoored from my own body. I couldn't shake the feeling that this would be the last time we would ever be together. Since we started dating, we had not been away from each other for more than a day or two. Was this a normal feeling, this unfathomable and pervasive fear? Or was this something else?

"*Are we okay?*" he said, repeating my question. "Why wouldn't we be?"

"I don't know. Will I ever see you again?"

"What!" He moved closer, eyes tightened to slits, and cradled my face in his palms. "Kercy, I am crazy in love with you. But sometimes I get the feeling that you think our relationship is made of helium, that at any moment it will float away and be gone forever."

That was exactly how I felt. I imagined there would be a kiss, then Gerald would open his eyes, his face screwed into pain as he shoved me away, like some kind of backward Frog Prince story, as if Gerald would kiss me one day and turn me back into the tailed, warty amphibian I was born to be. I would never forget the nurse the day I was born; *Oh my God, what is it?*

After breakfast, Gerald brought his duffle down to the kitchen. I didn't want him to leave, and I didn't want to cry, so I grabbed the boat keys from the rack. "Coffee for the boat ride?" I said, handing him a thermos cup.

"Yeah, that sounds great." He paused, as if gauging my mood. "What's going on?"

"What's wrong with your nose?" I noticed he was holding a tissue under his left nostril.

"Nothing. Just a little nose bleed."

My insides went to paste, picturing the scene so clearly, as if it was happening in real time, the creature pushing the instrument up Gerald's left nostril, his inability to fight back, the pain he must have felt. My world started to spin, ready to topple.

"Do you get nose bleeds?" I said.

"No. I figure it must have to do with all this fresh air up here... my nostrils need their daily supply of taxi exhaust." He smiled at me, until his expression suddenly shifted to one of concern. "What's going on, Kercy? You look absolutely ashen..."

"I'm fine... let's get going." I felt sick to my stomach, no longer able to discern between what was illusory and what was real. Did I have a terrible nightmare that my mind had somehow morphed to sync with reality? Was I imagining these connections between the dream and Gerald's nose bleed? I had to get outside. I headed for the door, Gerald hurrying to catch up.

The brisk morning air was a rejuvenating blast to my sour mood as we cut a path across the bay. Noise from the outboard drowned out any possibility for conversation during the ride to the harbor, and my acute attention on the GPS chart unit made it nearly impossible to think about anything else. I was relieved that the dream was fading under the cold draft of the boat ride. Even so, it left behind a sickening residue, like the slimy trail of a slug.

"Do you need that to get back to the harbor?" Gerald shouted over the outboard, referring to the chart device I was looking at intently.

"Yes," I shouted back. "It will take me a while to learn all the islands." That realization had become painfully obvious my first day back on the lake after all those years. From all my summers in this area, I assumed I would know exactly where to go, but the truth was,

I had no clue. After I bought the cottage, I had mentioned to Ben how lost I felt on the water, and he'd assured me that I'd get the hang of it. "Unless you're actually driving the boat, you never really learn the water," he'd said. He explained that that was why everything seemed so foreign to me. I trusted Ben and it made sense; all those summers coming up I had never once driven the boat, just sat there gawking at the surroundings without context.

I was trying to put Gerald's mind at ease, but his expression was telling me I failed. Suddenly my mind switched to a totally different subject, something I had wanted to speak with him about but we never got around to it. Unsure why, I was questioning my desire to work on my dissertation for the next two weeks, or even complete the PhD program at all. Did any of that matter anymore? What did I need a doctorate in Anthropology for? What would I even do with it? The overwhelming feeling to escape caught me off guard. Was this born of fear over the dream? Was my resolve to work at the cottage disintegrating...? Then, like an unwelcome visitor, my mother's words were in my head; *Promise me you'll never go back to the cottage...*

Gulls winged and screeched as I pulled the skiff to the harbor dock. Ben came out to meet us, and just seeing him brought me great relief, and I felt as if I could breathe again. He grabbed the bow line and swung a couple of swift knots around the cleat. I cut the engine and tied off the stern.

"You folks had nice weather this weekend..." Ben said.

"Yeah," Gerald said. "Real nice." Gerald slung his duffle onto the dock and then stepped from the boat. I followed him out and hugged Ben. I guess I held him longer than he expected.

"There's hot coffee in the office," he told Gerald, then said to me as Gerald headed for the little white building, "Everything okay, Kercy?"

"Yeah, yeah... I'm fine." I released my hold on Ben.

"Do you see Cindy?" Gerald asked, returning from Ben's office with coffee for each of us, then taking his eyes to the parking lot.

"She's not always punctual," I told him and felt terrible lying. "She'll be along."

Gerald picked up his duffle and we headed to his car. Since we'd known each other, we never felt it necessary to fill each and every moment with conversation, but this silence was awkward and uncomfortable.

"I've been thinking," I said to Gerald. "Maybe I should just bail on the whole doctorate thing. My heart's not in it right now anyway."

He stopped. "Why would you even consider that?"

His reaction surprised me. I thought he might be happy about that decision. We could spend more time together. No more schedule balancing. What difference was my education to him anyway? People went to school when they didn't have other options, but I had lots of options. I didn't need to go to school. I didn't need a job. I had this beautiful man who loved me. I had an amazing brownstone in Manhattan. I had everything. Gerald reacted the way my mother would have if she were still alive.

"What's the big deal, Gerald? It's not like I have to work."

"Work? Wow, Kercy, education isn't about getting a job. That's just using knowledge to assimilate yourself into the workforce. It's about fulfilling your potential as a human being. It's about fostering ideas and the ability to think, about expansion, about consciousness—"

"Hey, okay. Sorry I brought it up." I suddenly felt like one of his students getting the education-is-a-privilege speech.

"Kercy?" Gerald dropped his duffle to the pavement. "What's going on? This isn't you."

When I started crying, Gerald pulled me close. That's where I wanted to stay, against his chest, the smell of his sport coat, his hands wrapped around my back, his aftershave, his lips pressed to the top of my head, my tears spoiling his shirt.

"Maybe I should stay until Cindy gets here," he said.

Why the fuck had I lied to him about when she was coming? Now I had to lie again. I wiped my eyes. "No, I'm sorry. I'll be fine.

She'll be along soon. You need to get to the border before all the fishermen or you'll be waiting to get back into the U.S. until the next ice age." That was true during fishing season—long lines of cars hauling boats back to the states after a weekend of fishing in Canada—but not now. Few sportsmen came up this time of year except to hunt moose.

Walking Gerald to his car I couldn't help but notice his silence. It was different somehow. "You're worried you're going to miss me so much you won't be able to concentrate on all your little coeds, right?" I said, trying to raise the fog of my own discomfort.

Gerald wore the pained expression of someone who'd just heard a close relative had died.

"What is it?" I said.

"Nothing. Just a weird image that popped into my head."

"Like what?"

"Your naked body washed in green light..."

I felt as if I'd been punched in the gut, my air gone, my chest tight. "Gerald..." I finally said in a whisper, unable to form a sentence. After Gerald started his engine, he rolled his window down.

"I'll call you this evening, when I get back to the city," he said, a new burnished edge to his features.

"You okay?" I said, my question reflecting my own anxiety in that moment.

"Of course. How about you?"

I leaned in and kissed him again. "I love you," I said.

"I love you, too. I'll talk to you soon."

I watched his car pull from the parking lot and disappear behind the sugar maples lining the road, half expecting him to turn around and come back to get me, and believing if he did I would go with him in a second.

When I walked back to the harbor, Ben was nowhere to be found. Instead, a young man was in the office talking on the phone. He looked to be almost six foot and built like an Olympic swimmer, around my age. He wore a wave of crazy black hair on top of his head, shaved to stubble on the sides, his nose pierced. I waited a moment for him to hang up.

"Is Ben still here?" I asked.

"Grandpa just left," the young man said.

"You must be Jacob, Ben's grandson."

"Yes, ma'am."

I remembered that name. The last time my mother and I were leaving the lake, Ben had mentioned his daughter and her son had moved back to the area.

"Your mom's name is Gladys, right?"

"How did you know that?"

"Blessed with a great memory. How is she?"

His expression darkened. "She's gone."

"I'm so sorry. What..." I decided to let it drop. It wasn't any of my business.

"She took her own life a few years back. Is there anything else I can do for you, Ms. Powell?"

"Yes... please call me Kercy." On the wall behind Jacob were some posters I hadn't noticed before. They mostly looked like young women, all adults. In large letters at the top of each poster was the word MISSING. Jacob spun his head to see what I was looking at, then turned back toward me.

"Some of those are from before the end of the millennium, but Grandpa leaves them up just in case...you never know..." Jacob said.

I nodded my head in agreement, my attention caught by one in particular. "That one." I pointed toward a poster. "You can take that one down. It's my dad." I always knew how handsome he'd been, but this picture made him look like a movie star. For a second I was going to ask for it. I had no pictures of him, but it was too macabre.

"Grandpa told me about that. Really sorry."

I nodded.

"Grandpa said you were going to be up for a couple of weeks. If there's anything you need don't hesitate to call, Ms. Powell... Kercy."

"Yeah, thanks, Jacob." I guess I stood too long staring at the poster of my dad. Jacob went over and took it down, handing it to me.

"No. Thanks." I couldn't tell if he was disappointed or surprised. When I walked from the office, I noticed two men on the dock, one was climbing out of my skiff.

"Hey, there, can I help you?" I called out, hurrying toward them. I had never seen either one before, and wondered if they worked for Ben. The man with the beard, the one who'd been in my skiff, looked at me and smiled.

"Hello, ma'am. Just admiring your boat. That's a fine GPS unit you have. You been happy with it?"

I looked down at the unit and realized it was still on, the blue path from my cottage to the harbor still displayed on the screen. I had been trying to wean myself off using the GPS, attempting to learn the route so I didn't need to use it. But with so many islands and so many ways to get lost, I wasn't having much luck. Plus, the GPS allowed me to traverse the water at night if I needed to get back to the harbor for any reason. Even with the electronics, I still had to be wary of the enormous rocks that reached up just beneath the surface. They were the most unnerving obstacles, sending a sickly charge up my chest when I grazed one.

I climbed down into my boat. "Works just fine," I said, switching the unit off. What good would that do now... they had already seen it. He could have taken a picture with his phone. Paranoia gripped me. I tried to push it away.

"Are you running a shuttle service?" the other man asked. He wore sunglasses and a cap and I couldn't see his eyes. He stood with hands in pockets, unshaven. "We saw you drop off that black fella here at the dock. We were wondering if we could get a tour of the area. The regular outfits are all closed for the season."

Black? How odd for them to refer to Gerald as a "black" fella. Gerald was African American, but why not just refer to him as a "man" or a "guy" or something. Why the race distinction? And where had they been when I pulled in? I hadn't seen them hanging around the dock.

"No, I'm not running a shuttle," I said, undoing the stern line from the cleat. They were starting to creep me out and I just wanted to get away from the dock. "Ben rents boats. You might talk to him."

"Ben?" the bearded man said.

"The owner of the harbor." I turned the key to fire the outboard, and then walked to the front of the boat to release the bow line. The man with the beard squatted down to untie it for me, bringing us face-to-face. His breath smelled of alcohol. His eyes snagged on mine. It was unsettling.

"We have a boat," he said, motioning his head toward the parking lot, toward the blue pickup with the boat and trailer. "We've just never been up before and thought we might get a guide to show us the area. You know, learn where all the hazards are."

Their boat appeared to be a deep-V aluminum rig, very popular on northern lakes. I wanted to remember it just in case.

"My sonar and GPS stopped working," he said. "Need to get me a new unit in town."

"Well, good luck," I said, grabbing the steering wheel and slowly guiding my skiff from the marina. I was relieved to be putting more and more water between us. When I passed the No Wake buoy, I stabbed the throttle forward until the boat was gliding along the smooth surface of Georgian Bay. The day was gorgeous, sunny, with an infinite blue sky, belying the approaching winter and frigid temperatures only weeks away. A few white clouds gathered above the trees. It was still early in the morning and the wind had yet to pick up.

Distracted by the two guys at the dock, I had forgotten to switch the GPS back on. I was about to when I decided to follow my instincts and see if I could find my way back to the cottage without it. If I got lost, I'd use it to find my way back. So, I just drove. It was too pretty to head straight to the cottage and crack open the books.

The area I found myself in felt familiar, especially when I saw the first behemoth rock pass a few feet beneath the skiff. I knew immediately where I was. Boat Eater Bay. I jerked the throttle back and the boat quickly settled to the water. My heart was pounding as gigantic rocks passed beneath me, larger than my boat, some maybe six feet below, some only inches. I steered carefully and was almost out when the prop dinged a rock. "Fuck!" The boat moved forward but the prop was surely screwed. When the depth started dropping I knew I was free of the huge boulders. I cut the ignition, then held the tilt button on the engine control until the lower unit was free of the water. From the transom I could see the prop. One blade was nicked, the white paint gone revealing a shiny spot. Other than that, it seemed okay to drive. I would have Ben look at it when I went to pick up Cindy.

I started the engine and everything seemed fine. As I motored between two islands, the bay opened up, treating me to a breathtaking vista of sky and water with no land on the horizon. I eased the throttle back until the boat was almost stopped, then switched off the outboard. Silence. Complete and absolute. I glanced at the sonar unit in the dash. The LED readout gave me a depth of 107 feet. I looked around and the closest land was well over a mile away, while the water off the bow stretched to infinity.

Was this where we had found our boat that afternoon all those years ago, the empty beer cans, my father gone? I couldn't know for sure, so much of the area looked the same. I took a deep breath and gazed down into the water. Did I expect to see him there? I sat a moment and forced my thoughts toward Gerald, then forward to the day, forward to my visit with Cindy. I could hardly wait for her to get here.

The sun felt so good I decided to take off my blouse and jeans. The air temperature must have been close to 65 degrees. I removed my tennis shoes, then my bra and underwear. I placed my clothes on the seat so they wouldn't get wet, then stepped up onto the front deck.

What are you doing, Kercy! my mother would be screaming, frantic. *Get off there!*

How long had it been since I'd been swimming? At least ten years. No, more than that. I let my head fall forward, allowing my eyes to travel down into the gin-clear water. I always felt like I should be able to see directly to the bottom, as if there was nothing except air between me and the rocks below, as if I were floating, but that wasn't the case. The water, as clear as it was, still devolved into a greenish blue blur, maybe twenty feet down, maybe more, impossible to tell as there was nothing to draw focus, nothing to bring form to the formless depths.

My stomach was butterflies when I raised my right foot to the gunwale, then stepped onto it with my left. A moment of teetering, then perfect unswerving balance, until I stepped from the boat. The bay engulfed me, the frigid water wrapping me like an icy blanket as I sank, the cold stinging my skin until the familiar thermostat kicked in. Sudden, inexplicable warmth. Fully immersed, I could see perfectly, all the colors, the rocks over a hundred feet below coming up to meet me. I could see small imperfections in the boulders, fissures and discolorations from millenniums of glacial toil. Small fish darted around my feet in a rainbow of colors and bubbles. I tilted my head back to see the sky above me broken by the water's surface, like a stained-glass window changing colors, shifting shapes. It was breathtaking. When I reached the bottom, I pushed my fingers into the silty bottom and sparkles rose up, swirling around me as I lifted my palm, colorful rocks and grains of sand pouring from my hand. I watched as plankton drifted past my eyes. At times I felt I could see actual water molecules, spinning and flipping in and out of view. I wanted Gerald to see what I could see so he wouldn't fear this magical place. Then, in the strangest twist of logic, Gerald's words from just a couple of hours earlier came back to me: "Education isn't about getting a job. That's just using knowledge to assimilate yourself into the workforce." But it was the word *assimilate* that stood out in my mind. Growing up, I heard that word over and over from my mother. When she home-schooled me, she would take me to Central Park during our lunch breaks and stop my wheelchair next to a park bench and tell me to watch the joggers and people walking by. "What am I supposed to be looking for?" I asked her. "Watch how they move," she'd tell me. "Imagine their muscles working beneath their skin. Observe how their arms swing in rhythm with their step. Pay attention to their stride, how each foot comes to the ground, how it pushes them forward, the toes bending, the foot rising off the ground ever so slightly, shifting forward to begin the next step. Feel how that feels." "Why?" I asked. Without taking her eyes from the passersby, she would say, "Assimilation, Kercy. You will walk again. You will be able to do amazing things. You are special... you have the power to assimilate. You just have to observe with your entire being, see every detail, feel the movement in your own muscles." I had asked her how she knew I was special, that I had this *special power*. "You are *enhanced*." By all the operations I had? I was confused. She said, "By a force greater than ourselves..." She seemed to struggle with the words. I said, "Like God?" At this, tears formed at the lower borders of her eyes and froze there, her features carved with pain, as if some protective veneer was being stripped away inside her...

Just then something at the corner of my vision wrenched me from the memory. Swimming toward me was an enormous creature I thought at first might be a sturgeon, or maybe a bull shark which are euryhaline and can live easily in either salt or fresh water, but as it approached I realized it was neither of those, that this creature was much larger than I had originally thought, and as it swam above me it blocked out the sun and everything went black.

SEVEN

When I opened my eyes, I was lying in my bed at the cottage, the blankets pulled up to my chest. Daylight filled the room but I couldn't recall how I had gotten back after my swim. I pulled the comforter off and saw that I was still naked, but didn't see my clothes. I glanced at the alarm clock on the bureau. It was one thirty in the afternoon. Where had the morning gone?

I pulled my robe off the hanger and carefully wound myself into it, cinching the belt at my waist. As I reached for the door, a noise rose from the kitchen, the clapping of wood on wood, someone rummaging in the kitchen cabinets and drawers and not putting forth much effort to be secretive about it. I eased into the hallway and stood near the banister. Muffled voices traveled up the stairwell. Men's voices. Those creepy guys from the harbor was my initial reaction. But how could they have found my cottage? Had he taken a photo of my GPS as I had imagined?

I retreated back into the bedroom and locked it. A moment later footfalls approached up the stairs. I rushed to find a weapon more dangerous than mouthwash. Searching the closet, I dumped my outfits and jeans on the floor, then wrestled the wooden clothes bar from the side holders, nearly dropping the damn thing when a knock came at the door. I tried to quash the pounding in my chest, my eyes fixed on the door handle. Another knock. I raised the bar to a batting position when someone spoke.

"Kercy, are you awake?"

"Ben? Is that you Ben?"

"Yeah, Kercy, are you okay?"

I dropped the clothes bar and rushed to unlock the door. When I swung it open, Ben stood in the hallway.

"I heard voices downstairs. I didn't know who it was," I said.

Ben inhaled sharply and hung his head a moment. "I thought you were..."

"Grandpa? Everything okay?" a voice issued up from the kitchen.

"Yes, Jacob," Ben said, looking down the stairwell. "We'll be there in a minute."

When we got to the kitchen Jacob was sipping a cup of coffee with a towel around his shoulders. His hair was wet and stringy, and he was wearing some ragged bib overalls with a flannel shirt that seemed a little small for him.

"What happened?" I said. "Is Jacob okay?"

They both stared at me. Jacob's eyes grew wide and Ben was shaking his head.

"You nearly drowned out there, Kercy," Ben said. "If Jacob hadn't seen you, you... well... you'd be dead."

I sat down across from Jacob. I didn't understand what they were talking about. Ben brought me a steaming cup of coffee. I thanked him and looked back at Jacob who gave me a weak smile.

"I really don't understand, Ben," I said.

"Jacob forgot to give you those groceries you ordered," Ben said. "Luckily, he got right after you and was able to follow your boat wake and figured you were lost, since you were going the wrong way. But when he saw your boat, well..." Ben hesitated, obviously reluctant to finish the sentence.

"I saw you step into the water," Jacob said. "You were naked... and just stepped right off the bow into the water."

I remembered stepping into the water and all the things I saw on the bottom, the huge fish, everything...

"How did you find me?" I said to Jacob. "I mean it's really deep out there. How could you see me on the bottom?"

Jacob shook his head as if confused by my statement. "You were floating, Ms. Powell," he said. "You were floating face down on the surface of the water. When I pulled you into my boat you weren't even breathing. It took me nearly five minutes to revive you. Your skin... your lips... they were blue... I didn't think I could bring you back."

"Jacob," Ben said. "If you've warmed up, why don't you head on back to the harbor and help Liam get those boats out of the water. Don't forget to take your wet clothes back with you. And grab that heavy jacket out of my boat. I won't need it." Ben handed Jacob a plastic trash sack bulging with soaked clothes.

Jacob paused at the back door. "I'm glad you're okay, Ms. Powell... Kercy."

"Thank you, Jacob..." I said, confused, hollow.

He pulled the door closed behind him. I turned to Ben. "I'm so sorry, Ben. I don't know..."

Ben sat down across from me, palming his coffee cup. "I've known your family nearly all my life, Kercy. Your grandmother was one of the most beautiful and generous women I ever met. Your mother was like a saint, lent me money when my daughter Gladys was going through her own stuff, seeing a psychiatrist and all. Then Jacob came along, all kinds of problems as a baby, operations and such. But your mother helped me with that, too. Needless to say, I am indebted to your family, Kercy. They have shown me a brand of kindness that's rare even for family."

Never had I felt so terrible. I didn't know what to say. Ben had always been in my corner, and now I felt like I'd let him down.

"That summer your daddy went missing... that was a terrible time for you and your momma," Ben said. "I wasn't surprised to get that call from her just a few days after you left asking me if I could help sell the cottage. Made me sad to think I wouldn't see any of you again, but I understood. It was hard on her."

"Hard? What do you mean?"

"She loved it up here, but she was scared to death."

"Scared of this place? Of the lake?"

Ben stared at me a moment, his eyes sympathetic, yet stern. He exhaled roughly and shook his head. "Of you, Kercy. She was scared to death of losing you, of you pulling a stunt like you did today and nearly drowning yourself."

Ben sipped his coffee, then set the cup down in front of him. "I don't know how you and Jacob didn't both get hypothermia from the ride back here in wet clothes. He had you wrapped in some old blanket he found in his boat, but him... he was soaked. He made sure you were okay, Kercy, even before he called me, getting you upstairs under those blankets... then going back to get your boat. I am proud of him for that. But... he's my whole family, now, Kercy. He's all I got left since my daughter... if I lost him, I don't know..."

"I am so sorry, Ben. I really am." I couldn't look at him, couldn't stand to think I had hurt this caring and compassionate man who would do anything for me, who showed me the kind of warmth my own father found impossible to muster. I didn't deserve Ben's love but he came over and put his arm around my shoulders.

"I'm glad you're okay," Ben said. "Losing too many people I care about lately." He sniffled and kissed me on the cheek. "Now, when's that friend of yours coming? Cindy's her name, right? She coming tomorrow?"

I wiped my nose with the back of my hand. "Day after tomorrow. I'm so sorry, Ben. Can you ever forgive me?"

"Nothing to forgive." Ben brushed my hair back from my face. "I'm just worried about you. You have to promise me you won't go in that water for any reason, Kercy. This is exactly what scared your mother. Can you promise me that?"

I nodded, wiping my nose again and sniffling. "I won't, Ben. I really won't. I promise."

Ben carried his cup to the sink and rinsed it under the faucet. "I'm gonna have Jacob or Liam check on you later. I have to run to Toronto this evening, but I'll be back after lunch tomorrow. I'll run out and see how you're doing."

I walked Ben to the back door and threw my arms around him, hugging him close.

"Take care of yourself, okay?" he said. "Do that for me?"

I nodded and wiped my hand across my nose. He walked down to his skiff, and waved as he pulled from the dock. Something was bothering me and I couldn't quite bring it into to focus, until I replayed the words Ben had said to me in the kitchen, that Jacob forgot to give me the groceries I had ordered. I never ordered any groceries, which was neither here nor there, I guess, and was just grateful Jacob had been there to pull me from the water. But the disturbing detail I couldn't quite let go of, was, why Jacob had followed me in the first place? And why had he lied to Ben about it?

EIGHT

The sky outside the kitchen window had turned dark by the time I came back downstairs after putting on my pajamas. I brewed myself a cup of tea, then headed to the living room to work on my dissertation. I hadn't given much thought to it, and suddenly my books seemed as foreign as flying saucers. If I just started reading where I'd left off, I'd get back in the groove. I had just settled into the sea of papers and books, when my cell chimed. It was Gerald.

"I miss you so much," I said, as soon as I swiped my screen.

"I miss you too."

"How was your drive back?"

"No problems. The border was empty. Just a couple of cars in front of me. What time did Cindy get there?"

I couldn't take anymore drama today, but I couldn't lie either. "She... texted me and said she got hung up on her project."

There was a long pause. "She's still coming, right?"

"Of course. Yeah."

"Tomorrow?"

"Uh, day after tomorrow. In the morning."

Another pause, this time longer.

"It's okay, Gerald. Really. I'm okay up here by myself." But with all that had happened, even that statement felt like a lie. I hadn't fully processed the events of the day, or the night before with Gerald, the dream with the creatures, the green light...

"I just..." Gerald started to say. "I wish you were back here with me."

We talked a while longer before we agreed to hang up.

"Will you marry me?" I said.

Another long pause.

"Hey, I'm messing with you!" I finally said. "Don't lose your sense of humor."

"Yeah. Okay if I come up next weekend?"

"Can I see how much I get done first?"

"Sure."

I could tell he was disappointed. The thing was, I was more bummed than he was. The thought of sleeping alone tonight made me miserable. I wasn't even sure I could get any schoolwork done this week. My own research seemed like hieroglyphics to me now.

"Talk soon," he said. "I love you."

"I love you, too." I was glad we'd gotten that hurdle out of the way and were now able to express ourselves freely in that department; it seemed far easier to convey affection sexually than it was to say I love you.

The resulting void after disconnecting from the call was always troubling. My tea was getting cold so I was about to stick it in the microwave and nearly dropped the cup when someone rapped on the glass at the back door. The curtain over the window hid the visitor from me, and me from them.

"Who is it?" I said, wondering who the hell would be visiting?

"Jacob."

I went over to open the door, more relieved to have company than I thought I'd be.

"Hey, come in," I said, pulling the door open.

"No, that's okay. I'm just checking to see that you're okay. Grandpa was concerned."

"Well come in and have a beer or something." I wanted a chance to tell him how sorry I was, and maybe quiz him on why he'd lied to his grandfather.

"My girlfriend's in the boat waiting. We're headed over to Kurry for some kind of poetry reading or something."

"By boat?"

"Yeah. Faster than car. More fun, too."

"Hey, sorry about today, Jacob."

"No worries. Call me if you need anything, Ms. Powell."

"I'm kind of embarrassed... you know."

He looked down and shook his head. "It's fine, really. Have a nice evening."

"Hey, before you go, I was wondering something and wanted to ask why you had—"

"Have a nice evening." Jacob smiled and headed back down the walkway to the water, as if he hadn't heard what I was saying, or didn't want to face the question he must have known was coming. With the security light illuminating the dock and his boat, I could see his girlfriend, bundled in a heavy coat, sock hat and gloves. I couldn't imagine driving the lake at night, but thought it must be breathtaking, once you moved past the paralyzing fear.

When he pulled from my dock, I thought maybe the lie to his grandfather had been nothing at all, that maybe he needed to get away for a while but wasn't supposed to leave the harbor. I was busy making all kinds of excuses for this young man who I desperately wanted to afford the benefit of the doubt. Nevertheless, something about the whole affair clawed at me.

A few hours went by and I was proud of myself for getting so much done on my research. I deserved some kind of treat for all my hard work and went to the kitchen. Donuts sounded good, but I hadn't bought any. It was uplifting to be productive again; it seemed like weeks since I'd accomplished anything of substance.

There was the coconut cream pie I bought for Cindy and me, a kind of celebratory indulgence for purchasing the cottage. She and Gerald drove up with me several weeks earlier after the closing and helped me clean and paint for four days. It was a blast, working all day, drinking all evening. It gave me such a sense of purpose and connection. And I was glad Gerald finally had a chance to meet Cindy, my dearest and best friend on the entire planet.

I finally settled on a bagel and was sitting at the table eating, thinking about Ben and Jacob, about Jacob's lie and his rationale for spinning it, my mind shifting to the unsavory fact that I had nearly drowned again. Contemplating the events of the day brought me to a realization that was harsh and hard to accept, which was, that every time I had been underwater during my life and believed I was seeing amazing colors and sparkling fish and exotic details, I was actually drowning, hallucinating from lack of oxygen, the last images before death, the brain misfiring, tricking the retinas into seeing things that weren't there. All this time I had believed myself to have some meta-physical relationship to water, that I was more alive underwater; nothing could have been further from the truth.

The spell water held over me was powerful. Just being around it often tossed me into some fugue state. Water was mesmerizing. Captivating. Drawing me into it. Plunging me beneath the surface, the colors, the synapses in my brain misfiring, flashes of light, stun-ning fireworks, lucidity, ecstasy, free and floating...

Then a knock. I looked up from my bagel, which I had barely touched. Another knock. I couldn't pull myself fully out, trapped in my reverie. I glanced toward the door. The handle was jiggling. Was the door still locked? I think I locked it. A harder knock. The handle trying to turn. How odd, the handle trying to turn. I struggled to clear my head, but the water... the flashes of light. I felt lightheaded.

"Hello?" someone said. A man's voice.

I swiveled my head toward the sound. The door handle. The knocking. The deadbolt. Was it engaged?

"Hello? Anyone there?" the voice called again.

I didn't recognize it. I swallowed and shook my head. The room was tilting, flimsy, bending. I got up and went to the sink and splashed water on my face. Inhaling deeply, I felt the room gaining cohesion, the feeling in my legs returning, a low voltage energy coursing along my skin. My fingers tingled.

The door rattled.

"Jacob," I said. "Is that you?"

"No ma'am," a man answered. "We're having boat trouble. Seems to be damaged, may be taking on water."

My stomach lurched. I quietly made sure the deadbolt was set, then went to the kitchen counter for a butcher knife.

"I'm sorry," I said. "Have you called for help?"

"No signal out here, ma'am."

I held one hand against the door. My other hand, the one holding the knife, was trembling. "Fuck," I said, under my breath. "I have service," I said. "I'll try to call someone for you. Wait down on my dock."

I leaned my back against the door and brought my ear closer, not wanting to open the curtain yet to see who was there, or for them to see me. For a few moments I stood perfectly still, listening. Maybe someone was hurt? Why hadn't I asked. I went to the living room to peak between the blinds. From that vantage point, I could see the dock, my boat, and another boat behind mine.

I was headed back to the kitchen when the back door crashed open. A man with a beard rushed in, throwing me backward to the floor. The knife flew from my hand and spun across the tiles. Another man followed and forced the door closed behind them, the deadbolt hanging broken and useless. Two men towered over me. It took a moment before I recognized them.

"What do you think you're doing?" I said, pushing myself up off the floor and getting to my feet. The knife had flown across the kitchen floor; I'd never get to it.

"We're having boat troubles... like I told you," the bearded man said. The other man, who had been wearing sunglasses the first time I saw him at the harbor, now had on a red ball cap, and was surveying my home, seemingly uninterested in the conversation.

I went to the kitchen counter and grabbed my boat keys. "Here..." I said, tossing them over. "Take mine. Bring it back in the morning."

He caught them in his right hand and laughed. "Well hell, that's why we're having boat troubles in the first place." He shot an amused look toward his partner who was now gawking at me. "It's too damn dark out there to get around. We hit a damn boulder or something and the engine stopped."

"Really," I said. "How did you get here then?"

The bearded guy looked at his partner. "Tell her, Rags."

I could see why he had that nickname; the shabby gold and red flannel shirt, the tattered red ball cap.

"We paddled," Rags said. "Would've been out there the whole damn night if we hadn't seen your lights."

"Remember, I have that GPS unit you were so interested in," I said. "I'm sure you know how to use it. You'll find your way back with that."

"Truth is," the bearded man said. "I bought a new one, but hell, that damn thing wasn't much help. We still hit a damn rock."

"I'll drive you back to the harbor," I said. "We'll tow your boat back. You can have it looked at in the morning."

The bearded man looked over at Rags and shrugged. "What do you think, Rags? Want to take a boat ride with a professional tour guide?"

The conversation was bending in a troubling direction. I was hoping to diffuse any further confrontation by getting them outside, but it was starting to feel unavoidable. My hand started to tremble. I hid it at my side.

Rags stared at me. This was going sideways in a hurry. Maybe these two morons really had just wandered into something, seeing the lights, but then finding me in my night clothes gave them new ideas about the evening. Maybe I could tilt the scales by being aggressive, give them second thoughts about what they might be contemplating.

But if they had intentionally come here to do harm, the aggression may only fuel the frenzy.

"Get out," I said. "Get out or I am calling the police."

"Whoa, hold onto your pantyhose, little lady," the bearded man said. "We don't mean no harm. And we're real sorry about the door. We'll pay for that... but... we're just lost out here. We just need a bit of help, is all." He turned to his partner. "Rags, want to try for the harbor? She's willing to drive us."

I didn't want them to see how hard I was breathing. Was there any chance Jacob would stop on his way back from Kurry? Probably not. Maybe if he saw a strange boat...

Rags wouldn't take his eyes off me; he was going to be trouble.

"I'm going to grab my coat and then we're going," I said.

"Seems like a big place here," Rags said. "How about we just stay the night. Be easier to get back in the daylight."

"That's not a good idea," I said, and went to get my jacket, but I had to get around Rags to do it. I was almost by him when he grabbed my arm. I turned to face him.

"It's dark out," he said. "And cold. So much warmer here."

I jerked my arm free of his grip and pushed past him. If these clowns decided to party, they were going to have a fight on their hands. I have been through a lot of shit in my life and I wasn't about to be taken down by these two assholes. When I reached the closet, I was shaking like a wet dog. I was scared, but I wasn't about to give in to these knot-heads. I grabbed my jacket off the hanger, then sat on the floor and put on my tennis shoes and headed back to the kitchen.

"Let's go," I said, purposely keeping my head down so they wouldn't see the fear in my eyes. But near the edge of my vision I could tell one of them was gone.

"Where's your buddy?" I said to Rags.

"Marty had to piss. Hope that's okay. You know how the cold gets you."

"I'll be down in the boat waiting," I said. Marty and Rags. How brazen were these clowns? When I closed the door behind me, I was relieved Rags hadn't followed me out. I wondered if they were really stupid enough to let me get in my boat with the keys? Didn't they know I would drive off and leave them? Did they think I cared about the stuff in the house? I turned the ignition and the motor cranked but wouldn't start. I tried again. Same thing. The engine churned but wouldn't fire. What had they done to my boat? I tried again. No luck.

Regardless, there was no way I was going back in the house. And if they had done something to the engine, then they came here with fucked up shit in their heads. Whatever it was, I wasn't about to be a part of it. Time to find a different part of the island and wait them out. Ben would be by in the morning. I wished I had grabbed my phone.

I picked my way carefully over the rock and sand. Uneven surfaces were still tricky for me. I walked away from the house and the further I got from shore the sandier it became, and easier to walk. The grass was high and I headed for the thickest growth of trees. The island was nearly three quarters of a mile long and about a quarter mile wide. Not huge, but plenty of places to hide.

"Kercy?" someone called from the house. It sounded like Marty. I couldn't believe we were on a first name basis. They must have gotten it off my notebooks. The far west end of the island would provide the best cover.

I heard Marty call my name again, but it was farther away this time as I made my way through the brush and grass. Despite the fact that it was extremely dark, I felt I was doing fine until a log tripped me, throwing me to the ground. I sat a moment, collecting myself before I got up. Not much farther I figured. This part of the island had been off limits to me because of my wheelchair. I had only seen it from the boat a few times. Even so, I recalled thinking it looked like a jungle.

I found a thicket and hunkered down. The sound of the water was nearby even if I was unable to see it. Resting my back against a shagbark hickory, I wondered what time it was. I guessed it had been around ten o'clock when they came to the door. Maybe later. I closed my eyes and tried to settle the knocking in my chest. The water lapping against the rocks was soothing, but it wasn't long before someone called my name again. This time it sounded like Rags.

"Kercy?" It sounded like he was swinging some kind of branch or stick through the brush as he walked. I scooted down flat to the ground and pushed myself under the plants.

"Oh, Kercy," another voice called. It was Marty. He sounded far away, but it was Rags I was concerned about.

"Kercy?" Rags was much closer now. He stopped walking. A second later I heard him crush a beer can and toss it to the ground. "Hey, bitch! The longer it takes me to find you, the worse it's going to be..." Then he belched.

Even though Rags was fat and out of shape, there was no way I could outrun him; my legs were stronger than they'd ever been, but I wasn't going to be running any marathons.

When I realized he had a flashlight my heart collapsed. I felt along the ground and found a baseball-sized rock. I put my face close to the earth and laid as still as possible.

There was a long silence, just the sound of Marty calling in the distance. Then the beam from Rags light went over the leaves near my feet. My tennis shoes were mostly blue, with some white. The heels, however, had reflective strips for night jogging. I panicked and tried to pull my knees up tighter to hide the shoes.

Rags grabbed me by the hair and pulled me free of the cover, across the sand and rocks. My scalp burned. Rags dropped down on top of me and ripped my jacket open and was tearing at my T-shirt when I banged him in the temple with the rock. He screamed. I rolled him off me and kicked him in the head. He grabbed for me and caught my ankle, and almost had me down when I stomped his arm. He moaned and released me and I ran as best I could.

Marty was shouting now. "Rags? Did you find her? Where are you?"

I headed for the shore on the other side of the island. If I could get to the house, I could grab my phone, get the knife, and make my stand in the upstairs bathroom until someone arrived.

Marty called out one more time, but I couldn't tell how far he was. I ran, more like a crippled jog, soon falling with the house in sight, maybe forty yards away when I saw Marty.

He started laughing. "Man, this evening just gets better and better." He jogged toward me. My fingers crawled the cold sand for a sizable rock but found nothing. Marty got to me before I could get up. Even in the dark I could see his big stupid grin.

"Hope Rags doesn't miss the party," he said, as he got within a couple of feet of me. When he started to unbuckle his jeans, I came up with a handful of sand and flung it in his face. He squealed and rubbed his eyes and I kicked him in the groin. He went down but I was losing traction in the sand and kept falling. I was almost up when he grabbed my tennis shoe, pulling it off. I crawled away as fast as I could until he grabbed my other leg, this time by the calf. I kicked at him with my bare foot but he wouldn't let go. With his free hand he grabbed my gym shorts and started pulling them off. I kicked at his head but he just laughed. Sand and rocks dug into my bare bottom as he pulled me toward him, using my own weight to pull himself up on me. I kept fighting him, my shorts down to my ankles making it harder to kick.

"Marty?" Rags shouted "You have that bitch?"

"Over here," Marty said, running his hand up under my T-shirt, squeezing my breast. It hurt and I tried to hit him in the face, but he was able to fend me off with one hand while he fumbled with his jeans with his other. I got another handful of sand and tried to grind it into his eyes. He just slapped it away, then slapped me and laughed. When I felt him trying to penetrate me, I twisted and squirmed to get him off.

That's when Rags shrieked like he was being skinned alive. A piercing, high-pitched squeal. It stopped Marty cold. I struggled to free myself while his attention was elsewhere, but he was too heavy for me to throw off.

"Rags! You okay?" he said, pushing himself up on one elbow.

The screams came again and again, trailing off, moving farther from us. While Marty's attention was focused on Rag's horrible shrieking, I punched him in the throat. When he started choking, I kneed him and pushed him off. He was rolling on the sand, moaning roughly, as I scrambled away, pulling up my shorts, heading for the house. Rags had stopped screaming at that point. I glanced back to see Marty still writhing on the ground.

When I got inside, I grabbed the knife off the kitchen floor, then ran to the living room and picked up my phone. I wedged one of the kitchen chairs beneath the door knob, then hurried up the stairs. Once inside my bedroom, I locked the door, then pushed my reading chair in front of it and hurried to the bathroom and locked myself in. Seated on the floor, I pressed my weight against the door, trying to calm my breathing. That's when I heard muffled screams coming from outside. The screams kept coming, horrible shrieks and yelps. It went on for another minute or so, followed by a silence so eerie my breath sat like a ball in my throat.

I phoned Ben and left a message. Then I called Jacob. No answer. I left a message, then sat there for over two hours before I felt it was safe enough to take a shower. It was after three in the morning by then. I showered with my eyes on the bathroom door and the knife on the shampoo shelf. I hurried out and puked, then sank to my bottom, squeezing my knees to my chest, crying.

Around five in the morning I unlocked the bathroom door and opened it a crack. It was still dark outside my bedroom window, but the chair was still at the door. I hurried to my bed, grabbed my pillow and blanket, then rushed back to the bathroom and locked the door. I spread the blanket on the floor and put my pillow against the door and laid down. I pulled the excess blanket over me and tried to sleep, the big knife clutched in my hand, but I couldn't close my eyes without seeing Marty and Rags.

NINE

I never really slept, but I dozed off a few times. I checked my phone. It was half past seven. The sun would be up by now. I unlocked the bathroom door and went to my bedroom window. A beautiful day, the sun just above the horizon. Marty and Rags' boat was still moored to the dock. Why hadn't they left? Then I remembered the screams.

After getting dressed, I carefully pushed the chair away from the door and slowly padded down the steps, butcher knife in hand. My heart was trying to beat its way free of my chest. At the entrance to the kitchen, I saw that the back door was still shut—the chair propped against it—the jamb splintered and cracked. Apparently, no one had tried to get in after I went upstairs.

After pulling the chair away from the door, I walked out onto the back porch carrying the knife. I probably should have called Ben and Jacob again, and just stayed put with the doors locked until he got there, but for some reason I believed Marty and Rags were dead. Those screams left little doubt in my mind. Little, but there was some.

Regardless, I needed to know.

The first place I checked was close to the cottage, where I had fought off Marty. Replaying the screams, my mind called up an image of a *bear*. If a bear had gotten Marty, he'd be pretty messed up, but he would be there somewhere, some trace. I must have searched at least twenty minutes finding only one ragged boot, which I couldn't even be sure was his, maybe left there by the previous owners, the ones I had bought the property from. Why would a bear drag him off? There were no marks along the ground, no furrowed trails of dragging heels digging into sand. And where would it take him? Surely a bear couldn't cross a body of water this large dragging Marty's fat ass along. No, even badly injured, Marty would have tried to get back to his boat to escape the attack, and maybe had fallen in the water and drowned.

After spending the next half hour checking out my theory, coming up with no sign of Marty (as if he'd vanished from the planet), I decided instead to head to the far end of the island where I'd scuffled with Rags; the decision turning my knees to jelly. For whatever reason, maybe because it was so desolate there, so much more flora than this end, it occurred to me that Rags could still be alive, injured for sure, but feisty none the less, hiding in the thick cover. But wouldn't he have tried to get away in the boat as well if there had been a bear stalking him? Perhaps, but Rags' bone-chilling screams still reverberated in my head, making it seem implausible that Rags had survived.

Walking toward the west end, something deep and primal and previously undisturbed stirred inside me. It was as if I were traversing an alien landscape, an unknown universe closing around me, seeping inside me. I held the knife out in front of my body like a lance as if it might protect me from a surprise attack, my head on a gimbal, jerking side to side, swiveling so far at times it seemed I was able to see behind me.

I had considered that maybe another person had driven out with Rags and Marty, one I hadn't seen... then decided to kill them? To protect me? Okay, so far so good. Then what... he escaped the island by swimming in frigid waters all night? Or was still here on the island, hiding, and for what reason? No other boat had arrived or left, including Marty's. None of this added up at all. I even allowed for the possibility that some stranger boating past the cottage the previous evening had heard my screams, pulled his boat to the dock and came to my rescue. I really liked that scenario, made me feel a bit more secure, the thought of an altruistic protector just happening by, though it was completely implausible; boat motors were too loud to even hear yourself think, much less screams from a hundred yards away in a craft traveling forty miles an hour!

I continued on, sand sinking beneath my feet, gradually firming to pebbles and stones, then hardening to glacial rock, scattered with weeds and long slender grasses that brushed past my shins and knees, sticker bushes that picked at my clothes. Large shrubs and small gnarly trees sprouted along the path, blocking the view, making it difficult to see. This end of the island was feral and forgotten. A wilderness of sorts. How did Rags ever find me here? I certainly couldn't find him. Maybe he was gone too, like Marty. Then, a few minutes later, there he was, at least I thought it was him. I recognized his faded red and gold plaid shirt at first, but the dreadful and grue-some butchery of his body left me numb.

No longer concerned about Rags wanting to *party*, I eased my knife down to my side. Rags' *partying* days were definitely over. He was now a collection of anatomical parts, some angled oddly, distorted, wrong. There was blood to be sure, but more disturbing was his flaccidity, as if some of the bones in his body had been pulver-ized, his chest on one side deflated. I mentally tried to reassemble the puzzle of his bloody limbs, trying to account for all the pieces. Nothing seemed to be missing, his torso intact, all those juicy organs untouched just beneath his torn flannel shirt. That made no sense. Winter was coming. For bears, that signaled a long hibernation. And Rags' body was left uneaten. Not even gnawed on a little bit. Why would a bear, or any animal powerful enough to kill a grown man, leave this tasty buffet behind? No, this wasn't the work of a bear, or wolves, or coyotes, or anything else I could imagine. This was something else altogether, but for the life of me I couldn't figure out what. I tried to account for this degree of savagery. If this slaying wasn't for food, then what?

As I turned to head back to the cottage, I was seized by the sensation of being watched. I let my eyes drift past the scrubby bushes and pines, listening to the waves swell and break along the shore just out of view. Pushing branches and limbs aside, I stepped carefully toward the sound until the foliage opened, the bay reaching toward the horizon, latticed with small islands, white caps staging across the gray-green water. Pine boughs bent and swayed, their needles whispering. I stood like a post, watching, my breath leaking out slowly. Before me nothing but water and sky. Yet, I felt a presence, something out of place, unmoving, hidden beneath the surface of the bay. Seconds fell away. Minutes. The air was charged. From the edge of my vision, I saw movement, but when I turned, it was gone... or was never there.

I decided to head back. The wind had picked up bringing a frosty chill off the lake. I moved briskly, attentive to my surroundings, knife outstretched. The uneven glacial rock softened to loose stones and rocks, then to sand and grass as I approached the cottage.

Standing on the deck, about to open the back door, I was struck by a sudden, inexplicable fear—Marty was waiting inside for me, standing at the kitchen island covered in blood, his wounds oozing black and yellow puss, half his face scraped clean to the bone of his skull, one eye remaining, blood soaked, staring. Jesus! Get a grip, Powell! I pushed the door open slowly. A moment later, my breathing approached normal again. I stood shaking my head over the crazy chimera my mind had tossed up. Once inside, I closed the door and wedged the chair back under the knob. Crazy or not, it doesn't hurt to be cautious. I went to the stove and put the kettle on, my nerves frizzling in some heightened state of fight or flight. Details from the previous night rushed at me, Marty and Rags, their stupid faces, their vicious square yellow teeth, their insidious rabid grins. Call Ben, the voice said, cutting through the static in my brain. I was leaving the kitchen to go find my phone when I heard a knock at the back door.

I froze, sliding that big fucking butcher knife back off the island counter top, my knuckles white from clenching the handle, my heart beating a weird, frenetic cadence beneath my skin. I waited, not certain what to do...

"Kercy, are you there?"

"Jacob!" I pulled the chair from the door. "Come in!"

His eyes were fixed on the damaged jamb, then on the butcher knife in my hand. When he walked past me, I pushed the door shut and wedged the chair back into place. I set the knife on the kitchen counter.

"Sit," I said, turning up the flame under the kettle. "Tea okay? I can make coffee. I know Ben prefers coffee. I like coffee okay, but prefer tea, but I think it's—"

"Kercy, what happened?"

"Huh?"

"There's blood all over the back of your shirt," Jacob said.

I went to the full-length mirror in the hallway and twisted to see my blouse. I hadn't realized how scraped and scratched my back was.

Jacob and I sat at the table and I told him everything that happened. I got through most of it without crying. But I was glad he didn't come over and try to comfort me. I needed my space, a little buffer between myself and mankind, and was so glad Cindy was coming. I only wished it were sooner than the next morning. Jacob phoned Ben.

It wasn't long before Ben arrived, followed by a police boat and officers. One was asking me questions and taking notes at the kitchen table while the others were checking the boats, the dock, searching the island for Marty and Rags. When the officer taking my report finished, he told me there was another team on the way out to talk to me.

"About what?"

"More details about the attack. They'll have a rape kit and..."

"I wasn't raped. I already told you that. He tried... that's all."

The officer cleared his throat. "I understand. They'll still have questions for you. They'll want the clothes you were wearing. Take pictures. That sort of thing."

"Is that it then?"

"Yes ma'am." He let himself out the back door.

Ben and Jacob waited outside on the back porch. The fresh air was a blessing when I went out to join them. Police milled about everywhere, checking under bushes, around the trees, in the boats, both mine and Marty's.

Jacob was getting ready to leave. "I'm really sorry about everything that happened, Kercy."

"Thanks for coming out."

Ben stayed with me while the police searched the island trying to figure out how Marty had fled without his boat. I had told the officer about the screams, and where I had found Rags' body that morning, and offered my theory on Marty drowning trying to get to his boat. No one was much interested in my speculations, only actual details.

"You come back with me, Kercy," Ben said, looking out over the water, his hands gripping the rail. "You can't stay out here by yourself. Too dangerous."

I didn't say anything, but I wasn't going to leave because of those two assholes. Nobody was going to frighten me off. Although, whatever had killed Marty and Rags gave me pause.

"My skiff wouldn't start last night, Ben," I said. "It's brand new. It always starts. I think they did something to it."

He turned toward me. "You tell the police?"

"Yeah, sure."

"Probably pulled the kill switch cable."

I hadn't even thought about checking that, and started to say something when a policeman shouted, "We found something down here." The officer was carrying a dark bag, walking toward the west end, where I'd found Rags earlier. "We've got a body," the officer shouted.

Two other policemen walked in his direction. They all disappeared back into the trees and underbrush. Not long after that the other team arrived. They wanted to question me in the house. The woman introduced herself and asked if there was somewhere private we could talk. I showed her to my old bedroom; the couple I bought the cottage back from had turned it into a guest bedroom.

"How's this?" I said.

"This is fine," Lisa said, closing the door behind us. She asked me questions, much more personal and detailed than the first officer. She took swabs, had me undress and took pictures of my scratches and cuts, put the pajamas I'd been wearing into a plastic sack. It took about an hour for everything. When she finished she told me she'd be in touch if they needed anything else.

"You doing okay," Ben asked when I stepped outside.

I wiped my eyes and nose. "Yeah, sure. Hey, Ben, you don't have to hang around. Thanks so much for coming."

"I'm not going anywhere."

"Hello, Ms. Powell. I'm Officer Randall," a plain clothes officer said.

I nodded, shaking his hand.

"Can I have a word with you?" He looked at Ben.

Ben smiled at me and started down the walkway. "I'll be right down here, Kercy."

Officer Randall waited for Ben to leave before he spoke. He looked at his notebook. "It says here that you fought off a man by the name of 'Rags?' Is that right? Can you tell me how that struggle went exactly?"

I went over it in detail, how he'd grabbed my foot and dragged me from the brush, how I smashed the rock into the side of his head.

"Did you hit him with anything else?"

"No, I didn't have anything else."

Officer Randall scratched his head. "His real name was Kenneth Ragsdale. We found his body and he was pretty mangled."

Mangled? That was a fitting description. "Yeah, I know. I saw him this morning when I went back down there. But that's not how I left him. He was rolling around on the ground moaning when I started running back to the house."

"Did you hear anything else?"

"Besides the screaming?"

"Yes, anything other than the screaming. An animal perhaps?"

"Like what?"

"A bear? Maybe growling or something?"

"Nothing like that." I shook my head, knowing it was no bear, or any other animal, but if I told Randall that he'd expect an answer to what I thought it was, which I had no ideas about.

He flipped a few pages in the notebook. "You said that the other fella, 'Marty,' knocked you down and was on top of you and that you were able to get away. It says here that he was a big man. You're fairly small, Ms. Powell... how did you manage that?"

I explained that Marty got distracted by Rags' screaming and that I was able to punch him in the throat, then kneed him in the groin. "He was choking when I ran for the house."

"How do you think he got off the island?" Randall asked. Before I could answer another officer approached.

"The other man was Martin Dowry," the policeman told Randall. "Boat was registered in his name."

Randall examined the notes again, then repeated the same question.

"I told the officers earlier that I thought he probably beat a path back to his boat to escape and probably drowned," I said.

"Escape? From what?"

"From whatever killed them!"

Officer Randall cleared his throat, as if he thought my supposition was faulty in some way, then flipped through the pages of his notebook. "Did you know either of these men?"

"No. They were messing around in my boat at the harbor." I told Randall the story. He seemed satisfied.

"Thank you, Ms. Powell," he said. "Is this the best way to reach you?" He showed me my cell number in his notebook. "Says you're planning to stay up here for a couple of weeks. Is that right?"

"Yes."

"Okay... let's see... you have a friend coming up to meet you tomorrow? Ms. Cindy Baxter? She's going to stay with you for the next two weeks? Is that right?"

"Yes."

"Okay, well, good to know you'll be close by if we need more information? I'm sorry this happened, Ms. Powell. Are you sure you don't need to visit the hospital?"

"No, really. It's not necessary. I've been through much worse than this."

Officer Randall's expression fell gloomy at my comment and I wished I hadn't said anything. He let it drop, then nodded his head and left the porch, walking toward the two policemen who had just set a body bag on the dock.

I was rubbing my forehead when Ben came up and stood next to me.

"Can you look at my boat and see what's wrong with it?" I said.

"After they leave."

It was another two hours before the last boat left the cottage. Crime scene tape was draped over bushes and tied to trees throughout the island like the last remnants of a rave. The police impounded my boat and towed it back with Martin Dowry's boat. I was glad they hadn't ruled the cottage a crime scene and made it off limits. I wasn't ready to go back to New York and tell Gerald what had happened. I didn't plan to ever tell him.

"Ben, I'm going to need to rent a boat from you."

"For what?"

I braced myself for the argument to come. Ben insisted I stay at his place, or in town, anywhere but at the cottage. I told him I didn't want to stay in town or anywhere else, that I needed to be here. "I've struggled my whole life to get out of that damn wheelchair, Ben. I'm not about to be handicapped again. Especially by a couple of losers like Marty and Rags!"

Ben just stared at me, his features hard at first. Then his eyes softened. He swallowed and twisted his jaw to the side, thinking about what I'd said.

"We'll ride back and get you fixed up with a boat," Ben finally said.

I hugged him. "Sorry I yelled at you. I just..."

"No need to explain... I wish my Gladys had had a bit more fight in her."

TEN

Ben pulled the boat to the dock at the harbor and tied the stern while I got the bow. I had already decided to stay at a motel in Elico for the night and have Cindy pick me up in the morning. By then Ben would have a boat ready for us and we'd head back to the cottage.

On the way to the Aubrey Motel, Ben told me that Officer Randall had talked to him about Rags and Marty. "Over the past three years we've had multiple break-ins up here after the end of the season," Ben told me. "Randall thinks these two birds might be responsible." I sat and listened and wondered if I had just been an opportunistic distraction during their night of larceny, or the target of their miscreant minds. It had seemed planned, at least the part of them disabling my boat engine. Maybe the rest of it they improvised, but either way, none of it felt good. I was still wrestling with how Marty had gotten off the island, though it brought me a moment of solace believing he had drowned. I never wanted to tangle with him again.

Ben pulled in front of the Aubrey Motel. "It's nice enough," he said.

"I've stayed here before. When I was little. Thanks, Ben, I'll see you in the morning."

"Call if you need anything."

They had my reservation at the front desk. My room was on the second floor. It was nice, clean, television, microwave, refrigerator. The bathrooms weren't at big as I remembered as a kid, but nothing ever is. I thought I might go over to the Food-n-Fuel across the street for a few TV snacks before I got out of my jeans.

Cindy texted me on my way to the convenience store: *Be at the Aubrey in the am. Can't wait to see you!*

I texted her back: *Me too!*

After buying a few things, I walked back to the motel. I put on my gray sweats and NYU long-sleeve shirt and climbed up on the bed, thinking about Cindy coming, about my first day as an under-grad. Cindy had been the first person I saw when I arrived at the dorm. I had just turned nineteen, she was a year younger. She was putting her clothes into the dresser when I pushed the door open with my feet and rolled in. My mom had wanted to help me move in but I told her I needed to do it myself. I think she was proud and hurt at the same time. With my suitcase in my lap, I stopped at the oppo-site side of the room and looked down out the window between the beds. Standing below me was my mother, looking up, frail and flimsy, a handkerchief to her nose.

"Need help with that, Wheels?" Cindy had said to me.

I looked over at her. *Wheels?* It was kind of funny how relaxed she felt calling me that. Most people couldn't even look at me. "What, with this?" I said, motioning to my suitcase. "No, thanks, I'm good. I'm Kercy,"

"I know. *Kercy Powell.* It's painted on the back of your wheelchair."

Yeah, I guess it was. What a fucked up first meeting, like I was in kindergarten with my name written on everything. Nevertheless, there I was, an adult, still looking like I was in the fourth grade. I was just glad she hadn't questioned my gender by informing me that it was an all-girl floor.

"I'm Cindy." She grabbed her lacrosse stick from her bed and left the room. She was beautiful. And she didn't seem to care that I was a malformed troll.

The sudden urge to pee chased me from the memory and the bed. My ringtone sounded as I was coming from the bathroom. The coolest notion seized me; wouldn't it be crazy if that was Cindy calling just as I was thinking about her. Cool to me only; Cindy hated hearing my thoughts on synchronicities.

"Hello," I said, after rushing across the room to grab my phone off the nightstand.

"Ms. Powell?"

"Yes. Who is this?"

"Special Agent Samuel Mallory. Do you have a moment to talk?"

"Yeah, but my phone's a bit low on batte—"

"Can I come up? I'm outside the motel."

"How did you get my number? How did you know where I was?"

"Officer Randall, Elico Police."

I couldn't figure out how Officer Randall knew I was at the Aubrey Motel. Had Ben told him? Within minutes Special Agent Mallory was knocking at my door. I looked out the peep hole. He seemed to be about forty-five or so, and gaunt. "You have I.D.?" I said through the door.

He reached inside his jacket and held his badge and picture up for me to see. What would the FBI want with me? And why were they in Canada? I pulled the door open.

"Hello. Can I come in?" he said.

"I guess."

He walked by me and stood in the middle of the room. I motioned for him to sit on the only chair, the one by the small wooden desk. I sat on the edge of the bed.

"How are you doing, Ms. Powell?" he asked, sitting down.

"You know..." I wasn't sure how I was doing, except for a pervasive and oddly comforting numbness. "FBI? This isn't about the attack, is it?"

"Well... sort of." Agent Mallory cleared his throat. "I head up a special task force. The U.S. has been collaborating with the CISO and the OPP up here, sort of pooling our resources, if you will."

"Does it have a name? Like... what is the purpose of your task force? What do you investigate?"

"Anomalous crimes," he said, never taking his eyes from mine.

"*Anomalous!* What does that have to do with me?" I couldn't understand why the FBI was interested, especially a division whose primary focus was abominations and aberrations. "Do you think this attempted robbery and rape was somehow *anomalous?*" Anomalous would explain a few things, I thought, but the term made me uncomfortable.

"Not really."

"Do you want a Coke or something?" I asked, trying to warp the moment toward the ordinary.

He shook his head and pulled a notebook from inside his jacket. "It says here, while Martin Dowry was attacking you that you heard screams, presumably from the other man, Kenneth Ragsdale. That it so distracted your attacker, Mr. Dowry, that you were able to overpower him and escape? The screams must have been... quite disturbing to interrupt the attack? Wouldn't you say?"

"They were unnerving." I explained how I had left Rags lying on the ground, hurting certainly, but not in agonizing pain.

"Agonizing?" Agent Mallory said. "That's how you'd describe what you heard?"

"Yeah. He was hurting... I mean... it sounded bad. But I'm not even sure it was Rags... I mean Kenneth Ragsdale."

Agent Mallory adjusted himself in his seat. "I don't understand..." He referred to his notebook. "It says here you described the shouting as coming from the other man... the suspect... Ragsdale..."

"Well, yeah, that's what I told the police officers. But I also told them I couldn't be certain. That it may have been coyotes... or wolves.

It was an eerie sound. I just assumed at the time it was him." That was what I had told the police, but knew it wasn't wolves or coyotes, but the sound freaked me out.

Mallory absently massaged his temples with his thumb and forefinger, his attention on the notepad in his hand. "Have you seen wolves or coyotes on your island?"

I shook my head, placing my Coke can on the floor.

He was intent on the notes in his pad, fidgeting with his pen, thumping it on the arm of the desk chair.

"No tracks of any kind?" he said, breaking the silence.

I had to laugh. "What's this really about? You come up from the US from some special division of the FBI and start asking me about critters and animals? Something doesn't jibe here... if you tell me what's really going on, maybe I can help..."

"Ever see any bear on your island?"

"Oh, for Christ's sake." I was quickly becoming frustrated with Mallory. "You couldn't have come all this way to talk about fucking bears!"

Mallory ran the back of his fingers over the stubble along his jaw, his eyes back in his notebook. After several minutes he shoved the pad back inside his jacket and looked up at me. "We have Mr. Ragsdale's body at our forensics lab." He stared at me as if that should mean something, as if waiting for my face to register some emotion. All this intrigue over something that seemed better suited to a Game and Wildlife investigation, not the FBI.

"Is there anything else?" I said.

"Was there anything strange that night?"

"As strange as this?" I felt heat rising in my chest. "I'm sorry, but the whole night was fucking strange. I mean these two bastards break down my door, then..." Suddenly my stomach was in my throat. I took a deep breath. "What do you really want?"

He stood and extended his hand to me. "I'm very sorry for what happened to you, Ms. Powell. If you remember anything else that stands out, could you give me a call? You have my number in your phone."

"Fine." I locked the door behind him and went for the remote. How odd... why was he so evasive about what he really wanted to know? Anomalous crimes? What the fuck was an anomalous crime anyway, I thought, flipping through channels until I came to a rerun of Lost.

ELEVEN

I woke early to banging truck doors and metal toolboxes, talking and laughing, motel doors slamming, diesel engines rumbling. Evidently, the Aubrey Motel was a popular lodging spot for workers from Toronto. Unable to get back to sleep, I decided to busy my mind with schoolwork and give my dissertation some attention.

Reading papers all morning on The Human Genome Project, I found the findings from the multi-billion-dollar project fascinating. It was wildly successful in mapping the human genome, isolating defective genes that accounted for terrible diseases, and much more. A major scientific coup, no doubt.

In the end, scientists discovered that the human genome was essentially interchangeable with a chimp, or a mouse. There was less than two percent difference between humans and our cousin vertebrates, and nothing whatsoever to account for the obvious differences.

The subject of my paper was Evolution in a Technological Age. I had already explored the barf bag phenomenon, how early passengers flying on airplanes experienced nausea. Over time the sensation resolved itself and millions fly every day without a problem. Evolution? Or adaptation? And is there a difference between the two?

Before I could move beyond my last question, Rags and Marty were suddenly sucking up all the space in my brain, sparking new questions. I grabbed my notepad and pen—Does rape, or any violent crime for that matter, trigger some kind of microevolution? In other words, does the victim evolve in some way after a violent crime? It seems they would, but how? By developing a new fear? Or a better brand of caution? Could fear and caution reside in the genes? If so, could they be passed along to offspring?

Sitting in the middle of my motel bed, I started questioning whether that was a valid assumption and worth pursuing. I didn't know. I couldn't hold any thought for more than a few seconds. A moment later, I was questioning the past eight months of my work.

By now, the sun was up, pouring through the thin curtains of the motel room. My head was spinning with ideas, none of them pertinent to my paper. The events of the previous evening now played over and over behind my eyes; shadowy images of running past trees, hiding under bushes, the cool feel of a hand full of sand. Instead of trying to hide on the island, should I have gotten in my boat and just paddled away from the dock and gotten as far as I could before Marty and Rags discovered I was missing? If Marty had lied about their boat being broken, then they would have found me anyway. Then what? What if I had pulled the drain plug on Marty's boat so it filled with water and was truly unusable, then paddled away from the island in my boat? The only way they could have gotten to me then was by swimming, but they were too out of shape for that. That would have worked. Then they would have been stuck there till morning when the police could have just come and... Stop! Kercy. Stop the review! It's done, it's over! Let it go.

I looked down at my legs crossed on the bed, at my feet, the polish on my toes scratched and chipped, at my notepads and books, the dark spots on the papers and pages where my tears had just landed. I wiped my eyes, sniffed, trying to force the recollections away; Rag's horrible breath on my face, Marty's stupid laugh, standing over me unbuckling his jeans...

"Hey, Kerce! Open up!" A muffled woman's voice issued from the motel hallway.

"Cindy!" I said, jumping from the bed scattering papers and pencils. When I jerked the door open, I don't think Cindy was ready for the body slam hug I put on her. She stumbled backward, trying to get her balance. I couldn't let her go, tears rolling off my cheeks.

"Hey, Wheels, what's going on?" she said, tenderly easing me into the room so she could close the door. "Did you and Gerald break up?"

I wiped my nose with the back of my hand. "Can we go to breakfast first?" I said. "I think I need to eat." Even though I wasn't experiencing ordinary hunger pangs, my insides felt disassembled, like there was a vacancy in my stomach.

Cindy drove us to the diner several miles from the Aubrey Motel. I related the events of the previous evening, trying to recall the details, my recollection becoming like a smeared canvas of incoherent brush strokes. I buckled over in the front seat of her car and started wailing. It surged in waves, more flow than ebb, as if some dam had collapsed.

We sat in the diner parking lot until my composure returned. Cindy popped the glove box on her Volvo and handed me a box of tissues. I was about to tell her about the FBI agent, Mallory, who visited me the night before, but decided not to. Not just then. Maybe later I would. It felt good to tell her stuff. There was nothing we didn't know about each other.

While we waited for our omelets, I wanted Cindy to tell me about her new boyfriend, how things were going.

"That's over," she said. "Didn't I tell you?"

"Are you okay?"

Maybe she had and I'd forgotten, but I doubt it. She'd been seeing him for almost a year and now I was wondering why her relationship ended. It made me nervous. Cindy was beautiful and smart, a talented artist and visual effects expert and freelanced for studios all over the world. If she couldn't make her relationship work, what chance did I have with Gerald?

"Trevor was a mess," Cindy said. "He was still carrying a picture of his ex-girlfriend in his wallet. They were texting all the time. Jeez."

Cindy checked her phone, then placed it on the table.

"Anyway, time away from the city is much needed, Wheels," Cindy said. "The lake cottage is going to be great..." She reached across the table and placed her hands on mine. "You sure you still feel like staying out there?" She squeezed my hands gently. "We could just hang at the Aubrey and do stuff around here. You'd still get work done and it would be fun."

"No, I'm good. Rag's is dead, and Marty..."

"What happened to them?"

I scoffed and shook my head side to side. "I have no fucking idea! The police think it might have been a bear..."

"Do you think it was a bear?"

"No. No way..."

Cindy seemed content to let it drop. "You have Internet up here yet?" Cindy asked, taking a bite of her toast.

"At the cottage?" I said. "No. Same as when you were here a few weeks ago. Is that a problem?"

Cindy had an awesome loft in the Village. But sometimes she would fly to the studio that hired her freelance and work at their location if the "pipeline" required it. She tried to explain the "pipeline" concept to me, but not knowing much about CG work, I didn't really grasp it.

"Don't worry about it," she said. "If I have cell service I can get emails and texts. And if I need Internet, I'll set up a hotspot with my phone. I don't think I will, though. Biz is slow right now. I'm looking forward to boat riding, hanging out and eating junk food."

After breakfast we drove back to the Aubrey. Cindy took a shower while I packed my things. She said she'd left the city in the middle of the night so she could hit the border before it got too busy and she felt like a grungy sweat sock.

We stopped at the grocery store for supplies and I guess Cindy could tell I was distracted. "Let's just stay at the Aubrey for a couple of weeks," she said. "Or we could drive to Toronto and stay in one of those fancy four-hundred-dollar-a-night hotels. Sit at the bar, order breakfast in, wear our bikinis in the hotel spa. It would be a blast, Wheels."

I took Cindy's hand in mine. "That all sounds great, baby, but... and this is going to sound crazy... but, I can't give into this... insanity or fear or.... I can't let those fucking jerk-offs run... my life. I know that doesn't probably make sense, but..."

"No, it does, Wheels. It's cool. I think you're handling it great. I just wanted to give you an option... you know.... I love you, you know that. Let's go... go to the cottage."

"You scared?" I said.

"No, not at all... just a little, maybe... but hell, it's cool. I'm not afraid of being afraid."

We both laughed a little. "'I'm not afraid of being afraid.' Is that one of your dad's Yogi Berra-isms?" I said.

"All I know is this," Cindy said, "When you come to the fork in the road, take it."

We laughed again. Cindy's father was a huge fan of the famous baseball player... and he had a Berra-ism for every occasion.

When we reached the harbor, it was just after noon. Cindy slung her grip over her shoulder, then helped me carry my stuff down to the dock. We set everything outside Ben's office, then went in. Sitting behind the counter was a lanky middle-aged man with shaggy brown hair. I was fairly certain his name was Liam. I sort of remembered him from when I was a girl. He had searched for my father and seemed to feel bad about not finding him.

"Is Ben here?" I asked.

"Mr. Bouchard is not around right now," Liam said. "Maybe I can help you."

"Hi, I'm Kercy Powell," I said. "Ben was going to have a skiff ready for me this morning."

Liam's expression dissolved from pretend friendly to reserved annoyance. "Umm," he said, checking some ledger book as if my name would be in it. "I don't see anything here. Might try back around four. Ben should be back by then."

"You sure?" I said. "Ben told me any time after nine this morning would be fine."

Liam stood and placed his palms on the counter, then looked over his shoulder at the clock on the wall. "It's after noon," he said.

I didn't get his meaning. I looked over at Cindy, then back to Liam. "What difference does that make?" I said. "Can you just tell me where it's parked?"

"Somebody rented that around half past nine this morning," he said. "I held it long as I could."

I shook my head and walked out. "I don't know what this fucker's up to..." I said to Cindy, spying Jacob pulling into the parking lot. "Come on."

We walked up toward the parking lot. Jacob stepped down out of his pickup and walked toward us carrying a box.

"Who is that?" Cindy said, obviously interested.

"Hey Jacob," I said.

"Morning, Kercy," he said. "Liam get your skiff for you? I told him to bring it around when you showed up."

"Jacob, this is my best friend, Cindy."

"Nice to meet you, ma'am." Jacob shook her hand, balancing the box in the other. He turned back to address me. "You all set?"

"Uh, well, no. Seems there's a problem." I explained what had happened.

"Hmm, Liam's just being a douche. Sorry for the language. I wish Grandpa Ben would fire him. Come on, I'll get your boat."

We walked down to the dock with Jacob. He asked us to wait a minute, holding up the box, saying that he wanted to put the new prop in the office. Cindy and I stood outside and waited. After a bout of muffled arguing, Liam huffed out of the office and brushed past us, but not before giving me a hard look.

"What was that about?" Cindy asked.

I shrugged and shook my head. I had no idea what his problem was. I'd never even spoken to him before, and only remembered him as a nice young man. Nevertheless, it bugged me. Jacob came out soon after, picked up a couple of our suitcases and asked us to follow him. Cindy and I grabbed our groceries and stuff and walked behind him. I was watching for Liam, but never saw him. Jacob led us to a slip with a twenty-foot center console rig with T-top canopy and 200 HP Yamaha engine.

"Wow, that's a lot of boat," I said.

"You can handle it." Jacob hopped down into it. He put the key in the ignition and fired the engine. "It's got GPS just like yours. Throttle's the same, all the gauges. Cooler, compass, Sony stereo. That's about it. Hand me your stuff there."

After the boat was loaded, we got in. "Tank's full," Jacob said, climbing out. "I'll get the lines."

We hadn't gotten past the No Wake buoy when Cindy asked about Jacob.

"He has a girlfriend," I said.

"Is it serious, Wheels?"

I looked over at her and smirked. "First hunk comes along and you abandon me?" I said.

"Hey, the sisterhood is only so strong," Cindy said, looking back at the dock where Jacob was working on an engine. "I should have put my bikini on at the motel."

"He's seen me naked and it didn't even faze him," I said.

"What...? You've been holding out on *me*, big sister."

I told her the story on the way back to the cottage, shouting over the engine noise. When I glanced over, her expression had soured. She put her hand on my arm. "Hey, can you stop?"

"You have to pee?" I said. "Sure." I pulled the throttle back and the boat slid to a smooth stop.

"I'm worried about you, Wheels."

"What?"

"You told me you had that under control."

I thought I did. I had assured her several years ago that it wasn't like when I was a kid and had this goofy idea that I could breathe underwater. I knew I couldn't.

"Yeah... I'm not sure what happened that day," I said. "But I know it won't..."

Cindy wrapped her arms around me, pulling me close. "You have to promise me," she whispered in my ear. Tears rimmed her eyes when she drew back. "You can't do that shit anymore. You know I wouldn't be able to save you, right? I don't know CPR. I'm a terrible swimmer. You know that, right?"

"Hey, sweetie. There's no need to worry. It's fine. I understand it now." I explained about my revelation, about my hallucinations, about the trance I would fall into. As I was sharing my insights and new comprehension about the incident, I was simultaneously replaying my stupor the night Rags and Marty came to the door, how they'd caught me off-guard, how I was still a bit off kilter, and was convinced the attack was one of those "perfect storm" situations that would never happen again; a lightning strike.

She sat back down across from me and I started the engine. We rode in silence back to the island.

TWELVE

Back at the cottage, I noticed that Ben had repaired the door and installed a new heavy-duty deadbolt with a steel keeper. After Cindy and I got settled in, we baked a pizza and carried it out to the dock. We brought beers along. Although the afternoon sun was warm, there was a cool edge to the gentle wind coming off the water.

"It is so beautiful here," Cindy said, tipping her bottle back. "I don't get why Gerald is so freaked out by this place. What was it he saw?"

"I don't know. He said it wasn't a boat... but... I don't know..."

"Maybe it was that bear?" Cindy said.

"Hadn't thought of that," I said, both of us chuckling.

I told her about Gerald, that he said he was in love with me, how he wanted to stay, or me to go back with him. I told her how amazing he was, how wonderful the sex has been, about his unhappiness with me considering quitting the doctorate program. We talked about Cindy's work, my school, some projects she's worked on. She asked me if I'd seen any of the movies she'd collaborated on, the ones she'd created special effects for.

"I haven't been to a movie in a while," I said.

"What do you guys do all the—?" Cindy stopped herself and scoffed. "Oh, never mind. You should try going out on more dates. You've turned into such a slut..."

I wondered if Gerald felt that way, if he thought I was a nymphomaniac.

Cindy caught me crying. "Hey, what's going on?" she said.

"I can't even think about... you know... without Marty..." I said, putting my pizza down, my stomach roiling. "I can't help but feel it's always going to be this way. Like that bastard's always going to be right there in my head, his fat face laughing at me ..." In that moment it didn't matter that Marty was probably dead... something inside my brain was keeping him on life support, alive and living in my head without a lease.

"Come on, let's go back to the house," Cindy said. She carried the plates and beer bottles. I put the pizza on the kitchen table and we ate the rest of it there. By the time we finished, it was dark outside.

"So," Cindy said after finishing the last dregs of her beer. "What are we going to do tonight to kick off our two-week sabbatical in paradise?"

"What sounds good? We have food, beer, wine, DVDs, a body of water the size of an ocean..."

"Do you need to work? I know that's why you came..."

"Not tonight. I got a lot done this morning. I need to ease back into this school business."

"Okay, then," Cindy said. "So, first, how would you feel about putting on our heavy coats and taking a little ride in the boat, maybe take some wine, and sit out in the water and look at the stars?"

"You know it's illegal to drink alcohol in a boat in Canada, right?"

Cindy shrugged. "Who's going to know?"

"Right! That sounds incredible," I said. "If we leave the lights on in the house and drive straight out from the dock, I think we can get back okay."

Cindy had decided to take my old bedroom on the main floor next to the living room. I told her she could stay upstairs with me in my bedroom, but she said her sleeping habits had become erratic. "I get up at all hours of the night to work now and sleep when I can." She came out wearing her coat, knit hat and gloves.

"Are you just wearing tights?" I said.

"Yeah, why? You think it'll be too cold?"

I went into the hallway closet and grabbed a couple extra blankets and set them on a kitchen chair. We put the wine and cheese into one of the empty grocery sacks. Cindy grabbed the bag of chocolate covered raisins.

The security light on the post near the dock illuminated everything within about a fifty-foot radius, but beyond that the world was a solid black mystery. I figured I'd be able to see once we got away from the dock, and when the moon came up it would be easy getting back. I fired the engine, a bit of blue smoke drifted across the surface of the water. I switched on the GPS, placed a waypoint where we were sitting at the dock, then adjusted the unit so it would leave a trail of breadcrumbs to show me the way back.

About a hundred or so feet from the dock, my eyes were already adjusting to the dark. I didn't really have to see well; there was nothing to hit in the direction I was heading. Only open water. What an amazing feeling, the boat rising from the surface as I pushed the throttle down, picking up speed, the fiberglass hull gliding across the water, the fresh night air cold against our faces. Cindy was holding the blanket in her lap and started draping it down over her legs for warmth.

"This is fucking fantastic!" Cindy shouted over the engine, her long black hair whipping out from beneath her knit cap.

We were out a couple of miles from the cottage when I eased back on the throttle. I turned to find my house lights to make sure I could still see them. They were pin pricks on a featureless black horizon. The GPS had drawn a bold blue line on the screen from our current position back to the cottage. I left the unit running, but turned off the engine. The silence was heady.

"God, I needed this," Cindy said.

I grabbed the other blanket and spread it across the front deck. The area was large enough for both of us and we laid down next to each other. Above us only stars, billions upon billions, as if God had just created several billion new ones since last I'd seen them. A strange and sudden sound broke the silence; the high-pitched chortle familiar to me.

Cindy shot upright. "What the fuck was that!" she said, her eyes darting back and forth trying to find traction in the insoluble gloom.

"A loon."

She eased back down. "Kind of a cool sound..." she said. "Once you know it's not like an alien or something."

We both laid there in our own thoughts, holding hands at times, only sitting up to take swigs from the wine bottle. Cindy broke off a hunk of cheese from the block and handed it to me. It had been so long since Cindy and I had done this together, just lay next to each other.

Feeling her next to me, the smell of her hair drifting over, brought back one of my earliest, and first of many embarrassing memories of sharing a dorm room with her. When she'd come back from jogging, she would undress in front of me, leaving her clothes where they fell. Then she'd grab the towel off her bed, wrap it sarong like around her breasts and go down the hall to shower. She was not the least bit self-conscious over being naked in front of me. I was surprised at first, probably because my body was so freakish and ungainly, like spare parts from different creatures, that I would never let anyone see me without clothes, not that there was anyone who'd want to. But even with Cindy, I would wait until she went out somewhere, or was asleep before I changed into my pajamas or put on fresh underwear. At that time, I didn't even wear a bra; there was absolutely no reason to.

One Saturday morning when she came back to the room after her shower, I hadn't realized it but I guess I'd been staring at her after she took her towel off and was using it to dry her hair.

"Wheels," she'd said brusquely. "What's the deal?"

"What?" I said, sitting on my made bed, my legs hung over the side as if I were sitting in a chair.

"Why are you staring at me? You're creeping me out."

"I wasn't staring," I said.

With her towel wrapped around her head like a turban, she walked toward my bed, her arms at her sides. I couldn't believe how beautiful her skin was, how soft her pubic hair looked. She was standing less than two feet away.

"Do you want to touch it or something?" she said.

"No," I said, trying to focus on her eyes. But I wanted to study her breasts, in order to imagine my own chest so wondrously endowed.

She caged her fingers around her breasts and pushed them up together. "Do you want to touch these?" she said.

"No," I said, despite the fact I wanted to so badly. The truth was, I wanted to touch every inch of her and wondered if her vagina was different than mine. I was so tight and dry and I often wondered if that was natural. One night I used a drop of lotion on my middle finger and had succeeded in inserting it completely inside myself. There was no pleasure whatsoever, regardless of what my mother had led me to believe.

"Wheels! A shooting star!" Cindy said, sitting up, wrenching me from my troubling reverie. "Look at that. I've never seen one last so long."

It was amazing. Usually they streak through the sky so fast you barely have time to make a wish. This one remained long enough to make an entire list. Cindy wiped her eye. "You crying?" I said.

"I'm so happy right now... being with you... like this. Being with you is so easy, so nice." She started talking about Trevor again, along with a whole string of men she'd dated over the past six years. "It's like they're all the same, like they have this gene that sends a message to their brains that says, hugging should automatically lead to fucking within a few minutes or something's wrong, and that hand holding should only be endured for no more than thirty seconds without some kind of follow up groping! And kissing, jeez, it's like I would kiss Trevor, just the slightest little kiss, you know, just a tender kiss, and, I'm serious here, his hand would shoot straight up my blouse! He was like a contraption, like when his lips were kissed, that would throw a lever in his elbow, sending his hand upward and instructing his fingers to squeeze my tit. Do you know what I mean?"

"Not sure what I'm supposed to say here."

"I forgot who I was talking to. Your time will come, when the novelty of sex wears off and Gerald grabs your ass while you're trying to explain how you want to repaint the spare bedroom before your mother-in-law visits."

I couldn't imagine a time when I wouldn't welcome Gerald's hand on any part of me, but I did like the image of Gerald and I sharing a spare bedroom that needed painting, his mother coming to visit. Though I had yet to meet her.

"Want to know what I wished for?" Cindy said.

"I'd love to, but if you tell me it won't come true," I said.

"I don't think making a wish on a shooting star is like blowing out birthday candles."

"Okay, so what did you wish for?" I said.

She looked up at the sky, then over at me. "I wished that if neither of us has found the love of our life by the time we're sixty, that we move in together and live like a couple of old dikes and travel the world and go to art openings and book readings and run naked with the bulls in Spain and get our portraits painted by some old lech in Paris and hang glide off the Cliffs of Dover and live happily ever after."

I looked over at her, at the soft glint in her eyes. "I love you, Cindy," I said.

She leaned in and kissed me on the lips, and although I didn't want to spoil the moment, I couldn't help but think about her ex-boyfriend, Trevor with the automatic arm response, so I raised my right hand up and squeezed her breast.

"Ohhh!...very funny!" she howled, both of us laughing like

refugees from an insane asylum. We handed the wine bottle back and forth until it was nearly gone, and finished off the block of cheese.

We laid back down and looked at the stars, holding hands under the blankets, and fell asleep.

Cindy woke first and shook me. "Wheels, I'm freezing my ass off. Let's go."

I sat up and rubbed the sleep from my eyes. Cindy wrapped herself in the blanket and went back to her seat. I brought the other blanket back with me and wrapped it around her shoulders. A minute later I had the engine running and was studying the GPS. It was obvious we had drifted quite a distance from where I had initially stopped the boat.

"Turn the heater on, Wheels," Cindy said, joking, but still shivering under her parka of blankets.

"I wish." I surveyed the horizon, unable to find the glow of the cottage. The moon was probably up but clouds had moved in sealing off any of its light. When I switched on the running lights it became obvious why I couldn't see anything; a light fog had settled on the water. Visibility was still probably at least fifty yards or more, so the cottage wouldn't come into view until we got closer.

I started following the GPS back toward the cottage. Since we had drifted east, we weren't going back the same way we'd come out, so I wasn't sure what to expect. I decided to run about third throttle. Even at that speed, we were still clipping along at probably twenty miles per hour when we hit something in the water. The impact jolted Cindy off her seat, hurling me against the console. I jerked back on the throttle and tried to regain my balance. Cindy was lying on the floor tangled in the blankets, trying to get up.

I turned the engine off and hurried over to her and grabbed her under the arms. Struggling to her feet, she found the seat behind her with her hand and flopped onto it. "What the hell was that?" She was rubbing the side of her head.

"You okay?" I inspected her ear and cheek. There was no blood.

"Yeah, sure. What did we hit?"

"I don't know." I knew it hadn't been a rock. That would have felt like we hit a wall and surely would have thrown Cindy from the boat. At times it was disorienting to be out at night and sometimes the GPS gave a false sense of security with its clean bright screen and blue navigational line, a flawed testimony to the hazards that abounded here. But whatever we'd hit was soft, like a muddy or silty bottom, maybe dense with weeds, something that gave a bit. I searched the compartments for a spotlight. In the back storage I pushed aside some rope and rubber boat bumpers and found one. The plug end of the cord was dirty so I wiped it on my jacket, then pushed it into the auxiliary receptacle on the dash console. The spot burned bright when I switched it on. Pointing it toward the horizon didn't help, the beam only serving to illuminate the fog, making it appear as if the air was filled with a fine white dust. I trained the beam down into the water expecting to see the shallow bottom, but what I saw looked like blood, or an oil slick swirling through the water.

"Can you see that?" I asked Cindy.

She tried to turn in her seat, her movement hampered by the blankets. "I can't see anything. What is it?"

If she didn't see it then there was no reason to cause alarm, so I didn't answer. I shined the beam back around the boat, unable to see anything. I wondered if I had hit a moose, perhaps, or some kind of fish that was feeding near the surface. I checked the depth on the GPS sonar. Twelve feet deep. Not shallow enough for us to have hit bottom, but certainly some kind of a submerged island, as I was fairly certain the surrounding area was at least a hundred feet deep. Maybe we'd hit the shallow end of an underwater point. I wondered if I had done damage to the engine's lower unit. I held the trim switch until the prop was angled completely out of the water, then walked to the back of the skiff and pointed the light at the bottom of the engine. I bent over as far as I could to access any damage. Everything seemed fine.

I went back to the center console and was about to trim the motor back down when I heard a sound, out beyond the range of the beam, out in the fog. It sounded like something was swimming roughly along the surface, splashing a bit, then as quickly as the sound had started, it was gone—followed almost immediately by a thunderous crack, like a gun, or a bomb going off, throwing water everywhere.

"Holy shit!" Cindy screamed. "What the hell was that?"

"A beaver," I said. "It must have been a beaver."

"That's one big fucking beaver."

I had heard beavers do that before. And they sounded like sea monsters when they did, which was the point. When beavers are trying to scare off intruders, they slap their huge flat tails on the surface of the water. And since there is no warning of the impending explosion, the defense mechanism is abrupt and unsettling, sounding much more ominous than it really is. The thing that bothered me, though, was that he was so far from shore. That seemed odd. A beaver certainly had the ability to swim across a great expanse of water, but it usually roamed closer to its lodge. Plus, I couldn't imagine that hitting a beaver could jolt the boat the way it had. It seemed that maybe I might feel a small thump or something, but nothing that could have thrown me against the steering wheel.

After switching off the spotlight, I started the engine. Cindy had her head hung, her chin to her chest, her eyes closed, holding the blankets tight around her from inside.

I glanced at the sonar and saw that we were now in fourteen feet of water. We must be drifting off the deep end of the underwater hump. That's when the sonar started to bottom out, the depth dropping rapidly. Thirty-six feet. I looked at the water to see if we were moving. It was rippled from a slight breeze, but the skiff seemed to be sitting still. Forty-eight feet. It finally stopped at fifty-three feet deep. I figured it for some kind of dramatic underwater ledge.

Just then, something hit the boat, a dull sound but enough to rock it a bit. I looked over at Cindy but she hadn't moved. I glanced back at the sonar, the bottom coming up quickly, thirty-feet, twenty-, ten-, five-, another bump against the bottom of the hull, this time a bit harder, enough to throw me off balance. I grabbed the spotlight and shined it down in the water. My breath caught as I saw what looked to be the bottom only a few feet beneath the boat, moving steadily, yet the boat was sitting still. In seconds it was gone, the sonar reading nearly sixty-feet deep again.

"What the fuck," I said under my breath.

"Wheels, let's get to the house. I'm wrecked."

I pushed the throttle forward, keeping my attention on the GPS, and ran the boat at idle speed. We were only a few miles out so I figured it was best to take a little extra time to get in safely than try to hurry. Cindy woke when we got to the dock. Half asleep, she helped me carry our stuff up to the house. When we got inside, she headed straight for her bedroom and closed the door. The clock on the stove read half past one in the morning. I was just starting up the stairs when I heard her door open.

"Kercy," she called, still groggy from her nap on the boat ride back.

"Yeah, sweetie. Need something?"

"Sleep with me tonight. Okay?"

"Sure." I was thankful for the invitation. At the motel I had felt safe, but not here, not yet anyway, and as soon as I heard Cindy's door close a ripple of dread crawled through me, recalling the weird evening. "I'm just going to grab my pajamas. I'll be right back."

It had to have been a sand bar, I convinced myself, grabbing my PJs from the drawer. There had probably been a long point out there that I hadn't seen. That would account for the beaver. It made perfect sense. It was very disorienting on a body of water that huge, especially at night with a bit of fog. It's easy for the imagination to commandeer the brain in those situations, especially on too little sleep, too much wine, and a bit of weed.

THIRTEEN

When I returned to Cindy's bedroom, she was already asleep. Before getting into bed, I went to the window, still thinking about the evening when I noticed someone walking out near the side of the house, a dark figure. The fog made it difficult to see, but when a second figure appeared my stomach lurched, as if it was in free fall. Could it be Marty and some crazy friend of his? Surely he was dead. Then I saw the two figures walk along the shoreline for a moment before they walked into the water and disappeared beneath the surface. That wasn't possible, I told myself. Divers, maybe? But what were they doing out here?

I hurried to the kitchen to make sure the deadbolt was secure, grabbing a huge fucking knife from the kitchen drawer before checking the front door. The house seemed secure, but how secure was it? recalling how easily Marty and Rags kicked the door in. I rushed back to the bedroom to wake Cindy. I didn't want to be alone right now.

By the time I slid under the blankets next to her, still holding the knife, she was snoring like a hamster, a soft little fuss I would normally give her shit about in the morning, but right now, morning seemed a long way off. She rolled toward me, draping her arm over me, though she never stopped snoring. I carefully slid the knife under my pillow.

Should I wake her? My mind was tumbling over itself trying to rewind what I thought I'd seen. Had I seen two people? Or was it the wine and weed? Or maybe Jacob and his girlfriend had stopped by to check on things, then went into the water for a late-night swim. Right. The mist was so thick I couldn't be sure if they had really gone into the water or not, or if anyone had ever been there. What a strange fucking night. I had to settle my mind, trying to focus on anything but the dark walls closing in on me. I looked over at Cindy who was sleeping so peacefully. I put my face against hers to feel her next to me, hoping I didn't wake her, and at the same time, selfishly hoping I did.

That's when Rags appeared, not *partying* Rags, but dead, *mangled* Rags, the guy who looked as though he'd taken a spin in a concrete mixer. It wasn't the image of that poor bastard that bothered me, it was trying to imagine the thing that killed him, that made him suffer and squeal like a helpless child.

I checked for the knife under my pillow, my fingers crawling over the wooden handle. Then I slid my other arm beneath Cindy's neck and pulled her to me. She stirred just a moment before rolling toward me and resting her head against my chest. Having her near relaxed me, made my eyes heavy (holding the knife under the pillow helped too) and I would have fallen right off if not for hearing someone jiggling the kitchen door knob. Had I been upstairs in my own bedroom, I would never have heard it.

I slid the knife from under my pillow and sat up slowly. I wasn't going to wait this time for someone to burst in. The kitchen was dark, so I felt I had the advantage. I watched the door knob move once more, then ripped back the curtain on the window. Spare light from the dock lit the intruder in such a ghastly light, its eyes glowing, I yelped and fell backward, losing my balance and crashing to the floor, the knife banging against cabinets in the dark. Before I could get my bearings, I heard a loud commotion, then felt someone's hands beneath my underarms...

"Wheels, what the hell happened?" Cindy said, helping me up.

"There's someone trying to get in."

"Come on, get up!"

"Kercy! Ms. Powell!" the voice called from the other side of the door.

Jacob. He looked panicked when I opened the door. "I'm so sorry," Jacob said. "I saw the lights were out and wanted to check the doors before I went back home."

"It's okay, it's just been a hell of a—" I stopped cold, movement down by the shoreline marshaling my attention. "What the fuck is that?" I pointed toward the water. Jacob spun his head, then looked back at me.

"It's just Lola. Are you okay?"

"Wheels, what's going on?" Cindy said, turning the kitchen light on. "And what's this?" She bent over and picked up the huge knife.

I didn't know what to say. I suppose the two figures I had seen earlier had been Jacob and his girlfriend, but that had been some time ago. "Have you been here long?" I asked Jacob.

"No, we just pulled up a few minutes ago."

I looked back in Lola's direction. "Is she looking for something?" I said, my attention on her. I could have sworn she was standing in the shallow water near the bank, but I couldn't be sure with the fog.

"No, she just wanted to get out and stretch her legs while I checked the doors and everything."

"You sure you've only been here a short time?"

Jacob seemed to puzzle a moment, his face sagging under some new weight. "Well, actually, it's been more like fifteen or twenty minutes, I guess. We checked the entire island first, making sure no one was hanging around or anything..."

"Hm," I said, suddenly noticing something very disturbing about Jacob's pants. "You look soaked!"

He glanced down at his jeans, then brought his eyes back to mine, forcing an uncomfortable smile. "Stupid me, I stepped off into the water back there..."

I just shook my head. I didn't want to keep hounding him, but his story sounded more like fiction every second. Regardless, I wasn't scared of him, or his girlfriend. Though I was at a loss as to why he was lying... again. "Well, thanks for checking."

"I'm really sorry I scared you like that."

"Be careful driving back."

"Always," he said, turning from the door and pulling his sock hat down over his ears.

I watched as he walked to his boat, signaling for Lola that they were leaving. She cut a quick glance up at me, then hurried to catch up to Jacob. I waited until they pulled from the dock and sped away before I pushed the door shut and bolted the locks.

"What was that about?" Cindy said, setting the butcher knife on the counter.

"I don't know." I was troubled by their odd visit.

Cindy came up and held me from behind. "You're trembling. Come back to bed. I'll rub your back until you fall asleep."

I grabbed the knife, and Cindy—obviously reading my state of mind—didn't ask any questions. Once I shoved it under the pillow, I pulled my shirt up and laid on my side. Cindy, rubbed gentle swirls along my skin. The back-rub offer was a nice gesture on Cindy's part, but I knew she'd fall asleep before I ever did; sure enough, within five minutes she was gone. I didn't care. I turned toward her and watched her in the dark. I fell asleep that way, feeling the warmth of her body against mine.

The next morning, while eating breakfast, Cindy told me she'd had the best sleep of her life. "Except for that little fracas in the kitchen last night..."

"Yeah, weird, huh?" I was still a bit miffed and confused by Jacob's lies.

"So, you ready to get at it today?" Cindy said. "Know what you're going to work on?"

"I think so." But I had no idea. I felt I needed to reposition my paper from my original proposal, but I knew my doctoral advisor would freak out.

After we finished with the dishes, I topped off my coffee and went to the living room where my papers and notebooks waited like a toxic spill across the floor. I read more about evolution, and the mechanisms that bring it about. In spite of Professor Leiden warning me about using too much *biology* to prove my hypothesis in *anthropology*, I found it impossible to separate the two disciplines.

The theory of evolution holds that all living creatures have the same ancestor, and that the myriad of species on the planet today all evolved from that single ancestor into millions of other species by some form of gene mutation brought about by issues surrounding survival. And that mutation would result in a diversity of species each now possessing a new gene structure different from its brothers and sisters. Some would thrive in the oceans, some by air, others would spend most of their time crawling along the dirt. So, the first problem with the theory seemed to be that most gene mutations are rare, and when they do occur, they usually reveal themselves in the form of diseases or defects, and are rarely advantageous.

But reading the documents published by the Human Genome Project and all the subsequent animal genome findings, it was now obvious that the diversity in gene structures between different species that the project had hoped to discover, did not exist. Not only were we no closer in understanding the secret of genetic inheritance, but we could no longer hold onto our previous notions about mutated genes.

But there had been another question that haunted me when I was going for my Master's in Biology, and that was, if all species evolved over millions of years as supposed by evolution, and humans evolved from apes, then why had no other species evolved along the line of humans? How is it that with millions of different life forms evolving, adjusting to changing conditions, that humans were the only species to have come about with the ability to create art, master language, compose music, build skyscrapers, engineer trains and cars and fly massive steel planes through the sky, and rocket to the moon and send huge telescopes into deep space? No other creature has even come remotely close to evolving to that extent. That doesn't seem possible if evolution works according to its theory. With the current thinking, the odds would seem to rule in favor of hundreds, if not thousands, or millions of species evolving to the extent of humans, creatures that wouldn't necessarily have the appearance of humans, but would evolve in myriad forms with the ability to utilize languages, create art, engineer amazing structures and machines, communicate over thousands of miles and reshape the very world they inhabit. But that has never happened.

I had been stuck there for some time, burdened with more questions than answers, and I was fairly certain Professor Leiden wouldn't accept a paper riddled with question marks. After two hours of reading and hair pulling and anguishing over this stupid paper all morning, I decided I needed something more than coffee or juice. I was on the back porch drinking a beer when Cindy walked out. She looked at her watch.

"It's not even ten thirty, Wheels. But... I think I'll join you."

She returned a couple of minutes later with a beer and an opened bag of pork rinds and sat on the chair next to me. The crunching sound she made was like a belt grinder on my brain.

"Jeez, do you have to chew so loud?" I said.

"It's loud*ly*," she said, correcting me jokingly. "And they are pork rinds, after all. Impossible to eat quietly."

I got up and walked down to the skiff, frustrated with everything. I walked to the end of the dock and stared down at the water, listening to the waves lap against the shoreline. Stretching my neck, I felt tightness in my shoulders. I inhaled deeply, holding the cool fresh air in my chest. Just then Cindy came up and wrapped her arms around me.

"Hey," she whispered. "I'm sorry. I know you're struggling. I wish I could help somehow."

"I can't do this," I finally said.

"You've overcome way harder stuff than this."

"I know I have. And I'm tired of it. I want easy stuff now. I want fun stuff."

Cindy fired up a joint and handed it to me. I took a long drag and held it in my lungs till it burned, then exhaled, handing it back. We sat and finished it and our beer and said nothing for the longest time.

Feeling somewhat renewed and ready to tackle evolution again, I was about to head back up to the house when I heard a motorboat heading toward the cottage. Moments later a blue and white Sea Ray pulled up to my dock. Special Agent Mallory in casual attire; puffy down jacket, shirt and jeans. I almost didn't recognize him. Cindy and I went over to tie the lines. I introduced him as Samuel Mallory, detective with the Elico police. He shook Cindy's hand and asked if he could speak to me alone. Cindy looked over at me.

"I'm going up to start lunch," she said. "You're welcome to stay, Detective Mallory."

"No thanks, Ms. Baxter," he said. "But thanks."

Mallory turned to me and asked if I was up to a little stroll around the island. He headed in the direction where Rags had attacked me. I figured the trees and bushes down there were still draped in yellow crime scene tape.

"No, let's go this way," I said, leading him in the opposite direction.

Mallory's awareness abruptly shifted toward the cottage. "So, this looks like the front of the house here. I'm surprised you didn't put your boat dock out there with a walkway from your front porch. It looks like no one even uses that porch."

"Yeah, this is the front, or, was the front, when I was in a wheel-chair years ago. But my mother had the dock added to the back of the house so she could see me from the kitchen or dining room, which she converted into our living room. There was a boat dock out here as well, but it got crapped up over the years and she had it removed. I don't even use that front door anymore."

We started walking along a path through the trees.

"You were in a wheelchair?" he said. "An accident?"

"No. Birth defects."

Mallory stopped, his eyes narrowed on me like *I* might be guilty of some anomalous crime. "Birth defects?"

"Yeah, but I'm not listing them for you." I walked away from him. He caught up to me.

"You know Jacob, right, from the harbor?" he said. "Ben's grandson?"

"Well, of course, but... I wouldn't say I know him. But Ben, yeah, I've known him all my life. Ben is wonderful." Jacob, although he'd saved my life, was still basically a stranger to me. And over the past several days, it seemed he was hiding something.

"You two should get together... maybe talk," Mallory said.

"Ben and I talk all the time," I said, being flip. I knew what Mallory meant.

"Jacob..." he said. "You should talk to Jacob."

"Talk? Yeah, that may be a great idea." I stopped at the shore to look out over the water. It took me a few seconds to calculate Mallory's angle. "Are Jacob and you... you know... like, working together or something?" I was thinking that maybe Jacob's caginess had to do with Mallory.

Mallory scratched his nose and stood next to me. "Yes. For several years now actually..."

Things were beginning to make sense in a nonsensical way. "Then why are you asking me all these questions? It seems you know way more than I do. What is it you and Jacob are so protective of...?" I was tired of this game of cat and mouse.

"Look, just talk to Jacob," he said.

"Because of...?

"Just talk to him. Compare notes. He left for Toronto this morning, but he should be back in a few days. Drive your boat in, meet up with him, go get coffee in town... But do it alone, so it's just you and Jacob. Maybe your friend Cindy can see the sights, hang out in the shops. Most of them are still open."

"Did you want to print out an itinerary for her?" I was irked that he felt entitled to orchestrate a meeting with Jacob while excluding Cindy.

"Hey," he said. "I'm trying to help, that's all."

"Who?"

"You... both of us."

"Why don't you just tell me what Jacob knows and quit all this cloak and dagger spy shit? Maybe that will explain why he and his little girlfriend have been sneaking out here..."

Mallory eyes narrowed when I mentioned that, as if that were news even to him. "Look, I can see you're not in such a good place right now..." he started to say.

"What the fuck do you want, Agent Mallory? Just tell me!"

He glared at the earth beneath his feet like a schoolboy with a profound and disturbing secret. "It's just better if we're communicating, you know? Working together. It will be good for both of us..."

"Yeah, our own private snooper club."

Mallory scratched his head. "I've got to go."

Back at the dock, he climbed into his Sea Ray and I undid the lines and tossed them into his boat. The inboard rumbled when it started, bubbles rushing up along the transom.

"Give the meeting with Jacob some thought," he said.

He turned the big boat toward open water, idling out about fifty feet before throttling up. I watched the white froth of his wake cut across the blue water, spreading, dissipating, leaving a vague trail on the surface until the waves completely consumed it.

"Wheels!" Cindy called from the back porch. "Lunch is ready.

FOURTEEN

Over the next few days Cindy and I fell into a relaxing vacation rhythm, drinking and snacking and napping, sunbathing and boat riding and watching movies on DVD. Between junkets out on the water, Cindy landed a new client who needed a fresh approach to a HUD—Heads Up Display—so popular in movies. They wanted something that didn't resemble the hi-tech info graphs and graphics that had become so commonplace in sci-fi flicks. While she labored away on her laptop, I managed to get some work done on my research, tackling the problems of macroevolution, where one species actually transforms into a new and entirely different species, much like humans transforming from apes into their present form. A transformation that dramatic—from apes to humans over millions of years —would require an enormous amount of intermediate steps due to the problems of bone structure, vascular system, creature's center of gravity, nervous system, and numerous other changes. So, while all these necessary changes were taking place over millions of years, the intermediate creature enduring these transitional steps might likely be an inferior form at best, thus falling prey to other creatures.

When I explained it to Cindy, she said, "What about you?"

"What do you mean?"

"What about your transformation, Wheels? It's astonishing. I know you call it *assimilation,* but isn't the transformation you've undergone... I mean, wouldn't that be evolution?"

"Maybe... or it could have just been delayed maturation. With all my birth defects and operations, my body could have just fallen into some kind of stasis, perhaps, a sort of... uh, biological status quo."

"Really? You believe that?"

I didn't know what to believe. "But to answer your question, in order for my transformation to be some form of evolution, I would have to be able to pass it along to offspring. So... I guess we'll never know."

We tried to steer clear of such heavy subjects, and I had yet to tell Gerald I was unable to get pregnant. It had been a few days since I thought about Agent Mallory, and amazingly everyone was leaving us alone, to the point that Marty and Rags, while never completely gone from my head, occupied a portion of my brain that had to compete with Cro-Magnon man, a subject I mentioned to Cindy while she was sunbathing on the dock and drinking a beer.

"Big browed, knuckle dragging, hairy bastards," Cindy said from behind her sunglasses. "Dated 'em all."

"Yeah, okay... but that's not actually true, the big browed... whatever," I said. "Cro-Magnon's' artistic achievements in art are nothing short of remarkable. Their work exhibited dimension, perspective, incredible detail, and a sense of humor. It went beyond mere recording, rivaling any art created today."

"Apparently I never dated that particular Cro-Magnon," she said.

"The point is, it would seem they just happened on the scene thirty thousand years ago. There's nothing in evolution to account for this kind of dramatic shift in consciousness."

"While fascinating, my dearest pet," Cindy said, getting up from the dock. "We are presently not in possession of near enough beer for me to continue this discourse further. So, I will bid you adieu as I retire to the house for a much-needed slice of coconut cream pie. You, as always, are welcome to join."

"Okay, very funny, Professor Baxter. I'll just sit here alone trying to grind out thought-altering rhetoric on subjects as staggeringly engaging as evolution. But just so you know... the coconut cream pie is gone..."

"No way! When did we finish that?"

"Last night. Should we head into town for another?"

We slipped some clothes over our bikinis and took the boat into the harbor and got into Cindy's Volvo. At the grocery store we bought two pies, one chocolate and the last coconut cream. After restocking our dwindling beer and snack supply, we drove back to the harbor. When we walked past Ben's office, Liam was standing in the door-way. He said nothing. We climbed in the boat and headed back toward the cottage.

Along the way we found a quiet bay out of the wind. I loved watching the spruce and pine tops sway and roll, the sound of the needles brushing against each other, that soft hissing sound. Unusually warm and sunny for September on Georgian Bay often signaled a storm approaching, probably to hit in the next couple of days. There was an early June years ago when the temperatures were in the 90's at the beginning of the week, followed by a blizzard a few days later. Yet the deep blue sky today controverted any possibility of foul weather.

Our pies and beer were safely on ice in the skiff's huge built-in cooler, but our snacks were not faring as well. I counted at least four bags of salty snack foods opened on the front deck of the boat, when Cindy reached for another kind of really flat party pretzel designed especially for dipping.

She sat up and dug her hand into them and was reaching for another beer.

"Hey, let's go for a boat ride," I said.

She started stowing the chips back into grocery sacks, then

shoving the bags into compartments. I started the engine and asked Cindy if she wanted to drive.

"I just want to ride with the breeze in my hair," she said, tipping her sunglasses up to stare at me. She was seated in the bow on the front deck.

"You're going to have some breeze in your hair sitting up there," I said. "Why don't you come back here by me?"

She scooted down off the front deck onto the side seats, but still near the front. "How's this, mother?" she said, lighting up a joint.

"Fine," I said, cramming down the throttle, the boat shooting from the water, throwing her to the floor.

"Oh, real mature, Powell," she said, struggling to get back on the seat, the momentum of the skiff pushing her toward the back. We drove past islands I'd never seen, always with one eye on the GPS and sonar. The water was extremely deep and I felt okay opening the boat up, seeing how fast it would go.

Finally seated upright again, Cindy howled, her hair ripping behind her. She kept one hand on the railing, the other holding her joint. She held it up to me, offering me a smoke. We were at least ten miles out from the cottage, the shorelines of islands gradually disappearing. I wanted to see how far I'd have to go before it was like ocean, where the land would melt away leaving a seamless mirror of sky and water. We drove for over fifteen minutes before I eased back on the throttle, bringing the boat to a slow stop. I turned the key and the engine went off.

Cindy stood up and looked around. I went up and stood next to her.

"Is this unbelievable or what?" I said, swiveling my head, water stretching to the horizon in every direction.

"It is." Cindy crunched some kind of chip, then looked over at me. "But a girl's still gotta eat, right?"

I dug my hand into the bag and we sat there, drifting and eating, until they were all gone.

"Okay," Cindy said, after a long silent interlude. "So... I think I need real food now. Can you get us back, Wheels?"

"Yeah, sure." I slipped my thin wind breaker on and Cindy did the same. The sun was dipping slightly, the breeze picking up.

Shooting across the open water, my eyes on the GPS, I figured we should be back in less than forty minutes or so. I wasn't sure where we were, but the cottage was marked on the unit and we were headed for it. That seemed good enough for me... until we hit something that stopped the boat, hurling me against the console, first, then recoiling me back, stumbling to the floor. The engine raced for a moment, then clattered and made an awful noise before it stopped completely.

FIFTEEN

Still loopy, I tried to get to my feet. "Cindy, you okay?"

She didn't answer. "Cindy! Are you okay?"

I was dazed, blood on my fingers from where I grabbed my forehead. When I finally got to my feet, Cindy was gone.

"Cindy! Cindy!" I ran to the front of the skiff. "Cindy!"

Water and waves and no sign of her. A moment later she came up, flailing at the surface about sixty feet from the boat. "Cindy!" The wind was carrying the boat away from where she was struggling to stay afloat.

"Cindy, can you swim over?" I knew she wasn't a good swimmer, but making it even worse, the cold water was sapping her strength, her ability to breathe. She went under, then resurfaced, coughing, grasping at waves.

I wrenched off my wind breaker and dove in, trying to keep myself near the surface. But I couldn't, and started sinking. The colors came, then the acute clarity of the watery world, the bright fish slipping and darting... Stop, I told myself. Get to the surface and SWIM. CINDY IS DROWNING. The familiar calm was settling over me, warmth oozing through my body, the amazing... NOW,

KERCY! GET TO THE SURFACE, NOW! YOU'RE DROWN-
ING! After a moment, my senses dull and gauzy, I pumped my feet
and arms and reached the surface, sticking my head above the waves,
coughing, spitting up water. When I caught my breath, I started
kicking my legs to keep me up, spinning myself around, looking for
Cindy, until I glimpsed her at least forty yards away. She was splashing, unable to keep her head above water.

She kept sinking, resurfacing, and I could tell she was getting
weaker. "Cindy, don't give up! I'm almost there!" I wasn't even sure if
she could hear me. I was almost to her when she went under and
didn't come back up. I ducked my face beneath the surface just a
moment and saw her sinking, her limbs no longer moving, slumped
over.

I dove down and tried to force myself to focus on her, incredible
colors swirling around me. I shook my head and said her name over
and over. CINDY. CINDY. After an eternity, I reached her finger,
and held on, her weight pulling me down. With my other hand I
grabbed her wrist and then found a new hold with my right hand. I
kicked my legs and got her to the surface, then spun her around in my
arms to drag her backward. The boat seemed impossibly far away
now, and I wasn't sure I could make it back. I wasn't cold, but, for
some reason, I felt exhausted, like the water was leaching my
strength.

I kicked and kicked, using my free hand to push us along. And
after another eternity, I reached the skiff and tried to balance Cindy's
body at the transom while I climbed into the boat. As I was throwing
my leg over the side, she started slipping from the edge. I stretched
out and snagged her wrist. It took me several minutes to wrestle her
into the craft. I turned her head to the side to clear her air passages,
then put my lips over her mouth, held her nose and tried to resuscitate her, switching to CPR, pressing on her chest, counting between
each compression, then back to her mouth. "Come on, Cindy." After
several pumps of her chest, I went back to her mouth. "Damn it,

Cindy!" I had just started CPR when she coughed, gasping and choking, water spewing from her mouth.

"Oh my god, Cindy!" I touched her face. "You're okay! You're
okay!"

She coughed a few more times. Her head was bleeding, but just a
trickle. I wiped the blood away to see how bad it was. It was just a
cut, rather than a gash needing stitches.

"Cindy!"

She looked around, her hand going to her head. She was starting
to shiver. I got her out of her wet jacket, then grabbed my wind
breaker and wound her arms into it. "Wait a second." I rushed back to
the compartment hoping I'd find one of the blankets from the night
before, one we'd forgotten to take back up to the cottage. I pulled it
out and wrapped her.

"You better now?"

"Yeah. Yeah, I'm good" she said, sitting up. "Wheels, your head is
bleeding."

"It's nothing."

She coughed a few more times. I held her, surveying the area,
trying to figure out where we were. That's when I recognized a
familiar cabin in the distance. Boat Eater Bay. Fuck, how could I not
know that! We had entered from a different direction.

After Cindy got settled, I went to the controls and trimmed the
engine out of the water to assess the damage, afraid to look. My fear
was confirmed. Not only was the prop missing, the entire lower unit
was gone, oil dripping into a shiny, rainbow-colored pool along the
surface. My stomach soured. I looked over at Cindy. She now had the
blanket pulled to her chin, her eyes stark, her body shaking.

"It's going to be okay," I said. "We're not far from the cottage."

"Yeah, no, Kercy, I'm okay. Don't worry about me. I'm just a bit
shook up, is all. Can you grab my sweat pants from the back
compartment?"

"Of course." I felt stupid that I'd forgotten. I carried them back to her, then fumbled with the paddles from the side compartments and laid them on the floor. This was going to be a long afternoon.

"Can you get the motor running again?" Cindy asked.

"It's kind of... gone... at least the bottom half."

"Holy shit!" Cindy laughed a bit. "How fucked up is that!"

I was glad for her lightness, in spite of feeling completely horrible that I'd almost killed her. After slipping her sweat pants on she crawled out of the blanket and grabbed one of the paddles.

"No, you need to stay warm," I said, trying to drape the blanket back over her shoulders.

"I'll be plenty warm paddling this big-ass boat. So, let's get going here. Which direction?"

I checked the GPS. It was working, but its response time was inadequate in showing the boat's heading if we were moving slow. It would be no use, and I had no idea how to access the compass function on the GPS unit. I would have to rely on memory.

Standing up, I looked around, trying to recall times Ben had driven me through this bay. "That way, I think."

Cindy's eyes followed my pointing finger. "Okay," she said, pushing her paddle down into the water. I sat opposite her and we started paddling. After a half hour our efforts were starting to feel futile, as the wind continued pushing us off course, thick clouds rolling in. I stopped paddling and searched my pockets, the seats, the floor.

"What's going on?" Cindy asked, still paddling.

"My phone's gone. I wanted to call the harbor, see if someone could come out and help us." At this rate, with the wind, we were going to be farther from the cottage than when I knocked the lower unit off.

"Hey, Kercy, it's okay. We're gonna be fine."

"I know... it's just... I feel so stupid. You almost..."

"Hey, I'm fine. You're fine. Let's keep paddling. Didn't you say the wind usually dies around dusk."

I didn't answer because that brought up an entirely new list of problems, one being, I'd never find my way back in the dark if we were still paddling two hours from now. We had to get back before nightfall or we'd be stuck until morning with no real food and hardly any clothes. And if I didn't find an anchor, we'd be drifting all night. I checked the GPS again, trying to calculate the distance from our current position to the cottage. The screen made getting back look so easy; it didn't show wind pushing us off course. Or the dark clouds building, the storm rolling in behind them, or the exhaustion we felt from paddling.

"Where's your phone, Cindy?" I said.

She pulled her paddle in the boat and laid it on the floor, then grabbed her jacket off the deck and unzipped the pocket. Her phone was soaked, dripping in her hand.

"Damn," I said, looking around, then at Cindy. "I'm so sorry I got us into this..."

"Hey, Wheels, stop. We'll be fine. Let's just keep paddling."

Steering the boat with the paddles was impossible in the wind. We had rowed for over an hour and a half. Even with cloud cover, it was pretty obvious the bright spot of the sun was falling lower over the water. I was sinking deeper into my own self-recrimination when Cindy stood up and started yelling, waving her arms in the air. I followed her eyes to see what she was looking at, then dug into the console compartment for the air horn, blowing it several times toward the boat several hundred yards off.

"Hey! Over here!"

I blew the horn several more times. The boat rounded an island and was gone from view. I looked at Cindy. She shrugged, picking up her paddle. A moment later the boat shot out from the island and circled back toward us. Cindy and I started yelling again, waving our arms. This time the driver saw us. We laughed and dropped our paddles on the floor. I dug around in the back compartment for a heavy rope. Just as I was pulling it out, the boat slid up alongside us.

It took a moment for me to focus on the driver. It was Liam. I looked over at Cindy. By the way she was yucking it up with him, all smiles and bright eyes, I figured she hadn't recognized him yet.

"Hey, Liam," I said. "I've got boat troubles. Can we get a tow?"

"Yeah. I can see that. Wow." He was laughing, looking back at my engine trimmed out of the water, dripping oil. "Throw me your rope."

Holding one end, I tossed the bundle toward him. He grabbed it and tied it to a cleat on the back of his boat. I wound my end through the bow eye of my skiff.

"Anybody get hurt?" he said.

"No, we're fine," I said. Cindy looked at him, then me.

"Want me to tow you to the harbor?" he said.

I hadn't thought it through. Hoping Ben could come out and repair it, I had assumed we'd try to get a tow back to the cottage. But my phone was gone, and Cindy's, even if we could dry it out, may never work again. I wasn't sure how I would get a hold of him. Yet, I didn't want to be stuck in town. All of our stuff was at the cottage.

"Is Ben there?" I said. "At the harbor."

"Naw, he's gone. Jacob won't be back for a couple of days, but Ben will be in tomorrow morning first thing."

Liam seemed much friendlier this time, much more willing to help. "Well... could you get us back to the cottage so we can get our stuff, then take us to the harbor?"

"Yeah, no problem. It'll be late when we get in. Takes a lot longer towing another boat."

"Is that cool with you?"

Liam looked at his watch, then back at me. "Yeah, shouldn't be a problem."

He eased his craft away from ours until the rope tightened, jolting our boat a bit until we were tracking in his wake. Cindy came back by me and sat down.

"Is that the rude guy from the harbor?" she said.

I nodded, keeping an eye on the rope between the boats. "I guess we'll stay in town tonight," I said to her. "Maybe Ben can get us another boat tomorrow."

"Yeah, that's fine. We're going to get our stuff first, right?"

I nodded, not wanting to stay at the Aubrey again. I didn't want to stay in town at all and started silently berating myself for being so reckless and not paying attention to where we were.

"I'll drive you to the hospital when we get back to the harbor," I said. "There's one about sixty miles from town."

"I'm not going to the hospital," Cindy said. "I'm fine."

I took my eyes back out over the water and found myself staring at Liam's boat wake, the froth churning behind his skiff, spreading out, becoming wider as it drifted beneath our boat, getting smoother towards the edges, until finally merging back into a seamless statement of water and waves. Everything was gray now, the clouds so thick even the last dregs of sun could not burn its presence onto the last forty-five minutes of the day. The air was cooling and it was obvious the wind would become stronger through the night as the approaching cold front swept the islands and shores. I looked over at Cindy. She was bundled in the blanket, her eyes closed, her head hung, chin resting on her chest. Liam kept his eyes straight ahead, the occasional trail of smoke from his cigarette swept away from his dark shape. Dusk was coming fast and the ride back to the cottage was taking much longer than I had imagined.

The whine of Liam's engine became less frenetic as he slowed his boat. He pointed his skiff toward the house and idled alongside the dock so masterfully that my boat tucked right in behind his. Once he tied his boat to a cleat, he jumped out and grabbed the rope tethering our boats together, pulling us up snug to the bumpers.

I grabbed my deck line and tied us off. Cindy woke up and climbed out of the boat.

"It won't take us long to gather our stuff together," I said. "Do you mind waiting?"

"No, that's fine," Liam said, lighting another cigarette.

When we got inside the house, Cindy went to her bedroom and I started packing stuff from the fridge into the cooler. I gathered some of the food from the cabinets and was placing it in a grocery sack when a knock came at the back door.

"Hey," I said. "What's up, Liam?"

"I just wanted to apologize for how I acted the other day..." he said, his cigarette pinched between his finger and thumb at his side. "Problems at home... you know..."

"No worries." I held the door, not wanting to invite him in. "We shouldn't be long. Sorry to put you out like this."

He turned to go back to the dock, then stopped. "You know... if you want, you can stay out here tonight, and Ben and I'll drive a new boat out here tomorrow. That way you don't have to ferry all your stuff, right?"

Cindy came into the kitchen and announced she was packed. Still holding the door, I swiveled my head toward her and related Liam's proposal.

"That works for me. How 'bout you, Wheels?"

I guessed it would be okay, but something didn't feel right. I didn't like the fact that we had no phone and no way to communicate with anyone.

"I don't know, Liam," I said. "Probably best if we head back tonight."

Cindy came closer to me so Liam couldn't hear. "Are you concerned because we don't have a phone?"

I nodded.

"Listen, I can stick my phone in a bowl of rice. We've got that big bag we bought for stir fry," she said. "Phone should be good by morning."

Liam must have heard Cindy. "You can use my phone, tonight," he said. "I'll get it tomorrow when Ben and I come back out. We can be here by eight or so. We got plenty of boats."

"No, that's too much of an imposition..." I said. "For you. How you going to go tonight without your phone?"

Liam laughed. "I know... it's damn crazy how much we depend on those things. Probably do me good to go a night without it. Give me a chance to dig out my ice fishing tackle and get it cleaned up."

I smiled weakly, trying to be appreciative of his offer.

"Besides, I owe you for how I treated you the other day," he said. "You could have gotten me fired by telling Ben, and I feel terrible about how shitty I acted. Pardon my French."

"I'm okay with it, Wheels, if you are," Cindy whispered, standing out of Liam's line of sight.

"You sure?" I said to Liam.

"Really, it's no problem. Besides, it's already starting to rain. It'll be a slow cold ride back to the harbor towing your rig." Liam lit another cigarette and turned away from the door, jerking his collar up over his neck.

I agreed and Liam went back down to the dock and was about to pull away when I realized he hadn't given me his phone.

"Liam!" I shouted, trying to hurry down the walkway without falling. "Liam!"

He was pulling off and glanced back to see me and shifted his boat into neutral.

"What is it?" he shouted over the engine noise, rain slashing across the deck boards. I was getting soaked and his boat had already drifted several feet from the dock.

"Your phone," I said, my hands cupped around my mouth. "You didn't give me your..."

Before I could finish, he dug into his coat pocket and held out his phone as if to toss it. "Can you catch?"

"Yeah," I said, thinking what a klutz I was.

The phone cut a gentle arc through the rain and darkness, the security light flashing off its shiny surface as it twisted and rolled, then landed in the cup of my palms. I squeezed it tight, relieved I'd caught the damn thing.

"What's the password?" I shouted.

"Ain't locked. You're good to go." Carefully protecting his cigarette from the rain, he drew hard and left a long line of blue smoke as he swerved the skiff into the darkness, my broken boat trailing behind, the engine still trimmed up exposing a metal shaft and a tangle of machinery sticking from the casing.

SIXTEEN

Cindy was preparing burritos for dinner while I was upstairs showering, trying to push away the uneasy feeling I had about Liam. As he was pulling from the dock, I had quickly checked his phone to make sure it opened. It was unlocked, just as he said it would be. And it showed four bars, good signal.

I was soaked when I got back to the house. Cindy had already changed into dorm pants and a sweatshirt and offered to cook. I had gone upstairs and peeled out of my dripping clothes and wind breaker. And while the hot water was soothing on my skin, I couldn't help but feel stupid about hitting the rock, destroying Ben's boat, nearly drowning Cindy. Never once had Ben ever hit anything!

The afternoon kept rolling over me—the boat slamming the rock, Cindy struggling to keep her head above water, her limp body sinking —as if the sheer number of replays could somehow produce a different outcome. I twisted the shower handle off and was drying myself when Cindy called up to me.

"Dinner, Wheels," she said.

"Be right there." I put on my flannel pajamas.

We'd decided to watch a DVD after dinner before we got back to work. It was hard for me to focus, the accident playing over and over in my head. When the movie ended, Cindy got up to take the DVD out.

"I'm so sorry about today," I said.

"Wheels, you have to stop apologizing! I mean it, or I'm gonna go find a different island. As Yogi would say, 'Even Napoleon had his Watergate.'"

Laughing, I asked what that was supposed to mean.

"Hell if I know," she said. "My dad... whew, what a piece of work."

We laid together, Cindy breathing softly, me thinking back to the college dorm where we'd met.

Back in school, the first time Cindy asked me to take my clothes off I was mortified and started to cry. The second time, several months later, I was still reluctant, but felt we were close friends by then. After Cindy locked the door to our dorm room, I, with much trepidation, unbuttoned my blouse and slid it off my arms. Cindy was seated on her bed with me sitting in my wheel-chair in front of her. I left my T-shirt on and unsnapped my jeans and slid the zipper down. With my jeans lying on the floor in a heap, I crossed my arms over my chest, still wearing my underpants and T-shirt.

"Want me to help you with your top?" Cindy had said softly.

As I lay on the couch of the cottage, Cindy behind me, her arm draped over my tummy, I remembered that night in the dorm as the pivotal point in my physical development. But I had never answered her. I hadn't wanted help with my top because I didn't want her to see me naked. My body was a mistake. So she got up and came over to me and wrapped her fingers around the bottom seam of my shirt and slowly pulled it up over my head. My arms sprung back across my chest like trap doors. I tried to wipe my eyes on my bare shoulder.

When she removed my underpants, cool air brushed over me and I crossed my legs and hunched over.

"Is that enough?" I said. "Can I get dressed?"

She held my gaze until I had to look away. "Can you stand?" she said.

"No," I said. "I can't stand. You know that!"

"I'll help you." She held her hands out to me. For several breaths I refused to take them, but she never wavered, just waited silently for me. She had my mother's patience. I reached out to her and placed my palms in hers. "When you're ready," she said.

I nodded and she held firm against my pulling, never trying to hurry my ascent or force my progress by jerking on my arms. She provided a handle for me to pull up on. A moment later I was standing in front of her naked, my legs a bit wobbly at first, the plain, unattractiveness of my body on full display. Crushed, and losing resolve, I wanted to fall back into my chair and give up.

Her eyes traced an imaginary line down my body. I looked away. "You're beautiful, Kercy," she said. "I'm going to release your hands now. Will you be okay?"

I nodded. When she let go, I tried to cover myself but she gently guided my arms to my sides.

"Remember how you focused on my body when you touched me, Kercy?" Cindy had said, reminding me of the time she'd had me touch her a few months earlier. "I want you to focus on your own body as I touch you."

I think I was shaking when I first felt her touch. She held my face in her palms, something I was very used to; my mother held me that way. But even after a deep breath, I still felt an unbearable turbulence rushing through me. Her hands moved down my neck to my shoulders, and something wobbled so violently inside me I felt it was about to break loose. With her palms flat against my skin, she let them slip down my chest, and my breath caught, and I felt a bit dizzy and just as I was about to pass out, something released, as if a blockage suddenly dislodged, allowing this crazy new energy to swell inside

me, prickle along my skin. A surge of pleasure so overwhelming I
jerked back, stumbling against my wheelchair. Cindy reached out to
steady me.

"Do you want to stop?" she said.

I shook my head, then closed my eyes, my familiar focus returning, just as it would when I touched her. Her fingers found the soft
flesh of my tummy, slowly tracing the faint muscles beneath my skin.
There I was, seeing myself as if seeing through Cindy's eyes, feeling
through her fingers, but different; the absolute otherness of it causing
my breath to falter. A warm wetness filled me; it took a moment
before I realized Cindy's finger was inside me. I couldn't open my
eyes, for fear the feeling would vanish. Immersed in this alien sensation, I found it difficult to concentrate on assimilating it. I tried to
focus on it, master it somehow, and then just as quickly I found
myself lost in irrepressible ecstasy. Heat bristled beneath my flesh,
filled my abdomen. Cindy's hand reached behind me as her lips came
to my stomach. With my legs now weak and trembling, I leaned
forward and balanced myself against her, my hands on her shoulders.
Never had I experienced anything so intense.

After several minutes she helped me into her bed, where she laid
me on my back and kissed me. I could no longer focus, or process the
movement of muscles and tendons. I was lost, drifting through some
unsettled landscape, luscious shapes and colors, floating on a warm
zephyr of silk, the salty taste of skin on my tongue.

I don't even remember how that night ended, or if it ever did,
because those sensations never left me. For months after, when
Cindy touched me, held me, caressed my skin, exploring every part of
my body, I could no longer concentrate on movement, no longer
cared about picturing the inner workings of the anatomy and was
sure my development would end. But the opposite happened, and
over the next several years my body underwent miraculous transfor-
mations, my legs took shape, growing exponentially stronger. It
seemed I had only to release myself to this sensory pleasure to accom-

plish my most sought-after goal; to transmute my slapdash puerile anatomy into a woman's physiology.

"Hey, Wheels," Cindy said, stirring behind me on the couch. "You awake?" She sat up and yawned, looking around as if trying to figure out where she was. "Did you sleep?"

"I rested," I said. "But I need an incentive to get back to work?"

"Oh... what are you thinking?" she said, yawning again.

"Well, I'm thinking if *hot* sounds good, then pizza bagels," I said, sitting up to face her. "And if *cold* is more to your liking, then Coke floats!"

"Tough choice," she said. "And I'm too traumatized from the day's events to make that call... let's do both."

"God, it's going to take a crane to get us off this island!"

"I don't care, Wheels," Cindy said. "The future ain't what it used to be."

"Your dad?" I said.

"What do you think?" she said, smirking. She got up and stretched. "Don't make my float until I'm out of the shower, okay? You know I hate it when the—"

"You think I forgot?" I said. "We have deep depth."

Cindy laughed. "You've been around my dad too much. I'm cutting you off for the holidays."

Her parents had the dorkiest, best Christmases, complete with caroling, eggnog and more decorations than Clark Griswold. Cindy stopped in her bedroom to grab clean underwear, then bounded up the steps. The music came on upstairs and I heard her singing along, her voice lush and soulful.

SEVENTEEN

The pizza bagels were ready to go into the toaster oven, but I had yet to hear the shower come on. I went to the living room and spread my notes across the floor. Wind rattled the windows, rain hissing against the siding. The nice thing about the cottage was that the power lines ran under the water and were buried outside the house, so we hardly ever lost power. Even so, the possibility of trees falling on the roof was always a threat.

I had just cracked open my book when the shower came on upstairs. I glanced over at the small clock on the bookshelves and figured Cindy would be about another twenty minutes. She loved long, luxurious showers.

I had just started reading about an experiment that biologists had performed on house flies, manipulating one of the HOX genes to grow eyes on its wings and legs when the lights flickered for only a second, then went out.

"Shit!" Cindy yelled from upstairs. "Wheels, what's going on?"

"Power's out," I yelled up to her. "I'm grabbing flashlights. Stay put." Something must have happened in town, some transformer must have been hit by lightning. I figured the power company would get it back up fairly soon; Elico wasn't that big. But the power outage spelled the end of our pizza bagels.

I stumbled around in the kitchen, guiding myself along by holding the counter tops, having a difficult time adjusting to the absence of light.

"Wheels, how we coming down there?" Cindy called again. "I can't see anything up here."

"Yeah, it's fucking dark, isn't it?" I yanked drawers open, rummaging my hand through them, wracking my brain trying to recall where I'd left the flashlights. Ben had one in his boat, but the boat was gone. "I'll be there in a minute. Hang on."

The front door blew open, the wind banging it against the wall. How could that be? It should be locked.

"Hang on, Cindy. I'll be there in a sec."

I touched my way down the hall and was met by rain pouring in through the doorway. After forcing the front door shut, the wind fighting me every inch of the way, I latched the deadbolt. How did the deadbolt come open? Had Cindy gone out the front?

I was trying to get back down the hall when the phone in my pocket rang. Liam's phone. Why hadn't I thought of that, the flashlight on his phone. I looked at the number but there was no way I'd recognize it. I switched the phone off to stop it from ringing, then opened it again to activate the flashlight function.

When I did the beam caught on someone standing a foot away from me.

I thought it was Cindy until a hand shot toward me and snatched the phone. Someone grabbed me around the throat from behind and hustled me back to the kitchen. Their breath was rank with tobacco. I heard footsteps rushing on the stairs and thought Cindy was coming down from the shower, but the footfalls were too heavy and dull to be her... and were going up.

A moment later I heard Cindy screaming and all the air left my body.

"I needed my phone tonight after all," a voice said. There was no mistaking Liam.

But he wasn't the one holding me around the throat. Cindy was still screaming upstairs, but it was muffled now as if someone was holding a hand over her mouth.

"Here, give her to me," Liam said. "Go out and get the power back on."

I couldn't bear Cindy's screams any longer. By the thump of footfalls and dull groans of struggle above me, I knew she was fighting back. How many were there? Before the lights came on, I punched out into the dark, in the direction where Liam was standing. I caught him somewhere in the face, then ran for the steps. When he grabbed my arm, I elbowed him with the other, then hobbled up the staircase.

The lights of the house snapped on just as I burst into the bedroom. Cindy was on the floor, naked, and wrapped in the shower curtain, kicking at the two men who were trying to grab her legs. I charged the one nearest to her and he brushed me away with one arm, knocking me to the floor. I ran to the closet and swept the clothes to the floor, then yanked the thick wooden bar from the holders. When the other man, the smaller of the two, lunged for me, I caught him in the head with the wood stock and he went down howling.

I took a swing at the other guy who had Cindy trapped in the corner of the room, but when I went for his head, he grabbed the wooden pole and twisted it free from my hands, then swung it back at me, catching me in the temple. The blow knocked the light from my eyes. I went down, the side of my skull pulsing with fire. Strobes of light, spinning, flickering black and white. I was falling through space, flailing my hands and feet, no sky, no ground; a soundless descent.

When I regained consciousness, I was tied to a kitchen chair in the middle of the living room, my papers and notes spread about my feet, just the way they'd been when the lights went out. The upstairs was quiet. I looked around for Cindy. Liam was gone too. The house was still, except for the rain against the windows.

My head was throbbing, burning, a trail of blood running down my blouse. With my hands tied behind my back, my feet cinched to the legs of the chair, it seemed impossible for me to get free.

Able to get to a crouching stand, I managed to inch forward toward the bookcases with the chair on my back. When I was close enough, I twisted my body and slammed the chair into the bookcases, hoping to break it apart, or at least loosen the ropes. The impact of hitting the solid oak shelving knocked me off balance, throwing me to the floor. Lying sideways now, I found it difficult to get upright again, but I did.

After a few minutes of slamming the legs of the chair against the oak shelving, the rope around my left foot loosened. I twisted my leg, then struggled to my feet and busted the other legs from the chair until my feet were free. The back would be harder and I knew what I was about to do was going to hurt. With a running start, I hurled myself at the wall, twisting as I came in contact. The pain was excruciating as shards of the wood dug into my back, my wrists burning where the ropes sliced into flesh. The chair back was fractured and with a few more blows to the wall, the ropes opened enough for me to pull one hand loose, then the other. Once I was free, I went for the kitchen and grabbed a knife.

I rushed up the steps to my bedroom, to Cindy. When I saw her my heart collapsed.

"Cindy! Oh my God, Cindy!"

I fell to my knees on the floor next to her and tried to unwrap the shower curtain from her face. Her green eyes stared up at me, dull and fixed. Her mouth was still open, the plastic pulled tight against her skin, over her lips. Her flesh had lost all color.

"Cindy! No... No. Cindy, No!"

Blood trailed down her legs. I tugged and ripped at the plastic to get it off her face, to open a hole so she could breathe. I finally broke my fingernail through, ripping the plastic away from her. With her mouth finally clear, I laid her flat on the floor and gave her mouth-to-mouth. After a minute or so I gave her CPR, then mouth-to-mouth again. I felt for a pulse. Nothing.

"Cindy!"

I repeated the process, pounding on her chest to restart her heart. She was still wound in the shower curtain, so I tried rolling her over to unwrap the plastic cocoon. Condensation had formed between the impermeable clear material and her skin. I tried pulling it out from under her legs, tried pushing her free. I finally got one end out from under her, then started unraveling it. When I had her chest free, I started CPR again. More mouth-to-mouth. I pounded on her chest and screamed at her.

"Don't leave me! Don't you dare leave me!"

After probably ten more minutes of trying to resuscitate her, her eyes were still lifeless, her skin dull and cool. I knelt over her, sobbing, shaking. This couldn't be happening. I kicked the shower curtain from her body and tried to lift her. I wanted to get her to the bed, cover her up. I felt too weak to move her. I coughed and cried and pounded the floor next to her body. It was my fault. The whole day had been my fault. The whole stupid fucking shitty day!

I grabbed her beneath the armpits and dragged her near the bed. Just moving her that far exhausted me. My legs were trembling, my arms weak. Where was my burst of adrenaline, that miraculous strength capable of lifting cars?

Trying again, I managed to raise her shoulders to the bed, then fell backward on the sheets. I dug my heels into the mattress to slide her backward over the edge. I was lightheaded, about to pass out. When I got her hips onto the bed, I collapsed, Cindy lying on top of me, her back against my stomach. I laid there, catching my breath, starved for air. My body was covered in sweat. After a moment to recover, I wriggled myself out from under her weight. Only her legs hung off the bed now and the sight of her bloodied body crushed me. I fell to my knees, my head on the floor, crying into the carpet. This couldn't be happening. It had to be some kind of nightmare.

After several minutes I gathered myself, stood up, and carefully pulled her legs onto the bed, then positioned her, moving her toward the headboard to get her onto the pillow. I arranged her limbs so she looked somewhat natural, as if resting in a peaceful sleep. I gathered up the bedspread from the floor and covered her with it, smoothing the wrinkles, feeling her body beneath the material.

Her unseeing eyes stared at the ceiling.

I reached over and arranged her hair away from her face, then gently slid her eyelids closed. There was much to do, but I was so exhausted.

I went to the window and checked the dock. Rain beat along the walkway, but there were no boats. Maybe they were gone. Maybe they hadn't meant to kill Cindy and when they did, they got scared and left. But what if they came back? I had no way off the island.

I locked the door and went back over to the bed. I stretched out next to Cindy beneath the covers, clutching the knife in my right hand. I slid my left arm beneath her neck. Rolling toward her, I could smell the soap on her skin, the chai-vanilla shampoo in her hair.

"I am so sorry, Cindy. I am so—" Tears overtook me. Then exhaustion. Then the sleep I'd been so desperately fighting.

EIGHTEEN

"Wow," Liam said.

I barely had my eyes open. He was standing in front of me, soaking wet, his hair stringing down his forehead. Water dripped from his eyebrows and chin. I was tied up seated on the floor in the middle of my bedroom. Cindy was still on the bed, just as I'd left her.

My insides were numb, my head pounding, my hands hurting. My sweatpants were wet; obviously I had peed myself at some point. I was groggy, like I'd been drugged.

"That was some scene up here, you lying next to her corpse. Hell, for a minute I thought you were both dead."

"You bastard!" I said, trying to wriggle free of the ropes. "You killed her you fucker!"

"Not me," Liam said. "Those crazy meth heads did. Then they started crying about it. Can you beat that? They rape her, then kill her... I guess by accident the way they tell it. Hell, they were so scared they took off like their asses were on fire. Can you imagine that, driving across the bay at night in this storm? They'll probably kill their damn fool selves."

"Why don't you untie these ropes... we'll get this over with," I said, my only thought now was to kill Liam. I didn't care what happened to me, but before the night was over, I swore to myself he would be dead.

"Well, you were a busy little beaver while I was outside calming down the drug addicts," Liam said, holding a hunting knife. "I think they stole some of your shit on the way out, some TVs and DVD players and whatnot."

My mind was skipping, the macabre quality of the evening playing backwards and forwards, none of it making any sense.

"What do you want?" I said.

"You'll find out soon enough... when my partner returns. He's off handling a bit of business. In the meantime, let's get those little bagel things in the oven."

Liam went down to the kitchen. I struggled against the ropes but it was useless. He had bound my hands behind my back, then looped the rope around my neck once, then down to my feet. Each time I moved my legs, the rope tightened around my throat and pulled my arms up my back, causing excruciating pain in my shoulders. The knife I'd been holding when I fell asleep sat on the nightstand. How could I be so stupid?

I heard the oven door open and close. Liam couldn't really expect to get away with this, could he? When Ben saw the boat, he'd know it was the one he'd given me. And Liam would have been the only one who could have towed it back to the harbor. Jacob was in Toronto.

Liam came back up and sat on the edge of the bed. "You know, seeing you out there today, waving me down, well that couldn't have worked out better if I had planned it," Liam said. "I was headed to your place to have a look around when I saw you two. All the luck. Gave me a whole new plan finding you and your little girlfriend."

"What's this about?" I said.

Liam seemed to ponder my question momentarily, then leaned in close to smell my hair. He put the knife tip under my chin, then ran the point down my chest, the tip of it grazing the material of my sweatshirt.

"Do you know what an A.R.S. is?" he said, his eyes dropping to my waist.

I stared at him. He was small, not much bigger than me, and I felt I could overtake him if I got the chance.

"It's an Alternate Revenue Stream," he said, "You see, Ben don't pay shit for me to swab out boats and clean up rich folks' cabins and houses all season, so I had me a sweet little A.R.S. going. But then you ruined it... when you killed Rags and Marty. They were my A-team, so to speak. Dumber than bugs but I told them which houses to go to, and they brought back the goods. And I paid them shit, and they were happy to get it. I even gave them a boat to use on their runs. Not sure why they got so interested in you, though. I guess they were bored..."

Liam came down on the floor with me, then grabbed my arm and rolled me onto my side, then pushed my face down into the carpet. "Speaking of a sweet little A.R.S., you have one yourself. You could peddle that for good money in Toronto."

I tried to kick him away, but the ropes tightened, choking me. I moaned and Liam seemed to enjoy that.

"All this over that stupid Marty and Rags?" I said. "Were they really worth it?"

"Were they worth it?" Liam said, moving in close to my face. "What's a rich little cunt from New York worth? You fucking assholes come up here and think you own the goddamn place, like it's your own personal fucking Disney World. And people like Marty and Rags are just shit floating on the water that you have to swerve around in your fancy fucking boats... I'm sure you think I'm just a piece of shit, too..." Liam leaned in until his nose was almost touching mine. "Go on, say it, tell me I'm a piece of shit..."

"You won't get away with this," I said.

"Oh, I most definitely will, little lady," Liam got to his feet. "Because when our little soiree—that's what you call those fancy parties in New York, right? Soirees?—well when it's over, you and your little blue friend on the bed are going to just disappear, and the authorities are gonna find that busted up boat floating out there empty, with enough of each of your blood on it to make it convincing... You can bet that sweet little ass of yours I'm getting away with this...!"

"Fuck you, you piece of shit!"

"There it is!" Liam said, triumphant, his face breaking into a wide grin. "Ummm, those bagel things smell like they're done."

He went back to the kitchen. A while later he returned with one plate and two beers. "Hope you don't mind if I help myself," he said. "Brought you one too." He held a beer bottle out for me to take. I glared at him.

"Oh, yeah. Well, I could untie your hands but you're pretty feisty for a cripple. So here, let me help you." He reached over and put the bottle to my lips, tilting it so high against my closed mouth it spilled down the front of my sweatshirt. My top was soaked.

"Whew, you're starting to reek," he said. "That beer and piss smell remind me of when I used to go on week-long benders. But don't worry, we'll get you cleaned up..."

Liam got up and walked around the bedroom, looking at pictures, going through my dresser, pulling out my underpants and placing them under his nose.

"You're a pig!"

Liam glanced over at me, stuffing the bagel in his mouth. He pulled out his cigarettes, shook one from the pack and lit it. He blew smoke toward the ceiling, carrying one of my tank tops over, holding it up in front of me. He fished out a pair of my thong underwear and laid it at my feet.

"Those should look nice?" he said. He tilted his beer back and tossed the empty bottle toward the wall. He came over and held the cigarette near my lips. I turned my head away. He sniffed and cleared his throat and took another drag, holding it in his lungs, letting it out slowly. I wanted so much to kill the bastard, cut his fucking throat with his own hunting knife.

"Carlton should be back soon, and he won't like how bad you smell," Liam said. "So, we need to get you cleaned up."

He had to untie me to do whatever he was about to do. There was no way he could pick me up and carry me. He was scrawny, maybe five foot nine and rawboned. He reached down with his knife and cut one of my feet loose. I kicked out at him with the freed one, causing him to jump back. He pushed my face to the floor and jerked up on the rope behind my back, strangling me, wrenching my arms. I screamed, my shoulders burning like they'd been pulled from the sockets.

"Now, let's try to get along," he said, holding my face to the carpet, the knife against my throat. "Now don't move, someone could get hurt." He started undoing the buttons on my pajama top, slicing it from my arms, letting it fall to the floor in pieces. "Okay, the pants should be a lot easier, don't you think?"

He started to pull them down and I kicked back with my free foot until he jerked the rope so hard my shoulder was on fire.

"You motherfucker!" I screamed, tears dripping from my chin.

A moment later he had my bottoms off, then my underwear. He cut my bra strap and it fell to the floor.

"There we go," he said. "That wasn't so bad?"

He tugged upward on the rope and I winced with pain, trying to rise as quickly as he was pulling to take the pressure off my shoulders. When I was to my feet, he led me toward the shower. After pushing me in, he turned the knob and cold water came out first, then warm. He grabbed the bar of soap and rubbed it between his hands, as if he was going to start washing me. I was humiliated, crying, shaking. In that moment every bit of strength left my body. I gave up, and fell to the shower floor. It knocked him off balance but he yanked the rope upward to get me to my feet again, the pain excruciating. I felt like I was about to pass out.

Liam put the bar of soap back on the shelf, rinsed his hands, and started to undress.

With his clothes in a heap, he stepped into the shower with me. "I think I can do a much better job like this, you know, kind of hands on and all..."

He reached over and grabbed the shampoo bottle off the shelf, flipped the top, then squeezed a good bunch into his palms. "You really are quite beautiful," he said, proceeding to gently stroke the shampoo into my hair, starting in the front, squeezing it toward the ends at my back. He moved closer, his hands covered in suds, letting them slide down over my shoulders, to my breasts. He was no longer looking at my eyes, but at his own hands on me. I swung my head, slapping my soapy hair across his eyes. The shampoo must have burned because he screamed. "You bitch!" His hands shot up to his face. I kneed him between the legs, doubled him over. When I swung my knee up into his face, he dropped to the shower floor, groaning. The shampoo bottle lay next to him, so I squeezed my foot down on the side of it to squirt the liquid onto the floor, then ran my foot through it. Liam's hands were now at his crotch, so I ground the shampoo-soaked foot into his eyes, then kicked him in the ribs several times, then in the stomach, then in the head before squeezing past him in the shower.

I wanted to kick him until he was dead, but I had no idea where this Carlton guy was, or when he'd get back. Liam's knife was lying on top of his clothes and I tried to stoop down to get it, trying to keep my balance. Almost to a squatting position, I realized there was no way to grab the knife with my hands behind my back.

Liam was still groaning on the shower floor when he tried to grab my foot. I stomped his hand and kicked him in the face. Blood poured from his nose. I stood up, using the shower stall wall to steady my balance.

Reaching the nightstand, I turned my back to the butcher knife and picked it up, but I couldn't maneuver it to actually cut the ropes. I had no leverage. Liam was trying to get to his feet.

Hurrying to the stairwell, I made it down a few steps before slip-ping on the bare wood, my feet slick with the shampoo, tumbling the rest of the way, landing on my back. Get up, Kercy. You can handle the pain.

I struggled to my feet, first turning over to get myself to my knees, then using the wall for balance to get myself upright. The backdoor in the kitchen was locked, the deadbolt impossible for me to open with my hands secured behind my back. A strong draft blew through the house, as if coming from the front. When I got to the hallway, the front door was open again, blowing back and forth, banging occasionally against the jamb.

Liam came stumbling down the steps.

I dashed for the opening. That's when someone grabbed me under my arm at the bicep and jerked me into the guest bedroom, the one Cindy had been staying in. Her suitcase was open, her clothes dumped out on the floor. The grip on my arm was tight and I had yet to see who was swinging me in an arc.

The inventory of Cindy's things ended abruptly when the huge man tossed me toward the bed. I landed on my back, on my bound hands, which pulled the rope taught at my neck. It felt as if something ripped inside my arm or shoulder. I was dizzy from the pain, having trouble catching my breath.

"Hold that bitch down, Carlton!" Liam screamed as he burst through the doorway. His eyes were scalded red, blood covering his face.

Carlton was a huge man, fat and tall and broad at the shoulders, and climbing on top of me. He grabbed my breast, and when I kicked at him to get him off, he punched me in the face. I was dazed, a new pain shifting through me, the room turning red, then white. That's when I remembered the knife I had put under the pillow. But there was no way to get to it. Liam tried to get at me, but Carlton shoved him off, landing Liam on the floor.

"Get the fuck out of here," Carlton said.

Liam started yelling at Carlton, threatening him, and Carlton told him to shut up.

Just then, Liam flew across the room, slamming into the far wall.

So distracted with me, Carlton didn't seem to notice what was going on, and I couldn't tell either. Lying on the floor, Liam looked up, his eyes wide, his mouth hanging open. I wasn't sure what had happened. When Carlton turned to see, he was dragged from the bed.

At first I thought it was Jacob or Ben. The shadowy figure moved swiftly toward Carlton and with a high-pitched shriek, picked him up and tossed him toward the doorway. Carlton was stunned, unable to stand. The creature went over to him and thrust its arm into Carlton's stomach. Carlton screamed, his eyes bright white, shrieking and yelling as the creature carried him from the bedroom. Carlton's screeching continued, moving farther from the house until it finally stopped. Liam, shaking his head as if to clear it, stumbled toward the doorway.

Lying on my back on the bed, I tried to shake the cobwebs from my brain, unable to believe what I was witnessing. Liam seemed to run down the hallway toward the front door. I heard it fly open, slamming against the wall, then the grinding of his boat engine. Even over the wind outside I could hear his screams, his calls for help, but it was the sudden explosion and flash that shook the windows and brought the silence. No boat engine. No screams. Just the wind and rain.

I tugged against the ropes again, my struggle useless. There was no way to get loose. I had closed my eyes just a moment to compose myself when I felt someone grip my wrist. I tried to jerk away. That's when I saw it up close. It was exactly like the figures that came the night before Gerald left. It hadn't been a dream. Its hand was exactly like the one I had caught on the dock when I was seventeen, only the hand of this creature was larger, its digits fitted with sharp long claws, like talons.

Its eyes were dark and hard to see in the dimly lit room. It was almost as if they were shielded, not by an apparatus, but organic, like tinted eyelids or something. Occasionally they would blink open and I could glimpse the actual eyes, but only for a split second. The smell of ammonia and phosphorus drifted on the air.

The being regarded my body for a moment, as if scanning me from head to toe, then using one of its talons, sliced the rope at my wrists. I quickly backed away and tucked my knees to my chest, wrapping my arms around them. That's when I noticed two others standing at the doorway, watching. At first, I was startled, but the fear dissipated gradually, leaving behind a strange calm, especially given the circumstances.

They stood for a long while looking at me. The other two entered —and like the one that had freed my wrists—had skin that was shiny and iridescent, as if made of pearl, though much darker. They regarded each other, then looked back toward me. When one of them turned around I noticed a protrusion, a long tube-like growth or apparatus attached or growing from its back. It seemed to be connected to a hose-like growth, almost like a huge external vein, snaking up around its shoulder and ending somewhere at its neck where its chin should be, but there was no chin, its face angling back sharply to form the neck.

The one that had cut the ropes was becoming agitated and motioned toward the doorway. The others did not seem to want to leave and came closer to the bed. They stared at me. One of them reached out and touched my skin. As if gasping for air or something, the agitated one made a loud guttural noise, becoming increasingly more hostile toward the others. It fled the room and left by the backdoor. I heard it pad roughly down the walkway. Now also becoming agitated, the other two hurried toward the doorway making the sound of crinkling cellophane. I remembered that curious noise from when I was seventeen, before my mother sold the cottage. In a moment they were gone.

Getting up from the bed, I crept slowly to the hallway and listened. The front door was still open, swinging free and banging with the wind. When I went to the kitchen, the back door was open as well. I closed it and locked the deadbolt, then did the same with the front door. When I finished securing the house, I went upstairs. Cindy's body was only partially covered, but mostly undisturbed, still positioned the way I'd left her. I went to the bathroom and sat on the shower seat and turned the water on, letting it flow over me. I washed myself several times, crying, images coming at me when I closed my eyes.

When the shower finally ran cold, I turned the knob and dried myself. I put on a sweat shirt and pants, locked the bedroom door, then switched all the lights on. I looked over at Cindy in the bed, unmoving. It was surreal. I felt sick to my stomach.

I took a deep breath, then went to the bed and pulled the blankets up to cover her body. Sliding in next to her, I eased myself closer, waiting for dawn, my eyes on the bedroom door, my hand clutching Liam's hunting knife beneath the covers.

NINETEEN

Wind-blown snow scratched and etched the slate sky, the morning a silty gray. Huge white-capped waves broke across the bay, crashing against the shore, splashing in great explosions over the dock. When I slid the window up, frigid air flooded the bedroom. White flakes swirled and rushed through the opening, dying a second or two after they touched the carpet. Looking back toward the bed I hoped that the last twenty-four hours had been a bad dream, but the unmoving shape of Cindy's body beneath the covers dashed that possibility.

In the kitchen I found a large colorful ceramic serving bowl and carried it back upstairs. I filled it with hot water from the bathroom faucet, then retrieved a clean washcloth from the linen closet. My hair brush was in the drawer so I grabbed it and stuck it in my pocket.

Standing at the edge of the bed, I gently rolled back the blanket covering Cindy's body and sat down next to her, placing the bowl on the sheet. I soaked the washcloth in the hot water, wrung it out with both hands, then lightly wiped the dirt from Cindy's face. I used the brush to smooth out the chaotic tangles of her hair. I wanted to remember her the way she was. How could anyone do this? How could anyone hate to this degree? It was inconceivable to me that anyone's heart could be so dead.

Wiping my eyes with the sleeve of my baggy sweatshirt, I rinsed the washcloth again and started cleaning her body, washing the trail of blood from her thighs. It wasn't that I had forgotten about DNA samples and evidence, but I figured there would be traces of everything they'd need still inside her, as well as all over the room; fingerprints, hair, saliva, sperm. The shower curtain alone would probably have enough evidence to convict them all and send them away for life. But more than likely, they were all dead.

The water in the bowl cooled, the bedroom becoming like a refrigerator. With no idea when anyone would come to the cottage, especially with the storm, I wanted to make sure Cindy's body didn't deteriorate; I couldn't stand the thought of that.

When I finished bathing her, I took the bowl back to the kitchen and went to her bedroom for some of her clothes. There was no reason for her to still be naked when the police arrived. When I entered the guest bedroom, I gagged, the smell was so bad; Carlton's horrible body smell, the sheets rank with sweat, blood and stale beer. Her suitcase was across the room on the floor, still opened, her clothes dumped out in a haphazard pile. Seeing the soiled sheets, I vomited, the memory of Carlton inside me, his rancid breath, his noxious body odor.

I sniffled and wiped my mouth, then knelt on the floor by Cindy's clothes. She'd brought plenty of tops and jeans and even a couple of skirts. Maybe she figured we'd go out on the town one evening, maybe over in Kurry Sound, or maybe we'd hang out in Toronto for a couple evenings on the way back to New York.

Holding her blouse to my nose, I could still smell her, the way I could when we slept together, her hair next to my face, or when she would touch my cheek, or kiss my lips. Her parents would be crushed. *It ain't over till it's over.* How many times had her dad said that to me when I wanted to give up on school, on the master's program, on my doctorate, on walking again? It was over now, though. And he would be devastated. Cindy was his *little girl,* a distinction I had secretly coveted from my own father.

I picked up a pair of jeans and her favorite top, the worn-out T-shirt with the Annie Lennox graphic, then went back upstairs. After I finished dressing her, I pulled the blanket back up, kissed her forehead, her lips, then covered her face. After grabbing clothes from my own closet, I got dressed and went back to the kitchen.

The bowl of rice Cindy had stuck her phone in was on the counter. I dug my hand down into it and brought her phone out. When I switched it on, it flickered a bit, then a couple of thin horizontal lines flashed on the screen before it went black. Maybe it just needed a charge, but I was pretty sure it was shot.

I dropped it back in the bowl and went to Cindy's bedroom and packed all her clothes back into the suitcase and carried it to the living room. I returned to the bedroom and yanked the sheets from the bed, rolling them into a ball, along with the blankets until I was down to bare mattress, then carried everything outside and dumped it on the ground in an open patch about fifty yards from the shoreline.

Grabbing the charcoal lighter fluid from the back porch, I walked down and doused the bedclothes, lit a match and tossed it on the pile. Flames shot up five feet high. I went back to the house.

The mattress was a struggle, but when I finally got it to the back porch, I lifted one end, using the railing as a fulcrum, then dumped it over the side. After dragging it to the fire, I went back for the box spring. It was much lighter, just awkward getting through the door as it didn't bend. The flames shot higher when I tilted it up and dropped it into the flames.

The police might be upset that I was burning evidence, but what did it matter... I realized that Carlton and Liam were most likely dead; the loud crash... the explosion? Had there been an explosion? I was already having trouble sorting fact from fiction.

Smoke billowed up and, if not for the heavy snow, could probably be seen from the harbor. Standing in the heat of the fire, I let my eyes drift out over the rough gray water, wondering about the events of the previous evening. Even though I'd been awake for hours, my mind had not allowed me to think about the freakish creatures until now. Had they wanted only to protect me? Or had all of that been my imagination?

Special Agent Mallory came to mind. Did the FBI know about these creatures? Were they the subject of his investigation by the Anomalous Crimes Task Force? They had to be; nothing else made any sense. But if that were the case, why had there been no talk about these beings in the news? And where did they come from?

Georgian Bay was linked by the St. Lawrence Seaway to the Atlantic Ocean, all the way to Antarctica, and beyond, to every major body of water in the world. If these creatures were real, and there was a part of me doubting it, did they live beneath the surface of Georgian Bay, or had they come to the cottage last night by some other means?

Snow was wetting my blouse and jeans, but the fire seemed to be evaporating it almost as quickly. I hadn't bothered with my jacket, feeling numb, and a bit adrift. By now, Ben should have seen his skiff, the one I crashed, and would know that I had no boat. He probably tried to call, but my phone was sitting on the bottom of Boat Eater Bay. Eventually, unable to reach me and knowing I had no means to get off the island, he would certainly take a run out here, or at least send Jacob.

Jacob? Why was he working with Agent Mallory? Jacob must know about these creatures, too! And Ben? Did he know? And all the Missing Persons posters in the harbor office? Were the creatures somehow linked to them. And my own father? Had he fallen prey to... Stop! My mind was looping back on itself, the constant assault of chatter, the ifs and whats and whys; more questions than snowflakes.

I coughed and choked, then sneezed. The wind had shifted, sweeping smoke into my face. I moved to the side of the fire and thought about Liam, his screaming, the explosion. I decided to walk around to the front of the house where they must have parked their boat last night so I wouldn't see them tied at the dock. The front was mostly sand and easy to pull a craft up on the shoreline without being heard. It occurred to me that Liam probably knew this house as well as I did. I figured he was the one who winterized it every year. No wonder he knew how to turn the power on and off, where to land a boat undetected. Did he have keys to my cottage, to the front door, the kitchen door? Is that how they got in without me hearing them?

When I reached the shore, I saw how badly the beachfront was tore up and gouged out; more damage than just pulling a boat ashore. When I got closer to the edge of the water, I saw something beneath the surface. Part of the bow of a white skiff, blackened and burnt in places. The stern appeared to be completely gone, where the gas tank would have been, while the front was splintered and cracked. Looking around the area, I saw several pieces of boat, fiberglass shards and hull and decking, part of a compartment hatch, glass and a few remnants of life jackets, a rubber dock bumper.

Obviously the boat had exploded with Liam in it, but why? What could have caused it?

About to go back to tend my fire, something lying in the weeds near the house caught my eye. When I walked over to it, I gagged and held my mouth, trying to push my stomach down. I couldn't. After puking once, I gagged a couple more times until I was done.

Studying the head lying on the ground, I thought it might be Liam, but the face, if there was one, was completely unrecognizable. I walked through the trees surrounding the area and found other body parts, human... and not human. Some body parts were impossible to determine, but seemed to belong to one of the beings that had helped me. Had they heard Cindy's screams? Had they heard mine? How could they have heard us in the middle of the storm? Overcome with questions, I had to sit on the front porch a moment. Liam was dead, I figured, but what about Carlton? He had to be too, picturing the creature's appendage stuck through the huge man's torso.

Before continuing the search, I needed a large trash bag to gather the non-human parts, as well as something to pick them up with, a shovel maybe.

After searching the shed unsuccessfully for something to scoop up remains, I had to settle for a large trash bag and rubber gloves. I combed the area around the dock for any clues as to what had happened, but found nothing. After looking for nearly a half hour, I decided to take my search back to the front of the house.

Having perused the sandy beach area near the boat wreckage for only twenty minutes or so, the plastic trash bag was becoming heavy with parts, most of which I didn't recognize, except for an arm. It was like the one I caught from the dock years earlier. On the ground was something that appeared to be part of a head, with shielded eyes, or maybe translucent eyelids, I couldn't tell. The eye coverings had become a milky blue, making it impossible to see much detail of the actual eyes hidden beneath them. I left all the human parts; the police could gather those, if there were any left. Gulls were not on the island today, because of the snowstorm, but when the sky cleared, they'd arrive by the hundreds. None of this carnage would go to waste.

Venturing farther from the house I wasn't sure I'd find much else, and was about to turn back when I spied something large and pale near the edge of some tall grass. When I stepped closer, I could see it was a man, human, partially naked, and ripped in several pieces; a horrid jumble of anatomy caked with dried blood. Moving closer to get a better look, I saw that part of his face was gone, but there was no mistaking it was Carlton.

That's when I noticed tracks in the sand, non-human, all around what was left of Carlton's torso, but with the snow and wind, the footprints would soon be gone before Agent Mallory had a chance to make plaster impressions. If I had my phone, I could at least take photos. *That's the man that raped you, Kercy,* something inside me said. It was true, so why wasn't I more outraged at the sight of him, or at least vengefully jubilant over this expeditious and brutal retribution? The scientist in me was taking over, disconnecting from my victim role, pushing away the harrowing events of the previous evening. The scientist walked back to the house with a large black trash bag stuffed with some kind of alien body parts and was now going to gather up some candles, melt them down, and make a wax impression of a footprint while an early snowstorm raged around her.

My ability to compartmentalize had never been more evident and useful as it was right now.

Methodically, I stored the bag of body parts in the fridge—which required moving much of the food around. I then melted several large candles in a pot on the stove. I had to keep the wax hot, so I decided to use the front door which was closer to the footprints. With the pot wrapped in a towel, I wasted no time getting back to Carlton's body, darting between trees and shrubs.

Picking the most defined foot print, I carefully poured the wax until it overflowed the cavity. It took only minutes for the wax to cool and harden. Using my fingertips, I gently eased the casting from the ground, brushed off excess sand and carried it back to the house. It wasn't as great as a plaster model, but it would have to do. I left the mold on the kitchen table, then gathered up some of the jars that I had removed from the fridge to make room for the trash bag, planning to leave the jars on the back porch.

The wind met me at the door when I stepped outside to place the cooler full of pickles, mayonnaise, and other refrigerated food items on the back deck. I looked over toward the fire, which had burned to glowing orange embers in the dying light of evening. The snow had eased a bit, still limiting visibility to about fifty yards.

Despair was setting in. Cindy was lying upstairs in my bed, and I'd never talk with her again. I'd never touch her again, never hear her laugh, never enjoy her sarcasm and wit. I'd never be able to confide in her, never get advice, never have her hold me while I cried.

I sat down on the deck, under a crushing sadness, and curled myself into a tight ball, looking out toward the end of the dock.

Where was Gerald this evening? Was he wondering why he couldn't get through on the phone? He had gone back to New York less than a week ago but it felt like a year. Was he worried? I was having trouble calling up my affection for him, a pervasive lethargy marshaling my emotions. Heat rose inside me, an electrical storm of sorrow, hurt, and defeat and I couldn't stop crying. I buried my head in my folded arms. My stomach clenched and I felt myself falling away.

TWENTY

There haven't been many times in my life when I've been frightened.

Feeling alone, sad and damaged filled most of the space between moments of happiness. But never fear.

Until tonight.

And as the gray sky dissolved to black, a horrible dread seized me. I went through the house turning on all the lights. I checked the locks on the doors. The wind rattled the windows, shook the house. Snow gathered on the porch railing, growing deeper on the sills. Darkness entrapped me as if someone had draped a black velvet shroud over the entire cottage.

I cooked dinner but couldn't eat it. Cold drafts followed me from room to room. I turned the thermostat up. Wrapped in a blanket on the couch, I decided to put a comedy into the DVD player only to find a bunch of ragged wires where the player and the television had been.

Where was Ben and Jacob? I was sure they'd show up at the cottage when they saw the damaged boat. Then it hit me; Liam never took the skiff back to the harbor. He probably cut it loose somewhere...

From time to time the wind subsided and silence rushed at me from every corner of the room, allowing my mind to play its own movie. Dark figures coming at me, grabbing me, forcing themselves on me. Their stench, their fusty breath, their rough flesh.

I hurried up the stairs to my bedroom where Cindy was lying beneath the covers. Snow had gathered on the carpet near the opened window. The room was freezing. A dusting of snow had blown across the blanket covering her. I went to the bathroom and grabbed some candles. I arranged them on the nightstand, then closed the window. With all them burning, the rich glow of the flames flickered across the walls, bringing a counterfeit illusion of warmth to the freezing room. I sat for a long while, my eyes closed, remembering all the things we'd shared, how we'd met, how we'd loved each other... how she'd died.

The memory shot through me like a bullet.

I stood up from the floor, shuddering, trying to push her screams from my head. The sound of her helplessness was more than I could bear.

Before I went back downstairs, I decided to open the window again to keep the room cold. Grabbing the handles of the sash, I noticed a disturbance out by the end of the dock. A huge swell countered the large waves rolling in. The snow had eased somewhat, the security light illuminating the water.

I stood a moment to watch, and was about to leave when I saw something climbing from the water, hurrying to pull itself up onto the dock. The figure was dark and vague and I had trouble seeing what it was. It almost looked like a man, but I couldn't tell. My skin went cold. I hurried down the stairs, missing several as I slid and stumbled, despite my grip on the railing. Rushing to the kitchen, I grabbed the biggest knife I could find, not recalling where I'd left Liam's hunting knife, then switched off the lights.

Standing at the kitchen window, I watched a second figure climb from the water and pull itself onto the dock. They were like the creatures from the night before. I checked the lock on the back door, the deadbolt was set, then returned to the window.

What were they doing here? What did they want?

My mouth turned suddenly dry, my legs weak. I figured they couldn't see me with the lights off, but then they both glanced directly at me, as if they'd known I would be standing there. I shot back from the window, my heart pounding. I was about to sneak another look when I heard a loud crash. I checked the window to see what the commotion was—a huge section of the dock was broken and splintered. One of the beings was moving quickly toward the house. The other one was gone, or at least hidden from my view. Just then, something huge shot from the water throwing a spray nearly ten feet in diameter, grabbing the remaining figure in its teeth and dragging it back beneath the water. It only took a few minutes for the waves from the wind to erase any trace of disturbance from the attack, as if nothing had happened.

For a few minutes, I wasn't sure it had. I stared at the waves, almost hoping it would resurface to confirm that I had actually witnessed the extraordinary event. When the gigantic creature didn't show itself again, its image started playing on my retinas. A neck over twelve feet long and a head the size of an oven. And there was no mistaking the teeth, glinting like daggers in the dismal light.

Was this all an elaborate hallucination? Was I stuck in some crazy looping nightmare that I was unable to awake from? Nothing felt real. I grabbed the knife off the floor where I'd dropped it and went back to my bedroom. A part of me hoped to find my bed empty, Cindy coming from the bathroom wrapped in a towel, her hair still dripping from a shower. "Hey, Wheels, what's with the big-ass butcher knife?" She would smile and shake her head and use the towel in her hand to scrub her hair dry. "What's for dinner?" she'd say, then walk over and kiss me. "Come with me," she'd say, letting her towel fall away, taking my hand, pulling me toward the bed. I would fall in behind her, and she would lie on her back and I would lean over her and kiss her on the lips.

Her lips were like ice, her skin stiff and frozen. I sat up next to her in bed, her lips blue, her skin blanched, almost translucent. Her

eyelids resembled wax, with a filigree of blue veins, an unusual darkness filling the cavity of her eye sockets. Suddenly I was floating, the
moment timeless, a seamless never-ending second spreading itself
across space and time. Even the candle flames defied the slightest
movement, refusing to flicker or dance or sway. The room was illuminated, but how? I could not find the source of the light, even though
the candles threw shadows from their bases. I didn't even recall
lighting them again. I regarded my own hands, as if the very sight of
them could jolt me from this morbid fantasy. They were webbed, just
as they had been as a baby. Except now I could explore this strange
phenomenon, pushing my fingertip into each of the spaces between
my fingers to feel the flimsy skin connecting them, cold and bloodless.
But something shifted and now I was seeing through my hands,
through the bed, the floor, through the foundation, penetrating deep
into the Earth beneath the house until I reached water, as if the
island itself were a vessel merely floating on the surface. The water
beneath the island was filled with light, yet without life. Nothing
moved or swam or crawled.

And from the unearthly silence rose the sound of banging, a
persistent drumming from beyond the bounds of the universe, from
beyond the periphery of reality itself. It was in my head, then outside
me, surrounding me, floating me from the ground, from my own body.
Moving through undefined space I felt neither fear nor joy, sadness
nor elation, just a calm sense of existence beyond anything I could
imagine. Was I dead? I tried to pull myself back, but there was
nothing to pull back from. Sensations danced along my skin, my
arms, my legs, the source invisible to my sight yet unmistakable to my
sense of touch.

Then, as if a vast wave moved through me, or around me, the light
flowed past, in me, rushing and pulsing until a pain arose inside my
stomach, at the center of my being, increasing in intensity and dura-
tion until it gripped my insides and I felt the scream passing up
through me as if I were twenty-stories tall. I could monitor its

progress until it reached my mouth, blossoming from a small red rose into a magnificent and painfully massive eruption and the scream that shot from me felt as though it had ruptured my eardrums.

One being was on top of me, between my legs. Two other figures held my wrists gently, one on either side of me, stroking the skin of my forearms. I struggled for a moment, followed immediately by the most complete release, as if my body had emptied every memory and instinct from its cells. There was no reason to fight.

The beings were like the creatures that had killed Liam and Carlton the night before, like the ones eaten by an enormous sea creature at my dock only minutes earlier. Or was that hours ago? Or days? I wasn't sure. It could have been weeks, years. I wasn't even sure where I was. I could only see the ceiling above me. I could feel the carpet beneath my bare back. Was it the living room? Or some room I had never spent time in?

The being on top of me seemed to disregard my presence, as if concentrating on something else, as if I were just a creation of its imagination. What an odd thought, that I only existed in the mind of some other being, that I only derived my actuality from its ability to focus on me. But I could still feel myself. My consciousness had not abandoned me completely. I could feel the being inside me, filling me, as if searching deep within me. The sensation was neither pleasure nor pain, just a knowing that something was there, not unlike the feeling of the organs that fill one's body—the stomach, the liver, the kidneys—they're there, but they're not there.

Then suddenly, as if struck by some disturbing realization, the being pulled away abruptly, as if shocked by some discovery. Upon noticing the apparent agitation of the being who was now standing over me, the ones on either side of me released my wrists and stood, looking at the central figure as if some communication were taking place. I lay motionless, neither scared nor shocked, an observer in some drama that involved me, but was somehow outside of me. I was neither dizzy nor foggy-headed, but more like profoundly stoned, yet with a clarity of mind capable of recording multiple dimensions down to the smallest detail.

As the three beings exited the room, a bizarre sensation washed over me, as if I were waking from a dream very slowly, or the last vestiges of some mind-altering drug flushing from my brain. It took a few minutes to realize I was still in the house, in the living room to be exact, lying in the middle of the floor, naked. I did not recall getting undressed. It was almost like my sensation of drowning, the hallucinations, missing time, gaps in memory. I had no idea what day it was.

I got up and went to the kitchen. When I saw the clock on the microwave, I looked out the window. The snow had stopped but the sky was still black. How was it possible that is was four thirty in the morning? I tried to rebuild the previous evening from faulty memories—when I had lit the candles for Cindy, when I hauled the mattress, box spring and bedclothes outside and burned them, when I had prepared the pasta for supper that I was unable to eat. The memories seemed disjointed and non-sequential, making it nearly impossible to create a timeline of events.

The floorboards creaking above me wrenched me from the reverie. Instinctively I looked up. Someone was upstairs in my bedroom. Something tightened in my chest, my breathing strained. Could it be Cindy? Had this been a Byzantine nightmare? How many times would I have to wake from it? Were all my memories of the past few days nothing more than dreams, one inside another like Russian nesting dolls; waking from one only to find myself in the next.

"Cindy?" I called. "Is that you?"

I was about to rush up the stairs when I recalled the events of the previous evening, the eerie serpent-like creature attack down by the water. It felt weird to consider the thought. Had that happened? I pulled the drapes back on the window and felt like I'd been struck by a fist; boards missing from the dock, the gaping hole in the walkway cracked and splintered, water crashing up through the jagged opening.

My review of the earlier night's events was interrupted by foot-falls on the stairs. Starting toward the stairwell, I retreated just as quickly when my fear found its footing once again. Where was the knife I'd been carrying?

Hastily jerking the silverware drawer open, I accidentally sent it flying across the floor in a clash of forks and spoons and butter knives. Leaving the mess, I grabbed the meat cleaver from the magnetic strip on the side of the cabinet and squatted behind the kitchen island, peeking around the corner. A moment later I saw the beings walking past me, one of them carrying something in its arms... Cindy, her head, arms and legs hanging limp.

"No! No! No!" I screamed, rushing the beings with the meat cleaver raised. But before I could reach them, the meat cleaver fell from my hand as if all the strength had fled my fingers. It bounced and clattered on the floor.

"Stop! You can't take her!" I screamed, reasserting my attack. The lead being, the one carrying Cindy, had already exited the backdoor, followed by one of the others. The third one seemed to be hanging back, apparently to thwart my advance, blocking the doorway and when I moved closer. I slammed my fists against its chest, arms and face. It took the blows, never returning the aggression. When I grew weary of pummeling it, the being turned and followed its counter-parts down to the water. Out of breath, I followed, hurrying behind, yelling at them.

I wasn't sure if they were incapable of hearing me or had found it more expeditious to just ignore my protests. When I caught up to them, I rushed toward the one cradling Cindy and grabbed its arm. "Stop! You can't take her!" I yelled. "Please, please don't take her!"

The being wasn't entirely indifferent to my plea. For a brief moment, the large figure regarded me, its head slightly bent down, its gaze meeting mine. The strange translucent shields covering its eyes concealed any emotion that might lie behind them. It held Cindy's body out to me, as if prompting me to tell my friend goodbye. I burst into tears. "No, please, please don't take her."

It pivoted on the dock and a moment later stepped off and disappeared beneath the surface, Cindy's hair waving like a flag sinking into the dark water. I lurched forward toward the water only to be grabbed from behind by one of the beings. The other being jumped into the water and disappeared in seconds. The one holding me back, spun me slowly until I faced it, then gently cradled my face in its hands, just the way my mother always had. A calm flowed down through me as if every molecule, cell, and bone in my body was easing into perfect alignment. All pain vanished and I felt instantly weak, falling from the being's embrace, slumping to the wet boards. It reached out, briefly touching my forehead before stepping from the dock and vanishing beneath the water.

Waves crashed at the boards, insouciant to the scenario that had just transpired. The water spray covered me in countless droplets, icy pinpricks on my skin. I couldn't will myself to stand, to go back into the house. As a child I spent several years in therapy, dealing with my disfigurement, and Dr. Sheldon told me to follow my intuition, that it would guide me most of the time. "Most of the time?" I asked. She grinned and said, "Yes, dear, it's only accurate about fifty percent of the time." I had always wondered if that was true, or if maybe intuition was far more accurate, but that logic driven by ego was the trickster with the ability to undermine it. If I had followed my intuition, and not allowed Liam to tow us back to the cottage, Cindy would still be alive. But hadn't I followed my intuition when I bought the cottage this past year? Or was that just desire, getting what I thought I needed to survive; the home of my only comforting memories?

I eased toward the edge of the boards to peer down into the gem-black water. I could picture my mother there, the look on her face when she told me she'd sold the cottage, the disappointment that swept away all my resolve. Even now, I could hear her words, *Don't ever go back there, Muffin. Don't ever go back to the cottage.* If I had listened, Cindy would still be alive, still be in my life.

Every regret fueled my strength and determination to drag myself close enough to the edge, invoke the forces of gravity, which would have no choice but to obey the unbalanced weight of my body teetering at the lip of the wet wood, until finally, giving in, it would pull me down into the soundless, watery tomb.

TWENTY-ONE

When they found me, I was naked, and unconscious, lying on the dock. Someone placed a blanket over my body and pressed their fingers to my neck, searching for a pulse. "She's alive," someone shouted, starting a commotion that would last for several days.

"Get her inside," someone else said. "Get some hot coffee in her quick."

It would be at least fifteen to twenty minutes before I would recognize the faces that corresponded to the voices. I was seated at the kitchen table, wrapped in a thick blanket, steam rising from the cup of coffee clutched between my palms. At first I didn't recognize Jacob, but Ben's was a face I could never forget. Seeing his rugged, familiar eyes unleashed the contents of the past few days until I could no longer hold back the tears. Ben came over and put his arms around me, hugging me close. Jacob stood up and walked out the back door to join indistinct voices speaking in official tones. Ben stayed with me. I wiped my eyes and Ben handed me a box of tissues.

"Soon as you're warmed up, I'm going to drive you to town and get you to the hospital," he said.

"I don't need a hospital, Ben." I sipped the coffee.

"I know. I'm going to take you anyway."

I only had the strength to nod.

"How is she?" a man asked Ben, then looked at me. "Do you know who I am?"

I shook my head, but then remembered. "Mallory. Special Agent Mallory, right?"

"Yes, good." He squatted down to meet me at eye level. "We're going to get you taken care of. You're going to be just fine."

I felt my legs under the blanket and realized I was still naked. "Ben, could you get me some clothes?"

"Absolutely," he said, and left to go upstairs.

When he was gone from the room, I looked over at Mallory. "There's something in the fridge for you," I said. "You should probably take it before anyone else finds it. I also put a wax casting on top of the refrigerator that might interest you as well."

He studied me a second, then went over and opened the door. "This?" he said, pointing at the black bag.

I nodded. "Don't open it until you're by yourself. The casting is wrapped in aluminum foil."

He carefully slid the casting off with both hands and carried it, as well as the black plastic bag, out the back door.

There was no way to control the telemetry of my thoughts, the bits and bites of information ricocheting off the inner lining of my skull, then, like sparkling rockets, burrowing deep into the gray matter of my brain, only to resurface as random images and vague perceptions. Patterns fired chaotically, untamable, while pictures morphed and melted to the beat of some random cadence in my head. My forehead was pounding and my scalp hurt, as if an electrical current burned just beneath the surface of my skin. I was rubbing my head when Ben came back, his arms folded over a pair of jeans and sweatshirt and other clothes.

"You want me to help you to the bathroom so you can change?" Ben said.

"I'll be all right." I took the clothes from him.

Two police officers came into the kitchen. Ben pointed to the upstairs, as if they had worked out some secret code ahead of time. While I changed in the bathroom, I could hear the policemen above me, the clicking of a camera, the creaking floor boards, low muffled voices. I imagined them bagging the shower curtain, shooting photos of the candles, the bed, the bloodstains on the carpet. By now they probably had the sheets stripped off the bed and bagged; there would be so many questions. The thought of it further exhausted me. At best, most of the questions would be difficult to answer. Maybe impossible. Except for Mallory. How much did he know? He would certainly be shocked by the contents of the plastic trash bag if I had miscalculated his reason for being in Ontario. But his special investigation unit; they certainly weren't up here to research mysterious deaths due to bears and wolves.

Slipping my sweatshirt over my head it occurred to me that I couldn't recall how I'd gotten back onto the dock. I remember toppling into the water and sinking quickly, the cold enveloping me, prompting the familiar warmth to rise up, the magical colors, the exotic fish, then nothing. I didn't recall climbing back out.

When I went back to the kitchen a man was standing by the table. He looked familiar holding a small pad and pen.

"Hi, Ms. Powell," he said, extending his hand. "Detective Randall. Elico Police..."

I nodded. "Yes, I remember."

"I need to ask you some questions." He motioned toward the chair. I sat down, then he sat opposite me. He asked me about the human remains scattered around the house, if I knew who they were, what had happened.

I wasn't sure how to explain, wishing Special Agent Mallory was there to help me sort this. I wasn't even sure if Detective Randall knew why Mallory was here, but certainly they must know each other.

I explained about Cindy and me going for a boat ride, hitting the rock, tearing up the outboard motor. I explained how we had tried to row but the wind overpowered us, carrying us farther from the cottage. "That's when Liam came along."

Detective Randall looked down at his notepad. "Liam Stovin, right? One of Ben's employees?"

I nodded.

"What happened next?"

This is where it was going to get difficult. I explained how the winter storm and the wind had seemed to knock out the power, but that that hadn't actually been the reason for the outage. I told him about Liam grabbing me, then about Cindy's screams... and the next part of the story caught in my chest. I trembled and shook and couldn't stop crying. I sobbed into my hands until I couldn't sit up straight, and slumped over in my chair, my head on my crossed arms.

For a long while Detective Randall said nothing. Regardless, I could tell he was still there, waiting. I wanted him to just leave, just leave me alone. I didn't want to talk about it, flesh out the whole evening by focusing on every detail. I lacked the energy to lie, then be caught in the lies, and make up new lies to explain the previous ones. That's when I felt my stomach coming up and I rushed to the sink, dry heaving, a bit of water coming up, but not much else. My head was on fire, my eyes raw with heat. Holding to the edge of the sink, I tried to brace myself, my legs giving out, slowly melting to the kitchen floor. My body shook under its own volition, commanded by a much more powerful liege; despair.

Trembling, I gave into the impulse to give up and pulled myself into a ball on the tile, then closed my eyes and tried to push away the images and screams.

Detective Randall must have given up too, because when I finally opened my eyes Ben and Agent Mallory were helping me onto the living room couch. Ben took one of the throw cushions and placed it beneath my head, then lifted my feet onto the couch so I could lie down.

"I'm so sorry, Kercy," Ben said. "Police said it was Liam out there. I'm just... I'm just sick about this...."

I wanted to tell him it wasn't his fault, that I should have followed my intuition and never let Liam come back with us. With Cindy and me. Cindy. How could I have let this happen? Picturing her lying there suffocated in the shower curtain—the color draining from her body, her face smudged with dirt and sweat, the dried blood on her legs—flipped some switch in me, plunging me safely into darkness.

The thrum and thump of helicopter blades woke me. I bolted upright, looking for Ben. He was seated in the chair across from me. "It's okay, Kercy," he said, hurrying over to take my hand. "They decided to send a chopper. You're going to be okay. You're in shock."

EMTs pushed a rattling gurney into the living room. I stood up and Ben helped me onto it. They strapped me in and wheeled me to the waiting craft tied to my dock. Ben boarded the amphibious rescue helicopter and sat next to me.

"It's going to be okay," he said, holding my hand. His eyes were raw, as if he'd been crying. "You're going to be okay."

Within a few minutes the EMT had me hooked to machines. The chopper started to lift off, slowly rising above the trees until all I could glimpse out the windows was blue sky and a few white clouds drifting by. I wished I could have watched us take off, witnessed the land shrinking beneath us, the vast body of water dwarfing little spots of islands, the immensity of the planet, but I was strapped down, so I focused on Ben, and for the briefest moment I thought I had seen all those things reflected in the tear in his eye.

TWENTY-TWO

After the nurses left my room, I looked over at Ben seated in the chair next to my hospital bed. He'd stayed with me ever since we'd left the cottage. I needed to tell him about the two men who had raped and killed Cindy, that they had gotten off the island, but if he asked where Cindy was now, I didn't know what I'd tell him. And without Cindy's body, would it matter if the police caught the two men anyway. There was no longer proof of anything, just my word against theirs. And no one had asked yet, but the question of Cindy's where-abouts was going to come up sooner or later.

"Ben. I need to tell you something."

He sat up and leaned in toward me.

"Ben, there were two other men besides Liam and Carlton. They were the ones who—"

"I know, Kercy. Somebody found them this morning floating out near Trapper Bay."

"The police caught them?"

"No. Those two characters are dead. But they had the boat I gave you, so when the police checked the registration, they saw it was mine and called me wanting to know if I knew the two fellas. I didn't, but I figured something was wrong. That's why Jacob and I rode out to your place this morning. Then we found you..."

"How did they die?"

Ben cleared his throat and sat up. "Evidently they hit a rock in the dark and knocked the lower unit off. They were too stupid to paddle to shore, I guess. Authorities believe they died of hypothermia when the boat filled with water. The craft's floatation kept it from sinking."

The night Liam broke into the house he had said that Carlton was taking care of some business. Carlton must have killed the two men and stuck them in my boat, then dragged them out to the middle of nowhere.

"Why did their boat fill with water?" I asked.

"Big hole in the bottom," Ben said.

"Does anyone know how the hole got there?"

"Police said it looked like a shotgun blast. They'll know more after the lab boys have a look."

I explained to Ben that I had wrecked his boat on a boulder. I told him about Liam showing up, towing us back to the cottage.

"Liam," Ben said, shaking his head. "That young man had problems. He'd been with me a long time, but ended up being nothing but trouble. And that friend of his, Carlton, been in and out of jail since he was fifteen. Nothing but trouble, the both of 'em."

Ben cleared his throat again, then looked over at me. "I haven't wanted to ask, but where is your friend? That pretty young girl. Cindy, right?"

What could I say? Ben wasn't someone I could easily lie to. "She's dead, Ben."

Ben sat quietly, rubbing his left thumb over the fingernail on his right thumb. "I am so sorry, Kercy."

We sat for several minutes without talking. I grabbed a few tissues from the box and wiped my nose. Ben appeared pensive; his hands now clamped to his knees. He took a deep breath and looked over at me.

"Where is she, Kercy?" he finally said. "Police haven't found any trace of her."

What was I supposed to say? I still couldn't believe it myself. The past few days were impossible to untangle. "They won't find her," I said. "I think they dumped her body in the water."

"Those two fellas they found in my boat threw her in the water? Or did Liam and Carlton?"

"I don't know. The whole... the whole damn thing was a nightmare."

There was no way to talk about the events of the last two days without crying. I hated the secrecy, even knowing I was part of it. And Mallory would never tell me what his investigation was about. And I wasn't about to share stories of prehistoric sea creatures eating beings who apparently lived beneath the water.

"I'm sorry to bring it up," Ben said. "Randall kept on me about that... and... well... I told him you were in no place to answer those kinds of questions... but he just kept on me..."

"It's okay, Ben."

"Randall wanted me to give you this." Ben handed me a note from his shirt pocket. It was handwritten and brief; Randall wanted me to stay in Elico until he had a chance to clear up a few things. He said he'd be in touch. I tossed the note onto my tray.

"You look wore out, Kercy. You should rest. I'm going to the cafeteria for coffee. Want anything?"

"You should go home, Ben."

"Jacob's driving up later to take me home. I'll be here till then. Get some rest."

I was getting ready to roll over when Ben stopped at the door. "Oh, I meant to tell you, that friend of yours, Gerald, he's coming up to take you back to New York."

"What?" For whatever reason, I was not ready to see Gerald. I didn't want to answer more questions from him, or see the worry on his face.

"I thought... you seem upset," Ben said.

"No... Ben... I'm not upset. How did he...?"

"He called me, concerned about you. Said he hadn't been able to reach you on your cell for a couple of days, so I said that you... that, there had been, uh... I'm sorry. I guess I shouldn't have said anything... I... I'm so sorry."

"No, Ben, it's okay. No, I'm glad you told him. I'm sure he's been worried. No, you did the right thing. Thank you, really."

Ben stood at the door, shaking his head.

"Can you bring a coffee back for me?" I said. "That sounds really good."

He nodded, then stepped into the hallway. I should have asked when Gerald was supposed to arrive, but knowing him, it would be soon. Why wasn't I more thrilled? Had that been only a week ago we made love in every room of the cottage? Sat on the dock and drank beer? Hugged and kissed and soaped each other's backs in the bathtub, sipping wine by candlelight? I felt so in love then. But now it was obvious I had no idea what love was. Except for Cindy. That was love. Certainly that was love. But how could I know. Cindy was the only person in the world I could ask, and with her gone, I felt lost. How could I have been so stupid, allowing Liam into our lives?

I laid there drifting in and out of sleep, trapped in a grief beyond tears, a grief deeply lodged inside me, solid and heavy and damaging.

When Ben returned with coffee, I glanced at the clock. He'd been gone for over an hour. I must have been sleeping, but I didn't even remember closing my eyes.

"Did you get some rest?" he asked.

I nodded, sitting up. Ben pushed the tray to the bed and set the coffee down. I picked it up and sipped. We sat for a long time without talking, just drinking our coffee, closing our eyes.

"TV?" I said to Ben, holding out the remote.

"I don't watch much television. I mostly read."

I laid back and closed my eyes. Ben never seemed in need of conversation as a means of dispensing with silence. I was probably more guilty of that, but lying under warm blankets, feeling completely safe, I welcomed Ben's quiet presence. It was reassuring.

Someone knocked on the door jamb.

"Hey," Jacob said, carrying a suitcase and a small plastic sack. "Some of your things." He set the suitcase on the floor and the bag on the chair against the wall.

"What's in the bag?" I said.

He handed it to me. "Just some things I thought you might need."

I opened it. He'd brought my toothbrush, some makeup and other personal items. Underneath my brush was a cell phone. Cindy's.

"Looks like your phone may be shot," he said. "I don't know if they can fix those or not."

I held it in my palm. "Yeah, I don't know. Thanks, you're very thoughtful."

Ben stood and touched Jacob's shoulder. "We should get going, Jacob, let Kercy here get some sleep."

Jacob looked at Ben, then back at me. "Yeah, sure," Jacob said. "Could I just have a minute with Ms. Powell, Grandpa?"

Ben smiled and leaned over and kissed me on the forehead. "I'll be in touch. And anything you need, you let me know. And don't worry about your place. Jacob and I will go out and make sure everything's winterized and ship-shape for when you come up next summer." He sniffled and squeezed Jacob's shoulder, then went to the door.

"I'll be down in the lobby," Ben told Jacob, then gave me a smile before he walked away.

"You're so lucky," I said to Jacob. "Ben is the best."

Jacob nodded, then asked if he could sit a moment. I pointed at the chair. I had no idea what he could want, but I knew I had questions.

"I just wanted to clear some things up," he said. "This isn't easy to say, but both times I found you unconscious, you were... um... naked, like in the water the other day, and on the dock..."

Now I was confused, and just a bit embarrassed. Why would that be a topic of discussion given the current circumstances? I was a bit uncomfortable with his opening remarks.

He cleared his throat. "My mother," he said. "I found her numerous times. Naked, half-conscious. Sometimes unconscious. Outside in the cold. At night. Day. For no reason..."

I wasn't following. Jacob seemed to be drawing a comparison between his mother and me. Why? Was she a drinker? Did he think I was an alcoholic or something? Or a drug addict? Maybe his mother had been addicted... meth... heroin... opioids. Did he think I had a similar problem?

"Did she have a problem with drugs... or...?"

"Do you?" Jacob said, a bit defensively.

"I'm sorry, I didn't mean anything..."

"No, she didn't. She didn't use drugs. She didn't drink... but..."

I sat waiting for him to finish his sentence.

"Look," he finally said. "There is something going on up here. I think it may involve you... and... I think we should talk more about it, you know, when you feel stronger. Are you going to stay up here a while longer?"

"Is that why you've been following me, showing up late at night, just to talk?"

Jacob blushed, as if he'd been caught in his lies. "No, not exactly, not both times, anyway..."

"What does that mean?"

"You should stay. Just a few days. So we can talk."

We stared at each other so long it started to feel like a showdown, neither of us wanting to tip our hand. But secrecy and stealth were getting us nowhere. "Have you seen them?' I finally asked.

Jacob's eyes hardened. It seemed a full minute before he spoke. "You have... haven't you? Up close?"

Up close? That was an understatement. And I wasn't sure I wanted to say more. But obviously Jacob knew of them. Maybe he could shed light on what was happening. After all, he seemed to have

Agent Mallory's ear. They were somehow partnering in this investigation. How much did they know about these things?

"Tell me something, Jacob. What were you really doing out at my place the other night?"

"I told you. I was just checking on the way back from Kurry to make sure—"

"Bullshit! We both know that isn't true... and you didn't fall in the fucking water, either... What were you and Lola searching for...?"

Jacob flushed, but before I could push harder, Gerald walked through the door.

"Kercy, are you okay?" He rushed to the bed. He looked at me, then glanced back at Jacob, then took my hand in his. "Who's this? The police? Are you with the police department?" Gerald was now looking at Jacob. "What's going on?"

"Gerald," I said. "This is Jacob. He works at the harbor. Ben's grandson. I thought you met when you were here?"

Gerald shook his head as if he didn't remember.

Jacob stood and shook Gerald's hand, then looked over at me. "Just give it some thought... please," Jacob said, then excused himself, nodding at Gerald on his way out.

"Give what some thought?" Gerald said.

I picked up the coffee Ben had brought me and offered Gerald a drink.

He shook his head. "What did he mean?" Gerald said.

"Drop it, okay?"

An edgy hush settled between us.

"I've missed you so much," Gerald said. "Will they release you tomorrow?"

"Yeah, there's nothing wrong with me. I was a bit dehydrated, is all."

"Ben told me over the phone that you were in shock."

"Well... maybe... but what does that even mean? I'm fine now."

"You need anything?"

Gerald genuinely cared, but for some reason, I felt nothing going back his way. He was like a stranger, and that left an empty pit in my stomach.

"How is Cindy?"

"What?"

"Cindy? Is she here? Is she okay?"

I rubbed my forehead, heat rolling through my stomach. I exhaled, then tried a deep breath, wiping my eyes. Suddenly my mouth was dry. I wanted Gerald to stop asking questions. I wanted him to get up and leave, drive back to New York, teach his classes, and pretend he never met me.

"She's gone, Gerald."

"Gone? She went back to New York without you? I don't understand..."

"She's dead, Gerald."

"Oh, God, Kercy... no..." Gerald slid from his chair to the bed and pulled me to his chest. That's when the fucking floodgates opened. I couldn't stop wailing. My body spasmed and lurched and felt like it would break apart from the sheer violence of my grief.

Gerald held me tighter, his embrace calming, welcome, much needed. Something swept through me, a sensation that had taken leave over the past several days, my connection to him, my warmth toward him... at least as a friend. But I still felt no deeper ties, as I had before, the burning desire, the unmoored longing to be with him every moment. This new landscape was confusing, difficult to navigate. I was grateful for his love, yet felt like a cheat, taking all he had to offer, giving nothing back.

After several minutes I pulled away, then wiped the shoulder of his sport jacket, then my own nose. I grabbed a wad of tissues from the box and cleaned up my face.

"Gerald, thanks for driving up," I said. "I'm not going to be able to go back right away. I have some things I have to take care of first."

"Yes, that's fine."

"Maybe you should drive back. You can't hang around here waiting for me. I'll call you in a few days. After I get back."

"It's okay, really. I took some time off."

There was no need fighting about this now. I smiled and touched his face, then took him back in my arms. I needed his tenderness, his love, despite knowing that being with him over the next few days wasn't going to work at all.

Later that evening, Gerald fell asleep in the chair opposite my bed. The nurses bent the rules and let him stay the night, due to the circumstances and that he had just driven all the way from New York. For whatever reason I wasn't sleepy. The nurse had brought some pills that were supposed to help me with anxiety and panic, help me sleep. But I didn't take them.

I reached across the nightstand for the bag Jacob brought from the cottage. I pulled some keys from the bottom. They didn't look familiar at first, until I realized they were Cindy's, the little Wookiee hanging from her key ring. I pictured her silver Volvo sitting at the harbor, how excited she was the day she came over to show me.

"Wow, I love it," I'd said. "What made you pick silver?"

"Jeez, Wheels, it's *Mist,* not silver!" she'd said, and we both had a big laugh over the artsy names auto manufacturers assigned to their car colors.

I placed the keys back in the bag and pulled her phone out. I pressed the power button, half believing it might come on. Of course, it didn't, but the rice had seemed to dry it out, not that it mattered now. I thought about her nearly drowning that afternoon, and now almost wished she had, especially if it would have spared her the humiliation and torture of the attack. How horrified she must have been, how frightened and helpless. And as much as I wanted to, there had been nothing I could do to save her.

TWENTY-THREE

When I checked out of the hospital the next morning, I didn't leave empty handed. The morning nurse handed me the prescription for anxiety pills, which Gerald offered to fill while I settled in at the Aubrey Motel. I still lacked the courage to tell him I wanted to be alone, that he should return to New York.

At the motel Gerald offered to carry the suitcase but I took it from him. He set his duffle on the floor and said he was headed to the pharmacy and would bring something back for lunch.

"What sounds good?" he said.

"Nothing. But I'll eat whatever you bring."

He leaned in and kissed me softly on the lips. I can't deny it felt good, but I didn't return the tenderness, and was relieved when he seemed okay with that. He smiled and left the room. I heard his car start and pull away and the sudden aloneness should have been soothing, but it wasn't. I made sure the door was locked, then slid the chain into place and turned on all the lights. I found the remote and started clicking through channels when the picture came up. I had intended to shower and change clothes, but instead, just stretched out on the bedspread fully dressed, letting my attention sink into the drone of television noise.

Sometime later, I jumped when someone pounded on the door. "It's me," Gerald said

"Coming." I went to get the door. "Did you forget your key?"

"Yeah, sorry." He was holding a brown sack and a white sack. "Drugs for you," he said, handing me the white bag. "And lunch for us."

He told me he'd found a nice little deli just down the road from the pharmacy. The roast beef sandwiches smelled delicious. We ate chips and watched some talk show and just sat. Gerald went to the vending machine for a couple of Cokes and brought back the ice bucket filled. I prepared a couple of plastic glasses and it felt so normal I had nearly forgotten recent events.

The rest of the evening we watched television and grazed on the pretzels, chips and candy he'd brought back from the pharmacy. He laughed at the comedy shows and debated the political commentaries, and the normalcy of the evening had the effect of cementing me back into reality, even if it was only transitory. And as much as I was enjoying our simple evening, I knew it was going to make it that much tougher when I told him I needed to be alone. Both for him and for me.

I woke when Gerald turned the television off. The room was dark except for a bit of light leaking through the curtains from the Aubrey Motel sign in the parking lot. Gerald eased down beneath the covers, moving closer to me, wrapping his arms around me, one around my shoulders, the other on my waist. I pressed my back against his chest as he pulled me closer. I felt safe. Calm.

The next morning I went for a walk before Gerald woke. The day was brisk and windy, the early sun throwing long bluish shadows across the deserted street. I had no idea what day it was and didn't care.

After lying awake most of the night, I thought I'd be demolished by morning. But that wasn't the case. If anything, I felt revitalized. A familiar clarity filled me that I had forgotten about, that had eluded me over the past week. When I got back to the motel, I took the elevator to the second floor. I had just stepped into the hallway when I spotted Agent Mallory knocking on our door. I tried to get his attention before he woke Gerald, but the door opened, Gerald listening in his pajama bottoms, welcoming Mallory in.

I had hoped to have the rest of the morning before telling Gerald he should drive back to New York. And I didn't want him meeting Special Agent Mallory. Ever. Too many questions. Too many circumstances I would never be able to recount to Gerald.

When I entered the room, Mallory was seated on the desk chair, Gerald sitting on the edge of the bed.

"Agent Mallory," I said. "I didn't know you were coming." What was Mallory's excuse for being here going to be? Was he going to congratulate me on those alien parts I'd collected? Maybe remark on how handy that impression of the Creature from the Black Lagoon was to his research staff? Fuck, this was exactly what I didn't want. I felt like Moses trying to hold back the two walls of the Red Sea, not wanting Gerald's world mixed up in Mallory's.

"Hello, Ms. Powell," Mallory said.

"I can step out," Gerald said. "I'll go down to the lobby."

"You don't have to leave. I don't think Agent Mallory is staying long. This is just a follow up, right?" My eyes were fixed on Mallory's.

"Yes, I just wanted to make sure you got back from the hospital okay. There are a few things we still need to go over, but that can wait."

"Good." I showed him to the door.

"Uh... I think someone mentioned you lost your phone, and I'd like to be able to get in touch with you," Mallory said, reaching into his coat pocket. "Here, brand new. Maybe we can get together this evening if that works?"

He put the phone in my palm and I was about to ask if it was a *burner,* everything feeling so covert. I decided against the sarcasm and just hustled him out the door, dreading the interrogation that was sure to follow.

"I'll call you later," Mallory said at the door.

"Can't wait." I watched him walk to the elevator.

When I turned back, Gerald was lying on the bed. "Want me to heat up this coffee I made for you while you were walking? We have microwave technology here."

It was good to hear him joke. We sat and watched a morning news show on television.

"You know what's funny to me," Gerald said. "When I'm at a motel, I always turn the television on first thing in the morning. That's odd, because I would never do that at home."

"Yeah, well motel time is different than real time." I wasn't even sure what that meant. But even stranger than motel time was the fact that Mallory had been gone for more than an hour and Gerald had not asked one thing about him. What was going on?

"Hey, here's something else that's odd," I said a bit sarcastically. "You seem not the least bit interested in the FBI agent that came to our room. Isn't that crazy?"

Gerald's expression soured. He reached for the remote and hit the power button. "Kercy, I have a million questions," he said, turning to face me. "And at times I feel like I'll explode if I don't ask them... but I know you've been through something traumatic... and me badgering you for answers for my own edification doesn't seem to make any sense. I love you. And I hope in time you'll be able to talk to me about it. That you'll want to talk to me about it. But honestly, the only thing that matters to me right now is that you're alive. That you're safe. The rest of it we'll figure out."

I climbed onto the bed and nestled into his arms. Maybe I could just go back. Have Agent Mallory meet me in New York. We could talk there. I wanted this all behind me. I wanted time with Gerald and was thrilled to feel that way again. Maybe he and I could take a trip to the desert or something, somewhere without water. No more water for a while.

"I love you, Gerald," I said. It just came up. I hadn't thought about it. Hadn't planned to say it. He held me tighter and said nothing.

We napped the rest of the afternoon and that evening we went out to dinner at the restaurant Ben had told me about in Kurry Sound. There had been something I'd wanted to ask Gerald, and felt I could without a salvo of questions as to why I wanted to know such a thing. Over dinner, after a couple of glasses of wine...

"Do you think reanimation is possible?" I said.

"You mean like Cryonics?" Gerald said. "Well, it's been done successfully. Human embryos frozen, thawed, then implanted in the mother's uterus that grow into perfectly normal human beings. There was an experiment a few years back where a rabbit's brain underwent a cryopreservation, was then warmed and found to be in near perfect condition."

"Near perfect?" I said. "Near perfect doesn't sound reassuring when referring to brains."

Gerald chuckled. "Yeah, could cause a Frankenstein effect. Can you tell me more about what your interest in this is?"

I hesitated here. Maybe what he'd told me was enough. But his knowledge of earth sciences could help me with something I've been struggling with.

"Well... my interest is this... and don't roll your eyes. Is it possible, hypothetically, that when glaciers melt, that organisms frozen for millennia could somehow survive the thawing process and be... you know... reanimated?"

"Wow, is this part of your thesis work?" Gerald said. "You'll give Dr. Miles a cardiac if you propose that!"

I smirked and finished my wine. I shouldn't have asked Gerald about my theory. He was a scholar first, a scientist second, and what I had proposed was preposterous. He must have sensed my agitation.

"Hey, look," he said in a more conciliatory tone. "I'm not sure, but I doubt it. Cryonics uses liquid nitrogen, which freezes organisms at temperatures cold enough to halt the decomposition process. It's hundreds of times colder than any glacial ice, but I've not really had occasion to study that. I do know that permafrost halts bacterial decomposition as well, but to the extent to preserve an organism completely... I'm just not sure. I mean, let's face it, Cryonics still depends on future scientific discoveries to make thawing and reanimation even possible."

I knew it was crazy, but I couldn't help wondering about the prehistoric creature that smashed my dock. I was still fairly certain I hadn't imagined it. Before I was put on the rescue helicopter, I saw that the dock had sustained a fair amount of damage. And the beings the sea creature had been feeding on, where had they come from? Certainly evolution and our current scientific model had yet to account for such things, maybe because no one had ever witnessed them. But was that even true? What was Agent Mallory's special division about if not to investigate this unusual phenomenon? And was it an unusual phenomenon? Or was it just baffling to me? My questions resembled human cells that wouldn't stop dividing. It was maddening, and I seemed to be drifting further from any possible answers, like an untethered astronaut floating in deep space.

"I'm surprised you're asking me about this," Gerald said. "You're the biology major."

"We didn't study fricking million-year-old dinosaurs thawing out from glacial melt," I shot back, instantly sorry I had. I must have sounded like a lunatic. "Okay, so... sorry for that."

"No worries. I think it's a valid question given the current state of thawing."

"No you don't. You know my question is bullshit. Why are you patronizing me? Do I look that pathetic?"

Gerald put his wine glass down, shaking his head. "I'm not... but I don't want to fight with you. And you're not pathetic in the least. The truth is, no one can accurately predict what our future holds. Thirty years ago no scientist would have ever guessed that the Larsen B Ice Shelf could possibly disintegrate at its current rate of dissipation. Science can only guess at the outcome of climate change and its effects. We know the things that will happen, of course. They're pretty obvious. But it's the things we don't know that humbles scientific study. Of course, not many scientists will admit to that. We don't like *not knowing*. That's why we focus on what we know and stay mute on what we don't."

"Are you okay with that?"

"Okay with not knowing... or okay with staying mute?"

"Staying mute? Not talking about things? What about clearing the air, total honesty? Transparency?"

Gerald stared at me for a few moments. "Are we still talking about science here?"

"I don't know what the fuck we're talking about." I shot up from the table. I couldn't stay in this conversation another second. I walked from the restaurant and paced the parking lot. This is why I was beginning to hate anthropology, biology, the sciences in general. We pretended to have answers to things, but in reality, all we did was deal with what we could prove, or pretended to prove. Everything else was just ignored. Or theorized... or worse, taken on faith...!

Gerald came up behind me. "You okay?"

I spun myself into his arms. "Please hold me."

We drove back in silence, my head against Gerald's shoulder like some lovesick teenager, which I had never had the pleasure of being. A few blocks from the Aubrey my *burner* phone went off. "Hello Special Agent Mallory," I said, sitting upright.

He wanted to know if I could meet him later, around nine that evening, at Jacob's apartment.

"I don't know. Can it wait?"

"I would really like to sit down with you. Those remains... well, they're fascinating. We really need to talk."

I was surprised he had gotten some kind of results back this quickly. But he was the FBI, after all. Our tax dollars at work. I looked over at Gerald to see if he may have heard Mallory's comment about the remains. If Gerald had, he was wearing his best Phil Ivy poker face, because I couldn't tell.

I glanced at the clock on Gerald's dash. "I could make it around nine-thirty," I said. "Where's Jacob's apartment?"

Mallory explained that it was at the harbor, above the office in back. "Just go up the stairs."

"Okay." I disconnected the call, picturing a single forty-watt bulb burning over a long flight of dilapidated wooden steps covered in gull shit and termite rot. I'm not sure why I imagined it that way. Ben kept his place clean and well maintained. It was probably Mallory's furtive manner that was responsible for such sinister images in my head.

We got back to the motel and Gerald said he'd drive me to the harbor. I was about to protest. He couldn't attend my meeting with Mallory and Jacob. And I didn't want him hanging around outside waiting in the car. Then I remembered Cindy's car keys. He could drop me off, and I would drive her car back to the motel. I needed to get it back to the city anyway. That's when I remembered Cindy wrapped in the shower curtain, the men who had killed her. The thought renewed my anger and disgust. I wanted to know how much they'd suffered, dying together from hypothermia in the cold black of night, no one to share their miserable final moments on Earth except each other. Shivering. Begging. Warmth slowly leaving their bodies. Shaking. Convulsing. Trapped with full knowledge they were about to die. Even that still didn't seem enough torture for what they'd done...

Gerald snapped me from the morbid fantasy. "Want me to pick up some beer for later?"

"Beer sounds good. I can drive Cindy's car back from the harbor after meeting Agent Mallory."

"Perfect. We'll rendezvous back here at twenty-one hundred hours, or there about."

Gerald was standing in front of the mirror, shaving. I came up behind him and wound my arms around his waist. "Are you perhaps poking a bit of fun at me?"

"Maybe a little. These surreptitious meetings... well... they're more than a little hot."

"Yeah, well you won't think so when I leave here wearing baggy sweatpants, an oversized hoody, winter coat, ski gloves and galoshes."

"Wow, I didn't know you owned galoshes," He spun in my arms to face me. "The red kind?"

"Yeah, the red kind," I said, suddenly morose. I let go of Gerald's waist and walked back to the bed. Anytime I started feeling the least thing intimate, an iron wall fell on me.

Gerald drove me to the harbor. The parking lot was dark except for a few flood lights pointed toward the office.

"Why don't we start Cindy's car before I leave," Gerald said. We walked over and I unlocked the doors. When I turned the key, the engine fired immediately. I guess I knew it would, but I was glad Gerald was with me. Her smell was everywhere inside the Volvo. She kept a little angel on her dashboard. It was so weird to me; Cindy wasn't religious at all. She said she just liked it. Truth was, I think her dad gave it to her the year she started driving. I had yet to speak with them. Even so, I figured they had been contacted by the police. Besides, I wasn't sure I was up to giving them an explanation of the events. I couldn't.

"Can we head back in the morning?" I said to Gerald, turning the engine off.

"Whatever you want." He kissed me. This time I kissed him back and for a few seconds it was wonderful.

"I've got to go," I said.

"I'll walk you over," Gerald said, getting out of Cindy's car.

"Not necessary. Just find us some beer. I'm going to need it."

"Hey," Gerald said, wiping a tear from my eye. "It's going to get better."

"I hope you're right."

Gerald waited in his car until I rounded the harbor office to find

Jacob's apartment. The steps were just where Mallory said, and except for the gull shit and termite rot, looked pretty much how I'd pictured them. When I reached the top, I knocked on the wooden door. Someone padded across the room. I took a deep breath and pulled my coat tighter to my chest.

TWENTY-FOUR

Jacob's apartment was small but cozy. Mallory was seated at the kitchen table. Jacob offered me something to drink, showing me to a wooden chair across from Mallory. Anticipating how this meeting would go had filled me both with dread and enthusiasm; I would either learn things that comforted me, or things that would horrify me... or both.

"Thanks for coming, Kercy," Agent Mallory said, standing to pull the chair out.

"Wow, both formidable and chivalrous," I said, sitting down. "So how does this meeting start? A special handshake or something?"

Mallory chuckled but Jacob didn't seem amused.

"Well, as I mentioned, Kercy," Mallory began, "Jacob here has been helping us with this investigation for almost a year, now. He's been very—"

"What fucking investigation? Can we at least start with that?" I said.

Mallory and Jacob looked at each other. "We're investigating these creatures you encountered... I—"

"Where are they from? What do you know so far? What do they want with me? And why is all this such a big fucking secret?"

Mallory looked completely flummoxed. He sighed, then started talking. "If you let me finish, I think we can answer some of your questions. As I was saying, Jacob here has been instrumental in us making as much headway as possible. With that said, the samples you provided have taken the investigation to the next level. I'm not sure how you mustered the wherewithal to collect them, or thought to make the wax impression, but this is the closest we've come to understanding more about these beings. It's a breakthrough of sorts. I can't thank you enough."

"Okay, but, before we go on," I said. "What about Detective Randall? I want to go home in the morning? Randall left a message at the hospital for me to stay put until he's had a chance to speak with me. I need some cover here..."

Mallory scratched behind his neck, clearly vexed. "Well... as far as Randall is concerned, I have taken over the investigation for all practical purposes. He bitched about it, but I can't have you talking to him, so that's off the table... he'll just have to live with it."

I knew to wait for the other shoe. Mallory took a deep breath. "But I need you to stay, just a few more days, so we can sort things out..."

"Well... that's not going to happen. So... let's sort everything out tonight. We can do follow up in the city if need be."

Mallory glared at me, then glanced over at Jacob, his stern look returning to me. "Why are you being so difficult?" Mallory said. "I thought you wanted answers?"

"Difficult! I've been raped, assaulted, visited by amphibious creatures, and my best friend is dead! Sorry to be so difficult!"

I pushed up from the table and grabbed my coat off the sofa.

"Wait, wait," Mallory said, chasing after me. "I'm sorry... just... come sit down, okay."

I glared at him, then dropped the coat on the floor and went back over. "Can I have some water?" I said.

Jacob got up and filled a glass, returning quickly. "Here, Ms. Powell."

I drained it. "Can you please stop calling me that?" I said to Jacob.

Jacob refilled my glass and we sat around the table, no one speaking. Mallory finally broke the silence. "Kercy, I'm going to record your statement. I need to have an accurate record." He set his phone on the table between us. "So, can you tell me what happened out there?" Mallory switched the recording app on.

I told him about me running into the boulder on the lake, tearing up the engine, how we tried to paddle in, Liam coming along, towing the boat back to the cottage. Then the part about the power going out, then Cindy's screams, which was so difficult to talk about. I felt my lip quivering, my voice hung up in my lungs.

"Take a minute, Kercy," Mallory said.

I sniffed, then looked over at Jacob. He was expressionless and I started wondering why he was even here. I coughed and cleared my throat, then told them about breaking free from Liam and trying to help Cindy, how one of the men took the closet rod from me and knocked me out with it.

Mallory waited patiently for me to continue.

I took a drink of water. "Liam came in. Carlton had me on the bed. I couldn't get loose... and... you know what happened..."

"Can you be specific?" Mallory said.

"Why is that important?"

"I know it's hard..."

It took a moment, but I told him how Carlton had forced himself on me first, then Liam tried to join him and there was a short scuffle, Carlton pushing Liam from the bed. "Then I heard a commotion, and Liam flew across the room."

"What?" Mallory said. "How did..."

"One of the beings tossed him against the wall... like he weighed nothing. Then the other..."

Jacob leaned forward in his chair, the most animated he'd been other than getting me a glass of water.

"There were two of them?" Mallory asked.

"I don't know. I guess. Maybe more."

"Okay," Mallory said. "You want some coffee or something? Can you make some coffee, Jacob?"

Jacob got up, nodding, then opened and closed cabinet doors.

"So... then... Carlton was pulled off me and tossed across the room. Carlton was a big man but the being handled him just as easily, then thrust his arm through Carlton's mid-section and carried him out the back door. I heard him screaming and fighting.... Then a few minutes later, nothing."

"It killed Carlton with its arm?"

"Carlton was still alive at that point..."

"So where was Liam?" Mallory asked.

"Uh..." I tried to recall the order of events. "I'm not sure, but he fled the living room and must have run out the front door, which is actually now the *back* door. I think that's how they came in, the men, not the beings... I was in the kitchen when the men shut off the power... or the living room. I'm sorry." I was getting confused. The images had been seared into my memory, while the timeline and exact locations remained elusive.

"It's okay."

I watched Jacob measuring out coffee grounds. Simple things. When could I return to simple things? "I was still on the bed..." I said. "When I heard a loud bang, an explosion."

"An explosion?" Mallory said. "What exploded?"

"The boat they came in, I guess. That's how Liam and the being ended up all over the island."

"I was wondering how you managed to get the parts," Mallory said. "We had no idea what they looked like. Can we talk about that a minute?"

I nodded, the smell of coffee drifting across the kitchen. "They function quite well as bipeds.... at least when I saw them. And they are almost certainly some kind of humanoid species... but their skin... nothing humanoid about that. And their eyes... very unusual."

"What about their skin?" Mallory said. "They seemed to be very pale, almost white. Would you say they're albino?"

I shook my head, confused by Mallory's comment. "They're very dark. I'm not sure what you're talking about."

Mallory brought out his phone and showed me the pictures he'd taken.

"No... those parts have faded. Maybe the fridge did that. Or they fade after death. No, their skin is dark with some kind of iridescence, like mother of pearl, or oil. Their eyes... I never really got a good look at those... they're covered with some kind of shield I could barely see through."

Mallory was jotting notes along with his recording. "Any other details?"

I talked about their appendages, about the tube-like protrusions running over their shoulders connected to the hump-like formations on their backs, their rough skin, yet shiny, almost wet looking.

"If I brought in an artist, could you help them sketch one of these things?" Mallory asked.

"Probably." But I didn't want to. I just wanted to go back to the city and get on with my life.

"Okay, good. So, you heard the explosion, then what?"

"One of the beings came in and with a flick of one of its digits... they have sharp claws... cut the mooring rope like it was thread. Then it left. That was it."

"*That was it?*" Mallory scratched behind his ear. Jacob brought two coffee cups over for Mallory and me. I took a drink.

"Thanks," I said to Jacob. "That's good."

Jacob came over and sat down with his cup.

"What do you mean, *That was it?*" Mallory said again. "Your friend Cindy is gone. No trace of her. Your dock has some serious damage. There's all kind of burned crap in your front yard. Jacob found you naked on the dock during a winter storm. That can't be *it.*"

I explained about starting a huge bonfire with the mattress, box spring, and bedding from the guest room.

"Okay, but what about your friend? Cindy? What happened to her body?"

I rubbed my forehead, not wanting to talk about this. I explained that the next evening was kind of a blur, but that the beings returned. That things went a bit wonky and my memory was part fact and part hallucination.

"I don't know what that means," Mallory said.

"I sort of passed out or something. When I woke... the beings were... holding me down... but not really holding me... and one of them was on top of me.

"On top of you?" Mallory asked. Jacob put his coffee down and sat forward.

"Yes. On top of me."

"On top of you? Like... inside you?"

I nodded, wiping my eyes.

"Did you try to fight it off?"

I glanced over at Jacob. His eyes narrowed, his features hard. I looked back at Mallory, his expression unchanged.

"No... because... because... they do something to you... it's hard to explain. It's not like you're paralyzed, nothing like that, well, maybe sort of... but... they seem to be able to affect how you feel..."

"How you feel?"

"Yeah... like this calm comes over you, so... you feel no pain... no pleasure... nothing. There is no fight or flight response. But you are conscious... well, mostly conscious, I guess. Anyway, that was about it."

Jacob and Mallory shared some kind of look for just a split second. Then Mallory asked how long the assault lasted.

"I don't know. Maybe five minutes..." I was suddenly vexed by the private signals between Jacob and Mallory. "Why is Jacob even here?" I said to Mallory, then aimed my ire at Jacob. "Why did you come out at my place the other night? You and your girlfriend..."

Then like a lightning bolt, it hit me; the answer to my own question... "Oh my God, you were trying to make contact with these things!"

Mallory spun toward Jacob. "Is that true?"

Jacob must have felt ambushed, struggling to regain his composure, shaking his head as if he'd been slapped.

"I've got news for you, Jacob," I said, with a self-satisfied smirk. "I've seen four men, and maybe those other two jerk-offs, Marty and Rags, who encountered these things, and every one of those fuckers ended up in a body bag. I'd be very careful what you wish for, my friend... These things don't seem to like men very much..."

Jacob stood and left the room.

"Oh, for fuck's sake," Mallory said to me. "Was that necessary?"

"Are we done?"

Mallory turned back to me. "Is that true? Do you think they have an aversion toward males?"

"Hey, you've seen the carnage. You tell me."

Mallory was agitated. He sighed and took a breath. "So, after the attack, what happened next? Did they leave?"

I don't know why I felt bad about snapping at Jacob. I kept checking the door he'd gone through to see if he was coming back. "No. I thought they had," I finally told Mallory. "But that's when they came down the steps with Cindy's body. I tried to stop them but they walked past me. They never tried to hurt me or anything like that, even when I physically attacked the one carrying her, it just stood there a moment, then jumped into the water with Cindy and disappeared beneath the surface."

Mallory seemed like he was about to say something, then jotted notes in his little spiral pad. "I'm so sorry, Kercy." He looked toward the back of the apartment where Jacob had gone then, then said, "What happened to your dock?"

"I don't know. Maybe those clowns ran into it with their boat." I hoped Mallory could accept this explanation.

"Are you sure, Kercy? I didn't think they used the dock." He started flipping through his notepad, as if looking for some entry about what I'd said, but I never even talked to Mallory about it. "Yeah, here, Randall said their boat was out front, underwater, at least what was left of it. How do you think your dock got damaged?"

It bothered me that I was sharing everything while Mallory shared nothing.

"Well, Special Agent Mallory, a huge prehistoric sea creature shot from the water and grabbed one of the beings from the dock and ate it. Then the other being, in a futile attempt to save its own ass, started running, to no avail, and got eaten too. And the big ass dinosaur thing crashed down on my brand-new deck and fucked it all up. The end."

I tipped my coffee cup back and finished the last of it. "I wonder if there's any more coffee? It's really good." I got up and poured myself another cup.

Mallory was nonplussed by my fantastical story, still jotting in his little pad. I sipped the coffee, waiting for Mallory to finish writing.

"Could you describe the sea creature enough for an artist sketch?"

I scoffed, and shook my head in disbelief. "Really? You didn't find my sea monster story the least bit troubling, like, over the top? What do you know about these fucking things?"

Mallory's expression went unchanged. "Well, could you?" he finally said.

"Yeah, I guess. I may be able to do better than that, if I can get to a library." I explained that there could be drawings of it, that the creature reminded me of a *cryptocleidus*. I told him my mother was a marine biologist, that she had an interest in prehistoric sea creatures as well. "But I can't be sure about the creature until I research it more."

"You think it's prehistoric?" Mallory asked.

"It could be... maybe. So now it's your turn... tell me what you know."

Mallory looked toward the back of the apartment. "Well, Jacob has a theory. And if you hadn't chased him off, he could have shared it with us..."

"You share it with me."

Mallory cleared his throat. "He thinks all of this may have something to do with evolution."

"Evolution? Like Darwinian evolution?"

"He thinks... well... that these creatures are somehow trying to speed their own evolution in order to... be able to walk on land."

I shook my head, unable to understand how Jacob was making that leap. "They already walk on land. Does he understand evolution?"

"He's been studying it for the past several years. And he thinks—"

"You're kidding, right?" I knew I was being a bit snotty, but this was just crazy, especially considering everything I had been reading about the human genome project. "Evolution takes millions of years, if, in fact, it's even true. Evolution is just a theory. You know that, right?"

"Please, Kercy, we're just trying to understand things, here." Mallory now chose to defend Jacob and his hypothesis.

"No, really. He probably has one of those drawings by Thomas Huxley in his wallet," I said to Mallory. "You know the one, that clever line drawing depicting those five steps between ape and man, between walking on all fours to walking upright. Yes, the biggest load of bullcrap ever perpetrated on the public, signed off and endorsed by science itself to make everything fit."

Just then, Jacob came from the back room and joined the conversation as if he'd been there all along.

"Look, I know what you're saying about evolution theory," Jacob said, flopping back down in his chair. "But it is possible if genes are able to be mutated. And they can be. Science has proven that."

"But not without dubious and usually disastrous results. Mutated genes almost always end up as diseases. Destructive diseases," I said, impressed that Jacob had gone beyond the surface of the subject. "And why? Have you seen one of these beings? It's unlikely they'll be walking among us anytime soon. They're hideous looking." I couldn't believe I just said that given how I had looked, and was treated as a child. An awful backlash swept through me over my cruel remark.

"Look, all I meant was, these creatures perambulate just fine, so I don't think that's it," I said. "And given our current political and social climate, they're safer in the water." No one seemed to get my joke. But then another thought hit me about what Jacob had proposed... Maybe these creatures were utilizing human DNA somehow to become more adept at breathing air? That possibility was fraught with very disturbing potential.

"How about the sea creature you saw?" Jacob said. "Maybe that's why they need to live on land. Their very existence depends on it."

"Were you sitting back there listening the whole time?"

Jacob didn't react.

"Kercy, come on," Mallory said. "Please, let's keep this civil."

I scoffed, shaking my head. "To tell you the truth, that night was so freaky, I'm still not sure I saw anything."

"But your dock?" Jacob said.

"What about it? That could have happened lots of ways?" I wanted to believe that, but there was a part of me that could not easily deny the creature's existence. Then I remembered the night Cindy and I stayed out in the boat after dark watching the stars, how we'd hit something, the blood in the water, how the depth finder had given me a reading of only ten feet, but then suddenly shot deeper, even though the boat was sitting still. Could that have been one of those creatures passing beneath the skiff?

"What would even lead you to think about evolution?" I said to Jacob.

"Because... I think they... well... they are mating with humans," Jacob said. "Just like the one that mated with you."

"Mated? That's what you think happened? Are you kidding?" My tone was incredulous but my mind could not retire the possibility. Then I remembered my dream at a few months before my eighteenth birthday, the beings coming to me in the night, the pain, the confusion, the instrument inside me. But that was a dream, I told myself. But now I wasn't sure. And the time with Gerald... the scan... the blunt probe... what was all that... another dream... or something more nefarious?

"I think that's what's happening," Jacob said. "They have discovered how to mutate genes for a positive outcome before insemination. That's how they are speeding their evolution."

"Okay, well, then this little puzzle will be easier to solve than I thought," I said, climbing back up onto my soap box. "All we have to do is send down a few submersible ROVs and we'll find the underwater lab where they are doing all this highly specialized and sensitive work and Mallory here can arrest them for unauthorized tampering with the gene pool. That sounds simple enough."

"We've done that, Kersey," Mallory said.

"Done what?"

"We've sent numerous underwater ROVs all around out there," Mallory said. "I've got hundreds of hours of footage without a single frame that even hints at their existence. We've yet to glimpse any of these creatures on video. That seems peculiar to me."

"Do you have other eyewitness accounts?" I asked.

"A few," Mallory said. "Yours is by far the most sober of the bunch."

It was odd, but then what wasn't about all of this. "Okay, so, if there are no secret underwater labs, and no real proof of their existence other than a few accounts like mine, what brings you to such conclusions as alien beings trying to speed their evolution to walk on land and breathe our air? What... is their planet about to explode?" I couldn't avoid the sarcasm. The leap they were making seemed unfounded.

"There seems to be no other explanation..." Jacob said.

I shook my head. "So where are these so-called hybrid beings, then? Certainly, there must be a few of them around somewhere. It's not like they'd be very good at hiding."

Jacob looked down at the table, then over at Mallory. Mallory let out a sigh. "I think everyone's tired tonight." Mallory reached over and switched the recorder off.

"Just answer me that," I said. "Obviously you are going on more than what you've shared with me..."

"I really wish you would stay another day, Kercy," Mallory said. "You have no idea how helpful you've been. And our window of research time is shrinking."

"Shrinking? I don't understand."

"Winter. The water freezes. The activity ceases."

"That makes no sense. These beings are powerful. They'd have no trouble breaking through ice."

"I'm sure you're right. That isn't the issue. No one is up here in the winter. Once the season ends and everyone goes home, the activity ends."

That actually made a lot of sense, but I was tired and irritable and couldn't concede his point. "So can I go now?"

"Sure, but can I ask one last question?"

I stared at him.

"How do you think they knew you were being attacked?" Mallory said. "They hadn't come to you any other time, only when you were in danger. How could they know that?"

Mallory made an excellent point. But they had come at other times, recalling the encounter before Gerald had headed back to New York, which I hadn't told him about. I was fairly certain now that that incident wasn't a dream. But to his question, all I said was, "I don't know, Agent Mallory. But I'm spent. I have to go. Feel free to contact me in the city."

Mallory stood when I did. "Aren't you the least bit curious?" he said.

"Curious? I'm way beyond curious. I'm already at *terrified out of my fucking mind*. I came here tonight hoping you'd tell me that Navy Seals had been deployed to save my life that night, and that I had mistaken their wetsuits for alien beings. I hoped you would explain everything away by telling me this was all part of some elaborate climate experiment dealing with temperature changes across the northern hemisphere and something to do with underwater weather balloons and aquatic satellites or whatever stories government agencies fabricate to hide the unsavory facts. I came here prepared to believe any ridiculous story you told me, just as long as you hid those unsavory facts from me. What I wasn't prepared for, was for you to actually believe me! That way I could start working on not believing myself and get on with my life. But you didn't do that and now I am more discombobulated and frightened than I was before. So, yeah, I'm way beyond curious... I'm angry and tired and frightened and feeling powerless."

"There's nothing to be scared of," Jacob said.

"What? Nothing to be scared of? Seriously? Did you see those bodies out there, Jacob? These things are nothing to fuck with...! Okay... that's enough. I've really got to go." I grabbed my coat and threaded it on as I headed for the door. I hurried down the back steps, nearly falling when I got to the bottom. I was so angry I hardly knew what I was doing. Then I remembered Cindy's car. I rushed over to it, started the engine and spun a little gravel leaving the parking lot. How could Jacob be so nonchalant about what was happening. Even Mallory was disturbingly unfazed by sea monsters and amphibious creatures.

Passing flashing yellow lights and deserted dark streets, I was glad Gerald was back at the Aubrey Motel; I didn't want to be alone tonight. I hoped he had waited up...and that he had found a beer store.

TWENTY-FIVE

Gerald was asleep when I let myself into the room, but the television was still on. It was after one in the morning, but all the coffee had me so jacked up I knew I wouldn't sleep. I checked the mini fridge for beer and was pleasantly rewarded for my efforts. After popping the tab, I tilted it back and finished nearly half of it.

"Hey, can I join you?" Gerald sat up in bed.

I pulled one out for him and opened it.

"Thanks," he said. "Everything okay?"

"Yeah, peachy," I said, fighting back some smart-ass comments about evolution. I wasn't even sure what I was so angry about; Jacob and Mallory's cavalier attitude, or that some part of me actually agreed with Jacob's assessment. I wanted to reject his theory outright, but couldn't, even as I could see things didn't add up. Where were the hybrid beings? The beings that saved me, were they hybrids? Were they in the process of assimilating to a terra environment, breathing air instead of water? And what had they done to me that night? The theory of harvesting human eggs tested itself in my mind. Is that what they were doing, taking eggs from me? Did I even produce eggs? I wasn't even sure about that.

"You seem pensive," Gerald said. "Do you want to talk?"

"No. I just want to watch television and drink beer until I pass out."

We sat and watched a movie on HBO with the lights off, then another until Gerald rolled over and fell asleep. I had a buzz going and figured that one more beer should nudge me over the edge. It was after four in the morning. I figured if nothing else, I would sleep for a couple of days when we got back to the city. The thought gave me a rush of relief. Not so much the sleeping part, but the getting back to the city. I couldn't wait.

I was clicking mindlessly through channels when my burner phone lit up over on the desk. Why was Mallory calling me at this hour? Luckily the ring tone was off so it didn't wake Gerald. I decided to ignore it and continued searching for something on television to carry me through my last beer.

The phone went dark, then lit up again a few minutes later. Mallory wouldn't stop until I answered it. I got up and went to the desk. But it wasn't the phone Mallory had given me that was lighting up; it was Cindy's. I picked it up and tried to answer, but it wasn't actually a phone call. The screen was illuminated, but there was no text, no phone call waiting to be answered, no email alert, just a blank white screen. I held it for a moment, then tried to switch it off, but it was unresponsive. I set it down. After a few seconds it went dark. It must have been shorting out or something. That's all I could figure.

Nevertheless, there was probably a logical explanation, or at least an electrical one, for why Cindy's phone suddenly came to life, I couldn't stop thinking about it. Maybe it had finally just started working again.

I got up and went back to the desk. I tried the power switch. Nothing. I shook it then tried the power button again. It certainly seemed dead. I disconnected Gerald's phone from his charger cord and plugged Cindy's in. Nothing to indicate it was charging. Nothing at all. I plugged Gerald's phone in again and placed Cindy's back on the desk.

Whatever effect the beer had begun to have on me, was now gone, eradicated by the intrigue of Cindy's phone. It was unlikely I would sleep, but I switched off the television and rolled to my side and closed my eyes.

When I woke at half past seven, I was still zonked from the beer and lack of sleep. Gerald was already in the shower and I knew he'd want to be on the road by eight. I packed up the few things I'd taken out of my suitcase. Maybe I'd crash Gerald's shower instead of waiting to get my own.

"Hey, is there room in there for a scrawny anthropologist?" I said to the door, using the word scrawny because Gerald had made a comment at dinner the previous evening about how much weight I'd lost since he'd seen me last. Which I couldn't understand, given how Cindy and I had been eating.

He invited me in and I returned the favor of a back scrub, even though it wasn't equitable; his back was much larger than mine. He asked if I wanted to grab breakfast in town or stop on the way. "Whatever... I'm not very hungry," I said.

"Okay, then we'll eat in town," Gerald said.

"Why? Because I said I wasn't hungry?"

"Yeah, because no sooner than we get on the highway you'll tell me you're famished."

"Oh, you think you know me so well, buster." I was happy to be able to joke around. "And because of your ugly remark, I'm not washing your hair."

"Already did," Gerald said. When he turned to stick out his tongue at me, I kissed him.

"I love you," I said.

Gerald smiled and hugged me.

"I'm done if you want to turn the water off," I said. "Want me to dry your back?"

We dried each other, got dressed and packed up the car. I think Gerald wanted to make love, but I knew I wasn't ready. Nevertheless, it felt so wonderful to kiss him, to hold him.

I drove Cindy's Volvo, and Gerald followed me in his car to a small diner at the edge of town. When the waitress brought our coffee, I remembered about Cindy's phone and decided to share the story with Gerald.

"What would cause that?" I said.

Gerald shrugged and shook his head. "Dunno, but it lit up this morning on my way to the shower. I tried to answer it but it wouldn't do anything. It was weird."

Before the waitress brought the food, I excused myself to use the restroom. When I walked in and locked the door behind me, a ringtone went off in my jacket pocket. I reached in and brought out Cindy's phone. The tune, *Take Me Out to the Ballgame* was playing, the screen glowing, but no phone call to answer, nothing but a white screen, no icons, no time, no charge indicator. It wasn't even her ringtone.

When I returned to the table, Gerald was already eating. I moved my potatoes around with my fork, my mind transfixed by Cindy's phone. Then it hit me, her dad's love of baseball, his fixation on Yogi Berra.

"I have to stay," I blurted out to Gerald.

"What's that?" he said.

"I can't leave just yet. I can't leave Elico."

He cocked his head slightly. "What? What does that mean?"

"I need to stay a few more days. Finish up a few things."

Gerald set his fork down and wiped his mouth with his napkin. "Kercy, I don't... I thought you wanted to get back?"

"I do... you have no idea... but I need to do something first."

He paused, his eyes fixed on mine. After a moment or two, he nodded. "Okay... then... we'll just go back to the Aubrey until you're ready. There's no rush to get back."

His patience and understanding was making the next thing I had to tell him that much harder.

"I need you to go back to New York... without me," I said.

"What...? Why...? I thought we were going to—"

"I'm sorry, Gerald. I really am... but I need you to go back without me. I'll be home in a couple of days. Just say you will. Okay? Please?"

Gerald cleared his throat, taking his gaze out the window. He adjusted his neck to the side, something he did when he was flustered. He glanced back at me, then at the table. "If that's what you want..."

We finished breakfast in silence. When we walked to the parking lot, I pulled Gerald close. He returned the hug, but with less commitment than earlier. "I'm sorry," I said. "I'll call you when I get back." Gerald opened the trunk of his car and I grabbed my suitcase and book bag and put them in the trunk of Cindy's Volvo.

"Be careful," he said, then opened his door and got in behind the wheel. The window slid down after he closed the door.

I leaned in and kissed him. "Be careful," I said. "I'll see you soon."

I stood outside Cindy's car until Gerald pulled from the parking lot. Obviously, I wasn't cried out yet. I used my sleeve to wipe my eyes and nose, then got in Cindy's Volvo, undecided about what my next move was actually going to be. The only thing I knew for sure was that I had to go back to the cottage. That ringtone meant something, some kind of message from Cindy? How could that be, though? Had the creatures managed to bring her back to life? The only thing more ridiculous than the question was that I managed to ask it, and found myself suddenly wanting to believe in the absurd, needing to believe in fantastical schemes and outlandish possibilities. But I didn't believe at all. Not really. Nevertheless, my intuition was telling me that the answer was at the cottage. However, in order to get there, I needed a boat, and I couldn't bother Ben again. And for whatever reason, I didn't want to deal with Jacob. I dialed my burner phone.

"Hi, Kercy. Did you decide to stay?" Agent Mallory said when he heard my voice.

"Do you know where my boat is?"

"What boat?"

"The one the police, or the FBI, took into evidence a week or so ago."

"I can make a few calls... see what I can find out. But I have a boat if you need one."

"I need my own boat," I said.

"Sure, of course. Let me check on it."

I waited in the car. It took a few minutes for him to ring me back.

"They think it's in Toronto," Mallory said.

"They think? All right, so... where's your boat?"

"At the harbor. Is everything okay?"

Buying a new boat seemed easier than this conversation, but I knew it would be hard to get something water-ready in just a few hours.

"I have to run out to the cottage," I said.

"Sure, no problem. I can take you out there this morning. Give me about fifteen minutes. Meet me at the harbor."

"No... I need to drive myself. And I might need it for a night or two."

The long silence that followed was expected. I waited while Mallory processed whatever thoughts now plowed through his mind.

"Are you still there?" I said.

"Sure. Yeah... I just think that's a bad idea."

We went back and forth for what seemed like five minutes about why he felt it was a bad idea, and why it didn't matter to me if it was a bad idea or not, it was what I needed to do.

"You won't be able to get in," he said. "They have it taped off. Crime scene."

Now the silence initiated from my end of the conversation. How was this going to work? I wasn't even sure why I was going out there. It just seemed like that's what I needed to do, the ringtone still playing somewhere deep inside my head: *Take Me Out to the Ballgame...*

"You there?" Mallory said.

"I thought you took over the investigation?"

"I did... and your house is crawling with FBI agents. That's why I need to go with you."

"Just forget it, then," I said, and hung up. I dropped the burner phone on the pavement and smashed it with my heel. "This is so fucked up." I looked down at the phone, realizing I had no way to call Ben now. I went back inside the diner.

"Do you have a phone I can use?" I said to the waitress.

"Pay phones are all gone around here," she said. "Is it local?"

"Yeah, I have to call over to the harbor."

She handed me her cell.

Ben picked up on the third ring. I told Ben I needed a boat and apologized for the one I'd wrecked. He told me insurance would cover it, not to worry. Then he offered to take me wherever I needed to go.

"Ben... I need to go back out to the house," I said.

"But Kercy, those federal agents are at your place. I went out there today to get some of your things. They wouldn't even let me on the dock."

"Yeah... I've heard. Are they staying there at night?"

"I don't know... but, you don't want to go out there at night... I wouldn't think you'd want to go out there at all...!"

I couldn't think. My mind was spinning, options rising and dying faster than I could track them. For whatever reason, I didn't trust Agent Mallory anymore, or Jacob; they were hiding something from me and I didn't know why.

"You still there, Kercy?" Ben asked.

"Yeah, Ben, sorry... I'm just thinking."

"You know I'll get you a boat, Kercy," Ben said, interrupting my thoughts. "I'm just worried about you is all."

"Yeah, I know, and I appreciate that... If I ask you to just do this for me, could you? No questions?"

Ben paused just a moment. "Sure. Sure. You know where the guest stall is? I'll have Jacob stick it in there for you. Just see him when you get to the harbor. He'll have the keys."

I took a deep breath. This was getting so complicated. I wasn't sure how far Ben would go for me, but I didn't want to ask Jacob for anything. I didn't even want him to know I was going to the house.

"Ben, would it be possible to leave the keys in the boat?"

Another pause. "Sure, I'll tell him to just leave the keys in there. Nobody needs to know where you're going."

I had one more ask that I hoped wouldn't ignite a volley of unanswerable questions, or cause ill will. "Can we not involve Jacob?"

A deep silence spread between us like an ocean, until finally: "Sure, Kercy. But you have to promise you'll be careful."

"I will, Ben. I love you. Thank you so much. And don't worry."

Silence once again from Ben's end.

"You there?" I finally said.

Ben cleared his throat. "Kercy... you have to be careful... you have to..."

TWENTY-SIX

The boat was where Ben said it would be, the keys in it. I hoped Jacob wouldn't hear me when I started the engine. I backed out of the slip and pointed it toward the cottage. When I got there, it was just as Ben had described it; FBI agents everywhere. Two FBI boats rocked in the waves, tied to my dock, along with another one with the CISO logo on the side. I thought they'd be a bit stealthier, maybe unmarked boats or something. I decided to wait them out. I kept my distance, and it was the only plan I could come up with as I didn't want to try driving out in the dark again, relying on the GPS unit.

It was only two in the afternoon so I knew the wait was going to be long. I pulled up on the closest island to the cottage. From there I could see them without being too conspicuous, their boats small, but clearly visible, at my dock. I laid down on one of the bench seats in the boat and dozed off.

It was after six when I woke. The day had been fairly warm, but as evening approached the temperature dropped. I looked toward the cottage. One boat was gone, while a few agents milled about on the side of the house. A couple other men brought large yellow plastic bags down and placed them in the boat. Four agents then climbed in and untied from the dock. Soon they were headed across the bay toward the harbor, a sharp, white wake slicing a smooth trail across the water.

I hoped they had not left an agent behind. I fired the engine and shot across the bay. I expected to hear shouting as I tied the skiff to the dock. When I saw the lights on in the house my heart dropped. I went up the walkway to the back door. Yellow crime scene tape stretched across the opening. I reached under it to turn the knob. The door was locked. I got my keys out and opened it, then carefully ducked beneath the tape trying not to disturb it. It felt odd sneaking into my own house.

"Hello?" I said, not wanting to get shot if an agent had stayed behind. "Hello? I'm Kercy Powell. I own this place."

No one responded.

Checking the rooms, I found numerous tags marking all kinds of things. I wasn't even sure where I was going to sleep, or what I was doing. Obviously I had not thought this through.

I went to the living room. Not much to find, except for some tags where my DVD player and television had been, the ragged wires sticking out from the shelves of the bookcase. The books were still there. That was a relief, it would give me something to do until.... "Until what, Kercy?" I said to myself. I wasn't sure what I was expecting.

I fished Cindy's phone from my pocket and laid it on the coffee table. "Okay, so now what?" I said to the phone.

I hoped the agents hadn't taken my tea. I went out to the kitchen to put on the kettle. I filled it and placed it on the burner, then adjusted the flame. As I was pulling a cup down from the cabinet, I accidentally clipped a saucer, crashing it to the floor, along with the cup. I got the broom and was sweeping up the mess when I knocked the paper towel dispenser off the counter.

"Okay, settle down," I told myself.

I took a deep breath and opened the drawer and found the tea bags where they were supposed to be. My hands were shaking as I opened the packet to remove the bag. My heart was beating wildly. How was I going to last the night like this? My pills were in my pocket so I shook one out and took it with a glass of water.

When the kettle whistled, I almost came out of my skin. I fixed my tea, letting a dab of honey sink to the bottom of the glass. I wished for wind to crowd out the silence of the house.

After carrying my tea back to the living room, I perused my mother's books. When she'd sold the cottage years earlier, she at least had kept her library in storage, though I didn't find out until after she died. When I bought this place back, I knew it wouldn't be the same without her collection.

It didn't take long before I found the book I was looking for. I flipped through the pages until I came to a skeleton of the Cryptocleidus and an illustration of science's best guess as to how it must have looked. From what I could tell, this particular species only grew to around ten feet long. What I had seen had been much larger. The article went on to talk about the Elasmosaurus, one of the Upper Cretaceous types, which grew to over thirty-two feet long. I ripped the illustration out and folded it up to mail to Mallory when I got back to the city.

When I finished with that, I browsed some of her marine biology books, then came across some of her novels. What an interesting reading list; everything from Atlantis Rising to Zephyr's Trade, a satirical spy novel.

I chose the spy novel as it seemed to have a bit of humor. After an hour or so the meds kicked in, defeating any attempt the green tea had of keeping me awake. I got up and went to the hall closet and grabbed a blanket from the shelf. I hadn't even brought my toothbrush; all that stuff was still in my suitcase in the trunk of Cindy's car.

After going to the bathroom, I used my finger to brush my teeth with the toothpaste I'd left behind. There was no need to turn off the lights to sleep, the drugs were doing their job. Besides, I was feeling very drowsy and was afraid if I turned off the lights even the pills would lose their effect.

I laid on the couch and adjusted the blanket up around my shoulders and closed my eyes. I must have dozed off and had no idea what time it was when someone spoke my name. I listened for it again, holding my breath, my heart skittering. I was going to say something but I couldn't bring myself to make a sound. I exhaled carefully, quietly, and stole another breath. Maybe it was a dream. That's when I heard the back door open slowly, the tiny telltale squeak that was imperceptible during the daytime. A moment later the door slid slowly back into its jamb, followed by the faint sound of the latch clicking shut.

A weapon. That's what I hadn't thought to bring or grab from the kitchen.

However, I didn't hear footsteps, only the creaking of the floor as irrefutable proof someone or something was coming through the kitchen. As quietly as I could, I sat up and eased myself from the couch, deciding to hide behind it. I waited, my breathing increasingly unmanageable.

The house had fallen impossibly still, as if held in a vacuum. I felt an inaudible presence now in the wide entrance between the kitchen and living room; it was searching, seeing me hidden behind the sofa. Maybe I should jump up and run past it. Or stay still, hope it doesn't find me.

"Wheels?" a voice said. "Where are you?"

I shot up from behind the couch. "Cindy! Oh my God, Cindy!" I rushed out to hold her, tripping on the lamp cord and falling.

"Wheels, slow down."

"I'm okay! I'm okay!" I scrambled to my feet, tears running down my cheeks. I hugged her to me, my arms wrapping her tightly. I couldn't stop crying and laughing and looking at her, then hugging her again.

I kissed her cheek, her lips... then stopped, pushing back from her slowly, pulling my arms back, crossing them over my chest.

"You're cold as ice," I said, stepping away from her, creating distance between us. "You're soaking wet..."

She smiled weakly. "Wheels, please don't be scared. I'm sorry for this."

"Who are you?"

"I'm... Cindy... but I've been repurposed, so to speak."

"Repurposed?" I felt sick to my stomach. "What the fuck does that mean?"

"They thought you might feel more at ease with me. Plus, by using me, they can communicate through me utilizing my faculties of speech and language, as well as my memories."

"I don't know what the fuck you are... but you are not Cindy."

"I know... and I wish we had more time to talk about this, but we don't. Wheels, I need you to come with me."

"Stop calling me that!"

"Sorry. Kercy, please come with me. I need to show you something."

Cindy held her hand out to me. I pulled my arms closer to my chest and eased back.

"I won't hurt you," she said. "And if you want me to, I'll leave and that will be the end of it."

The end of it. I didn't even know what the *it* was, but having *it* end sounded like a great idea. I stood post-still staring at her, her eyes never blinking, never letting go of mine. They appeared soft, not dead, and her lips were pink, no longer blue. She was still wearing the clothes I had dressed her in. She looked down at them.

"Thank you for dressing me," she said. "And for the candles."

"How could you possibly...?"

"There just isn't time, Kercy. I won't be able to stay much longer."

I didn't know what to say. I was frozen, not with fear anymore, but disbelief.

"Before I go, Kercy, they want you to know it is not theirs."

"What? What's not theirs?"

She smiled. "The baby you're carrying, Kercy. It's not theirs. It's yours and Gerald's."

I could only shake my head. I was on overload, my mind trying to shape this information into something identifiable.

"But I'm unable to get pregnant, Cindy. You know that. It's impossible."

"Yes, I know. But you are." She turned to leave.

"Wait..." I said, but didn't know why. She smiled again, then walked from the living room. "Cindy, wait. I want to go with you."

I didn't really want to go, but I had to, or at least I felt I had to... I was so confused, anxious, so fucking scared. She must have sensed my hesitation. She stopped, looked at me a long while, then took my hand. We walked down to the dock, past the skiff I had borrowed from Ben, then picked our way around the damaged decking boards. The air had grown cold and still, the water perfectly calm. When we reached the end of the dock, she turned to me. "Just trust me. Nothing will harm you. I promise," she said, then tightened her hand on mine and jumped from the dock, pulling me along with her, down into the water.

TWENTY-SEVEN

Incredible lights, amazing colors, magical fish, unprecedented details, everything I had come to associate with drowning. The darkness that engulfed us when we first plunged into the depths had evanesced into this vibrant, animated world. The cold had left my body, replaced by a calming warmth. There was so much to see, so much to touch and I tried to dive to the bottom, but Cindy held my hand tight, moving us forward.

"I've drowned, haven't I?" I said, speaking without difficulty or consequence. I felt no panic, no trouble breathing. If anything, mobility was effortless.

"No, you haven't. Just wait a moment longer."

We swam toward a glowing barrier of light. When we glided through it, Cindy swam upward pulling me along. It took only moments it seemed, to reach the top. We broke the surface, but it was nothing like I expected. Fish swam above us, all around us, beneath us. Billions of sparkling life forms floated about, some no larger than a speck of dust. A clear delineation between these two environments was clearly visible, yet no place that wasn't liquid. We swam over to what appeared to be a shoreline, but when we stepped out onto it, we were still breathing water. There was no sky, no air, no above and below, and yet there was a substrate to stand upon, gravel and shiny colorful rocks, shy exotic plants that closed in on themselves sensing our presence. One water source seemed denser than the one we were now standing in. An enormous sea creature swam just above us, its tentacles brushing across our heads and shoulders. I crouched down and Cindy squeezed my hand.

"You have nothing to fear," she said.

I stood slowly, reaching up to touch the creature's tail. I looked over at Cindy. "I don't understand. Am I dead?"

"No. As a matter of fact, you have never drowned. All those times before when you believed you could breathe underwater and had to be saved... you were just passing through to this... our realm, our world, where you actually can breathe underwater, though it is not water in the sense that you are used to."

"We're not in Canada anymore, are we?" I said.

This time she laughed. "No. Far from it. Twelve generations away, to give you some idea."

"Twelve generations?"

"That's approximately how long it would take to travel from this planetary system to yours by conventional space travel. It would take twelve generations, being born and dying, to pilot a ship this distance, if it would even be possible. But because time and space are holographic constructs, it is possible to travel to Earth in the flash of a moment, and you here."

"What is this place?"

"No translation is possible, and the name would be inaudible to your ears," she said. "Nor would my vocal cords be able to reproduce the sound. As a matter of fact, the only reason we are able to communicate with you at all, is because of Cindy's vocal cords. But I can tell you that our planet is not unlike Earth was a few billion years ago, a planet completely covered in water, no land masses."

"What about cities, structures, dwellings? And the beings that came to me, the ones that took Cindy?"

"We have cities and living centers, yes, but you won't be allowed to visit those, not at this time anyway. And you won't encounter any of the beings here. This is a very remote area, and very near one of our largest research facilities. Your appearance among our general population would cause a great stir and negatively impact our societal well-being, just as the knowledge of our existence could upset the balance on Earth. That's why your visit here is so rare... no human has ever been to our world, even though we have been in contact with humans for generations, studying your species and your habitat."

"Why me in particular?"

Cindy studied me a moment. "You are special, Kercy. You were born with numerous birth defects, far exceeding the normal range we had come to expect during our trials. Discussion over bringing you here to study you more closely had begun—to find out what went wrong—until it was ultimately decided against. But more amazing, was your ability to overcome these deformities almost on your own, your ability to assimilate through your singular brand of tenacity, utilizing the gene alterations we had provided you. But even more than that, you've shown no extravagance of curiosity, nor fear, upon meeting our scientists face to face. That is most unusual among humans, a neutrality that keeps you open."

We moved past gleaming plants and creatures that glowed like neon, yet even that description wasn't enough to truly explain what I was seeing, bursts and flashes of light swirling up from our feet. This was the most astonishing habitat. It was obviously some kind of fluid enfolding us, yet I had no difficulty with drag or resistance. The extant gravity I felt functioned quite differently than on Earth. The sensation was one of lightness, a kind of nonlocal force gently pushing from all directions, yet without defining the limitations of this realm. Some sensations I experienced I could find no words for.

At that moment a group of enormous creatures with legs and fins glided above my head, but in a direction away from me, almost like giant salamanders, but with fins and tentacle-like protrusions from their heads. If I had been on Earth seeing this, I would have described them as floating up and away in the sky, weightless and untethered by the laws of physics.

In moments they appeared as mere spots high above me, yet glistening, like stars, or distant planets. Instinctively, I found myself following them, effortlessly and with great joy and anticipation, until Cindy seized my hand to halt my progress. Startled by her presence, and upset by the interruption, I tried to pull my hand away but found I had no real jurisdiction over my movements which gave me a moment of panic, leaving me feeling disoriented and scared. It took a second to realize she had been talking to me, that she was my guide if you will, that I needed her to keep me grounded in this strange and intoxicating world. What I was experiencing was like a drug-induced euphoria, a complete and utter surrender of my corporeal self, a kind of fusion of consciousness with some nonphysical fluid awareness.

"I know it will be difficult, but I need for you to focus as best you can, right now, Kercy. I must cover a great deal in a very short time, as we are bound by certain laws. They can only repurpose me for what will seem like an hour to you, but time is very different here than where you're from. Do you understand?"

Sounds seemed to have substance, as if I could touch them, hold them in my palm. Before me was a cloud of dazzling fragments, like puffs of light that I presumed to be the words Cindy had just spoken to me. I reached out, took one between my fingers, then brought it to my lips and tasted it. A burst of light opened inside my head, exploding out in all directions like some never-ending firework, my tongue alive with flavors both sweet and bland, but bursting into other tastes as well, some bitter, then tart, spicy...

"Kercy. You mustn't touch anything. You must focus on my voice. This world will overwhelm you. Humans are not built for this degree of sensory input. Kercy? Kercy...?"

My mind seemed to be in several places at once, as if I had the eyes of a fly, but instead of those eyes working in concert to focus more clearly, each one was transmitting different information. I swayed with nausea, my brain trying to parse the thousands of colors and movements and shapes shuffling through my brain. When Cindy placed her palms on either side of my face, forcing my attention on her eyes, I felt myself return to my body, as if some part of me had journeyed outside myself.

"Are you okay?" she asked tenderly.

I started sucking at the inside of my mouth, as if it was covered with a film, swishing my tongue back and forth to remove it.

"Kercy, are you okay?"

"Yes." I felt as if I was trying to reassemble myself, my body feeling like scattered puzzle pieces slowly coming back together. "I'm okay now."

Cindy focused her eyes on mine.

"You said something about laws?" I said, able to finally regain some composure. "Laws that govern bringing the dead back to life?"

My tone was a bit sarcastic. Cindy regarded me with a look that I took as disappointment. I knew my comment had been judgmental. After all, if they had the power and ability to bring the dead back, how could laws even apply anymore? It would seem like anything goes at that point.

"Yes, these laws are not impediments to our freedom," Cindy said. "But instead, are collective agreements to assure our survival as a species, to insure the freedom of all. Our laws are choices, not mandates."

I was about to argue the semantics of her statement, then let it drop. Regardless, it made no sense to me. Cindy waited a moment, as if to give me time to realign my attention away from my silent protest.

"Humans are an idiosyncratic species, who are both predator and prey of its own kind, and nearly impossible to tell one from the other," she said. "We have found no other species who kills its own in such staggering numbers."

"We don't eat each other," I said, as if not being cannibals was some defense for the violence; as long as we didn't eat one another, then killing was okay. I couldn't believe the knee-jerk rationale I had offered.

"No, that is the most intriguing aspect. Humans kill out of hatred, jealousy, and greed, which are merely constructs of the mind, nothing more than perceptions, emotions, words. Killing for actual survival among humans makes up such a small portion of the destruction. All other killing is based upon a "feeling" or "prejudice," one usually founded on defective assumptions and misinformation."

Where was this all leading?

"No other creature on your planet has the ability to alter the Earth in the way humans can," Cindy continued. "With that power comes great responsibility. But humankind, while very adept at utilizing the power, seems incapable of self-restraint, of actually being responsible. You pollute, destroy, and eradicate, and set off nuclear weapons with a "let's see what happens" attitude, all in the name of progress, but it's really born of power and greed. You appoint business, the free market, to be the voice of reason and responsibility, to solve the problems society faces: How can profit motive ever be expected to enact humanitarian solutions to anything? It is irrational to think otherwise. Profit motive's goal is profit, not eliminating human suffering or safeguarding your planet."

"What does any of this have to do with me... why am I here?" I said.

"Marine life on Earth is disappearing at an alarming rate, as well as many other species. Humans will soon need to adapt to a dangerous new environment, one mostly of their own making. Oceans will rise and expand, growing ever warmer, while land masses will be greatly diminished, forcing ever growing populations into even smaller, less inhabitable areas."

Maybe that was true theoretically, but not a foregone conclusion. Measures could still be implemented to curb expected disasters. I wasn't sure why I was debating everything Cindy was telling me. Was it fear? On some level, did I agree with her, or should I say, *them,* and their assessment of the situation?

"What does this have to do with me?"

"You are one of the milestones along the evolutionary track. You are able to breathe water, at least thin water at this point. You are able to assimilate. You are able to adapt with amazing speed."

An emptiness opened in my chest. I didn't like the trajectory of this conversation.

"We have the knowledge to mutate genes to positive effect," Cindy said. "Your science is just barely breaching the horizon of this important biological technology, but lacks the restraint to fully implement it in a responsible and safe fashion. No sooner than you are able to, you will turn this newfound power into a profit enterprise and a mechanism of militarization. That is why we would never share our knowledge of gene mutation with humankind. The governments of your planet cannot seem to help from turning every new discovery into a weapon. Atomic energy was weaponized. Computers are weaponized. Vehicles and aircraft and ships are weaponized. Even your religions have been weaponized. And this deity you call God has been weaponized to eradicate each other. And that notion, for some reason, doesn't seem to strike humans as psychotic, deranged..."

I didn't know what to say. I wasn't sure how counter their claims. Yet something still bothered me, irritated me, and I needed clarification. "Are you saying that I am some kind of experiment?"

"You are an important link. Your mother was a second-generation host to receive mutated genes, altered, then implanted, to speed the evolution of humans. Her mother, your grandmother, had been the first-generation host in your lineage."

"You... what the fuck? How could you...? You had no right! My grandmother committed suicide before I ever met her. My mother suffered horrible birth defects, as did I! How could you? What you did was psychotic... deranged! Fucking monstrous!"

Cindy stared at me, waiting for me to calm down. I couldn't look at her. I hated they had chosen her to bring this information to me.

"One of humankind's more destructive and misguided beliefs is Survival of the Fittest," Cindy continued after a minute or so. "It's based on inaccurate observations and faulty conclusions. If survival of the fittest was an actual law of nature, then soon you would see only one lion, one tiger, one elephant, until they decided to find out among themselves which was the fittest. There can only be *one* that is the 'fittest.' The last one standing. All others would be inferior by the very nature of the law itself. Do you see? The so-called law is fraught with fallacy. The myth itself is based upon faulty logic. What your science has observed are not creatures that will destroy themselves to the last organism, or creatures battling over which is the fittest, but animals that remove the weakest among them out of instinct, creatures that will suffer and be unable to prosper, or could draw predators to the pack. But humans have made this their excuse for preying upon the less fortunate, killing those who can be overpowered, who are *unacceptable*. Once killing becomes acceptable for emotional reasons, then hierarchies and ideologies can prosper, along with edicts that restrict freedoms, and all in the name of just and right killing based on survival of the fittest."

"You killed," I said. "I saw what you did to those men. It was ghastly."

"We did kill... to protect you. We had no malice toward those humans. But those men revealed themselves as predators as soon as they attacked you. In many ways, those men were a product of the survival of the fittest myth; they believed it was okay to prey upon beings they deemed unworthy of their ideology, that they viewed as weaker or less valuable."

Then why hadn't they protected Cindy? Why had they allowed those bastards to kill her? "What about the sea creature that attacked two of your own on my dock?" I said. "Why didn't you protect them from your predators?"

"That creature was not our predator, and no being was harmed. What you witnessed was a simulation, a repurposed sea animal allowed to follow its instincts so we could study it. We are working on ways to repopulate your oceans and waterways. The two beings you thought were destroyed had been repurposed for that end."

"What is repurposing?" I asked. "What I mean is, how does it work? How do you perform this literally death-defying feat?"

Cindy seemed a bit frustrated with me, then brought her eyes level with mine. "I shudder to think what humans would do with that knowledge, weaponizing this ability without a second thought, all in the name of protecting the free, while in reality creating super soldiers, repurposed authoritarians and corporate magnates, promoting suicide missions, and prolonging life for the richest among you past its normal limits, on and on... that's why we have rules governing repurposing... Besides, what's the point in explaining things to you that you cannot possibly understand."

"Try me," I felt a bit cocky in the moment; I didn't like being spoken down to.

"Okay, but first you must answer me this. If you can, I will gladly explain the mechanism of repurposing..." She paused a moment. "Explain to me the force that marks the difference between life and death on your planet. Not the mere functioning of the organs, brain and body, but the life-compelling influence that animates all humans and creatures on your planet? What is that called? Where does it exist? What happens to it when you die?"

I thought I knew the answer and started to tell her, but the thoughts in my head weren't really ideas I could verbalize, but more like vague impressions clustered around an unknowable truth that had to suffice for knowledge. Was it soul? If so, what was *soul* but a word that we seemed to have no real definition for, using an inadequate description of *spirit* to explain it, the idea of spirit in and of itself undefined? Consciousness then? What was that after all, but an awareness of itself and the world? Could that really spark the difference between life and death. If so, what was the source of consciousness? Was it the mind? But what was the mind but a storage unit, a hard drive of memories and thought processes and data? And where was it really? In the brain? Science couldn't answer this most basic tenet of life and in the end, I had no idea what the animating force of all life was, where it existed, where it went when we died.

"I don't know," I finally said.

"That is the problem. You must know that animating source

before you can manipulate it, or work with it. Humans call it spirit, or soul, or even God, with no greater understanding, or should I say, no *experience* of this force other than to cling to those empty words and use them to express what is inexpressible. That's not enough. You must enter that animating source with your entire being, immerse yourself fully. Then, and only then, can you begin to understand how this works. It involves not knowledge, but *knowing*."

"Aren't they the same?"

"Knowledge is the work of the brain. Knowing is the essence of your being, of the force underlying all things..."

"So, why do you have laws governing repurposing? I mean, doesn't that impede your progress?"

"Progress. I know humans pride themselves on progress. But the truth is, human progress has been repeatedly hindered by greed and hatred. Why do you still drive petroleum-powered vehicles even when they are destroying the very planet you depend on for survival? Why do you continue to burn fossil fuels for energy with so many alternatives available, ones you've yet to find because no one is looking for them? Why does widespread poverty exist on Earth amidst so much wealth? Why do your technological advances come in the form of enhanced gaming for the bored, or new ways to purchase things over a phone, or social networking which makes people even more faceless and alienated from one another and them-selves? Or products with built-in obsolescence, which only manages to bloat your landfills and ruin your oceans? Or medical devices and procedures too expensive for average humans to benefit from? And now the richest among you have hopes of colonizing another planet in your solar system and profit from joy rides into space, all the while diverting resources away from Earth which you have still failed to learn how to care for. That is truly gluttonous and insane and we fear you don't even see that. Your so-called *progress* is dubious at best. True progress benefits all, not just the few who profit from it."

"If you judge us so harshly, then why do you purport to help us?

What even gives you the right to think you can just affect our evolution?"

At this, Cindy scoffed a bit. "Humans still believe they don't need each other or anyone or anything else to survive. They don't even need their planet, or the universe for that matter. You don't realize you are part of a larger system of existence. That is your worst self-deception."

"Why won't you answer me?"

"I just did. Now it's time to go."

"No, you can't just lay all that on me without answering my question."

"Actually, I can. Let's go now... or you will have to find your way back alone. And that could be dangerous, or impossible."

"But I have a thousand more questions! You can't just leave things like this!"

TWENTY-EIGHT

Cindy guided me through a maze of exotic plants, past a short stand of shimmering tree-like growths. I thought I spied a domed structure in a distant valley. "It's time to go." Cindy said.

"What about that?" I pointed toward the rounded edifice, wondering if it was some kind of laboratory or something.

"Even if I was able to take you to it, you'd be unable to breathe the water. It is too dense. You're not ready for that yet. But we must go now..."

"No... I need more answers... this isn't enough!"

"Unfortunately, Kercy, it will have to suffice. We hoped to give you enough so you could come away with some understanding of what is happening. The rest of the answers will come in time..."

"In time? From whom?"

"In time... when you're ready. And the answers will come from you. Your own wisdom and knowledge, Kercy, will provide you with everything you need to know."

I wasn't at all satisfied with her answer, when Cindy took my hand and walked me back to the demarcation between the dense and thin water. We swam out from that waterline until Cindy flipped her body and started swimming downward. I held on, kicking my legs, but she seemed to require no help, her movements effortless. The strangest feeling poured through me, a vibration starting in my toes that sizzled up along my limbs and torso like electric current, an intense tickling sensation that bordered on pain and filled my head and I could tell I was losing consciousness, unable to stay focused. Cindy continued pulling me, while near the frame of my vision I spied a large creature moving toward us. We approached the bottom or something, I guess, the rocks and stones glistening like gems, so sharp and clear. The tickling had turned to heat, and I was acutely aware of the blood rushing through my veins. Cindy was trying to move me quicker, but I had become sluggish and distracted, colors and lights flashing and surging all around me. The creature was drawing closer as Cindy dragged me toward a bright obstacle of light. I didn't want to leave this world, my sense of self fragmenting into particles of awareness, as if I existed in thousands of different places all at once, my consciousness capable of processing infinite threads of sensory input. I was everything and nothing and Cindy pulled me harder toward the light. I fought with what little strength I had, certain that if I passed through it I would no longer exist.

"You must go through, Kercy, or you will die an unbearable death here," she cried, pushing me toward the light.

"You said I would be safe here! I thought you said I would be safe!"

"Go, Kercy! Now!"

The creature grew larger the closer it came.

Cindy pointed past me and told me to swim in the direction she was showing me. "Go now, and don't turn back for anything," she shouted, a fear in her face I hadn't seen before.

I kicked my legs and started swimming away from her, glancing back a few times to see where she was. That's when I saw her slumped over, unmoving, suspended above the bottom as if hanging by a rope from her waist. Just then the huge fish-like creature that had been pursuing us, swept toward her, engulfing her completely, then slowly finned away until it disappeared from view.

In spite of knowing she wasn't real, or was at best some kind of simulation, it was horrific to watch just the same. I swam away, not quite sure where I was going, suddenly disoriented. I felt a great pressure on my body, pushing in from all sides as if about to crush me, the pounding in my head unbearable. I glanced around, everything looking the same, but the glowing water was gone. When I looked to my right, I saw a huge silhouette headed toward me. In seconds I could see it clearly, the same creature which had just devoured Cindy. I panicked and started swimming away, knowing it was impossible to outdistance it as it swept above me like a huge shadow. My heart stopped. The huge creature passed so close that the backwash from its gigantic body pulled me sideways, sending me tumbling head over heels.

Before I could regain my balance, confusion overtook me, my mind a muddle of sensations, making it difficult to reorient myself. The creature had disappeared momentarily but was now returning, coming directly for me, moving deliberately but with such a casualness that it seemed odd that it meant to harm me. But when it opened its huge maw with rows of teeth glistening like polished glass, my mind went blank.

It was upon me now; trying to escape was futile and I gave in. The darkness of its huge jaws closing around me suffused me with an eerie sort of peace, a liberation now just seconds away.

I still don't know how the being snatched me from certain death, but the creature, like the ones that came to the cottage, swam briskly, dragging me along, toward a patch of glowing water. When we reached it, it pushed me toward it, imploring me with body gyrations to go through. I tried, but the resistance of this new medium was palpable and unpleasant. I fought past the barrier, as if clawing my way through a solid wall. When I got to the other side, the water changed again, becoming so heavy and cold and dark and I found myself struggling to hold my breath, frantically swimming for a faint smudge of light above me.

Time seemed to slow

My lungs felt as if they'd burst, the diffuse area of light growing more brilliant, expanding in all directions. When I finally reached it, I exploded from the water gasping and coughing and trying to get my bearings. The sun glistened across the surface of the water and I felt warmth on my face, even though I was freezing.

Daylight?

How could that be?

Then someone called my name. I spun around, the cold beginning to steal my strength.

"Kercy," Mallory yelled from the dock. "Over here."

I put my head down and started swimming in his direction, my heart pounding. It was hard to breathe, my legs growing heavy, pulling me down. It must be the cold, I figured. Never had I experienced such acute pain. Just when my arms became too sluggish and numb to move, Mallory grabbed my wrist, while someone else grabbed the other, and they hoisted me onto the dock. I landed on the boards unable to move, shaking, shuddering.

"You're freezing to death," Mallory said, trying to rub heat into my limbs. "You're covered in goosebumps."

I glanced at my arm to see what he was talking about. My skin was covered in tiny bumps. I had never experienced that before.

"Find some blankets, quick!" Mallory shouted to no one in particular. "Tony, help me get her into the house.

Together the two men lifted me, then Tony slung me over his shoulder in a fireman's carry while Mallory patted me on the face and arms.

"Stay with us, Kercy," he said, tracking along with the man carrying me, who was almost in a full run now.

When they got me inside, the man placed me on the couch and someone dragged a blanket over me, then another. Mallory sat down next to me.

"Jesus, your lips are blue. Crank that heat up," Mallory yelled toward two men standing near the hallway, then turned back toward me. "I'm sorry, Kercy, but I've got to get you out of those clothes."

He closed his eyes and fumbled with my jeans, then my top. I was shaking so badly I was no help. When he got my clothes off, he yelled toward one of the men, "Tony, let's get her onto the floor. The couch is soaked from her wet clothes. Somebody find some more damn blankets!"

Mallory continued rubbing my arms, then my legs. "Come on, Kercy," Mallory said. "Don't close your eyes." He slapped me on the cheek, then rubbed my arms again. It took several minutes before I could stop shaking.

"Anybody think to put some tea on? Let's go people, I can't think of everything here," Mallory shouted.

"Got it right here," a woman said, rushing in with a steaming cup.

"Thanks, Ronnie," Mallory said. "Sit up just a bit, Kercy. Get some of this in you."

I bent up and took a sip. The cold was beginning to leave my body, the shakes subsiding.

"There you go," Mallory said. "There you go. The color's returning. Here, drink some more."

In a few minutes I was able to sit up. Mallory wrapped another blanket around my shoulders.

"Thanks," I said, holding the cup between my hands. I had never experienced cold like that before.

"That was some scare," Mallory said. "I thought you were—"

"I'm fine."

"Good, good. You've been gone for two days and I didn't know where—"

"Two days? Seriously?"

"Yeah, my agents found your boat here two days ago. They called me and I've been here ever since. I'm glad you're okay. I called a chopper to get you off this rock."

"No! No more helicopters, no more hospitals. If your men haven't packed up all my clothes, I'm going to change and drive Ben's boat back to the harbor."

"No, let's get you checked out first," Mallory said. "I'll get his boat back. Take the bird."

"You really are kind of sweet when you're not holding out on me. I'll be fine. Let me up." I was a bit shaky when I stood, but quickly regained my equilibrium.

"What do you think I'm not telling you?"

I stared at him. "You knew all along that I was one of the *hybrids*. Even when I asked you and Jacob the other night, you both acted like you had no idea what I was talking about."

"I didn't know. Jacob suspected, but he didn't know either. How could he?"

I shook my head. "I'm getting dressed, then I'm driving back."

"Wait. How did you find out for sure?"

"That's a long story."

TWENTY-NINE

After dressing, I found an old jacket in my closet. Much of my bedroom furniture was trashed, except for a few screws on the floor, and a lamp. After checking the bathroom for anything I might need, I noticed how quiet the house was. In the living room I found my wallet on the coffee table where I'd left it. On my way to the back door, I could see from the kitchen window that the only boat left at the dock was mine. With the FBI boats gone I figured Mallory probably left with them, until I heard someone come up behind me.

"Can I get a lift?" Mallory said.

"What if I said no? Had you thought about that when you sent everyone away?"

"Sure... I'd call the chopper back."

He followed me down to the dock.

I started the engine, then untied the ropes. Mallory climbed in and offered to drive. I shook my head and pushed down on the throttle, pointing the skiff toward the harbor. The wind, though it was freezing, was an invigorating rush of reality. I had no time to process any of what had happened. The sun was about an hour from setting and the water was smeared with pinks and yellows, like oil paints on a shiny steel surface.

"We need to talk about where you've been the last two days," Mallory shouted over the outboard noise.

I kept my eyes straight ahead, my hands on the steering wheel, pretending not to hear him. When I pulled into the harbor, I guided the boat toward Ben's office. Mallory jumped up on the dock and secured the front of the boat when I cut the engine.

"Let me buy you dinner," Mallory said.

"Can't." I hurried past the harbor office and up the back steps to Jacob's apartment. I pounded on the door calling his name. He seemed surprised to see me when he pulled the door open.

"I want to know everything you know," I said, pushing past him into the apartment. Beyond him was a young woman sitting on the couch. She looked up from the television.

"Ms. Powell," Jacob said. "This is my girlfriend, Lola. Lola, Ms. Powell."

I nodded toward her. "I want to talk to you," I said to Jacob.

"Can it wait? We're watching a movie."

"The movie can wait. Pause it... or switch the damn thing off... whatever..."

Jacob nodded toward his girlfriend and she picked up the remote and aimed it at the television. Jacob walked toward the door so I followed. We went down his back steps and walked down the dock away from his apartment.

"What's this about...?" Jacob said, more curious than upset.

"Why did you lie to me? When I asked you about the hybrids, why did you lie?"

"I didn't..."

"You knew I was one of them and you didn't say a word."

Mallory ambled over, not saying anything. Jacob looked over at him, then back at me, then exhaled and took his eyes briefly to the weathered deck boards. "I told Agent Mallory that I figured you were, since I had observed some of the same behaviors in you as I had in my own mother."

"So, your mother was one? A hybrid?"

Jacob nodded. "So was her mother."

"Ben's wife? But didn't she...?"

"Yes, she died in an insane asylum."

I remembered when Ben had her committed. She'd been hurting herself and had become despondent. She'd been institutionalized for several years before she passed. Ben had been devastated.

"And my great grandmother," Jacob said without affect. "She threw herself out a window."

"They were all hybrids?"

"Don't know for sure? Except for my mother. She told me about the beings, how they'd come to her, what they looked like. She thought they were angels at first, then she thought Satan had sent them. Then she just didn't talk about them anymore and one day I came home and she was dead. Overdose on sedatives."

I felt bad for Ben. He'd been through so much and I wondered if he'd known about any of this. Mallory stood by, just listening, as if he was hearing it all for the first time.

"Then you must be a hybrid too?" I said to Jacob.

He nodded, then walked over to the edge of the dock, and stepped off into the water. Mallory gasped as Jacob sank in the clear water. But then Jacob stopped about three feet below the surface. He looked up at us and it was unsettling seeing his hair drifting atop his head, tiny bubbles on his face, his features distorted by refraction. Mallory and I both froze, staring. Without taking his eyes from us, Jacob opened his mouth wide and paused a second before inhaling deeply, filling his lungs with water, his chest swelling, then just as smoothly, a second later, exhaling water and bubbles. He repeated the process several times, smiling once before exhaling. His arms and legs hung motionless, as if he had attained some kind of neutral buoyancy and was not required to tread water to stay suspended.

Mallory was shocked and stared on wide-eyed and speechless.

Jacob could breathe dense water. I was amazed as well. He climbed from the water and I could tell he was not the least bit cold.

"Does that answer all your questions?" Jacob said.

"You were wrong," I said.

"About what?"

"Their motivation. They are not trying to speed their own evolution. They are trying to speed ours! They have decided that it is in our best interest to direct and accelerate the evolution of the human race to adapt to a changing and, in their belief, a soon to be inhospitable planet."

"What?" Mallory said.

"They've mastered the ability to mutate genes, to change life, create new forms," I said.

"What difference?" Jacob said. "Look at what I am able to do? Who cares what their motivation is?"

I was flabbergasted. "That doesn't bother you? They took it upon themselves to alter the human race, our life on this planet? They just removed free will."

Jacob scoffed. "You are making way too much of this. If anything, they're helping us. No charge."

"No charge? What about the price your mother paid? And Ben's wife? Ben's wife's mother? My mother? All the women whose lives have been ruined? Is that just collateral damage for the greater good?"

Mallory was pensive, seemingly annoyed by Jacob's ambivalence, yet he still said nothing.

"How about your girlfriend Lolita up there?" I said. "Does she know what you are?"

"Lola..." he corrected. "And yes, she does. She is one as well. And she's pregnant with my child. Do you know what that means?"

"No, and neither do you," I said. "You have no idea what the long-range effects of gene mutation are? They can lie dormant for years, until adulthood or middle age, then suddenly, for reasons unknown, become full-blown life-threatening diseases. No one knows the long-term effects of such manipulations. They are experiments based on theories and incomplete science. And even if these beings have figured it all out, they still have no right to choose unwitting test subjects. No scientist does, no matter how intelligent or accomplished. No matter what the supposed greater good is!"

"I've got to get back upstairs," Jacob said.

I shook my head. How could he accept what had happened to his mother, his grandmother, himself? Was this super-human ability to breathe underwater worth the risk, the loss of free will, the denial of the right to choose? Was the payoff to him worth more than his own mother's life? Had the human race come to that point? Had we justified enough atrocities, given up enough civil liberties, made ourselves believe that the end is more important than the means? Were these baffling beings right about humankind, that we were nothing but profiteers and soulless speculators, that we had hampered our own progress in exchange for a bigger payday?

Jacob walked up the steps, never looking back. I glanced over at Mallory. He was scribbling in his notebook. I turned and walked toward the parking lot. Mallory hurried after me.

"Wait," he said.

I spun toward him.

"Let's get something to eat," he said. "I need to tell you some things."

"Like what, Mallory? Did you just hear what Jacob said? Or did you know already?"

"No, Kercy, I didn't know any of it. But I do know that we need to step up our game. This scenario is entirely different... and... unacceptable. I'm sure my superiors will agree."

"You're sure they'll agree? You don't sound sure at all. You seem a bit shaken by all of this. Maybe some part of you believes your superiors already know what is going on and haven't bothered to tell you yet."

Mallory scratched at his neck and shook his head. "I don't know what to believe anymore. But I need your help, Kercy. You are the only person who has actually communicated with them. Look, I have a couple of ROVs arriving tomorrow morning, as well as several Navy Seal divers. If you can help us, we can find—"

"Save your resources, Agent Mallory." I started walking toward Cindy's car, hoping I hadn't lost the keys during my journey to the underworld.

"What are you talking about? Wait, stop, will you? This is our chance—"

"No, it isn't," I said, glaring at him. "You will never find them... because they aren't there."

"What... not there? I don't get it."

"I don't either, but they are not in Georgian Bay, or Canada, or... even on this planet. They are not here. And neither is the sea creature I saw that devoured two of their beings. I was informed that that had been a simulation. These beings can repurpose the dead, reanimate them. But they have laws governing... ah the hell with it!" I glared at Mallory. "These beings are an enigma, and you will never ever find them, unless they want to be found. And while they seem benevolent, I believe they could also be extremely dangerous."

I turned away and walked to Cindy's car. Mallory followed, not saying anything, but staying close.

"Come on, Kercy, you can't just run out on me," he said when I unlocked the door.

"Yes, I can." I slid in behind the steering wheel.

"I can subpoena you to appear in front of a Grand Jury, you know," he said with a sour look, as if he'd bitten into some forbidden fruit. "I don't want to do that, Kercy."

"Then don't." I started the engine. I backed out of the space and headed toward the street. When I turned onto the road, I wasn't even sure what I was doing next. I just knew I needed to eat, get gas, then leave Elico and drive back to New York.

THIRTY

After packing, I figured I would get gas across the street, then start driving. It was dark, already seven-thirty when I filled the tank. It would be late when I reached the city, but planned to stop at a motel if I got too tired. As I was placing the gas nozzle back into the pump, someone called my name. It was a man's voice. I figured it was Mallory.

"Kercy," the man said again, walking toward me.

The light wasn't great around the pumps, so I didn't see his face clearly at first, but I knew it wasn't Mallory. Then I recognized him. I took a step back. "Dad?"

"Hi, Kercy," he said.

"How... I thought you were...?" I was stunned. He moved closer and stopped within a few of feet of me, beneath the light. He looked exactly the same as the afternoon he'd left me fishing on the dock fifteen years earlier. He hadn't aged.

"You are so beautiful," he said, shaking his head as if he was the one seeing the ghost.

"What's going on?" I was not at all comfortable with seeing him. "How did you find me here?"

He hung his head a moment, then brought his tear-filled eyes up to mine. "They promised me I could see you one last time. But that I would have to wait until you knew everything."

"You're repurposed."

"I guess. I don't know what they call it. They found me. I guess I had drowned. By the look of you, that must have been a lot of years ago. You're a woman now. It was close to your eighteenth birthday the last time I saw you."

I nodded. It wasn't that I was unhappy to see him, as much as I was angry that these beings played with life and death like it was some kind of game show.

"I don't have much time, the way I understand it," he said. "I've been milling around town since yesterday."

"How did you find me tonight? Here at this exact gas station? At this exact time?"

"I knew you'd be at the diner tonight, but I didn't want to create a scene over, so I waited until you came over here to get gas."

"But how did you know I would come over here?"

He shrugged. "I just did."

"I don't know what to say..."

"Is your mother gone now?"

I nodded.

"I figured as much." His head bobbed lightly as if agreeing with his own conclusions. "I've got a lot of regrets, you know. Some about how I treated your mother. Mostly about how I treated you. I'm so sorry about that."

"Yeah... well, it couldn't have been easy, your whole life getting turned upside down when I came along. And what a mess I was."

He stood looking at the asphalt a long time, his head shaking, his hands at his sides. "I knew about them. What they'd done to your mother, impregnating her. I knew you had come from them and not me. Every time I looked at you I thought of them." His gaze fell to the ground. Ashamed maybe, or angry?

"You knew?"

"Yes, I knew," he said, wiping his cheek. "But your mother, she said it was for a higher purpose. I didn't care about any higher purpose, until she explained."

I felt like I'd been kicked in the stomach. How could she feel that way? Everything they'd done to her, to our family, was all right as long as it fueled some supposedly higher purpose?

"I'm so sorry," I said.

"I'm not. I knew that the only reason she was able to get pregnant was because of them. If not for them, then you would never have been born. She knew that too. You were the higher purpose she was talking about. Even so, I still couldn't get past it, and that's what I regret."

"You shouldn't regret that. I'm glad you couldn't get past it."

He looked at me. "I've got to go."

I nodded, then decided to hug him. When he hugged me back, he kissed me on the cheek and the cold of his lips unhinged me. I took a deep breath and tried to convince myself that the sentiments were real, even while knowing *he* wasn't. He smiled and walked away in the direction of the harbor. He looked pathetic, still wearing the same clothes as the day he vanished. Was any of this encounter real? Or was it some attempt by the beings to win my consent, or garner some support for their plan? But why, they certainly didn't need it. Or had they used my dead father to mine more information from me? To what end? How did they even know where I was?

I started Cindy's Volvo and drove into the night for as long as I could, until the road melted into a mirage of infinite water and I knew I needed to find a motel.

THIRTY-ONE

I had been back in the city for a few weeks and still hadn't contacted Gerald. He'd left numerous messages on my service at home and although I wanted to call him, there were things I needed to do, clarification I needed to get. My nights had been restless when I could sleep, and terrifying when I couldn't. Most nights when I did sleep it was only because the blaring television detoured my brain long enough for unconsciousness to take root. And that wasn't really sleep as much as passing out from exhaustion.

Agent Mallory phoned several times on my landline. I avoided contact with him as well, until one night I took his call. We talked for almost an hour, recapping my visit to underwater world. That's what I called it as I had no other name for it. Mallory wanted me to join his task force.

"No thanks," I said. "I can't sleep as it is."

"Just think it over. You'll set your own hours. Basically consulting. You'd be invaluable to the team."

"No. I can't. Have you spoken with Jacob?"

Mallory hesitated. "Yeah, a week or so ago. Ice is starting to form, so activity has stopped."

"How is he?"

Mallory hesitated again. "Honestly... I think he's crazy. He and his girlfriend have been spending time out on the lake until it started freezing, trying to make contact with the beings. I didn't ask him to do it."

"But you wouldn't mind if he did, right?"

"I'm just trying to do my job, Kercy. You could be a huge help. Just give it some thought. I've got to go."

In the days to follow I bought a new cellphone and thought about having my landline disconnected, but then Gerald wouldn't be able to contact me. I had to admit, getting his messages were so comforting, even though I never meant to torture him by not responding.

Gerald dropped by a couple of times, but I never answered the door. I hadn't showered in a week, or brushed my hair. Mostly I stared at the television, while my mind rolled over the events of a few weeks earlier, especially the beings' assessment of humankind and our world. At the time I had rejected most of their theories outright, but now, after much unwelcome contemplation, I wasn't so sure they were wrong.

I went to the bathroom and got out the pregnancy kit the grocery store had delivered with my last order, and soon confirmed what Cindy had told me was true. I couldn't believe it, caught somewhere between elation and panic. How could I be pregnant? I remembered what my dad had told me in Elico that night, that if it hadn't been for the beings, I would never have been born. Had they lied to me about this child being Gerald's? And how long had I been pregnant? There had been no signs, so maybe it was recent.

I made an appointment with my gynecologist. Before the receptionist hung up, I asked if it was possible to determine the DNA of an unborn child. "Yes," she said. "It's called a Chorionic Villus Sampling. We collect a sample tissue from the placenta using a needle. But there is a risk of miscarriage."

"How large a risk?" I said.

"Small, but it's there nonetheless. There is no way of knowing ahead of time."

"What would I need to do this?"

"Just some DNA from the suspected father, then yours of course, but we'll collect that when you're here."

"How... what can you use to gather his DNA?" I said. "Would a toothbrush work?"

"Absolutely. If you have his toothbrush that would work fine."

"Even if he hasn't used it in a month or so?"

"That's fine, it would still provide a reliable source of DNA."

Four weeks later I went in for my appointment. We had agreed she would perform an ultrasound to determine the approximate date of conception, since my periods were too erratic and unreliable. Then a follow up CVS to collect the DNA sample. Imagining what we would see during the ultrasound put me in full panic mode as I sat in her waiting room. It was about twenty minutes before they called me. Doctor Conner and I talked a bit, but I wasn't in a chatty mood; I wanted to get this over with. Gerald had continued to call and I continued to avoid him. I thought about just phoning him and telling him I needed more time by myself, but that seemed unreasonable. So I opted to avoid him altogether.

"Your blood pressure is really high," Doctor Conner said. "What's going on?"

"Just scared. I'll be fine once we're done here."

"Want to talk about it?"

I shook my head, then raised my blouse up. She squirted gel onto my tummy. "Kercy, relax," she said, touching my hand clamped to the armrest. "Sweetie, your knuckles are white."

I took a deep breath, but it did nothing to untie the knot in my stomach. She gently moved the device in a circular motion through the gel, her eyes on the screen. "There we go," she said. "Don't you want to see?"

"How far along am I?"

"Six or seven weeks."

She had not cried out or shot back in her chair from revulsion or fear and that gave me a moment of relief. "Is the baby okay?"

"Everything looks fine."

I glanced toward the screen. "Boy or girl?"

"Too early to tell," she said, smiling. "Take a look. There's nothing to be afraid of."

If only that were true. "Are you going to perform the CVS now?"

"We can, Kercy, but I want you to know there is a risk of miscarriage? Is knowing the DNA of your child that important right now? There's plenty of time to determine the father after your child is born. Are you thinking of not keeping it?"

On my drive back from the lake cottage I had decided to establish if indeed I was pregnant, and if possible, to determine the DNA so that I knew for sure the baby was Gerald's and not theirs. It had been almost three months ago when I had made a trip up to the cottage by myself to check on the new construction. The first night I was there I had another experience like the one when Gerald was with me. A dream I told myself. The beings came to me the same way, three of them, they scanned me, the pain of the probe between my legs. But what if it hadn't been a dream? Even if the beings seemed benevolent, I still found it impossible to trust them. And if the baby was theirs, or if it had defects like I did when I was born, I had decided to terminate the pregnancy. But this child could be the only chance I would ever have at conceiving. That must have been how my mother felt.

"I'll give you a minute," Doctor Conner said, standing to leave the room.

"What is the risk?" I said.

"Pardon me?"

"What is the risk of miscarriage? Percentage wise?"

Doctor Conner smiled weakly. "What difference does that make, Kercy? Believe me, you shouldn't make your decision based on the odds. If I told you there was a ten percent chance, and then you miscarried, would knowing that the odds had been in your favor make you feel any better about losing your baby?"

I closed my eyes to rest my mind.

"I can tell you this, if the odds were not in your favor, I wouldn't even perform a CVS. But that doesn't preclude the risk, Kercy. We could reschedule if you like. I'll be back in a bit."

"No... wait..." I considered all I'd been through as a child, the operations, the taunting, the social vacuum. I thought of Jacob's mother and how she must have suffered unable to tell anyone but her son, and Ben's wife, landing in a mental hospital, my own mother and how it had destroyed her marriage. I thought about Gerald and if the child was his, then he should have a say, but if I knew the child was his, then there'd be no need to consider this. And if it was theirs, then I didn't want Gerald to even know about it.

"I need to know," I said.

"Are you sure?"

I nodded, wiping my cheeks, having difficulty swallowing.

THIRTY-TWO

Doctor Conner told me it would take at least two weeks to get the DNA results. I wanted so bad to call Gerald, but I'd come this far without contact. I could wait another fourteen days. I decided to hit the grocery store on the way home, then maybe the coffee shop. Walking felt great. The day was brisk, and seeing all the Christmas shoppers lifted me. The sound of traffic, car horns and the hum of tires on pavement, made the day real and tangible. I needed this more than anything.

Snow flurries had just started to fall when I stepped into the coffee shop. It was packed, but the murmur of strangers was reassuring, the smell of roasting coffee beans, the rush of the espresso machines. How I'd missed this.

"Kercy," someone said.

When I turned to see Gerald standing there, the day collapsed.

"Kercy, when did you get back?"

I wasn't going to lie. Again. I had lied to Gerald so many times.

"Several weeks ago," I said, watching his expression flatten.

"Why didn't you... have you gotten my messages?"

"I did, Gerald. And I'm sorry I haven't called you. It's been crazy since I got back."

"Are you free for dinner tonight?"

I wasn't ready for this, catching up, the questions, what happened at the cottage—but when would I be? How could I ever explain to Gerald what had happened with Cindy, with Jacob.

"Kercy? Everything okay?"

"Yeah, sorry... I've been distracted." The barista called my name. "That's my coffee. Did you order?"

"No, I saw you through the window..."

I went to the counter and grabbed it, then turned back toward Gerald. "What are you doing right now?"

"No classes the rest of the day," he said.

"Come back to my place. But please, no questions. Let's just watch movies and eat popcorn, okay?"

When we got back to the brownstone, Gerald took his coat off and found the remote. I changed into my pajamas.

"If you want, you can spend the night," I said.

"You sure?" he said.

"Yeah."

Gerald put on the sweats he'd left at my place. While he was changing, I made popcorn and grabbed the package of cookies. Later that evening, after watching a couple of movies, I thought about suggesting a bath, but instead opted for a shower by myself. Gerald graded papers. Life almost seemed normal. I had just soaped my arms and chest when I noticed blood running down the drain. I put my hands between my legs and came up with bloody fingers.

"No, no, no!" I shut the shower off and placed a washcloth between my legs. "No, please no!"

I hurried over to my phone and dialed Doctor Conner's service. The washcloth was soaked with blood. "Gerald!" I screamed. "Gerald! Come here!"

Gerald came through the door just as I heard my ringtone. "Doctor Conner, I'm bleeding pretty bad!"

"Call an ambulance. I'll meet you at the hospital," she said.

Gerald dialed 911, then helped me get dressed. The ambulance arrived several minutes later.

THIRTY-THREE

Doctor Conner came in the room. She looked at Gerald, then at me. "Gerald, would you mind giving us a minute?" I said. Gerald squeezed my hand, then left the room.

"I'm so sorry, Kercy," Doctor Conner said.

I was crushed. Why did I choose to do the DNA test? How would I tell Gerald?

"Kercy," Doctor Conner said, reading my expression. "Don't do this to yourself. The odds are very low the DNA test caused this. Miscarriages just happen sometimes. There are many factors that can cause it."

"The day I have the test it happens!" I blurted out through my tears. "What are the odds of that?" I couldn't stop crying, I was so ashamed. So stupid.

Doctor Conner waited. "Don't blame yourself," she finally said. "If you conceived once, you can again. We thought that wasn't even possible, remember? But obviously it is."

How was I going to explain this to Gerald? It was a fucking nightmare.

"Kercy, I need to go do something," Doctor Conner said. "But I'll be right back. There is something else I'd like to talk to you about if you are up to it. Or it can wait."

"No, now's okay. Can you send Gerald back?"

"Sure," she said, opening the door. A moment later he stepped in.

"Everything okay?" He came over to sit next to me.

"Not really. I have a lot I need to tell you, Gerald. But it'll have to wait until we get home."

I asked him how his classes were going. We talked about regular stuff, his parents, his sister who lives in L.A., his car breaking down. I wanted to share regular stuff with him, but nothing was regular anymore. I would often tell him about Cindy, or my doctoral advisor, or a movie coming out that I wanted to see because Cindy had worked on it, or needing advice on some research. But the marrow of my thoughts was either preposterous, gruesome or sorrowful. I wanted to tell him how Jacob had reacted to the beings tampering with human genomes, how proud he was of his ability to breathe underwater, how Cindy had been repurposed, how I'd had a conversation with my dead father.

"Oh my God," I said, struck by a notion that had not occurred to me before. Agent Mallory's agenda was suddenly crystal clear. How could I have been so blind?

"What is it, Kercy? Are you all right?"

"I'm fine."

Doctor Conner knocked on the door, then came in.

"Can Gerald stay?" I asked her.

"Um... probably best if we speak alone," she said.

Gerald leaned over and kissed me on the forehead. "I'll be right outside."

When the door clicked shut, Doctor Conner sat in the chair next to the bed. "I don't really know how to start this conversation, Kercy," she said. "So, I'm just going to jump right in." She reached into the pocket of her lab jacket and brought out a small clear capsule no more than a centimeter long and handed it to me.

"What is this?" I said.

"That came out when the surgeon performed the D&C..."

I inspected it closer, then held it up to the light. It was obviously organic tissue, but it was technological as well. Like a small diode, or computer chip, with some kind of faint, nearly imperceptible luminescence. This was how the beings knew my every move, knew when I was at the cottage, knew when I was being attacked. But when had they placed that inside me? It couldn't have just been last week. Then I recalled my dream when I was almost eighteen, the beings coming to me in my bedroom, my first period. It hadn't been a dream after all.

"I have to go, Kercy," Doctor Conner said. "You're going to be just fine."

"Have you ever seen anything like this before?" I said.

"No, but if I had to guess, I'd say it was some kind of tracking device." Before she left, she told me I should make an appointment for a follow up visit.

"Sure," I said. She smiled weakly and let herself out.

Gerald walked in.

"I think they'll release me in the morning," I said. "Can you come by?"

THIRTY-FOUR

Special Agent Mallory was still holding back information from me. And he wasn't answering his phone, letting everything go to voice-mail. Gerald was in the kitchen toasting raisin bread and making us tea. We'd taken a cab home from the hospital and Doctor Conner had given me a list of things to avoid after my D&C, and told me to take it easy. So, I was trying, except for my agitation over Agent Mallory's agenda. I finally figured out why he wanted me to join his task force, why I was so important to his investigation.

Gerald came in with the toast and tea and set them on the table. I smiled and thanked him and knew this was going to be one of the worst days of my life; I planned to tell Gerald everything.

We ate in silence as I tried to formulate an outline for how I wanted to proceed. I felt like I wanted to start with the baby, which would lead to why I had made the decisions I did, and so on. Of course, I knew that Gerald might be so upset over what I had done, that discussion of the miscarriage, and why I had withheld the pregnancy from him, may end things right there. Wasn't that rich? Me upset with Mallory for withholding information, and then not even telling Gerald I was pregnant with his child. Or at least it could have been his child; and that, after all, was the whole problem; the doubt cast over everything.

After a sip of tea, and a brief warning about everything he was about to hear, I launched into what was sure to end up being an evening of discussion that could easily spill over into the early morning hours. No sooner had I started telling him about the pregnancy, my eyes started leaking tears. He listened quietly, reaching over to hold my hand at one point, until the part about the CVS.

"Why did you need a DNA test?" he said. "Did you think the baby wasn't mine?"

I hadn't even allowed for the possibility that Gerald would think I had slept with someone else. I hadn't wanted to jump too far ahead and muddle the entire discussion by talking about the beings.

"Sort of. But not because I slept with anyone else. The truth is, I have never had sex with any man but you."

"You've never had sex with anyone before me?"

I should have set out some rules of interrogation before we started, that all questions would need to be held until the end of my explanation.

"Okay, so I planned to tell you this anyway, but no, I have had sex before you... just not with a man."

Gerald was puzzled for a second, then nodded as if he understood.

"It was with Cindy. In college. When we were roommates." I had not expected to tell this part until much later, but my outline was shot and I decided to just follow a more organic telling of my life story based partly on Gerald's reactions. I told him about my birth defects, about the many operations, about my arrested development, how Cindy had helped me, how we'd grown so close, how we both preferred men, but also shared a sexual bond with each other. I explained how that bond had ultimately been responsible for my incredible transition to womanhood. "That was back then, though, in college. Before you and I met." I wanted him to understand I had not been unfaithful. He listened patiently.

"So why the DNA testing?" he said. "Couldn't it have waited until the baby was born? I mean, why was it even necessary? Were you concerned about birth defects?"

This is where it was going to get sticky, and I asked him to please hold questions and incredulity and all eye rolling and smirking until I finished. I was going to tell him about the attempted rape, and the actual rape, and Cindy's murder and I wanted to prepare him a little. "Some of this is going to be hard to hear..." I said.

I gave him a brief background on Marty and Rags at the harbor that day, them showing up at the cottage, attacking me, their deaths. At this point Gerald wore a sour expression and I had to squelch any further questions until I finished. I continued my story by telling him how I had wrecked Ben's boat, then Liam finding us, then the two meth addicts attacking Cindy and killing her, and Liam and Carlton attacking me.

"Oh my God, Kercy! Why didn't you tell me?" Gerald said, crying. "That had to be horrifying." He hugged and held me tight, both of us crying.

I needed to go on, tell him about the beings. I was about to preface the rest of my story, then decided I couldn't go through with it. So, I decided to lie.

"That's why I asked for the DNA test before the baby was born," I said. "Because of the rape. I wasn't willing to give birth to a child that had been conceived so violently and cruelly, having a father so vile and disgusting. Maybe that's wrong of me... but, I just couldn't go through with it if it wasn't conceived out of love."

"No... that makes perfect sense," Gerald said, hugging me closer.

I couldn't tell him about the beings. I just couldn't. It seemed that it would ruin any chance of a normal life with Gerald. I felt I could bear the knowledge of their existence alone; I'd already lived a life of hiding with Gerald. I knew the deception would always lurk between us, yet my reasons for the DNA test had been the truth.

"I may never be able to conceive again," I said. "Doctors believed it wasn't possible to begin with."

"I'm so sorry, Kercy."

"Does that matter to you?"

"You matter to me," Gerald said.

We sat on the couch holding each other. I was feeling more spirited than I had for a while. "Do you want to go for a walk?" I said. "It looks like it's snowing out."

"That sounds great."

I was slipping my coat on when my new cell phone rang.

"Hello," I said,

"Kercy?"

"Yes?"

"Agent Mallory," he said. "I would have called you back sooner but I didn't recognize the number. Why didn't you leave a message?"

"There was no point," I told him.

Mallory was quiet for a few moments and I wondered why he was calling now.

"You know those body parts you gave me...? Well... I've gotten back the preliminary results. Very interesting."

Okay, so now he had my attention again.

"There is less than a three percent difference from humans," Mallory said. "They found hardly anything in the DNA that distinguishes them from us. Makes no sense."

"Well, from what I've been researching, it may."

"How?"

I explained about the findings from The Human Genome Project, that they discovered small variations between species, that it was nothing like what researchers expected to find.

"But these things are from another world?" he said. "Wouldn't there be a greater difference...?"

"I don't know, Mallory," I said, thinking about what the beings had told me about our connection to them, to the universe. "I really need to go, though."

"Wait... just a second. There's something else," Mallory said. "I wanted to warn you about Jacob. He's obsessed with meeting these beings. He wants me to force you to come back to Canada to set up some kind of face-to-face. He even talked about driving down to New York to plead with you direct."

"What did you say?"

"Nothing."

Mallory probably would have loved if Jacob had driven down to badger me into returning to Canada. We both waited for the other one to say something.

"So why were you calling me?" Mallory said, breaking the silence.

"Not now," I said. "I'll call you later."

"Hey, Kercy," Mallory said. "I want you to consider my offer. I need your help more than ever now."

Gerald had come back from the bathroom and was ready to go for our walk.

"Just a moment," I told Mallory, putting my hand over the phone. "Gerald, can you give me a minute?"

"I'll wait for you out front," he said.

After he left, I took my hand from the phone. "There's no way I'm going to help you," I said to Mallory. "You've not been honest with me from day one."

"I haven't kept anything from you," Mallory said. "I've been straight with you from the beginning. I couldn't tell you things I didn't know..."

"Really," I said. "How about what your investigation is really about. I finally figured out your angle... your agenda..."

"I don't know what you mean?" he said.

"I saw how you reacted when Jacob demonstrated his ability to breathe underwater. You weren't shocked or scared. Surprised maybe, but excited, scribbling in your little notebook. You probably couldn't wait to tell your superiors."

"I'm not following," he said.

"You don't want to stop these beings from mutating genes in a process of evolutionary stewardship," I said. "You want to know what they know. You want to militarize this phenomenon. How efficient would an army be if it could repurpose dead soldiers? And Navy Seals who could actually breathe underwater without equipment? How strategically advantageous would that be? You don't want to block them from doing this, you want their technology."

My accusation was followed by a long silence. This was the Federal Bureau of Investigation I had just accused of colluding with aliens to bring about the rapid and radical evolutionary change of humankind. With the adrenaline flowing, my heart was breaking new speed limits. I was wired and petrified at the same time.

"Kercy, do you remember me telling you what the purpose of my investigation was?"

"No, actually I don't," I said a bit testy.

"That's right, because I never did. You made those assumptions about my task force. You have some blind spot of righteousness that keeps you on the sidelines of reality. That actually surprised me. You're supposed to be a scientist; study the phenomenon, gather information, wait until the data is in before positing a theory. But you didn't do any of that. You jumped right to the End of the World scenario, and started spouting about free will and engineering evolution and the sins of gene manipulation. What these beings can achieve is nothing short of miraculous. They have knowledge that we would like to have before our enemies do."

"Please, spare me the enemy around every corner speech," I said, not even sure what that meant.

"They came to your rescue, Kercy," he said. "They probably saved your life. Does that count for anything?"

"Absolutely. Of course. But that doesn't give them a free pass to do whatever they please. If they own my free will for saving my life, then I'm no better off if they'd let me die, because that's what those bastards did when they raped me, took away my free will. That's what violence does! That's what human trafficking and rape does! That's what indiscriminate scientific research on people without their consent does!"

Mallory paused a long second before he spoke. "I'm sorry you won't join my team, Kercy. You'd be an enormous asset, but I can see we are fundamentally at odds. I do want to caution you about speaking to anyone, especially the press about any of this."

"Are you threatening me?"

"This isn't a game, Kercy. This is as serious as it gets. Other governmental agencies are now joining this investigation upon learning of these latest revelations. Those body parts you gathered for me and stuck in your fridge have been studied by no less than twenty labs in the U.S, Britain and Japan. Homeland Security is very interested in this. The President has set up a special division in the White House to keep informed of all new developments. The Canadian government can't throw enough money at this now. A global coalition is forming. That's why I want you as part of it. You are the only living human that we know of so far who has actually made contact with these beings. Spoken with them."

"You're chasing ghosts," I said.

"What?"

"All you can do it hope they tire of wasting resources on us," I said. "You can't find them anywhere. You can't go to them the way Jacob wants me to, and just set up a meeting. You can't get leverage over them because they exist outside our reality. They communicated with me through my dead friend, Cindy, for God's sake! You'd have more luck eradicating white supremacy in this country than trying to negotiate with these beings. They hate us."

"What?"

"They despise us. They think we prey upon our own species. They see us as arrogant and trivial and stupid and waste our intellectual resources on idiotic phone apps. They believe we care nothing for one another and that our only incentive for progress is to monetize and weaponize our discoveries. They will never sit down with you, or me, or anyone, and share their technology. They believe we haven't the discipline to handle the responsibility of gene manipulation, nuclear power, or even taking out our own trash! And after hearing what you just told me, I am starting to believe they might be right."

"They told you that?"

"In so many words. I was with them for two days, remember? We talked about a lot of shit."

"What did you tell them?"

"Fuck, I don't remember. Look, I didn't ask to be the U.S. Ambassador to underwater world. I didn't plan to meet them. They invited me, remember. They offered to share information... as well as a rather scathing critique of our global society."

"If they hate us so much, then why are they trying to help us?"

I remembered putting that same question to the beings, and when they didn't answer, I pushed Cindy further by asking her why they wouldn't answer my question, which she then replied, "They just did." At the time it sounded like a riddle, but eventually I got their meaning.

I said to Mallory, "They told me that humans still believe they don't need each other to survive, that that notion is our worst self-deception."

"And...?" Mallory said.

"And that's why they are attempting to help us..."

"I still don't get it," Mallory said, obviously confused.

"At the risk of sounding corny... because every living thing in the universe is connected, that every living thing needs one another to survive... That's why they help us... despite the fact they don't like us very much."

Mallory exhaled but said nothing, then cleared his throat. "Important people who want to speak to you, Kercy," Mallory said. "You don't just get to sit this one out."

"Did you hear anything I just said? You know what... fuck it! I'll talk to anyone who wants to talk, but the bottom line is, you don't get to win this one no matter what you do to me; water boarding or hanging me naked by my fingernails, whatever it is you guys do. It won't change the fact that you will never gain sway over these beings.

They move between our world and theirs the way you move between your television and the refrigerator. Don't you get it? You can't win this one. You could nuke Georgian Bay all the way up the Atlantic coast to the Arctic Circle, but it wouldn't matter... because they aren't there!"

"Where is their so-called world?" Mallory asked.

"Twelve-generations away," I said. "Now I've got to go"

"Wait. What is that supposed to mean?"

After I explained the twelve-generation theory to him he immediately started working on the math.

"That would be like..."

I hung up the phone, unable to continue the mind-numbing conversation, then hurried to the front stoop before the phone rang again. I ignored it.

"I'm sorry, Gerald," I said. "Are you frozen?"

"No, I'm good. How are you?"

"Not great." I threaded my arm through Gerald's going down the steps, concerned with what Mallory had meant by, *You don't just get to sit this one out.*

THIRTY-FIVE

A couple weeks later, in the middle of the night, I found out exactly what Mallory had meant, when a team of masked men wearing all black gagged and bound Gerald and me and took us from my bedroom, then loaded us unceremoniously into a black SUV parked in front of my brownstone. They drugged us. When I came to, the helicopter was racing above a dark landscape, the deafening rumble of the rotor pounding in my head. Gerald was seated beside me, eyes closed, hands cuffed in his lap, his head tossing side to side with the movement of the aircraft. It was obvious he was still out. In a few minutes we landed on some huge slab of pavement, maybe an old airstrip or something. The deserted facility had no lights, making it nearly impossible to see anything. I pretended to still be asleep when two military personnel wearing dark multi-pocketed jumpsuits and hooded puffer jackets escorted me from the chopper to the backseat of a waiting Suburban. One of them unlocked the cuff on my right wrist, attaching it to a bar on the door. A moment later, the other back door flew open and Gerald was pushed in next to me, one end of his handcuffs affixed to a bar like mine. Gerald groaned a little when the men slammed the door, then fell over, his head against the window pane. We drove for about fifteen minutes and ended up in the harbor parking lot. The agents jumped out of the car, the motor running, and joined a group of men all wearing black, loading gear and supplies onto sleds attached to several black snowmobiles. I was still groggy.

Outside the SUV was Mallory, also dressed in black, directing the operation. I couldn't believe he'd risk a kidnapping charge to force me to come back up here. Then I realized he wouldn't, and that was even more troubling; evidently someone with real pull in the government had authorized this little shindig, and that was more unsettling than the kidnapping itself. What was the plan, I wondered? And what would happen to Gerald and me when the operation was over?

Gerald stirred as the men outside seemed to be performing some last-minute checks on the equipment. "Gerald," I said in a hushed tone. "Wake up."

He blinked his eyes as if trying to clear his head, then attempted to bring his left hand to his face when the shackles on his wrist halted his movement. He jerked harder, trying to get free, the shiny chain rattling, then looked over at me. I held up my right hand showing him my matching bracelet.

"What the fuck?" Gerald said.

"Looks like the FBI has a little evening out planned for us," I said, trying to stay light.

"Where are we?"

"In Canada..."

Mallory jerked open the door on my side and unlocked my restraint. A masked commando opened Gerald's door and removed his cuffs. In a moment, Gerald was rubbing his wrists.

"Before you start yelling," Mallory said to me. "I told you I needed your help. Sorry it had to be like this..."

"Yeah, well, not as sorry as you're going to be," I said, trying to sound tough, realizing pretty quickly that it was hard to be intimidating dressed only in pajamas. And poor Gerald, wearing only what he'd gone to bed in, boxers and a short sleeve sweatshirt, had started shivering. An agent in a black ski mask brought over two insulated jumpsuits and instructed us to slip them on over our clothes. After we zipped our suits, he handed us two heavy parkas, ski masks, and thick insulated boots, making it obvious we were in for a very chilly night rendezvous.

Under a deafening roar, the snowmobiles shot across the snow-packed lake, Gerald on one of the vehicles, me on another across from him. Occasionally we exchanged glances, neither of us able to see one another's faces hidden beneath our ski masks. Our drivers wore full helmets to protect their faces from frostbite.

I counted two other snowmobiles leading the pack, pulling big sleds, with at least one bringing up the rear with more supplies. I wasn't sure where Mallory was in our little convoy, but I was sure of one thing, this surreptitious little operation of Mallory's wasn't going to be a one-night stand; it seemed we had enough gear for a fortnight.

I had always dreamed of taking a midnight ride across the frozen bay on a snowmobile, but this journey had none of the magic I had always imagined, and far too much intrigue and potential for disaster. I was glad when we started pulling to the dock. Regardless of the agents supplying us with thick mittens, my fingers were disturbingly numb.

With the covering of snow, the bay resembled some otherworldly landscape in a distant universe. Several men started carrying boxes up to my cottage, which surprisingly had all the lights on. When my driver quickly departed and headed up the dock toward the house, I climbed off the back of the vehicle and stretched my legs. Gerald started over but was ushered away from me, being pushed up the ramp to the back door by a man with an automatic weapon.

"You warm enough?" Mallory asked, walking up next to me carrying his helmet in his arms.

"What the fuck do you think you're doing," I said. "And who's staying at my house?"

"Jacob and his girlfriend are out here…"

"You people have no idea what you're doing, do you?"

Mallory turned away from me, taking his attention to an object way out on the ice. It was some kind of vehicle, but it didn't look like a snowmobile. Mallory, putting his helmet on, started walking back toward his snowmobile. "Hey, where you going?" I said.

He looked back for a second, then snapped his helmet and swung his leg over the seat. I stood dumbfounded by the whole evening. When he fired the engine, he twisted the front slides and headed back toward me. "Climb on," he said, his voice muffled by the visor of the helmet.

I resisted at first, then stupidly succumbed to my own curiosity. I threw my leg over the seat and wrapped my arms around Mallory's waist. It wasn't more than a hundred yards or so, and it took less than a minute to get out to it. It was obviously an ATV with steel-studded tires and a snow plow attachment on the front. We pulled up next to it.

Mallory turned off the engine and stood looking at it with the visor of his helmet flipped up.

"Is it Jacob's?" I asked. I remembered what Mallory had said about Jacob's obsession with meeting the beings. Maybe he thought if he hung at the house long enough, they'd come for him. Maybe they had.

Mallory said nothing, his eyes finding something new, pointing at some objects lying on the slick frozen surface. We stepped carefully and found an auger and an ax. Someone had drilled two large holes through the ice, then chopped away between them to make the opening larger. I could see a couple of the little "puck" devices Ben sold in the harbor store. They were shaped like canister lids, that agitated the water in the hole to keep it from refreezing while one was fishing. It appeared the batteries had gone dead some time ago, the gadgets encased in fresh ice. Letting my eyes drift over the surrounding area, it was curious to me that Jacob had cleared a spot the size of a small skating rink with the ATV. The snow was pushed in high piles along the perimeter of the shiny ice, an open area maybe forty by sixty yards, far more than necessary to drill out a couple of holes. Why the huge amount of real estate? Then it hit me; he needed some trick to find his way back to the hole under the snow-covered lake surface. If he planned to swim a great distance, then the huge cleared surface of the lake would provide the perfect "window" of light that could be seen from a distance. But I had a sinking feeling; something obviously had gone wrong.

"Kercy," Mallory said, shining his light at the ice. "Come here." He was standing about thirty feet from me. I walked over slowly, careful not to slip and fall. When I looked at what he was shining his light on I gasped.

"Is that Jacob?" Mallory said.

With Jacob's eyes still open, he stared up at us from beneath the ice, his face bloated and white. Beside him was Lola, her red hair fanning out from her pale face.

"Oh fuck," I said. "We can use the axe to chop them out."

Mallory grabbed my arm as I started back for the hatchet. "Too dangerous," he said. "We'll have to wait until morning. I'll get an emergency crew out here."

"Ben will be devastated," I said, staring down at Jacob's lifeless body. Just then Lola's hair moved, swaying in the water as if under a sudden current. That's when we saw one of the beings come up beneath the ice. It didn't seem to notice us standing on the ice. It grabbed Lola's arm and proceeded to drag her body down.

"What the fuck...?" Mallory yelped.

A moment later another being came for Jacob. This one looked right at us through the ice, then at me, holding my gaze. When the shields covering its eyes raised up, I was dumbfounded. It had eyes like a puppy, round and sad like a Pug, just like my dream at eighteen. A moment later the being sank away slowly from the ice, taking Jacob's body down with it.

Mallory looked over at me, his eyes dark cavities against his pale face. I swallowed hard, unsure what to say to him.

"That was them?" he finally said.

I nodded.

"Do you think the creatures did that to Jacob and his girlfriend?"

I didn't, but couldn't be sure. To me it looked as if Jacob and Lola grew impatient waiting for the beings and tried to rush the introduction and got trapped beneath the ice after finding their way back only to realize the pucks had failed and the holes had iced up. But it seemed odd that they could've drowned; Jacob was certainly adept at breathing under water. But maybe the cold had retarded his abilities somehow. It was hard to tell.

Mallory walked over to the snowmobile and fired the engine. He waited for me to climb on and we headed for the cottage. All the gear was unloaded from the sleds when we arrived back at my dock. Men in heavy parkas and ski masks patrolled the perimeter of the island with automatic weapons and I could tell this wasn't going to end well. Mallory lifted his helmet off, taking his eyes back to the spot where Jacob and Lola had been trapped beneath the ice. He stared a long time before he spoke.

"Jacob thought he was close to making contact," Mallory said to the frigid air, the steam from his words suspended like tangible objects. He looked at me. "Are they that ruthless? These beings?"

I didn't think so, but I had no idea. I just shrugged, knowing I didn't trust them. They saved me, that's true, but how could I believe in them after what they'd done to Ben's wife, my own mother, my grandmother? Me? Maybe they weren't intentionally cruel, but some of the worst atrocities are committed under the guise of higher ideals.

Mallory looked over at me and snorted. "I guess this was all for naught," he said.

"Why?"

"Because they're dead."

"Why did you bring me out here?"

Mallory paused as if considering all possibilities. "You're right," he finally said. "I guess we'll just wait." He hesitated only a few seconds before turning toward my house. I followed, feeling oddly like a guest at my own residence. When we reached the back door, I said, "You really should reconsider the sentries with those automatic weapons…"

Mallory coughed a few times, then twisted the knob and went in. I followed, unsure what I'd find inside.

THIRTY-SIX

Gerald was seated by himself on the couch, perusing a book from my mother's collection, a guard sitting nearby with an Uzi in his lap. To my surprise, Gerald was wearing sweatpants and his shirt from Staten Island where his folks lived. I sat next to him. "Where'd you get the clothes?"

"They brought 'em," he said. "Yours are in a bag upstairs."

"Hmm," I said in a low tone. "You okay?"

"Yeah, I guess, all things considered," he said, almost in a whisper. "What's going on."

"I'll tell you later. Are you hungry?"

"I guess I could eat something. This is really weird though, I gotta tell you."

"I know. I'll be right back." I touched Gerald's leg but I'm not sure he even felt it. When I stood to go to the kitchen, the guard raised his weapon and told me to sit. Gerald glared at the man, then brought his eyes back to me. I was so glad Gerald didn't confront him.

Mallory, still deep in thought, waved off the armed guard and motioned for me to go do whatever it was I was going to do. Gerald rose to join me and the guard told him to stay put. He sat back down. I looked over at Mallory, who regarded me with a blank stare.

"I'll be back in a second," I told Gerald, then went to the kitchen. After hunting through the cabinets and pantry, I came up with an instant rice meal in a box.

When I went back to the living room with a bowl for Gerald and myself, Mallory was gone.

"Has anyone worked out the sleeping arrangements for tonight yet?" I asked Gerald softly so the guard couldn't hear.

Gerald cleared his throat and took a bite of the rice. "Yeah, our stuff is in your bedroom..." He touched my leg with his free hand. "Thanks, this tastes good."

When I finished my rice, I asked the guard if he knew where Mallory was. He ignored me.

"You ready for bed?" I asked Gerald.

"You think we can leave?"

"Let's find out.

When we stood at the same time, the guard raised his weapon toward us and told us to sit. "We're going to bed," I said. He glared at me a moment, then shooed us away with his gun. Gerald followed me up the stairs to the bedroom. It was a mess. We scooted some things into the corner so we wouldn't trip over them in the night, though I half expected it to be morning any moment. Mallory and his crew had brought us extra blankets and enough clothes for a couple of days. But no toiletries.

I searched my closet, while Gerald checked the bathroom drawers for remnants of toothpaste, maybe even a travel brush or two. He found a toothbrush from years ago, stuck in the very back of the lower draw, that was about four inches long with a little cartoon bear on the handle. We took turns using it, then readied ourselves for bed. Neither Gerald or I recognized the bedding and figured it was military issue or something. We spread a couple heavy blankets on the floor for our bed, then covered ourselves with the rest.

"I am so sorry about all this," I said, adjusting the covers over my shoulders.

"What the hell is going on?"

I didn't want to have this conversation, not now, not ever, but there was no other way. "Gerald, I wasn't completely honest about the DNA test on the baby... no way could I have gotten pregnant from the rape... it didn't go on long enough..."

"So why the test, then?"

I took a deep breath, then let it out slowly.

"What I'm about to tell you may strain all credulity, but... there are beings who are performing experiments on humans and..."

"Beings? What kind of beings? You mean scientists?" He looked hard into my eyes. "Aliens?"

"Yes, and they..."

"They experimented on you?"

"Yes, just let me finish, okay?" I explained about my mother, and her mother, and how these beings were amphibious and lived beneath the water, but had to qualify that somewhat by telling him about their world..."

"Their planet is twelve generations away?"

Gerald seemed to ponder that notion. "That's an interesting way of explaining distance, but..."

"Please... let me just finish." I told him about the experiments they were performing, their ability to mutate genes for positive effect, then went into detail about how they would impregnate human women, and their supposed end..."

"Climate change? But, we don't know how bad it will get yet..." The scientist in Gerald was considering the practical aspects of the alien agenda, momentarily forgetting why I was telling him all this, until it suddenly dawned on him. "So, you thought you were pregnant with one of these hybrids?"

"Yes... and just so we're perfectly clear, here... I am one of those hybrids..."

Gerald's breath seemed to catch for a second, his eyes fixed on me but focused on some examination inside his head; he had obviously not considered that. After a couple of very long seconds, he wrapped his arms around me and pulled me close. I was okay that he was still at a loss for words. I kissed him.

"Gerald, be prepared to witness some really strange things over the next few days," I said.

"Stranger than this?"

"Oh, yeah. Way the fuck stranger. Are you okay to hear more?"

"There's more?"

"Yeah, I'm afraid so." I told him about Cindy, and repurposing, at least as much as I knew...."

Gerald released me and sat up, the cover peeling down from his chest, his face wracked with alarm, his mind trying to assemble fragments from the past to fit into this new paradigm. "I guess I had always made room for the idea of aliens, but this *repurposing* business, I just don't know... it's so..." He sat a moment staring at the far wall, then shifted his attention toward me. "That's why you went back out to the cottage, because of Cindy's phone... I remember her phone lighting up that morning, like it was coming back to life... and... how did you put that together? That was quite a leap."

I shook my head, then scooted closer to him. He sat in silence, busy finding appropriate compartments to file all this new information. He twisted toward me, his eyes leveled on mine. "What were you and Mallory looking at out on the ice when we got here tonight?"

"Jacob. And his girlfriend, Lola. They were dead, beneath the ice..."

Gerald closed his eyes, shaking his head.

"I know, it's a lot to take in..." I said, touching his arm. "I'm really sorry, Gerald..."

At that point, telling him about the beings swimming up to retrieve Jacob and his girlfriend was sensory overload, so I avoided the subject all together. At least I thought I had.

"So, they're still out there, stuck beneath the ice? Jeez, that's messed up. Why doesn't Mallory send a couple of those guys out there and get them?"

"They're not out there anymore, Gerald."

"What? Where are they?"

I explained how the beings had come up and taken Jacob and Lola down with them. Gerald's eyes grew big as eggs. "You saw them?"

I nodded. Gerald gave a little gasp, his head on a gimbal, shifting gently back and forth. I hated laying all this on him, and at the same time I was relieved that everything was out in the open. My only concern now was what would happen to us, Gerald and me?

"You ready to sleep?" I said.

His head spun toward me when he scoffed. "Seriously?"

"Well, how about just lying here together, holding each other?"

He slumped down beneath the covers and rolled toward me. He looked wrecked and I felt horrible. I was just about to tell him how much l loved him when someone knocked on the door.

"Who is it?" I said.

"Mallory."

"Just a second." When I got up, Gerald didn't move, his eyes staring at a fold in the blanket.

"What is it?" I said, holding the door open a few inches.

"You have what you need?" he said to me, then apparently was searching for Gerald in the darkened room.

"Yeah, except for a bed," I said.

"Hope they weren't too rough on him..." Mallory said.

I held my tongue, wondering what had been going through Mallory's mind when he concocted this insane scheme.

"Can I talk to you in the hallway a second?" Mallory asked me.

I walked out and closed the door. Mallory apologized again for the inconvenience and I almost corrected him, reminding him it was a bit more than an inconvenience, it was an *abduction!* but I let it drop. He seemed particularly annoyed, a state I had not really witnessed in him before. "Why do you think I should get rid of the machine guns outside?"

I shook my head. "Well... these beings take umbrage with aggression, and those machine guns qualify, I think..."

Mallory stood like a bookcase and I thought maybe the conversation was over, but he didn't turn away or react, just remained perfectly still, his mind seemingly trapped in some vortex of deliberation. Just as I put my hand on the doorknob to rejoin Gerald, Mallory asked me to wait.

"Will you help me now?" he said.

"Help you with what?"

"Make contact..."

I didn't want him to see me smirking, but his request was ridiculous. How could he not know that contacting these beings was impossible, after all I'd told him? "I'm not sure I understand what you want. Are you hoping to score an invite to their world?"

Mallory didn't answer, but the sudden rise of his eyebrows made it clear that that was exactly what he wanted.

"You would drown," I told him. "You could never get there. I thought you understood that."

Mallory's jaw tightened like a vice and I could see the frustration across his brow. He turned to go back down the steps, stopping at the railing. He glowered at me in the dark and for the first time since I'd met him, he seemed dangerous, his expression bordering on psychotic. It was becoming obvious these beings had become his obsession and I started to wonder about this entire enterprise, the kidnapping, the snowmobiles and helicopter, the gear and guards and machine guns; was this all Mallory's brainchild, one of those off-the-book campaigns? Was this his own ad hoc project after Jacob led him to believe they were close to making contact?

Mallory's mouth parted slightly, his jaw shifting to one side before he turned and went down the stairs. Back in the bedroom, I locked the door and the room fell silent. Any other time, Gerald would have been asleep and snoring within minutes. I knew he was rattled and was lying awake. I looked over at him under the blankets. He had rolled over, his back to my side of the floor now. My heart sank. I walked to the window and shifted my attention toward the dock, then at the grounds along the shoreline, the guards standing by, machine guns at the ready, and wondered if Mallory would order them to stand down. If not, I feared this evening would turn into one long nightmare and regretted that Gerald had been exposed to any of it.

THIRTY-SEVEN

This absurdity went on for two days, paramilitary thugs surveilling the island with automatic weapons, Mallory walking around like a zombie, morose, unspeaking, making his way out onto the ice during the day to inspect the spot where Jacob and Lola disappeared, then returning to sit by himself in the house, or on the porch, or stop a moment along the shoreline to speak to one of the guards. Some days Mallory just stood at the end of the dock, or near the gaping hole of damaged boards where the huge sea monster had crashed it to pieces. I still believed that thing to have been an Elasmosaurus, but couldn't be completely sure.

One afternoon, with nothing else to do, I searched my mother's books again and found the artist's depiction of the Cryptocleidus, similar to the Elasmosaurus only much smaller. I couldn't find another image of the Elasmosaurus, and had misplaced the one I'd planned to send to Mallory. I carefully removed the illustration and handed it to Mallory. He just stared at me with blank eyes. "What's this?" he finally said in a flat tone.

"It's a Cryptocleidus, like the creature that busted up my boat dock, just not as big as the one I saw. I told you I'd get you a picture..."

Mallory regarded it a second, then handed it back like an incomplete homework assignment.

"Don't you want that?" I said. "You asked for my help?"

He walked away.

I found a few games on the top shelf of the closet in the living room. I was looking forward to the distraction, but Gerald was in no mood to play, spending most of his time on the back porch in his parka gazing out over the bay. Gerald and I ate together, but mostly in silence. The military types kept to themselves, and I have no idea when or what they ate. They were a somber, stony-faced group, and Gerald had adopted a similar temperament, keeping mostly to himself, avoiding me when possible.

Mallory completely ignored me, refusing to even make eye contact when we happened to find ourselves in the same room. That was fine with me, but Gerald's aloofness was intolerable. Several times I tried to make conversation, but he only listened, a canyon opening between us.

It must have been just after midnight, the sky a black sheet beyond the bedroom window, when I heard the dull staccato pops of machine gun fire. I bolted upright from the floor, thinking it was a dream, the rapid explosions raining out below my bedroom window. Gerald was motionless on his side of the floor, oblivious to the drama evolving down by the shoreline. I wanted to see what was happening but didn't dare walk near the window fearing a stray bullet crashing through the glass.

Down on the main level of the house, the noise of footsteps and urgency echoed through the void. The clatter of guns and ammunition clips, footfalls and boots, people talking in hurried, muffled tones swept up into our bedroom. The gunfire outside continued for another few minutes then stopped abruptly. The kitchen door opened and slammed a few seconds later followed by a brief barrage of gunfire, but then it all stopped. Silence fell over the island like a deep snow. My ears perked up under this new hush. Nothing. Was everyone dead?

"Gerald," I whispered. He didn't move but I could hear his breathing. I wanted to check on things but not alone. I waited another minute, then nudged Gerald. He stirred, then seemed to snap awake, but disoriented, as if he had no idea where he was.

"Gerald," I said again, a bit louder, not sure if he'd even answer me.

"What is it?"

"Something's going on. Gun fire, but now it's all quiet..."

He sat up and stilled himself. I could feel his eyes on me, then on the window, but said nothing, gazing back at me. I slid my legs out from the blankets and padded softly toward the door.

"Where are you going, Kercy?"

"I'm just going to stick my head out."

Gerald got up just as I pulled the door open. Voices echoed in the stairwell, but I realized it was only one person talking. With no urgency or fear, almost like normal conversation.

"Come down and join us, Kercy," the voice said. My chest tightened and it was difficult to breathe. Gerald's eyes narrowed, but even in the dark I could read the fear.

"They know we're here, whoever it is," I whispered. By the look on Gerald's face, I could see he was filled with the same dread that was marshaling me.

"Wait here," I said.

He shook his head *No* and followed me down the steps. When I reached the living room, Jacob was standing in the middle of everyone like some lurid ringmaster, two of the alien beings stationed nearby. Mallory sat on the couch, but his demeanor was frozen, his eyes straining to look up at me. Over near the kitchen entrance was one of the paramilitary guys, holding his machine gun with one hand, the weapon pointed at the floor, but he too was unable to move, the tendons along his neck strained and bulging under some force making it hard for him to breathe. His mouth was open, his eyes bright with panic, as if he was almost out of air. It was like witnessing a room full of mannequins, only alive, just barely, as if caught in some retarded stage of thawing. Another soldier stood behind the couch in a similar state of suspended animation; only his eyelids flickered. He too had his weapon, but it extended uselessly from his side, frozen like an unnecessary appendage.

Jacob came over. "Kercy, I am sorry about the baby," he said, in all sincerity. I wasn't sure how he even knew about that. He then spoke to Gerald. "Are you okay? There's nothing to be afraid of..."

Gerald seemed unable to speak. He grabbed my hand and squeezed it so hard I thought he'd snap my fingers.

"Jacob, what's going on?" I said.

"Well, Special Agent Mallory here really wants to make contact with the beings, and I kind of promised him that I could make that happen..."

"Is that a good idea? I mean... he would drown, right?"

"Well, maybe not. It may be possible to revive him once we're there..."

"Revive? You mean *repurpose,* right?"

"No, we think we can revive Agent Mallory. We want to speak to him, but as you know, there isn't much time. We'd need to get going. But Mallory seems to be in no condition to agree or disagree. What do you think? Should we take him?"

"We?"

"Yes, we want you to come as well," Jacob said, light reflecting in a peculiar way off his eyeballs. "I think you'll find it most fascinating."

I studied Mallory and it seemed he could understand what we were saying, and the way his eyelids shuddered, he was trying to communicate. Jacob walked over to him and bent down until his face was level with Mallory. "I think he's willing to try it..." Jacob concluded. My heart dropped about fifty stories; no way would Mallory live through this. Jacob glanced back at me, then over at Gerald, holding his gaze on him...

"No! Gerald's not going!" I said. "We'll take Mallory... but Gerald stays!" I wasn't sure what I was going to do if Jacob refused my demand.

"Okay then," Jacob said. "I just thought he might want to see what this is all about."

Jacob motioned for the creatures to get Mallory's unmoving body from the couch. They picked him up and headed out the back door. Jacob pointed for me to follow, so I fell in line, giving Gerald a backward glance.

"She'll be fine," Jacob said to Gerald. "Everything will be fine."

When I heard the back door close, I pictured Gerald standing alone, helpless and afraid, yet smart enough to refrain from heroics. Not against these creatures. Or Jacob.

Outside, numerous soldiers stood perfectly still, but alive, holding their weapons. Their eyes followed our departure, unable to turn their heads, trapped in strained standing positions, apparently held in stasis by some unfathomable and agonizing force. Maybe this wasn't the same power the creatures had used on me in my bedroom, inducing that calm state of immobility, but it seemed similar, except these men were definitely under duress.

The creatures carrying Mallory stood above a huge carved out area of ice, the calm pool reflecting the night. When the creatures dropped into the water with Mallory and disappeared, Jacob took my hand and walked me to the edge above the pool, then said,

"Everything will be all right..." At that, he pulled me over with him and we sank into a darkness so arrant I'd thought I'd gone blind.

THIRTY-EIGHT

The sensation was unlike anything I'd ever experienced before as Jacob guided me into a thick, syrupy blackness toward a vague smudge of light ahead. My breathing stalled, but I wasn't panicked, not yet, hoping we'd reach our destination soon, my lungs unaccustomed to this environment. And I had no idea where the creatures had taken Mallory. Maybe I should have protested more, although I'm not sure if I would have had much say in what was happening. I just knew I didn't like being here.

When we reached the light and entered a more breathable environment, my lungs convulsed until I expelled a blackish slop, like the ink from a huge squid. To see that billow from my own mouth made me shudder. A second later my lungs spasmed again, expelling more black gunk from my lungs. This time I felt lighter, almost dizzy, about to pass out.

"Stay with me, Kercy," Jacob said. "I didn't let you die before... I won't let you now."

It wasn't long before I spotted a structure in the distance. As we swam closer, I recognized it as the domed facility I had seen on my first visit to this world. Cindy had told me that I wasn't allowed to go there, and I wondered why they were taking me now. After a few timeless moments we were standing outside the huge rounded building. I looked over at Jacob, and for whatever reason, I trusted him. Even so, I wasn't sure how well Mallory was going to fare on this journey; I had sensed some hostility toward him from Jacob.

Jacob led me inside the structure, the interior filled with water so clear—if not for the slightly more difficult sensation of breathing—it was impossible to tell it was liquid and not air. He led me down a corridor, guiding us into a large space that appeared to be a laboratory, yet void of any technological equipment. For whatever reason, I had thought I was seeing just fine, but after a few moments, my eyes adjusted more perfectly to the interior. Indescribably brilliant flecks of color floated about everywhere, some sparkling like electric lights, yet as tiny as specks of glitter. They didn't hinder the ability to see, but actually enhanced the clarity of objects they clustered near. It was then, when the radiant particles moved across the room, that I saw Mallory, suspended in this substance, unmoving as if dead, lying on his back with no visible means of support, ten feet above the floor. The floor, if you could even call it that, was pearlescent, glimmering with a mystifying effervescence. The ebullience it exuded flooded up into my body with a vibrancy that nearly took my consciousness, making me light-headed, or more exactly, no-headed; all sense of my own corporeal self was gone. I was pure energy, a spell-binding mixture of buoyancy and boundlessness.

High above Mallory's body, the ceiling had the appearance of some kind of membrane, streaked with numerous luminescent veins that pulsed with shifting intensity and hue. Mallory, floating like an astronaut, was now covered in the rainbow particles, the speckles of light clustering and moving over him with frenetic urgency, lending him a clarity, a sharpness that I had to look away from; it was impairing my vision, causing me discomfort at the back of my eyes and I felt I was about to pass out. The substance surrounding my consciousness now vibrated so violently that I felt something was going to break loose, that I was going to splinter into a million frag-ments, each of them containing every cell in my body, perfect replica-tions, millions of replications controlled by one center, one profound yet enervating nucleus.

"Just a little bit longer, Kercy," he said. "Just let your conscious-ness go blank and you'll be fine."

At first, I found Jacob's suggestion absurd; how could I possibly know how to do that? And then, it just happened, the vibration stopped, my fragmentation became instantly whole like an implosion, my vision washed in nothingness, yet lucid, my entire being suffused with tranquility.

When imagery formed on my retinas, I noticed at least a dozen tentacled orbs floating just beneath the ceiling membrane. At first, they appeared to be some sort of lights the way they glowed, until I realized they were organisms, alive and pulsating. Slowly they convened around Mallory's body, morphing together into a solid mass to completely blanket him like a cocoon. A moment later Mallory was utterly encased by these entities, the surface translucent and undulating.

Jacob stood next to me. "He'll be fine now," Jacob said.

"Are you sure?" My voice sounded foreign to me, echoing as if reflected from multiple sources, amplified with a grandness and authority that unnerved me.

Jacob only nodded. "Time to go," he said.

The experience was so heady I felt inebriated, so light and discar-nate I thought maybe I had died.

You did not, Jacob intimated to me without speaking, leading me from the facility. In moments we entered the thick, blackish fluid again, my lungs straining, recalling what Cindy had said, "You won't be able to breathe the dense water."

Losing my ability to assimilate this glop in my lungs, I started feeling that Cindy had been right and I began to panic. Jacob sensed my distress and reassured me with a tender touch, squeezing my hand gently. Soon we entered a new realm where my lungs quickly spewed a cloud of dark water. Before I could move, my lungs spasmed another thick cloud of inky sludge. Jacob guided me forward until my breathing became effortless. We paused to rest a moment and I told him I had questions.

"We must keep moving," he said. "Do you feel better now?"

"Yes," I said wanting to talk a moment, but Jacob started swimming with me in tow. "Stop, please, I want to ask you something," I said. Jacob twisted toward me. "Why did you and Lola drown? I don't understand..."

Jacob wore a look of impatience, but finally said, "Jacob and Lola represented only one of innumerable different trials being explored simultaneously. Their transitions, while impressive, ultimately resulted in failure due to their inability to maintain their potential over an extended period of time."

Human guinea pigs. A horrible end to their lives, which they never deserved. And considering the scathing rebuke by these aliens of the human race, they seem to have a blind spot for their own shortcomings and dereliction. But there was so much more I needed to know...

"Jacob, you and Lola could breathe fresh water, but most of the Earth's water supply is salt water?" I said, confused over why they had chosen Georgian Bay.

"When the transition is complete, your species will be euryhaline, so it won't matter. You'll be able to adapt to either medium."

"But your experiments seem to be on such a small scale as to have no effect on the—"

"This research is taking place all over your planet... both in fresh and salt water..."

"Even so, how could you possibly expect to perform this extent of gene manipulation on the entire human race?"

Jacob seemed suddenly confused by my question. He turned to face me. "We don't. We never did..."

Now I was the one confused. "Then how will this work? I mean what will happen—"

"Millions upon millions will perish, Kercy," Jacob said, shaking his head as if I should have understood that. "We are not trying to affect the entire population, only enough to ensure the survival of your species. And gene manipulation alone was never going to be sufficient to that end. That's why you are so important, Kercy, with your uncanny ability to assimilate. The ones like you, the beings who are genetically enhanced to assimilate at the rate you've demonstrated, they will have the ability to transition swiftly through the necessary steps to an amphibious existence. Your species will not have millions of years for this shift. And if the planet is ultimately covered in water, you and those like you will be capable of adapting to an entirely subaqueous way of life. Now, we must go..."

"No, wait," I pleaded, "please, just a few more—"

Jacob spun away from me, the forcefulness of his maneuver causing a small vortex, throwing me off balance. Regaining my composure, I swam after him, trying to keep up and was suddenly unsteady, confused. It took a beat for me to pull it together. When I finally focused, Jacob was gone. New fear shot through me when I found myself unable to discern one direction from another. Even though I was breathing without difficulty, I was suspended in nothingness; I panicked as I had no idea which way to swim, trapped in this featureless void.

It seemed forever before I heard a dull, thudding sound. I swiveled my head to find the source, then became still to focus my attention. I waited. Nothing, then the sound came again, and off to my left I saw a disturbance. Even not knowing what it was, I decided to swim toward it, stopping abruptly when I spied something shiny and sharp that seemed to be attacking another creature, chunks of it sinking and rising. Yet no blood of any kind. The attack continued so I started swimming away, until I realized that what I'd been observing was someone chopping a hole in the ice with an ax.

I hurriedly pumped my arms and legs, propelling myself forward, which I finally understood was actually up, then shot through the watery breech, grabbed by a hand trying to pull me up. When I flopped on the dock, someone pulled me to their body. "Oh my God, I didn't think I'd ever see you again!" Gerald said, tears flowing down his cheeks.

In a few minutes I was sitting up, surrounded by the cold night air. Gerald quickly covered me with his parka and hustled me up to the house, and helped me out of my clothes, returning with heavy blankets from the bedroom.

"Didn't you hear me calling you?" Gerald said, patting my arms on the couch. "I could barely see you down below me under the ice. I shined the light and kept screaming at you, but you looked disoriented. I was getting ready to dive down, but then, like... I don't know how, you started swimming straight up at me..."

It took a moment to clear my head. "How did you know I would be there, Gerald. I mean... it looks like the middle of the night..."

"Jacob," Gerald said. "He came to the house and made me follow him. He told me to wait for you at that spot. And to keep the hole open with the ax..."

I was still a bit groggy, trying to remember where Jacob had gone. I couldn't piece it together, my memory fogged and blurry.

"How long have I been gone?"

"Two days. I was going out of my head here. Ben left a little while ago on his snowmobile to get more supplies in town. He's been waiting out here with me. I told him about Jacob, and... I hope that was all right, anyway..." Gerald stopped talking and hugged me again. This time I had the presence of mind to hug him back.

When he released me, I said, "Is everybody gone? The soldiers? The snowmobiles?"

"They left... with Mallory..."

"Mallory?" I said. "He was here?"

Gerald screwed up his face in an odd way. "Yeah, he showed up early this evening... and, he rounded everyone up and they left..."

"No one was hurt?"

"No, it was really freaky, all those soldiers like zombies for nearly two days. I will never fully parse that."

I felt so bad for Gerald, thrown unawares into this disturbing phenomenon. "You're okay, though?" I said, getting to my feet.

"Yeah, no, I'm fine. I'm just so glad you're safe," Gerald said. He stood, then bent down and kissed me on the lips. "I love you so much, Kercy."

THIRTY-NINE

Earlier in the week, I had asked Gerald if he would go back to the cottage with me. He had cleared his schedule and we packed our warm clothes, a couple of minus-ten-degree sleeping bags, and flashlights. Gerald offered to drive, giving me a chance to sleep on the trip up to Canada.

I was exhausted over the rehash of my life story with Gerald over the past few weeks since we'd returned to Manhattan. At times, the lengthy and often absurd Q&As about the creatures with Gerald—their powers, where they lived, the whole twelve-generations thing—became tedious. I had been amazed by how well he handled everything those days at the cottage, the immobilized soldiers, aliens in the living room, even Jacob. Especially Jacob. Since we'd been back at the brownstone, though, Gerald was obsessed with understanding everything. Out of the blue, he'd launch a question at me when something didn't add up. And to a point, I was happy to clarify anything I could, and it was actually helpful to me as well. But I needed a break from the inquiries. Nevertheless, I was keen to have things settled at the cottage, and get on with my life, but first, I had to meet Agent Mallory—by my invitation—at a coffee shop in Manhattan.

It was just after noon when we arrived. Mallory still hadn't shown and I couldn't be sure he would. We hadn't spoken since he'd kidnapped us, not until today, and the short conversation we had on the phone left me a bit uncomfortable; he seemed preoccupied and a bit rude and acted as if he didn't really want to see me. But I had to meet up before we left.

Gerald had just come back to the table with our lattes when Mallory walked in. I barely recognized him, his scruffy beard, his dark set eyes. He was wearing a heavy trench coat and beret, looking more like an NYU professor than an FBI agent. He surveyed the small interior, then walked over and stood by the table.

"Have a seat," I said. "Can I buy you a coffee?"

"Can't stay. What do you need, Ms. Powell?"

"Nothing, really. I'm heading back up to the cottage to put it on the market, and I probably won't see you again. I just wanted to say goodbye."

"We weren't that close."

"No, I guess we weren't. Did you get the answers you hoped to find?"

Mallory regarded me with mild disdain, then glanced at Gerald, his eyes severe. "What are you referring to?" he said, pointing his question at the center of my face.

"Your trip to underwater world... I would have thought it was enlightening for you." I was being serious but I know it sounded snarky.

"I have no idea what you're talking about. When Jacob's *repurposed-self* took you that night, I figured it was pointless hanging around any longer. I'm figuring out a new strategy... unless you're reconsidering assisting me?"

Mallory's comment threw me for a loop. How could he not remember anything that had happened that night? Or was this a ruse to throw me off. If so, it was working. But I still had to be sure of one thing. I stood to shake his hand, extending my palm. He reluctantly took it.

"This is silly!" I said. "We know each other better than this..."

When I pulled him into a hug, he stiffened. With my arms woven around him, I rested my face against his, then gave him a brief kiss on the cheek. I patted him on the back a few times, a gentleman's hug. He bristled but endured the gestures. When I released him, I smiled.

"Well?" Mallory said.

"Well, what?"

"Are you going to help me?"

"Take care of yourself, Agent Mallory."

He looked at Gerald, then me, then padded away from the table. A moment later he was gone. That was it. And even though I got what I came for, a part of me felt bad for him, how pathetic he now seemed, but quickly realizing that maybe his broken veneer was part of the subterfuge.

"You ready to hit the road?" I asked Gerald.

Gerald picked up his drink and we walked to the car.

"That was weird," Gerald said. "How could he not recall anything from that night. And why was he acting like such an ass? I mean, we could have pressed charges..."

"Yeah, I know."

Soon after, Gerald and I headed north up the highway. I slept for a while and Gerald seemed content with the radio keeping him company. When I woke, we stopped for a short bathroom break and a snack, then got back on the road. I felt revived and called Ben and asked if I could borrow his snowmobile for a day or so.

"Sure, no problem, Kercy," he said. "You gonna pick it up in the morning?"

"I wanted to get it tonight if I could?"

"Going to be dark," he said. "But you'll have a bit of moon... you should be fine. Call me when you get into Elico. I'll meet you at the harbor."

"Thanks, Ben."

We had several hours of driving ahead of us. Gerald played music on the radio, but even that couldn't stop the flow of thoughts when I closed my eyes. I was relieved that Gerald now knew everything about me, and while it felt touch and go there for a while at the cottage, everything seemed back on track with us, though probably never normal again. But I had to be sure. I reached over to turn the radio off.

"Sorry, was that bothering you?" Gerald said.

"Are you afraid of me?" I said.

"Afraid of you? Why would I be afraid of you...?"

"Because I am part them, the aliens. I have their DNA, their blood in my veins. I'm still assimilating, changing."

"You seem perfectly normal to me."

"You are the worst liar." When I moved closer to him, he wrapped his arm over my shoulders.

"One thing I need to ask you?" he said. I sat up to meet his eyes. "I am a fairly intelligent person, right?" he continued. "Why did you wait so long to tell me everything? Did you think I hadn't made room in my consciousness for the possibility of other intelligent life forms?"

"I don't know," I said. "I'm not sure I ever had."

He smiled weakly and pulled me close. I leaned against his side and felt my mind spinning slowly to a stop. I woke up with the street lights of Elico strobing by above us. I yawned and stretched and looked around. Then I glanced over at Gerald. "I love you."

"I love you, too. You going to ring Ben?"

"Looks like he's here."

We pulled into the harbor and Ben was waiting in his office, the lights on and the heater running. Gerald went back to grab the last of our stuff. Ben hugged me and kissed my forehead.

"You look good," he said. "How are you doing?"

"Fine."

Gerald walked up and shook Ben's hand. Ben asked how he was doing.

"I'm better, Ben. I am. That was some strange stuff, wasn't it? I don't know what I'd have done if you hadn't stayed out with me until Kercy came back..."

"It was good getting to know you, Gerald. So, I've got the tow bar and freight sled hooked up so you can haul your stuff out."

"I'm sorry to put you to so much trouble," I said.

"It's no trouble. Everything was already done. I planned to head out for some ice fishing next week and had gotten everything in ship shape. I love ice fishing, though I don't seem to have as much tolerance for the cold as I did when I was younger."

I smiled.

Ben said, "I'm glad you didn't come alone. To be honest, I didn't expect to see you back up here for a while... you know..."

"Yeah. This may be my last time."

Ben nodded. "I understand."

He helped us carry everything over to the snowmobile, showed us how to lash it to the freight sled, then handed us helmets.

"Now, we had a bit more snow since you were here last," Ben said. "But you'll be just fine."

Ben handed me the keys to the snowmobile. "Do you need the keys to your cottage, Kercy?"

"No, I'm good."

"Okay, so, after everything settled down, I winterized your place, but that's not a problem." Ben explained that we would have to turn on the gas, the water, the electricity. "I'll go back up and winterize the place again when you leave. You know where the water main is, right?"

I nodded.

"Okay, good. So, I put a padlock on the outside electrical box and I'm the only one with a key. Here, take this extra and keep it on your chain. I should have done that a long time ago..."

"Ben, that wasn't your fault."

Ben hung his head a moment.

"So, now I just need you to show me how to drive this thing," I said.

"You've never driven one of these?" Gerald said.

"Oh, she's a quick study," Ben said, proceeding to show me how to operate it. "My snowmobile is fan cooled, so you don't have to worry about burning it up if you hit bare ice. It's fitted with studs and carbide, so you'll have plenty of traction, and don't be afraid to open her up. I've got ice scratchers, so you won't have to worry about melting the slides. I always take a little dish soap with me if I'm going to ride long distances. Just squirt a bit right here on the slides, but the ride out to your place won't be a problem. But if you go any distance tomorrow you might want to keep an eye on 'em. Tank's full. You have my number. That's about it."

"Should I have been taking notes?" I said.

Ben laughed. "No, no, I was just going over the checklist in my head. Nothing to it. Just have fun."

"Thank you for trusting me with your snowmobile, Ben," I said.

"Aw, Kercy, you're family. If you have any problems, now, you call me. I've got a new ATV and I'll come right out. Give me an excuse to get out on the ice and enjoy this beautiful night instead of sitting home reading."

We hugged and Ben looked as if something was bothering him.

"Kercy, I'd like to talk to you about a few things before you head back to the city, but it can wait until you bring the snowmobile back."

"You sure, Ben? We can talk now..."

"No," he said, smiling sadly. "When you get back."

I climbed on and started the engine. Gerald climbed on behind me and wrapped his arms around my waist. My takeoff was a bit jolting, but it didn't take long for me to get the feel of it. It was exhilarating, the cold, the moon and stars, the sound of the slides gliding across the snow. Unbelievable. Ben had set up the GPS just in case I had a problem finding my way in the dark. When we first left the harbor, I had been a bit disoriented, but then everything fell into place.

When we rounded the last island, I got a bit distracted with the cottage being so dark. For a moment I thought I was lost, but as we got closer the damaged dock came into view. I pulled the snowmobile up alongside it.

"You stay with the snowmobile and I'll have a look around, okay?" Gerald said.

We decided to leave everything on the freight sled until we'd had a chance to get the lights on. When we started up the walkway, Gerald pulled a gun from his coat pocket.

"What are you doing with that!" I said, trying not to shout.

"After the last time up here, I thought I'd come prepared," he said.

When we got to the back door, I put the key in the lock and unbolted the door. We used our flashlights to get the power on, and the gas and water. It took us a half hour to get the place up and running, but I wasn't sure I wanted to spend the night after all.

"Wow, you were like fricking Jethro Gibbs back there," I said to Gerald. "I had no idea you were packing."

"Packing? Just being cautious," Gerald said, sticking the gun back into his jacket pocket.

"Let's go get our stuff," I said, wondering if Gerald believed he could actually shoot someone. We went down to the dock and had just started unlashing the gear from the freight sled when I turned to Gerald. "I don't think I want to spend the night," I said.

"I thought you wanted to get everything shipshape so you could sell the place?"

"I thought I did too, but this has to end," I said.

"I don't understand," Gerald said.

"Just wait here, and don't follow me," I said, leaving the snowmobile at the end of the dock. "Promise..."

"Yeah, okay..."

I left the engine running, and climbed off the snowmobile, then walked back up to the house. Once inside, I grabbed a candle from the bathroom and lit it and stuck it on the kitchen island. After getting a blanket from the closet, I draped it across the opening to the kitchen, attaching it with some pushpins from the toolbox. With the kitchen partially sealed, I blew out the pilot light, then turned all the knobs on the stove until gas hissed from each burner, and was almost out the back door when I remembered what I had wanted to take with me.

I had rehearsed this a million times during the drive up, but in my haste, forgot my mother's books.

I ran back to the library, giving the stove a quick glance, as if that would give me some idea of how much time I had. Standing in front of the bookshelves, I realized I couldn't take them all, so I grabbed the important ones, the ones she'd spent so many nights poring over, the ones where we'd sat together, her showing me pictures of sea creatures and ocean plants. The burners seemed to be hissing louder now and I was sure it was my imagination, but with the smell of gas seeping into the living room I needed to hurry.

I ran for the back entrance in the kitchen and pulled the door closed behind me, glancing at the candle as I went by.

Nearly off the porch I stopped, wondering if shutting the door so abruptly may have blown out the candle. Gerald yelled something, but I knew I had to go back in and check. *Don't go back, just run,* something inside me said. I looked at the backdoor and... *Run!* I looked down at Gerald, then at the door, and started jogging down the walkway, toward Gerald and the snowmobile, dropping books, tripping on them when the blast came, the force throwing me forward head over feet tumbling down the walkway, books flying from my arms. With my ears ringing, I attempted to get up and shake the humming from my head, when a second explosion ripped the fragile night apart, fiery pieces of the house flying through the air, landing on ice and snow.

Disoriented, I struggled to get my bearings when Gerald grabbed me, pulling me to my feet. We ran to the end of the dock, flaming boards and burning chunks of wood landing all around us.

Helping me toward the snowmobile, Gerald yelled, "What happened! Are you okay!"

"Yes! Get on!"

I never imagined a fire could be so loud. Sap in the trees popped and crackled as branches crashed to the ground, sliding along the ice. The fire roared with a terrifying fury.

Once Gerald was holding my waist, I gunned the throttle and raced the snowmobile out away from the house a safe distance. Obviously, I had not estimated the timing very well on the explosion. Gerald shouted something, grabbing me tighter. Fiery projectiles scattered across the ice, spinning like helicopter blades. Smoky embers and debris shot into the night sky, fire licking at all the trees around the property until the entire island was engulfed in flames. Even from a hundred yards away we could feel the heat, the fire illuminating the ice, the glacial rock, the shoreline. The dock was the last thing to catch, until it finally broke apart and burned on the snow.

Gerald and I watched from the snowmobile as the trees closest to the house spilled over onto the roof, weakened by fire, collapsing the walls and porch, sending a blaze of debris and sparks across the ice.

The cottage had been in my mother's family for over a century. It was the house of my childhood, the source of my fondest memories, the only place I had ever fit in. My summers had been spent on the water. The warm sun. The cool breeze off the lake. The weak scent of my father's aftershave. It was gone forever. Yet the normalcy I had always felt coming here had been taken away weeks ago. I couldn't even drive into Elico without thinking about Rags and Marty, without remembering Carlton, and Liam, and the beings.

And Cindy.

How could I sleep another night in that house, spend another day on the dock, constantly reminded of how she died that night.

I slid from the seat and looked down at the only book left in my hands, the only one I'd been able to hold onto from my mother's collection. The funny thing was, it didn't even look familiar to me. I had no idea what it was.

I took my eyes back to the house, remembering her, my life growing upon the island, the boat rides, playing games at the living room coffee table. Tears rolled down my cheeks and I hoped this would be the last of them for a very long time. Gerald placed his arm around me and pulled me close. After a few minutes, I got back on the snowmobile, Gerald wedging himself in behind me.

I drove away from the house, glancing back occasionally at the flames, the fire burning to the edge of the shoreline. In a few minutes we had rounded enough islands that I could no longer see the fire, only a faint orange glow over a black silhouette of trees. By the time we reached the harbor, no hint of anything out of the ordinary remained, just a billion stars frozen into a perfect night sky.

FORTY

After parking the snowmobile back where we'd picked it up, Gerald and I unloaded our stuff from the sled and stowed it in his trunk. Gerald was quiet and I knew he had more questions, especially after that little stunt. We drove to the Aubrey in silence until he asked me if I was going to phone Ben.

"In the morning," I said, sad I'd never see the cottage again.

Gerald and I talked until almost one in the morning about everything that had happened. I tried to explain why I'd blown up the house, that I needed something dramatic to end my connection with it. He suggested I could have just sold it. "I planned to... but then I couldn't," I told him. "What if someone with daughters bought it? How could I ever feel good about that?"

"There are hundreds of houses up here?" he said. "Maybe thousands. What about those? You can't do anything about them."

"I know... but I could do something about mine."

He seemed to understand, but said he still felt bad because he knew how much the place meant to me.

"But that's not the only reason," I said.

"What do you mean?"

"They lied to me," I said, explaining to Gerald how the beings had shown me miraculous things, that I had even started to trust them.

"But they lied."

"How?"

"When we met Mallory for coffee," I said. "I hugged him because I had to know if he had really been saved, or repurposed."

"You think he was *repurposed?*" Gerald said. I had told Gerald about this unique power the beings had, about Jacob, my dad, about Cindy, and how she'd come to the cottage that night.

"But, how could you tell? I mean, Mallory looked perfectly normal, well, maybe a bit scraggly..." Gerald said.

"Mallory was cold as ice when I kissed him on the cheek. Just the way Cindy had been when I kissed her. The beings said they had strict laws about repurposing, time limits and all kind of rules and... but it was all bullshit..."

"Why would they do that?"

I'd given much thought to their reasons and my conclusions bothered me. "So they would have eyes and ears in the FBI maybe. Through Mallory, they would have control over investigations and top-secret information... they now control what he says and does..." Pondering what I had just told Gerald, I couldn't help but wonder how many repurposed beings lived among us, in high places in our government, captains of industry, generals in the military... the possibilities were disturbing.

"But Mallory had just come in off the cold street," Gerald said. "Couldn't that account for it?"

It was possible, I guess. I hadn't considered that. But aside from something not feeling right about him, I felt I had witnessed Mallory's *repurposing.* Why the beings had wanted me there for that, I could never be sure, but something extraordinary transpired in that domed facility.

The next morning, after a late breakfast, Gerald and I drove to the harbor. Two police vehicles with empty trailers sat in the parking lot. I assumed they had hauled snowmobiles to get out to the cottage. Ben was walking up from the docks when Gerald parked. He stopped and glanced back out toward the bay, then back at me.

"I guess the police are at the cottage?" I said to Ben.

"What happened last night?" Ben asked.

"How did you know?"

"When I saw my snowmobile this morning, I wondered why you hadn't spent the night on the island. So, I took a ride out to check on things... there was nothing left..."

I didn't want to lie. "I blew it up, Ben. I couldn't have anyone else hurt by what was happening out there..."

"Yeah, I wish I had moved away a long time ago," he said, then glanced at Gerald, then back to me. "Is it true that Jacob is living with those creatures now?"

"What? What do you mean?"

"I knew what Jacob and Lola had been up to out there at your place, Kercy. And all that business working with Mallory. Gerald told me Jacob was at your house, and he was with the creatures now..."

Gerald shrugged when I looked over at him.

"Jacob isn't living with them," I told Ben. "Jacob is actually dead..."

"But Gerald said he saw Jacob..." Ben said.

"That wasn't really Jacob," I tried to explain. "He'd been repurposed, an ability the beings have to reanimate things that are no longer living..."

Ben seemed dazed, distressed.

"I'm sorry, Ben," I said. "Mallory and I found Jacob and Lola beneath the ice the night Mallory and his team abducted Gerald and me. They were dead, and there was nothing we could do. We figured they'd be there until morning and Mallory planned to get a crew out to retrieve the bodies..."

Ben regarded me a moment, then scratched the whiskers on his jaw.

"I'm sorry, Ben. They must have drowned trying to swim back to the hole they'd made."

"I didn't think that was possible... you know... for them to drown," Ben said.

"You knew?"

"Yeah." He sniffed and took his attention back over the bay. "So... are Jacob and Lola's bodies still out there?" he asked. "I don't understand..."

"No... they're not," I said. "I know it's all difficult to comprehend."

"Well, then... what happened to them?"

"The beings came up and took them back to their world. Then they repurposed Jacob so they'd be able to communicate with me through him."

"So, they are real?" Ben said. "You've seen them?"

"Yes."

"And those things are just out there in the bay somewhere?"

"No. They move between our world and theirs, Ben. Most of the time they are nowhere to be found."

Ben looked at the ground, then brought his eyes to mine. "Did you actually see them take Jacob?" Ben asked.

All I could do was nod. Ben's rugged face seemed trapped between grief and incredulity. After a moment, he shook his head, then said, "You should get out of here before the police get back."

"They'll want me to answer questions ... I'm still not sure what I'm going to tell them..."

"You were never here, Kercy," Ben said. "As far as the police know, I went drove out and found the house this morning. I told them there must have been some transients squatting out there, that folks do that in the winter because they know the houses are empty..."

"Is that true?"

"No, not really, but it could be. Anyway, if your insurance doesn't cover it, let me know... mine probably will," Ben said. "I mean, you hired me to winterize your property, so—"

"No, no, I'm not even turning it into the insurance company," I said. "I'm never coming back up here. I'm never rebuilding the cottage."

Ben nodded, as if in agreement. "I'm selling the harbor come this spring. This place has given me so much... and taken everything."

Ben stepped closer to me and took me in his arms. "I know you loved this place, Kercy," Ben whispered to me. "But please tell me you'll keep that promise. Don't come back here, ever. I love you. And I'll try to keep in touch."

Ben shook Gerald's hand, then looked at me one last time before walking to his truck.

FORTY-ONE

Two weeks after Gerald and I returned to New York, I contacted Dr. Conner about the CVS. I had thought a long while about whether I really wanted to know the results, and Gerald saw no point in finding out. But I couldn't *not* know, even though it would crush me if the baby had been Gerald's.

"I'm sorry," Dr. Conner said.

"Sorry? Does that mean...?"

"I never got the results," she said. "The sample and the fetus went missing. The lab has no idea what happened. I'm very sorry, Ms. Powell."

Ms. Powell? I'd known Dr. Conner my entire adult life and never before had she called me Ms. Powell. I figured the FBI must have seized everything.

Over the next few months I really focused on what had happened. I dropped out of the doctoral program and dedicated myself to writing everything down. Gerald moved in with me and continued teaching. I met with numerous people from the FBI, Homeland Security, as well as scientists and medical professionals. I never knew the results of all the tests they'd run on me, and didn't really care. And I never heard from Mallory again.

Jacob's drowning always perplexed me, and at the same time gave me hope. I knew I was still assimilating, but to what end I had no idea. I finally settled on the theory that I was becoming more human. As if somewhere within my genes, or cells, or some mechanism in my biology that science had yet to discover, or maybe some location outside my body, was a greater apparatus at work, where, no matter what experiment might be performed on me, I was still hardwired to be human. I considered that maybe that was what had happened to Jacob and Lola, that they had also continued to assimilate, becoming more human, losing the ability to breathe water. The part that gave me hope was that if the beings studied Jacob and Lola, they might come to a similar conclusion, that the evolutionary experiment had failed, that humans were not viable candidates for such an undertaking, not only because of our biology, but because of our psychology; that the human ego could not withstand such grandiosity, such power, without destroying itself.

Nevertheless, I would be forever changed, glimpsing a world that was inconceivable, rare and astonishing, so unlike anything I could imagine. A part of me wished these unusual creatures who had essentially forged my life, who were responsible, I suppose, for my very existence, who had saved my life at the cottage, would be a race we could collaborate with, could unite in some harmonious effort to solve many of the problems humans are confronted with on this planet, but that was not to be.

"Hey," Gerald said, setting my manuscript on the table. "Very interesting, what you've written."

"Really... that's all you've got to say?"

"No... I also want to say, Yes."

"Yes? I don't get it."

"Well..." Gerald picked up the manuscript, thumbing through the pages. "On this page right here, if you recall, you asked me to marry you... and I'm giving you my answer."

"Sorry, that's been off the table for some time."

"Yeah, right," Gerald leaned over and kissed my neck.

We eventually moved to Boulder, Colorado. A few weeks before we left, I was summoned to the White House. I never met the president. An advisor questioned me about the events in Canada, and my plans for the future, if I had spoken to reporters, if I planned to respond to invitations for television interviews.

I told him I just wanted to be left alone.

After Gerald and I moved to Colorado, I figured my involvement with intelligence agencies was over. However, just to be on the safe side, I left manuscripts with lawyers in several locations around the globe, detailing everything, with instructions that if anything happened to me or Gerald, or if our assets were frozen or tampered with in any way, or anything strange at all occurred, that all of those manuscripts would hit the public in one form or another.

Eventually Gerald and I moved from the U.S. to a secluded mountain home in a beautiful and forward-thinking country. One day while unpacking, Gerald caught me sitting on the floor against the bed looking at a book. "What's that?" he said. I handed it to him and he started thumbing through it. He looked at me quizzically.

"It's dedicated to you?" he said, almost as a question. I nodded. The book in his hands was the only one I managed to hold onto that night when the cottage exploded. A small book of poetry entitled "One and Other" by Marianna Duncan. That was my mother's maiden name. She had succeeded in turning her nightmares and haunting memories into art. I was proud of her for that. And I missed her terribly.

Gerald and I loved our new home. We lived simple lives, teaching at a tuition-free school we had established. The curriculum focused on science and philosophy, as well as art, dance, music, math, and of course, earth studies. Our goal was providing children with an environment where they could learn *how* to think, rather than *what* to think.

I don't spend much time near water anymore, and I still correspond with Cindy's parents all the time. Ben and I talked frequently for the first year, but after he left Elico, we fell out of touch. He does drop a postcard now and then, and has met a woman a few years younger than himself, though they don't plan to marry. Gerald and I discovered the mountains, and hiking, and with our second child on the way, there is less and less time each day to dwell on the past, and an abundance of opportunities for being in the moment.

And our beautiful daughter, Marianna, just turned four and loves the outdoors.

ABOUT THE AUTHOR

Lonnie Busch is an award-winning author whose short fiction has appeared in *South-west Review, The Minnesota Review, The Baltimore Review* and other magazines. Among his awards for fiction are the Clay Reynolds Novella Prize for his novella, *Turn-back Creek*, finalist in the Tobias Wolff Award for Fiction, the *Glimmer Train* Very Short Fiction Award, and others.

Busch is also a painter, animator and illustrator, and has created artwork for numerous corporations, ad agencies and institutions, including the "Greetings from America" and "Wonders of America" Commemorative Stamps for the USPS.

See Busch's other books at:
https://lonniebusch.com

www.ingramcontent.com/pod-product-compliance
Lightning Source LLC
Chambersburg PA
CBHW020215260626
47156CB00002B/397